P9-EJZ-841

A VICTOR LESSARD THRILLER

NEVER
FORGET

MARTIN MICHAUD

NEVER FORGET

A VICTOR LESSARD THRILLER

Translated by Arthur Holden

DUNDURN
TORONTO

Copyright © Martin Michaud, 2020

Originally published in French under the title *Je me souviens*, © Martin Michaud, 2014, Les Éditions Goélette.

All rights reserved. No part of this publication may be reproduced, stored in a retrieval system, or transmitted in any form or by any means, electronic, mechanical, photocopying, recording, or otherwise (except for brief passages for purpose of review) without the prior permission of Dundurn Press. Permission to photocopy should be requested from Access Copyright.

All characters in this work are fictitious. Any resemblance to real persons, living or dead, is purely coincidental.

Publisher: Scott Fraser | Editor: Allison Hirst
Cover designer: Sophie Paas-Lang
Cover image: istockphoto.com/Instants
Printer: Webcom, a division of Marquis Book Printing Inc.

Library and Archives Canada Cataloguing in Publication

Title: Never forget / Martin Michaud ; translated by Arthur Holden.
Other titles: Je me souviens. English
Names: Michaud, Martin, 1970- author. | Holden, Arthur, 1959- translator.
Description: Series statement: A Victor Lessard thriller ; 1 | Translation of: Je me souviens.
Identifiers: Canadiana (print) 20190117400 | Canadiana (ebook) 20190117409 | ISBN 9781459742734
(softcover) | ISBN 9781459742741 (PDF) | ISBN 9781459742758 (EPUB)
Classification: LCC PS8626.I21173 J413 2020 | DDC C843/.6—dc23

We acknowledge the support of the Canada Council for the Arts and the Ontario Arts Council for our publishing program. We also acknowledge the financial support of the Government of Ontario, through the Ontario Book Publishing Tax Credit and Ontario Creates, and the Government of Canada.

Care has been taken to trace the ownership of copyright material used in this book. The author and the publisher welcome any information enabling them to rectify any references or credits in subsequent editions.

The publisher is not responsible for websites or their content unless they are owned by the publisher.

Printed and bound in Canada.

VISIT US AT

dundurn.com | @dundurnpress | dundurnpress | dundurnpress

Dundurn
3 Church Street, Suite 500
Toronto, Ontario, Canada
M5E 1M2

To Guy,
after more than twenty years
I remember

To my own

To make war upon fortune is the heroes' will.
— Victor Hugo

The best-laid plans of mice and men go oft awry.
— Robert Burns

MAY 20TH, 1980

REFERENDUM

I just saw René giving his speech on TV, the eternal cigarette between his lips: "If I've understood correctly, what you're saying is, 'Until next time.'"

The fact that he used my words made me smile. I won't see him again. I suppose I should feel some kind of emotion about the situation, or about the result of the vote, but I feel nothing. What's really important?

Is it what I am, or my impression of what I am?

Is it what's going on in my life, or what I tell myself is going on?

I'm just a void, an abstraction. I'm nothing like what I thought I was.

I am without identity. A little like Quebec today.

One day, perhaps, someone will come along who can read between these lines and tell me who I am.

THE FUNNEL OF TIME

1

THE YOKE

Broken, emptied, reprogrammed, recovered.

The woman with the frizzy grey hair knew everything there was to know about the workings of the brain, but she'd never dealt with one more twisted than her own. The time for terror, for shouting and weeping, had passed. The pain was numbing her.

The yoke that had been fastened to her was piercing her flesh, impaling the bones of her sternum and chin, forcing her to tilt her head back in full extension. Her clothes had been removed, to humiliate her. Her feet were bare, her hands manacled behind her back, her legs immobilized so she couldn't bend them.

The moon, coming in through the window, projected a rectangle onto the cement.

The woman knew she was being watched. She relieved herself one last time and felt the satisfying sensation of urine running down her thighs. "Fu ... fuck you!" she stuttered, struggling to swallow.

One thought etched a grimace onto her face: the brightly coloured plastic numbers ...

The woman crossed the red line and, after many failed attempts, was able to seize the key, laughing wildly. The laugh of a madwoman.

After an arduous effort to insert the key into the lock, she turned it. For a fraction of a second, she thought the impossible had happened: she'd managed to free her wrists.

Then the dart whistled through the air, pierced the back of her neck, and came out her throat. Blood welled up, seething, gushing from the wound, spurting between her teeth.

2

SNOWSTORM

Montreal
Thursday, December 15th, earlier that day

The weather girl cocked her head to one side, pressing two fingers to her ear, a glum expression on her face. When the voice in her earpiece barked that she was on the air, her face lit up and she began confidently declaiming her prophecy: "Winter storm. Thirty centimetres expected. Blowing snow. High winds."

The woman got up and turned off the TV. An impetuous, almost savage smile crossed her deeply lined face. She rinsed her cereal bowl in the sink and put it on the counter. The liquid crystal on the stove showed 6:00 a.m. There was no better moment to go for a walk than during a morning blizzard, when time stood still, and, under the milky dome that purified it of its filth, the city caught its breath.

The woman always followed the same route. Bundled up in a down coat, she left her building on Sherbrooke Street, near the Museum of Fine Arts, and headed south on Crescent. Here, on summer nights, urban wildlife, laden with bling and eager to be seen, pressed up against the bar entrances. Now the woman met only her reflection in the storefronts. She turned onto De Maisonneuve Boulevard and passed by Wanda's strip club.

Crossing Peel at the traffic light, she watched, amused, as a car fishtailed its way around the icy corner.

Snow was piling up on the sidewalk. The wind howled in her ears; flakes whirled in the air.

She stopped on the esplanade at 1981 McGill College, where the trees, strung with lights, were contending with the gale. She was admiring the sculpture — *The Illuminated Crowd* — when the touch of a hand on her shoulder made her start.

Fleece jacket, combat pants tucked into fourteen-hole Doc Martens, multiple piercings, black-shadowed eyes, dreadlocks spilling out from under a skull-and-crossbones beanie: the young punk looked like she'd just stepped out of a Sex Pistols show.

Terrified, the woman staggered back as this angel of death cupped her hands around black lips, drew close, and spoke into her ear: "I didn't shoot anybody, no sir!"

Wondering if she'd heard correctly, the woman wanted to ask the vampire to repeat herself, but before she could, the punk straddled a bicycle and was swallowed up by the storm. The woman stood for a moment, staring down the street, eyes wide, body buffeted by the squall.

The woman got home at 11:22 a.m. Hurriedly, she left her boots on the hall rug, threw her hat and mittens onto the couch, and dropped her coat on the bathroom tiles. She relieved herself in the darkness with a long sigh.

Pressing the light switch, she looked at her face in the mirror, smiling broadly. Her lips were tinted blue from the cold. From downtown she had walked to Mount Royal, where she had spent hours wandering the park paths, admiring the conifers bent under the weight of the snow, observing, from the elevated vantage point, the city in its transparency.

She hummed as she went to the kitchen to make tea.

As the kettle was whistling, a feeling came over her that something wasn't right. She had a sense of some object being out of place. Her gaze moved along the cluttered counter, dipped into the sink, and traced the line of cupboards. Seeing the date spelled out in colourful number magnets on the refrigerator, she jumped. When she'd taken out the milk five minutes earlier, the magnets hadn't been there.

She'd given no further thought to the incident that morning, but now her whole body was trembling, sounding the alarm.

She froze at the sound of a voice behind her; the hair on her scalp rose.

"*I didn't shoot anybody, no sir!*"

She turned, saw the Taser's threatening mouth, and screamed. The barbs burst through the air, penetrating her skin. The force of the charge knocked her down. As she fell to the floor, her body gripped by convulsions, she couldn't help but be haunted by that voice — a voice she had recognized without difficulty. The delicate voice of President Kennedy's assassin.

The voice of Lee Harvey Oswald.

3

HANGMAN

Friday, December 16th

With surprising agility for a person in his seventies, the man mounted the stairs leading to the Stock Exchange Tower. Without a glance at the decorative wreath draped in red ribbon hanging over the entrance, he pulled open the glass door and, preceded by a screech of wind, plunged inside.

Winter had sunk its hooks into the tatters of Montreal. While Jesus shuddered on his cross, Christmas and the merchants of the temple were jostling at the gate. Snow fell from his overshoes and twirled across the mirror of marble.

In the empty elevator, the man barely heard Bing Crosby's smooth voice crooning about a marshmallow world. On the forty-eighth floor, he greeted the receptionist with a winning half smile of the sort that had once made Walter Cronkite the most trusted man in America.

"Good morning, Mr. Lawson."

He had encountered no one in the submarine.

Every morning, the secretaries' desks and the piles of boxes blocking the hallway gave Nathan R. Lawson the suffocating impression of moving through the cramped entrails of an underwater vessel. Baker Lawson Watkins, the law firm at which he was one of the principal partners, had undergone many changes since he'd joined it in the early sixties. Numbering fewer than twenty lawyers when he'd arrived, the firm had grown exponentially. At the turn of the new century, a series of shrewd mergers had transformed it into a nationwide partnership. Now it employed more than 600 lawyers, 174 of whom practised in Montreal.

Over the years, palatial offices had given way to more austere workspaces. The tiny cubicles with yellowed partitions in which the associates now toiled were at odds with the firm's high-end image. But clients, whose only wish was to be pampered, had no access to the bowels of the submarine; they were confined to the luxurious conference rooms on the forty-ninth floor, where they could enjoy the panoramic river views and admire the art collection.

Nathan Lawson removed his coat and brushed himself off in front of his assistant's workspace. She was wearing headphones, transcribing the memos he had dictated the day before. Other secretaries were available to work evenings and overnight, but he trusted no one except her.

"Have a nice night, Adèle?"

"Not bad."

For twenty-six years they'd been repeating the ritual, willingly engaging in this daily charade. For twenty-six years they'd been lying to each other every morning: Lawson couldn't care less how his secretary's night had been; Adèle had spent it, once again, contemplating the cracks in her ceiling. Following their custom, they would exchange no further civilities for the rest of the day, their interactions being limited to a few work-related monosyllables.

In a couple of seconds, he would step into his office to go through his mail, while she, during the next half hour, would bring him a cup of steaming coffee and two sugar cubes.

Nathan Lawson was often the first lawyer to set foot on the floor, but he never arrived before Adèle. This rule had been broken only once — the day, eight years ago, that she had buried her mother. Over the years, by a sort of involuntary osmosis, they had come to a complete understanding of each other's lives, without ever talking about them.

"Did you put this in my correspondence?"

Standing in the doorway, Lawson held up a sheet of paper.

He'd just found it, stuck between the Bar newsletter and the billable hours report for the month of November. Waiting for Adèle's answer, he flicked a speck of dust from the lapel of his jacket.

Absorbed in her work, eyes fixed on her screen, Adèle continued to tap at her keyboard. "Lucian handles the mail, not me."

Mystified, Lawson returned to his office. Leaning back in his chair, he stared for a moment at the row of Christmas cards on the corner of the table as his thoughts spun idly. Suddenly, an idea came to him, erasing the puzzlement from his features.

No one else in the firm could have imagined a practical joke like this. Smiling, he recalled that Louis-Charles Rivard had struck again just last week. The prank on that occasion had consisted of switching family photos between the offices of two litigators.

The numerous deficiencies in Rivard's level of professional competence hadn't prevented Lawson from opposing several attempts to fire his protégé. Sexy and entertaining, Rivard made up in social skill what he lacked in lawyerly ability.

The ringing telephone roused Lawson from his reverie. "Your clients have arrived," announced the forty-ninth-floor receptionist.

"All right."

He got up and looked at his watch: 7:02 a.m.

As he picked up his file folder, his gaze strayed once again to the paper lying on the desk:

Good morning, Nathan.

Let's play hangman: _ V _ _ G _ _ _ N

Hint: Company filled with corpses.

Ain't this fun, Nathan?

•   •   •

The meeting dragged on. Even the man in the Jean Paul Lemieux painting on the wall looked like he was bored stiff. Armani-suited and aristocratically perfumed, two other partners in the firm were on hand to assist Lawson.

"We have to set a redemption price for the preferred shares before closing," Lawson said, looking at his clients.

"We'll get back to you with a number," came the assured response from the chief financial officer of a large pharmaceutical company, an elegant man with manicured hands. "By the way, we haven't yet received the closing agenda."

Lawson turned to one of his juniors. Responsibility for the agenda and documentation fell to his protégé. "Carlos, ask Rivard to come and join us."

"He's out of the office, Mr. Lawson. Tania's replacing him. I'll call her."

Lawson nodded. He had forgotten that Louis-Charles Rivard was in a daylong meeting at the office of another client. The discussion resumed, but Lawson was lost in thought, still pondering the drawing.

During a break, while the others were getting coffee, he took the sheet discreetly from his pocket and examined the hanged man more closely. The man looked sinister, his tongue sticking out. Or maybe it was a moustache. Nathan R. Lawson hadn't played hangman since his childhood — even in his youth, he'd never had much time for games — but he remembered that the man was supposed to be drawn piece by piece, with a limb added whenever the other player guessed a letter wrong. In this case, the man seemed fully drawn. What did that mean?

Suddenly, a thought flashed through his mind, making the hairs stand up on his forearm. Using his pen, he filled in the blank spaces with letters. The secret word exploded off the page.

"Mr. Lawson?"

"Nathan?"

Four pairs of eyes were trained on him. Had he cried out? Distraught, he stammered a vague apology and hurried from the conference room.

His vision was blurred, his fingers hesitant over the cellphone keypad, his voice weak. "I need some documents from the archives, Adèle!"

Retrieving a forty-year-old file was no easy job, Adèle had remarked pointedly. Lawson had barely heard the complaint. Though it had taken him a while to recognize it, the face of fear now seemed to lurk in every corner.

Lifting the lid from one of the boxes, he saw with relief that the seals, stamped *Never Destroy*, were still intact. Picking up the phone, he called Wu, told him he was going away for a few days, and asked him to prepare an overnight bag and to include his passport.

Before leaving the office, he spoke briefly with his secretary. Adèle was visibly surprised; he rarely treated himself to vacations. "What about the active files?" she objected.

"Rivard and the others will step in. That's what they're paid for."

One by one, the floors evaporated overhead until the elevator doors opened at the sub-basement. As Lawson wiped his forehead with a handkerchief, the mail boy lifted the heavy boxes onto a trolley, revealing a Celtic knot tattoo on his left bicep.

"My car is there, beside the black truck," the old man said, nervously pocketing the checkered fabric.

A row of neon lights threw their wan glow onto the concrete walls of the subterranean parking garage. Walking rapidly, the lawyer glanced anxiously over his shoulder, never losing sight of the two boxes on the trolley bed. "Hurry up, for God's sake!"

When he was within a few metres of the Mercedes, he activated the keyless entry. "Are you sure you don't remember, Lucian?" he asked insistently as the mail boy transferred the boxes to the trunk.

"Like I said, Mr. Lawson, I handle hundreds of documents every day. I don't know how that message landed on your desk."

Displeased, the lawyer put a ten-dollar bill in the young man's hand and got into the car.

"Stupid Romanian," he muttered, watching in the rear-view mirror as Lucian walked back to the elevator.

Struggling to overcome the terror that paralyzed him, Nathan Lawson rolled furtively out of the parking garage. For several minutes, he drove around at random, checking the mirror constantly to see if he was being followed.

His mind was focused on solving a problem: apart from calling the police, which wasn't an option in this case, what would an ordinary person do in the face of the threat hanging over him? Of the possibilities that occurred to him, one stood out as the obvious response: an ordinary person would put the greatest possible distance between himself and the danger. Therefore, Lawson would do the opposite. He'd hide nearby, where no one would think to look for him.

His adversaries had considerable resources at their disposal. Their actions would be calculated and ruthlessly executed. And, if his supposition was right, train stations and airports were already under surveillance.

What was happening didn't surprise him unduly. But why now, after all these years?

As per his instructions, the building's doorman met Lawson in an adjacent alley and handed him the overnight bag that Wu had prepared. After making sure his passport was inside, Lawson drove away, wondering why he had received this warning instead of being coldly executed. He considered the question from every angle and kept coming back to the same answer: the aim was to scare him, to force him to make a mistake.

Lawson slapped his forehead. The file he was carrying in the trunk … he had blundered in removing it from its hiding place. He'd exposed himself.

Lawson stopped at a convenience store and bought garbage bags. He placed the documents inside the bags to protect them from water and humidity before putting them back in the trunk of the car. Next, he went to a business centre and sent a fax. Finally, back on the sidewalk, he extracted the SIM card and battery from his cellphone and threw them into a trash can, along with the phone.

After assuring himself that he wasn't being followed, Lawson drove to the Mount Royal Cemetery, where he pulled up in front of an old family vault. After discreetly placing the garbage bags inside the vault, he relocked the rusted iron door and left the key on a gravestone a hundred metres away. Lawson then got back into his Mercedes and left.

Shortly before arriving at his destination, he feared he was being followed, until an unremarkable woman driving an unremarkable car rolled past without so much as a glance in his direction. As he turned onto Summit Circle, he began to feel calmer. He'd won the first round; he'd succeeded in evading them. A little Tchaikovsky was in order.

His finger touched the power button on the CD player. A familiar voice broke through the background noise of the recording. It was Oswald's voice, running in a loop, making Lawson's blood run cold: "*I emphatically deny these charges … I emphatically deny these charges … I emphatic …*"

4

WALLET MAN

Saturday, December 17th

Decorative spotlight beams wrapped themselves around the brick facade of the New York Life Building, magnifying the clock and the sheen of the turret. From the roof, the man gazed over the other heritage buildings on Place d'Armes, all brightly lit for the benefit of tourists. After a moment, he resumed his unsteady progress through the semi-darkness.

"That's just how it goes … goddamn shitty life." A stream of saliva blackened the snow at his feet.

For any other vagrant, managing to get up here without being noticed would have rated as an accomplishment. Not for André Lortie. Picking locks, hiding in the shadows, waiting for the right moment to move: he'd been doing those things for most of his life.

"They've gone fuckin' crazy, putting their machines all over the place," he said, climbing over an air-conditioning unit. "The place isn't what it used to be, Sylvie. But don't you worry, I'm on my way. Old Dédé hasn't forgotten you."

Lortie fished a gin bottle from a pocket of his grease-stained coat and took a long swig. "Ahhhh. Jesus, I'm gonna miss that."

The homeless man advanced uncertainly toward the brick wall. "I'm sure it was around here someplace, Sylvie …" By the glow of his lighter, Lortie scanned the wall as though seeking the meaning of life between the mortar joints.

"I remember, the weather was hot. I think it was a couple of days before they killed Laporte. The dates have gotten mixed up in my head. But I remember how fuckin' beautiful you were. You took off your dress, Sylvie. Right here."

The drunk looked tenderly at the trodden snow in front of him. By the light of the tremulous flame he was shielding with grimy fingers, he resumed his careful inspection of the wall. "I'm sure it was here," he muttered.

Several minutes later, defeated, he went to the edge of the roof and sat on the parapet, his legs dangling in space. "They changed the bricks in the wall," he said with infinite sadness. "You remember? Your name and mine, Sylvie, inside a big heart. I wrecked my knife blade. And you were kissin' me like crazy while you were puttin' your dress back on …"

The man drained his bottle and let it fall into the emptiness. Then he began to cry like a child.

The bottle shattered on the sidewalk. Shards of glass struck a passerby, who dialed 911 at 9:47 p.m. Twelve minutes later, patrol officers Gonthier and Durocher arrived at the scene.

"Are you all right, sir?" Constable Gonthier asked, trying to keep her voice steady.

The dishevelled old man turned in their direction without seeming to see them. Encased in his own parallel universe. But when the policewoman looked like she might approach, he retreated along the balustrade.

She stopped dead. "What are you doing here, sir?"

A bitter smile appeared among the creases gouged by a hard life into the man's face. "I woulda liked to have memories."

"I understand," the policewoman said, glancing at her partner.

"I'm tryin' to remember Sylvie. I can't see her face anymore."

"Do you want us to call her?"

The tramp laughed out loud. "I don't think they've got phones in heaven." The man looked at the policewoman with a desperate expression. "And the heart I carved isn't there." Lortie pointed to the wall.

"You carved a heart into the bricks?"

The homeless man's face lit up. "Back in seventy. My name and Sylvie's."

"I understand. Come on down from there and we'll look for it together, okay?"

"I woulda liked to have memories."

"You do have memories, sir. You remember Sylvie."

Lortie's face had taken on the appearance of a death mask. "No, I checked real carefully. There's nothing on that wall. They scraped out my brain too many times. There's nothing real left inside my head. And it's starting again. I'm sick of it …" The tramp lowered his gaze, looking down at the street.

The policewoman realized the urgency of the situation. "Don't move. I'm coming."

Before he jumped, Lortie took something from his pocket and placed it on the balustrade. Constable Gonthier's fingers missed the fabric of his coat by centimetres.

As he neared the ground, Lortie saw Sylvie's celestial smile bloom in the reflection of the street lights. His head exploded on the pavement ten floors down, under the horrified gaze of a hundred people emerging from the Montreal Symphony Orchestra's Christmas concert at Notre-Dame Basilica.

In a state of shock, with her partner's hand on her shoulder, Constable Gonthier stood for a moment and stared down at the red jellyfish crawling over the snow.

Then she noticed the two wallets that the victim had left on the balustrade.

5

JANE DOE

Sunday, December 18th

Hands on his thighs, head bent forward, Victor Lessard was trying to catch his breath and regain his composure. From the depths of the warehouse, he'd had to run twenty metres before reaching the door and bursting outside.

Still panting, he turned away from the yellowish puddle at his feet and straightened up.

Wiping his lips, the detective sergeant took out a pack of cigarettes. The first puff set fire to his throat; the second lit up his lungs; the third calmed him down.

As his face returned to its normal colour, Victor zipped up his leather jacket and, putting his hands in the pockets of his jeans, paced among the junk in the snowy courtyard: an old boat sitting on wooden pallets; the carcasses of eviscerated cars; misshapen, rusting metal parts.

With a little imagination, one might almost have expected to find this fractured, postapocalyptic scene in the backdrop of a picture by Edward Burtynsky.

Worried that someone might be looking for him, Victor glanced toward the warehouse. From where he was standing, he could read the sign over the entrance: METALCORP. In the distance, to his left, he saw the gaunt silhouette of the Décarie Expressway ramp leading to the Champlain Bridge.

For a moment, Victor watched the unending flow of vehicles, hypnotized. Then he walked toward the Lachine Canal. He stepped carefully to prevent snow getting into his black-leather Converse high-tops.

His gaze drifted briefly to the canal's far bank. Though the district was still largely industrial, residential buildings were sprouting up here and there; but nothing like the disused factories farther east, now converted into high-end condos, that he had visited with Nadja.

Tossing his cigarette butt into the skeleton of a Plymouth Duster, Victor ran his fingers across the stubble on his cheeks. With a shake of his head, he turned and headed back toward the building, limping slightly. That limp was the only visible remnant of the attack that had nearly cost him his life. But neither the passage of time nor the psychotherapy could altogether erase the scars that the King of Flies had left on his soul.

"You're too sensitive, Lessard. You puke every goddamn time."

Victor's square jaw clenched and his green eyes looked straight into his partner's. "I just stepped out for a smoke."

Jacinthe Taillon responded with a skeptical little smile as she plunged her thick fingers into a bag of Cheetos and crammed a handful into her mouth. "The trick is never to go in on an empty stomach. Do you eat breakfast every morning?"

"There's orange stuff on your face, Jacinthe."

She was in her forties. With her doughy features untouched by makeup, her short-cropped hair, and rolls of flesh visible under her clothes, she was affectionately nicknamed "Tiny" Taillon by her colleagues. She wiped her mouth with the back of her hand. Direct, unsparing, practical, she was known for bluntness and a resolute refusal to beat around the bush. Ever. "Okay, big guy, let's go. We haven't got all day."

With that, Jacinthe set her massive body in motion and headed toward the back of the warehouse, crumpling her bag of munchies. Victor rubbed his temples for a moment, took a deep breath, and followed her.

The interior was as chaotic as the courtyard, but it was organized chaos: dirt, debris, metal stacked in layers or contained in wooden crates. Two Forensic Identification technicians were spraying luminol on a stretch of floor, looking for blood spatter. Victor tried to remember the techs' names, then gave up. Since his return to the Major Crimes Unit, there'd been so much information to absorb that his brain sometimes failed to keep up.

"What's the latest on Mr. Horowitz?"

Taillon sighed with frustration. "He had a heart scare. He's in the ICU at Saint-Luc Hospital."

"Put yourself in his shoes," Victor said. "He didn't expect to find a corpse in his warehouse on a Sunday morning."

"Maybe not, but now we'll have to wait before getting his deposition. And the clock's ticking."

"Anyway, we've still got our Jane Doe to deal with. This'll take as long as it needs to take."

"Are you deliberately trying to get on my nerves?"

The cleanliness and elegance of Horowitz's office contrasted with the rest of the place: lacquered concrete floor, glass-topped desk, leather armchairs under industrial windows, computer, papers, meticulously aligned pens, metal file cabinets, adjacent washroom, Toulouse-Lautrec prints on the walls, small kitchen with sink, microwave, and espresso machine, and a laminated table surrounded by several chairs for mealtimes.

Only the yellow plastic crime-scene tape and the body disturbed the harmony of the space.

For an instant, Victor hoped that by closing his eyes he could erase the dead woman. But when he opened them again, she was still on her back, pallid and naked, at the foot of the table, where he'd first seen her before the nausea overcame him.

A shaft of sunlight coming through the window cast singular patterns on the skin of the corpse, whose posture recalled the twisted forms of Delacroix's paintings.

Her sphincter muscles had relaxed at the moment of death. Her legs, bent to one side, were bathed in urine and feces. Victor raised his T-shirt over his nose to block out the stench that was pressing at his nostrils.

Jacob Berger turned to him, smiling. Berger had refined traits and a delicate chin. He wore little glasses and his hairstyle was too perfect. "Feeling better, Lessard?"

Both men were nearly six foot three, but the resemblance stopped there. While the detective sergeant's hard features and athletic physique gave him a threatening appearance, the medical examiner was long and lean, the prototype of an intellectual.

"How can you stand it, Jacob?" Victor hung back, not getting too close to the body.

The dead woman's rolled-back eyes made him shudder, but he couldn't look away from the wrinkled arms, the limp, toneless flesh dotted with droplets of blood.

"You get used to it," Berger said, kneeling beside the victim.

"I don't think I ever will."

Jacinthe rolled her eyes, then noticed the clothes piled in a corner. "Save the touchy-feely stuff for later, girls. Was she killed here?"

"Yes."

"How long ago?"

"I'd say a good forty-eight hours. Probably sometime Thursday night."

Victor made a mental note, then hesitated for an instant, trying to find the right words for what he was about to ask of the examiner. Berger had a touchy streak, and Lessard was eager to avoid seeming to micromanage him. "Since we don't have a purse or ID, I'd like you to be on the lookout for anything that might help identify her — dental work, physical particulars, labels, distinctive garments, details of that sort."

"No problem."

Maybe, like him, Berger was getting softer as he aged.

"How old would you say she was?"

"In her sixties. I could be wrong."

"She left behind an impressive body of work," Jacinthe said, laughing loudly at her own joke before turning serious. She used a fingernail to pry an orange blob from between her teeth and asked, "Cause of death?"

"She bled out. Something went right through her throat — from back to front, I believe."

"Is that the hole?" Jacinthe pointed to a circular wound just above the trachea.

Gently, Berger turned the dead woman's head and inserted a finger into the opening. The *sploosh* sound made Victor queasy. He averted his eyes, close to retching. Taillon watched, fascinated, as the examiner's expert hands moved over the corpse's throat.

"This is the exit wound. The object used by the killer entered the back of the neck and exited here, severing the carotid artery along the way. The vertebral arteries run through the cervical bones on their way to the brain. Hemorrhaging was massive. She was dead in minutes."

"The object used by the killer …" Victor paused, still struggling to hold down the contents of his stomach. "You mean that's not a bullet wound?"

"I could go into details, but —"

"Forget the details," Taillon snapped.

"Short answer: no, that is not a bullet wound."

"Okay," Taillon said, "so what was the murder weapon?"

"I'll know more after the autopsy, but I'd say it was a sharp object propelled by some kind of mechanism."

"Mechanism?" Victor asked, intrigued.

Berger looked at him over the rims of his glasses, which wavered in precarious balance on the bridge of his nose. "It took considerable velocity to cause a wound like this. More than human strength alone could generate."

Their gazes met for an instant.

"There's something else," Berger said.

"Oh, yeah?" the big woman growled.

The examiner ran his finger along two cuts, one above the sternum and the other beneath the chin, near the throat. Each wound had two distinct entry points.

"I don't know what made these punctures, but they're deep."

The image stayed with Victor wherever he looked: the dead woman's head and frizzy grey hair lying in a red lake, a Mona Lisa half smile clinging to her lips as though she'd been at peace when she was struck down.

"There are abrasions on the wrists and neck."

"Caused by what?" Jacinthe asked.

"On the wrists, could be handcuffs."

"And the neck?"

"It looks like the murderer made her wear something extremely tight and heavy."

"A dog collar?" Victor suggested.

"That," Berger answered, "would be one very large dog collar."

6
ROOM 50

Chronicle of a marital disaster foretold: Detective Chris Pearson looked at the picture of his wife and two daughters on the corner of his desk and sighed. It was Sunday. The week hadn't yet begun, and already Corinne would be making dinner and giving the girls their baths by herself. He would try, at least, to get home a few minutes before the children's bedtime.

Taking a sip of coffee, he couldn't help recalling his motives for requesting reassignment to Station 21. The myth of downtown police work. Plenty of young detectives were hungry for the challenge, hungry to be where the action was. But only the best got the chance. Pearson was one of the best, as the recommendation letter from his former mentor, Victor Lessard, had confirmed.

Lessard's departure for the Major Crimes Unit had been a factor. Lessard was tortured, surly, and stubborn, but Pearson had loved working with him. He was a loyal boss who never gave up and who knew how to protect his team from the abuses of the higher-ups. After his departure, Commander Tanguay had started arbitrarily poking his nose into active investigations. The atmosphere at Station 11 had become so bad that Pearson had longed for a change of scenery. That was when he'd set his sights on Station 21.

But the adrenalin rush of frenzied activity he'd expected to find downtown hadn't materialized. Instead, he was deluged by petty case files that piled up faster than he could deal with them.

Lessard had often urged his protégé to pay attention to his marriage and home life, warning him not to make the mistakes that he had made. At the time, the young man had only half listened to these warnings, convinced that he knew better. Chris Pearson wouldn't fall into the same traps. Now he and Corinne were in counselling.

A call during the early hours of the night had roused Pearson from his dreams. Corinne hadn't woken up. Before leaving, he had stood for a moment in the doorway of the children's bedroom, gazing with love at the two blond heads that emerged from the covers. Then he'd gone straight to the New York Life Building.

André Lortie's body was covered by a sheet, and a security perimeter had been established. A short distance away, their faces awash in the glow of the emergency lights, two attendants waited to take the body to the morgue.

Upon arriving at the scene, Pearson had gathered the usual information. Lortie had managed to evade the night watchman's notice and slip into the building stairwell, picking several locks before gaining access to the roof. The beat cops who had responded to the emergency call were shaken, but their accounts were clear and concise. There was no ID on the body, but a fingerprint check yielded a match.

André Lortie was known to police on the basis of a few minor convictions. For the past little while, he'd been spending his nights in a rooming house with other vagrants. Because Lortie's file contained no emergency contacts, Pearson had gone to the rooming house at 8:00 a.m., hoping for information that could help him locate next of kin. But neither the other roomers nor the toothless female caretaker had been able to point him toward a family member. After being let in by the caretaker, Pearson had looked through Lortie's filthy bedroom, but he'd found nothing that connected the homeless man to anyone in the outside world. The detective had also visited the Accueil Bonneau and the Maison du Père, two shelters where Lortie occasionally made appearances. No one at either shelter knew him to have any friends.

Those who had spent some time in his presence described a quiet, solitary man. "He wasn't outgoing or communicative," a caseworker at the Maison du Père told Pearson. "He slept here, but he never used our other services. He wasn't looking for help."

Lortie had also stayed at the Old Brewery Mission, but he'd been banned after an incident in 2006. "He hit a volunteer," a shift supervisor had explained concisely, unable to tell the detective anything else about the attack. Pearson had looked up the incident report on the Quebec Police Information Centre database, but the report didn't contain the personal information he was seeking. After a stop at Tim Hortons, he'd gone back to Station 21.

Sitting at his desk, Pearson tore open the envelope the patrol officers had given him and extracted two wallets. They'd probably been stolen, though the dead man might simply have found them. An initial database search yielded no results; neither of the two individuals in question, a man and a woman, had been reported missing, and neither one had filed a complaint for theft. Pearson wasn't surprised. The suicide had taken place during the night. People often went several hours before noticing that something had been stolen from them.

The woman's phone number appeared on a hospital card; Pearson found the man's number using his driver's licence. He left them both the same message: had they lost wallets or been victims of a theft? If so, they should get in touch with him to recover their possessions.

Tucking the envelope with the two wallets under his arm, Pearson got up and headed for Room 50, where, following protocol, the items would be barcoded and stored until their owners showed up to claim them.

On the required forms, he wrote the names of the wallets' owners: Judith Harper and Nathan R. Lawson.

7

DEPOSITION

A few cars were heading south on Saint-Denis, bound for the Ville-Marie Expressway. Victor took a drag on his cigarette and turned up the collar of his jacket, shivering. Taillon, her coat wide open, was eating a chocolate bar.

Maintenance workers, nurses, patients wearing bathrobes over their hospital gowns and pulling their IV poles after them: the usual bestiary was out snatching a smoke along the wall next to the entrance of Saint-Luc Hospital. Victor empathized with the people huddled there, but he would willingly have turned and fled their misery for fear it might prove contagious.

Clouds sped headlong through a sky streaked with flakes. Wind, cold, and humidity stung the skin.

He tossed away his butt, carving a black furrow in the snow. Taillon was at his heels. It was 10:37 a.m.

"Who'd you get for Secret Santa?" she asked with a chuckle.

"Not telling."

While Victor peered at the directory near the elevator doors, trying to figure out which way to go, Jacinthe pragmatically put two fingers in her mouth and whistled to the security guard who was sitting at the counter in an open-eyed doze. Startled, the guard told them which floor their destination was on.

"Stop being such a pussy, Lessard," Taillon insisted as the steel doors slid shut. "Who'd you get?"

"Gilles."

Gilles Lemaire had been Taillon's partner prior to Victor's return to the Major Crimes Unit. Apart from his work in the field, Lemaire was now responsible for the digital component of the unit's investigations. He was a short man and a father of seven, making him a target of choice for mockery within the team.

"Gilles? Hah! What are you giving him?"

"None of your business."

"I got you."

"Seriously?"

"Yep. I was thinking I'd buy you some moisturizing cream, seeing as you're such a retrosexual. When a man's in his forties, he needs to start taking care of his complexion." Her raucous laugh drew stares as they walked along the hospital corridor.

"That's *metro*sexual, Jacinthe," Lessard said, not letting himself be provoked.

"Same difference."

Victor shook his head. "Going to the gym and watching what I eat doesn't make me a metrosexual." He sighed. "And if you're wondering what to give me, there's a new biography of Muhammad Ali that looks interesting. I'll find the title for you ..."

The long face of Robin Horowitz, the warehouse owner who had discovered the woman's body, was the same chalky colour as the bedsheets on which he lay. His cardiac scare hadn't, in the end, been serious, but a nurse had nevertheless asked the two detectives not to stay too long.

Victor was sitting beside the bed, an open notebook on his knee. Horowitz had been quickly ruled out as a suspect. The warehouse was closed to customers on Fridays and weekends, but the owner had gone in that morning to catch up on some bookkeeping.

"So," Victor said, "you were in the habit of leaving the key on the back-door lintel?"

"Yes," Horowitz answered in a weak voice.

"I didn't see an alarm system."

A coughing fit shook the man as he lay on the bed. "Apart from the computer, there's nothing of value. Nobody steals scrap metal."

"Who knew about the key?" the detective sergeant asked.

"We're a family business. My two brothers are in China, negotiating a contract. My sister-in-law helps with the accounts three times a month. The kids drop by now and then. That's a lot of people."

"Well, Mr. Horowitz, we're going to need a list of names," Jacinthe said. She was standing at the window, hands behind her back.

Victor shook his head to reassure the man. "We think the killer used the key to get in," he said. "Aside from family members, did anyone else know about it? A supplier? Customer? Acquaintance?"

Horowitz made a mental effort that seemed to drain the last of his energy.

"I can't think of anyone."

More out of habit than chivalry, Victor stepped aside to let Taillon board the elevator first. More out of manliness than habit, Taillon didn't thank him.

"You've gone soft!" she brayed. "The guy's story doesn't add up. He's lying, I'm sure of it."

"Calm down, Jacinthe," Lessard said, pressing the button for the ground floor. "The poor man is practically at death's door. How about we cut him a little slack?"

"Like I said, you've gone soft."

"Maybe. Or maybe I'm getting more laid back with age."

"You? Laid back? Fat chance. Gimme the keys. I'm driving."

"Suit yourself," he said, handing them over.

"I'm hungry. Let's go eat."

*   *   *

Jacinthe's foot on the accelerator was as heavy as the rest of her. Paying less attention to the traffic lights than if they were red Smarties, she kept the gas pedal down. In minutes they were at the corner of René Lévesque and Saint-Urbain, where La Maison Kam Fung offered a dim sum menu she loved.

The noisy restaurant was full of Asian families enjoying their Sunday meal.

"There's no point in making a list. I'm guessing the killer observed Horowitz from the bicycle path along the canal. That's how he knew where the key was hidden."

"What makesh you shay that?" Taillon gargled, slurping her noodles.

"A hunch. I had a look around the property this morning. You can see the warehouse door from the canal."

"I'm still going back to the hospital tomorrow. I want that list. I'm not taking any chances."

Deep in thought, Victor had barely touched the food. "Why do you suppose the killer chose that place?" he asked.

"Hmm? Fucking chopsticks … I don't know. Because it's isolated?"

"He must have noted Horowitz's comings and goings. He knew he wouldn't have to worry about the victim's screams."

Jacinthe put her hand in her bag and pulled out her buzzing cellphone. "It's Gilles," she said, looking at the text. "Our Jane Doe's prints aren't in the database, and her profile doesn't match any missing-person reports."

"I'm not surprised," Victor said, but he looked disappointed. "Let's ask Berger to take pictures of the body to distribute to local police stations."

"You think a beat cop might recognize her?"

"A beat cop, a detective, you never know."

Victor was already tapping out a text to the medical examiner.

"Good idea." Jacinthe hesitated. She pointed to a bamboo basket of steamed *baozi* meat buns. "You want any more?"

"No. Help yourself." He paused. "Maybe we should have divers drag the canal."

"If they find the weapon in the canal, I'll go on a diet. The surface is frozen."

"It isn't frozen everywhere. The ice is unstable. And I thought you were already on a diet."

Jacinthe gave him a sidelong look. They talked for another few minutes, time enough for Victor to finish his green tea, Jacinthe her apple fritters, and the waiter his bill.

Though it was only a fifteen-metre walk from the restaurant door to the service vehicle, Victor hunched against the chill. The wind was blowing hard.

In the passenger seat, he listened to the thrum of the engine before breaking the heavy silence. "I wonder what he's doing right now."

"Who?" Jacinthe asked, not taking her eyes off the road.

"The guy who killed Jane Doe."

8

AIR BUBBLE

Nathan Lawson tried to make out the indistinct form manipulating the air bubble, but his vision was blurred by a viscous substance, as though he had ointment in his eyes. Before lapsing back into the netherworld, as he hovered at the brink of unconsciousness, he thought he must have had too much to drink. A rapid succession of images unspooled through his cortex.

After parking the car in the garage, he had gone into the house. Knowing the place well, he had settled in without turning on any lights. When the sun went down, he had lit a candle, placing it so that its glow wasn't visible from outside. Later in the evening, he'd allowed himself a whisky. And then another …

Staggering to the bedroom, he had tried to calm his fears, reminding himself that no one would look for him here. A name had risen up, floating in his memory as he slipped under the covers. Why had he suddenly thought of him? He had received assurances a lifetime ago that André Lortie was in no condition to cause problems. Nothing suggested that the situation had changed.

Lawson had woken up in the middle of the night, hungover, urgently needing to urinate. Groping through the blackness, he'd stepped into the hall. As he looked up, he was shocked to see the outline of a person in the bathroom doorway.

He had tried in vain to reach Peter's hunting rifle …

Nathan Lawson half opened his eyes. A powerful beam of light blinded him. He felt as though he'd been asleep for months. A metallic taste filled his dry mouth. Turning his head, Lawson noticed that the indistinct form had disappeared. Only the air bubble remained. His gaze focused on the bubble, which, he finally realized, was in fact a vinyl bag containing translucent liquid. Widening his eyes, Lawson saw his own milk-white body strapped to the bed, tubes connecting the solution to his veins.

How long had he been kept like this, on a drip?

Fear flowed into him, releasing a current of adrenalin.

He was trapped. He began to scream.

9

RESIDUE

Though located in the Place Versailles retail complex, the head-quarters of the Major Crimes Unit was nothing like a royal palace. Even so, cops had gotten into the habit of referring to it simply as "Versailles." Standing at the intersection of Sherbrooke and Highway 25 in Montreal's east end, the large building also housed the anti-gang squad, the sexual assault team, and the fraud unit.

As they strode past a series of large outlets and smaller boutiques, Victor smiled at the thought that this time, at least, he and Jacinthe had managed to avoid the shopping mall's food court.

They emerged from the elevator and walked through the impersonal beige office, passing a row of workspaces piled with computers, boxes, and stacks of documents. At the far end of the row, they saw Gilles Lemaire in the midst of a phone conversation, gesturing energetically.

Taillon tiptoed forward, slipped behind her former partner, and touched his ear. Lemaire whirled around. Clamping one small hand over the mouthpiece, he glared at Taillon. With his slicked-back hair, impeccably tailored and creased suit, and silk tie, he looked like a dandy. His nickname within the unit was "the Gnome."

"Do you mind?" the diminutive cop said, his eyes at the level of Taillon's ample bust. "I'm on a call with Forensic Identification."

Jacinthe scowled and sat down, grumbling, on the chair in front of Lemaire. "Nobody can take a joke anymore ..."

Seated at the neighbouring desk, Victor went through his emails. Berger had sent him photographs of Jane Doe's lifeless face.

Within minutes, the detective sergeant had drafted an electronic alert detailing the circumstances of the body's discovery and inviting anyone with information to contact him. As soon as the alert was complete, Victor emailed it to all the police stations on the island of Montreal, with Berger's photos attached.

Then he opened the message that he'd saved for last:

> Just heard about the homicide.
> Hope you're having a good day anyway.
> Still on for tonight?
> ILY
> N xx

A smile lit up his face.

He and Nadja Fernandez, his ex-partner at Station 11, had been in a relationship for several months now. She'd often stayed at his tiny apartment on Oxford Avenue while he was in rehab. Nadja and Victor's son, Martin, had become thick as thieves, working in shifts to look after him during that difficult period. Recently, she'd begun to raise the possibility of their moving in together. Perhaps because he feared losing her, Victor hadn't yet admitted that he didn't feel ready for that. Nadja gave him balance, helped him stay organized, endured his moods. She was smart, funny, sexy, and unfailingly upbeat. He loved her. But he hadn't yet found the courage to say so.

What was he afraid of?

Maybe he wanted to avoid the pitfalls that had ended his marriage. Having sunk into comfortable complacency, he and Marie had lost sight of each other so completely that when professional trauma plunged Victor into drinking and depression, they'd been unable to reconnect.

Maybe he feared himself.

Victor became aware that Jacinthe was behind him, reading the reply he was typing. When he turned, he saw no trace of mockery in her expression.

The detectives both looked over when Lemaire slammed down his phone. "The techs found a piece of metal near the body."

Jacinthe rolled her eyes with impatience. "Jesus, Gilles. It's a scrap warehouse."

"I'm aware of that, Jacinthe. I was just filling you in."

"What else?" Victor asked.

"How do you know there's something else?"

"You speak more slowly and your voice deepens when you're hiding something."

The Gnome smiled, impressed. "I'll have to remember that next time I lie to my wife."

"We're waiting," Taillon said impatiently.

"There was adhesive residue on the concrete floor at the foot of the table."

"What kind of adhesive?" Jacinthe asked.

"The kind used on duct tape."

Feeling the onset of a migraine, Victor pinched the bridge of his nose between his thumb and index finger. It always took some time for him to settle on an impression of a new case. If his dawning premonition was right, this one wouldn't be easy. "What does Horowitz say?"

"He didn't tape anything there. Berger also told me the same adhesive residue is present on our Jane Doe, around the ankles and thighs."

10

IDENTIFICATION

After eating his lunch hunched over a crossword puzzle, Chris Pearson had resolved to go for a walk along Saint-Catherine Street. But when the icy wind had forced him back indoors, he'd returned to his office and poured himself a cup of sludgy coffee.

A call home to see how the girls were doing had earned him a scolding from Corinne, whom he'd disturbed mid-nap. Pearson had apologized and hung up.

Looking out his window, lost in thought, he'd spent some time watching the sprays of slush thrown up by the cars speeding along René Lévesque.

Medical files often contained an emergency contact name. Administrative offices were closed on Sunday, but Pearson hoped a few calls the following day might help him find André Lortie's next of kin.

Checking his emails, he saw the alert Lessard had sent out a few minutes earlier and clicked on the link to download the attached photographs.

Pearson had noticed long ago that when life departed a body, the remaining husk no longer seemed quite real, as though it were stripped of its essence. He had that impression now as he looked at the Jane Doe's ashen face, which, at first glance, he didn't recognize.

But as he was about to shut down the computer and go home, he took a second look at the dead woman's photograph. The penny dropped. A moment later, he was sprinting up the corridor.

Hurriedly, Pearson filled in the requisition forms and signed out the items he had logged in to Room 50 that same morning. The attendant handed him the wallets. Pearson took the one belonging to the woman and rifled frantically through the cards until he found the driver's licence. One glance was enough.

Lessard answered on the first ring. "Your Jane Doe ... her name is Judith Harper. I have her wallet in my Room 50."

SEPTEMBER 1964
YOU WON'T GO TO HEAVEN

Near Joliette, Quebec

The nasal ringing of the bell, the teacher's sharp voice, the squeals of the other children. Running madly down the hallway, coat in hand, Charlie barrels through the door into a flood of sunshine, slowing down at last in the schoolyard.

A look to the right: Lennie's massive form looms on the other side of the fence, under a shelter of trees. Heat wave, rain, blizzard, ice storm — nothing can keep Lennie from showing up on time.

Baseball cap pulled low, Charlie hurries over.

"Hel-lo, Cha'lie."

The slurred speech seems barely comprehensible, but Charlie's used to it. "Hey, Lennie. Help me with this." The schoolbag changes shoulders and the small hand disappears into the big one.

"Di' you have a ni' day, Cha'lie?"

"Pfff. Nothing special. You?"

"It won' l-l-lea' me al-l-lone, Cha'lie."

"What?"

Lennie stops walking and looks into Charlie's eyes. "The v-voice in m-my 'ead."

The giant crosses himself, and the two of them disappear into the brightness at the end of the sidewalk.

•　　•　　•

The blond stalks of grain are rocking gently in the wind. Léonard loves to run his hand along the tops of their heads. A '57 Chevy roars past on the gravel road, kicking up dust, enveloping them in a fine, gritty cloud. They walk by a decrepit farm. The Boivins' dog runs in circles around them, barking. Terrified, Lennie cowers behind Charlie.

"Don't worry, Lennie. He's nice. You can pet him."

Lennie reaches forward tentatively, but his nerve fails him. Charlie takes the immense hand and guides it gently toward the animal's back.

"There. Like that. Good dog."

"Goo' doh," Léonard repeats. There's still a faint note of worry in his voice.

"Don't be scared."

Little by little, the giant's anxious features relax, brightening at last when the border collie rolls onto its back to be rubbed. Now he's smiling broadly. "He's s-s-soft …"

Voices call out behind them. Charlie turns quickly, darkening.

René Desharnais, a big jackass with sunken eyes and holes in his pant legs, is swaggering toward them, flanked by his cronies. "Hey, Charlie! Having fun with your buh-buh-brother?"

The children's laughter claws at Charlie's ears. One voice rises above the rest. "Your idiot brother!"

One of the kids brushes a lock of hair out of his eyes and, with a sleeve, wipes away the snot hanging from his nose. "My dad says he's a retard."

Retard. Handicapped. Slow. Charlie's parents have never explained the mystery of Lennie's condition. Charlie flares, stung by the slur. "Lennie's different, that's all. You're the one who's a retard!"

"Oh yeah? Come here and say that!"

Charlie flies at the snot-nosed kid and the two of them roll in the dust, fists flying, until an overwhelming force lifts them both off the ground. The yells fall silent. Jaws drop. Mouths gape in awed silence.

"Let me go!" Charlie rages, spitting a gob of blood onto the dirt.

Léonard is holding them both effortlessly by the seats of their pants.

"Th-this is b-bad, Cha'lie. You … you … you won' go t' heav'n."

The last shimmers of daylight are licking the treetops, and the breeze is rustling in the woods as Charlie, riding the giant's back, sings lustily. "The ants go marching ten by ten, hurrah, hurrah …"

"Again, Cha'lie, again," Léonard begs, his face illuminated by a beatific smile.

In the distance, the glow of the house is visible through the trees. Two strange points of brightness dance in the air, and suddenly they're caught in the headlights' beam. The '57 Chevy slows to a stop beside them. The driver's window is open. Two men are in the car. In the half light, Charlie makes out the malignant gaze of the man at the wheel.

A stream of saliva lands at their feet.

"It's a goddamn shitty life, kids. I'd watch out for the boogeyman, if I was you. I hear he's prowling in these parts."

The evil laugh is drowned out by the rasp of tires on gravel, then by the engine as it thunders away.

Léonard and Charlie arrive in front of the house. On the porch, a man is on his hands and knees, gasping for breath. A woman is bent over him, her hand in his hair. Charlie knows something is wrong even before hearing the stifled sobs.

With the cry of a wounded animal, Léonard rushes into the driveway.

Climbing the steps, Charlie freezes at the sight of their father's swollen face.

11

WARRANTS AND SEARCHES

A lava flow couldn't have ignited the atmosphere at Versailles more completely than Pearson's phone call did. After giving instructions to his colleagues, Victor had moved quickly to brief his boss, Paul Delaney.

The detective sergeant was now coming to the most delicate aspect of the operation. "We're drawing up the warrants, Chief. Can you fast-track them the way you did last time?"

Victor was referring to a previous case in which his commanding officer had secured a judge's approval with impressive speed.

His face dotted with acne scars, the head of the Major Crimes Unit sighed and scratched the crown of his head, where, for the last few years, a bald spot had been widening. "I'll see what I can do, Vic," he answered, clasping his hands across his round abdomen, against which several shirt buttons were straining. "But in case you hadn't noticed, it's Sunday …"

"I know. Thanks, Paul."

Delaney's best friend from law school was now a provincial court judge. Godfather to one of his daughters, Paul Delaney called the man on his cellphone and pulled the strings he'd pulled before. Perhaps because it was a murder case, the warrants were issued even more promptly this time.

•   •   •

Siren screaming, emergency lights activated, the patrol car raced through the darkness, zigzagging through traffic on René Lévesque Boulevard. The unmarked car followed in its wake.

"Who's going to Judith Harper's place with Gilles?" the detective sergeant asked, keeping his eyes on the road.

Taillon leaned back in the passenger seat and sighed. "The kid."

Victor frowned and shook his head, displeased. "Loïc? I'm not sure that's a good idea."

"The kid kept asking. Gilles finally gave in."

Victor executed a tight turn onto Berri Street. "He'd better not screw up again."

Irritated, Taillon looked at her BlackBerry for the tenth time. "Still nothing from the patrol unit we sent to Lawson's place …"

The officers who'd been dispatched to the lawyer's residence were under instructions to call Jacinthe as soon as they found him. At this stage, the detectives had no cause to fear for Lawson's safety, nor any reason to think he was involved in Judith Harper's death. Nevertheless, the fact that they'd been unable to reach him, combined with the circumstances surrounding the wallets' discovery, required explanation.

"Give them time. If they find him, we'll know soon enough."

"I bet you a tenner Lawson's body will be lying in Lortie's room."

"You lose. Pearson had a look around the room earlier." Victor glanced in the rear-view mirror before speaking again. "And you know as well as I do that we're getting ahead of ourselves. The fact that some homeless man had Judith Harper's wallet, and Lawson's, doesn't make him their murderer. We can't even say if the lawyer's dead."

Jacinthe raised a finger. "Yeah, but the homeless guy killed himself."

Victor's expression changed. "Speaking of bets, you still owe me ten bucks."

"Fucking Habs," she grumbled. "You'll get your money." She paused. "By the way, how did Pearson get involved in the Lortie case? He wasn't on duty last night."

"He'd been trying to find Lortie for a couple of weeks. Patrol cops at Station 21 were under instructions to get in touch if they found him."

"Why?"

"Lortie stole a parking officer's ticket pad."

Jacinthe laughed and opened a package of candy. "They should give him a posthumous medal. Licorice?"

"No, thanks."

"Wasn't Lortie staying at the rooming house?"

"Apparently he bunked in other places, too." He looked at the licorice package. "Ah, what the hell. Gimme one."

After chewing a sticky mouthful, Victor ran a finger along his teeth to be sure he hadn't lost any fillings. "Disgusting," he muttered.

"Pearson didn't find anything of interest in the wallets?"

"Nothing."

"And he didn't insist on coming with you?"

As they rolled across Saint-Antoine Street, the hulk of the Château Viger, a former train station and hotel, slid by on their left. Victor pulled up at the corner of Saint-Louis and parked next to a patrol vehicle at the curb. "Not when I told him you'd be in the car," he said as he opened the driver's door.

Taillon laughed loudly. A joke after her own heart.

A few blocks to the east, white vapour rose from the Molson Brewery's brick chimney.

On this stretch of Saint-Louis, carefully renovated heritage buildings were interspersed with rundown structures and vacant lots. Real estate signs had gone up in front of several properties.

Unsurprisingly, the building they stepped into was the shabbiest on the block. Victor looked up the stairwell: grimy streaks disfigured the yellowing plaster, which, in several places, had caved in altogether. As the cops ascended the stairs, the stench of piss filled Victor's nostrils.

On the landing, a single bulb cast its weak light.

According to standard procedure, the detectives should have called a locksmith. But since Lortie was dead, they asked the caretaker to let them in.

The caretaker was about to open the door when something made her step back. Jacinthe and Victor had also heard a noise inside the room.

Unholstering his Glock, the detective sergeant banged on the door. "Police! Open up!"

The partners didn't need to say a word. Taillon threw open the door and Victor rushed in. He took a fraction of a second to evaluate the situation before running to the open window. He pulled aside the curtain that was fluttering in the wind. A man in his underwear was hurrying down the spiral fire escape, which overlooked a tiny backyard and, beyond it, a vacant lot dotted with skeletal trees.

Victor was about to take aim at the fleeing man and order him to freeze, but the two patrol officers who had stayed downstairs appeared in the yard, weapons drawn.

Barefoot in the snow, the individual stopped and offered no resistance. The officers took him into custody at the base of the stairs.

In the corridor, a drunken man came out of his room wearing jeans and an undershirt. Another, dressed in rags, stepped onto the landing.

"There's nothing to see here," Victor announced, holding up his badge. "Get back in your rooms."

The urinous fumes rising off the mattress were enough to convince him to leave the window open. The grey-walled room contained a filthy bed, a broken chest of drawers, and a rickety chair. In a corner, a balled-up bundle of clothes reeked of sweat and mildew.

Through the paper-thin wall, Victor heard occasional exclamations from the next room, where Jacinthe had taken the fugitive for questioning. "I'm leaving him with you," Victor had said. "No rough stuff."

"Maybe just a little," she'd answered with a malicious smile.

"Jacinthe!" he had cautioned through his teeth.

His partner had a knack for getting under his skin.

"Relax. I was joking."

Wearing latex gloves, Victor searched the pockets of a pair of pants extracted at random from the bundle and found nothing but cigarette butts. In a drawer of the chest, he found a Polaroid photograph: a woman in her early thirties with a generous bosom. She was gazing at the camera, unsmiling. After trying and failing to make out the faded handwriting on the photo's white border, the detective sergeant slipped it into a plastic evidence bag.

Under the bed, he found two empty De Kuyper gin bottles.

For a moment, Victor gazed at the flowerpot on the chest of drawers. It was astonishing to think that Lortie, who had manifestly struggled to look after himself, had managed to keep a plant alive.

He suddenly realized that he was hearing nothing in the other room. Could he trust Taillon? He decided not to dwell on the question.

Overcoming his repulsion, he lifted the mattress. A pill bottle lay on the box spring. The detective picked it up, examined it briefly, then slid it into a bag.

Next he inspected the box spring, turning it over completely. Several sheets of cardboard had been inserted between the posts and the wooden frame. The detective sergeant removed them carefully and laid them out on the floor; it took him a few seconds to assemble the six eighty-by-sixty-centimetre rectangles in the right configuration.

Victor's head spun: a complicated filigree of words had been inscribed on the cardboard sheets, some in blue or red ink, some in black felt pen. Hundreds, if not thousands, of letters and symbols were set out in a chaotic maze; a system that followed its own rules, an undefinable handwritten quilt.

Some would have called it the product of a disturbed mind. Others might have hailed it as a work of genius. Barrelling into the room, Taillon made her choice without hesitation: "Whoa ... fucking whack job."

12

NEWSPAPER CLIPPING

After studying the cardboard sheets long enough to understand they weren't going to decipher the inscriptions on the spot, Jacinthe and Victor agreed to call forensics and have some technicians come and take photographs. Then, before Lessard could speak, his partner informed him that the man who had tried to flee was named Michael Witt. He occupied a room on the floor below. At first, he had claimed he was trying to recover a bottle opener that he'd lent Lortie a few days previously. But Witt eventually admitted that, having learned of Lortie's death, he had sneaked into the room to steal his belongings. Jacinthe had searched him and found nothing in his possession.

Victor hardly dared wonder what she had done to make Witt talk so fast. He shook his head, tight lipped, visibly displeased. "Jacinthe, tell me you didn't mistreat him ..."

"Oh, come on, you know me!" she exclaimed, looking offended.

Nothing was more likely to increase Lessard's worry than his partner's assurances that there was nothing to worry about. "Okay," he said, making an effort to stay cool. "Anything else?"

"The caretaker confirmed that Lortie would often go missing for long periods. She thinks he was sleeping outdoors or at shelters."

"I have an idea where he was going."

Victor showed her the plastic bag containing the pill bottle that he'd found between the mattress and the box spring.

"Pills?"

"Antipsychotics. The name of the prescribing physician is on the label."

Taillon, who was nearsighted, held the bottle up close to read it. "Doctor Mark McNeil … How does this tell us where Lortie was going?"

"McNeil works at the Louis-Hippolyte Lafontaine Psychiatric Hospital. We haven't seen Lortie's file yet, but it wouldn't surprise me to learn that he was a patient there from time to time."

"How do you know McNeil works at Louis-H.? Because of your father?"

Victor stiffened, his hands closing into fists, his jaw muscles tensing. "I just know," he said abruptly and stepped out into the corridor.

There was a single bathroom on the floor, serving four bedrooms. Victor entered the filthy space and slammed the door behind him. Leaning over the sink, he splashed cold water on his crimson face, then massaged the veins bulging at his temples.

He was seething; blind anger surged uncontrollably in him. His fist shot forward, splintering the mirror into a spiderweb of cracks. The detective's pent-up aggression then flowed out in a volley of kicks aimed at the ceramic wall.

Victor took a moment to catch his breath, then opened the window and lit a cigarette. These fits of rage had begun during his rehab and were growing more frequent. Random and overwhelming, they would come on suddenly, often triggered by some minor annoyance. Jacinthe took perverse pleasure in pushing the emotional buttons that provoked such outbursts — a dynamic that left him exhausted. This time, though, her words hadn't been calculated to set him off. She had touched a nerve without meaning to.

Shards of glass had pierced his hand; he drew them out carefully and flushed his skin with a stream of water. Then, for want of any better bandaging, he wrapped half a roll of toilet paper around his knuckles. Drained, he sat on the edge of the grimy bathtub and took a long drag of his cigarette.

That was when he saw it: under the hail of kicks, a tile had shifted. Victor leaned forward and noticed that the grout was broken at regular intervals. Had the fragments been inserted into the space to create the impression that the joint was still intact?

Using his car key, Victor scraped out the grout entirely.

His pulse accelerated. With his thumb and forefinger, he tugged on the tile and removed it from its space. Poking his fingers through the opening, he searched the cavity and removed a cylindrical object. He held it up to the light. It was an aluminum Montecristo cigar tube. With trembling hands, Victor opened it and found a cracked, yellowed newspaper clipping inside. He unrolled it cautiously and saw that the article was dated October 11th, 1970.

At the end of the corridor, Taillon was talking to one of the roomers. She turned to Lessard. "You okay?"

He barely looked at her. "We're going back to Versailles."

"We haven't finished questioning the others."

"Call forensics," he said sharply. "Tell them to go over every inch of the bathroom."

"Did you find something else?"

Victor walked quickly into Lortie's room. He took the plastic bags and the plant off the chest of drawers, then went down the stairs.

After he had instructed the patrol officers to guard Lortie's room until the forensics team arrived, he and Jacinthe walked in silence to the car. Getting behind the wheel, Victor handed the clipping to his partner.

"What's this?" Jacinthe asked, buckling her seat belt.

He gunned the engine. The car leaped forward. "A story on the abduction of Pierre Laporte."

"That guy the FLQ kidnapped during the October Crisis?"

"He was a government minister, and they ended up killing him," Lessard said.

"Fucking whack job," Taillon murmured, referring to André Lortie.

Victor had to hit the brakes hard. Wearing a soiled parka, Michael Witt had stepped out from between two parked cars. The detective sergeant waved a hand, allowing the man to cross. Then he turned and glared at Taillon.

"I knew it."

Witt was holding a bloodstained cloth over one eye.

13

THE BIG BOARD

After bandaging his hand, Victor watered the plant that he'd just installed on his desk. Then he went to the conference room, where Jacinthe was ordering barbecue chicken in anticipation of a long night.

On the big Plexiglas board, someone had arranged the photos of Judith Harper's body taken by Forensic Identification and the pictures of Lortie's body provided by Pearson.

Using adhesive gum, the detective sergeant stuck copies of the newspaper clipping and the Polaroid found in the rooming house to the panel.

After returning to the office, he had checked Lortie's criminal record — something he hadn't had time to do earlier, while the warrants were being hurriedly drawn up — and learned that the homeless man had been arrested a few times for vagrancy and disorderly conduct. More importantly, Lessard had confirmed his suspicion that police officers often brought Lortie to the psychiatric hospital. The most recent episode had occurred in November: Lortie had been brought to Louis-H. by patrol cops because he was having suicidal thoughts.

It was no surprise that Victor had found antipsychotics in Lortie's room.

As he placed the bag containing the pill bottle on the table, he was reminded of something he had to do. He consulted his watch, then pulled a container of pills from his pocket. After downing two tablets, he became aware of Taillon standing in the doorway, watching him with a frown. He hastily pocketed the pill container, looking ill at ease.

"Tylenol. I have a headache."

Jacinthe knew he was lying. And he knew that she knew.

"I ordered you a chicken leg and creamy coleslaw."

"Great. Thanks."

Trying to look composed, Victor sat on a chair and started reading a document summarizing the information that had been gathered, in their absence, on the subject of Nathan R. Lawson. Jacinthe went out, holding the information summary on Judith Harper.

Lawson was seventy-one years old. A native Montrealer, he had inherited a considerable fortune from his mother. The family money had been made in the import-export business. Lawson lived in a luxurious downtown condo and also owned a sumptuous country house on Lake Massawippi in the Eastern Townships and a villa on the Côte d'Azur.

Victor smiled. *Born with a silver spoon in his mouth* would have been the mocking reaction of his former partner, mentor, and second father, Ted Rutherford.

Single, gay, childless, Lawson was a Harvard graduate. He sat on the boards of a variety of companies, foundations, and other charitable organizations. He enjoyed a personal friendship with a former artistic director of the Montreal Symphony, held season tickets to the prestigious Théâtre du Nouveau Monde, and was often seen at high-society galas. Naturally, he dined at the city's best restaurants.

Victor got up and went to the kitchenette for a bottle of water. On his way back, he exchanged glances with Taillon, who had sat down at her desk to look over her summary. He wouldn't have sworn to it, but she seemed displeased.

Resuming his reading, he skipped a few passages, but began reading with care when he came to the account of a conversation between the lawyer and his secretary, whose name Lessard wrote down in his notebook.

Cupping his hands around his mouth, he called out, "Jacinthe?"

"Mmm?"

"Any news from the patrol cops we sent to Lawson's place?"

"Nothing. I just left them a message."

Victor looked at a photo of Lawson printed from his firm's website: ruddy face, thinning hair, weak chin, sleek moustache.

"Wanna trade?" Taillon was standing in front of his desk, holding out the Judith Harper summary. How had she managed to move her considerable bulk without his noticing?

"Sure. Here you go."

Lessard looked down at the document his partner had handed him. Then he realized she hadn't moved. He lifted his eyes.

She was gazing at him with a severe expression. "Tell me you haven't started up again."

"What are you talking about? I told you, it was Tylenol."

Taillon left the room, muttering. Lessard went back to his reading.

Born in Montreal, aged seventy-six, Judith Harper was a retired medical professor at McGill University, where she had taught in the department of psychiatry for more than forty-five years. She had never treated patients, devoting herself to research instead. She had written numerous papers that, in their way, had made a mark on the discipline. Widowed, childless, she belonged to the Friends of the Canadian Centre for Architecture and did volunteer work at Fangs, an animal-rights organization.

Victor coughed and took a sip of water.

Assembled in a hurry by a researcher, the summaries were rudimentary. Still, these preliminary reports gave the investigators an overview of the situation, one that would become more detailed as the case progressed. Victor wrote a note in the margin: in Harper and Lawson, the investigators were dealing with respectable people, both advanced in years.

He heard voices in the corridor. The sound of youthful laughter alerted the detective sergeant to the fact that Gilles Lemaire and Loïc Blouin-Dubois, a tall, skinny young man in his twenties, had just arrived.

Everyone converged on the detectives' room. Paul Delaney stepped out of his office, looking like he had the weight of the world on his sagging shoulders. "Debriefing in fifteen minutes. I ordered barbecue chicken."

A greedy smile appeared on Jacinthe Taillon's features. With the chicken she had already ordered, there would be no shortage of food.

The smell of grease and french fries hung in the room. Empty take-out boxes were piled on the grey rug in one corner. Taillon and Loïc were still eating, Taillon having reluctantly agreed to split one of the two extra meals with her youthful colleague.

Victor had just texted Nadja that he'd be home late, Gilles Lemaire was meticulously cleaning his fingers with moist towel-ettes, and at the head of the table, Paul Delaney suppressed a burp and tossed a few Rolaids into his mouth as he consulted his notes.

"The patrol cops didn't find Lawson, but they've brought in a witness," Delaney said. "Victor, you'll deal with him. Loïc, you can sit in on the interrogation and —"

"Yesss!" the young detective said, smacking the table.

"But this time, Loïc …" Delaney left the rest unspoken.

Loïc took an elastic from his pocket, gathered the long, blond hair that fell in a disordered cascade in front of his eyes, and tied it back in a ponytail. Before starting to eat, he had pulled off his hoodie, revealing a Nirvana T-shirt and colourful, labyrinthine sleeve tattoos that ran up both his arms.

Blouin-Dubois's contrite expression made it clear that he had understood his boss's allusion. "There won't be a problem, Chief."

"Who's the witness?" Victor asked.

"That's still unclear," Delaney answered. "He's a young man who was living at Lawson's place."

"Lawson has no children," the detective sergeant said.

"Then it's not unclear at all," Taillon said. With her tongue in one cheek, she mimed an obscene act. Slapping her thighs with amusement, she sent an inadvertent squirt of barbecue sauce onto the sleeve of Gilles Lemaire's suit. Lemaire, who took scrupulous care with his appearance, scowled at her.

"Jacinthe, please ..."

"Sorry, Chief."

"Gilles, bring us up to speed on what you found in Judith Harper's apartment," Delaney said.

For the moment, the Gnome had nothing of significance to share with his colleagues. Apart from some winter clothes lying on the floor, everything seemed to be in order. A preliminary search hadn't turned up any next of kin for Harper. Residents of the neighbouring apartments didn't know her well, nor had they seen or heard anything out of the ordinary. A search of the dead woman's belongings had, however, yielded the name and contact details of one Will Bennett, who seemed to be her lover. Attempts to get in touch with him had so far been unsuccessful.

"It's important that we talk to him soon," Delaney declared.

No one needed to ask why. Violent crimes against women were usually the work of an estranged husband or lover. Lortie was still the principal suspect, but the longer Will Bennett remained unreachable, the more convincing his claim to the top spot would be.

"I left a message on his cell," the Gnome said. "The ringback tone made me think he might be out of the country."

This detail cast a shadow over the group. No one wanted to be chasing a murderer who'd fled to a foreign jurisdiction.

Lemaire finished up by noting that a Forensic Identification team had arrived at the scene and technicians were going over the place.

"Loïc …"

"Yes, Chief?"

"Wastebasket."

It was the third time the kid had popped a Bubblicious bubble.

With his jeans precariously low on his hips, Blouin-Dubois got up, shuffled to the wastebasket, and got rid of his gum.

"Victor? Jacinthe?"

The detective sergeant described their visit to the rooming house, with Taillon occasionally filling in details. This was followed by a lively discussion on the possible existence of a link between Lawson, Lortie, and Harper.

Delaney only half listened. He was waiting for Victor to continue.

"We should concentrate on the Harper murder, Chief. For now, we have nothing solid on Lawson. It's too early to say whether he's even missing. He could be dead, or he could be on vacation in Costa Rica. And we risk getting caught up in pointless speculation about why Lortie had Lawson's wallet as well as Harper's."

"What do you suggest?"

"While we wait to hear from Lawson, we could try to put together a timeline for Lortie. We may discover that he had an alibi at the time of the murder. In any case, it's a way forward. At the same time, Gilles can continue his efforts to track down Bennett."

"That works. Unless, of course, your interrogation points us in another direction."

"We're also going to send pictures of the hieroglyphics on the cardboard sheets to our documents expert," Victor added. "She'll look them over."

Delaney nodded. "Good idea."

Two uniformed cops had just entered the room, escorting a young Asian man.

"The witness is here!" Loïc exclaimed.

The kid jumped to his feet and hurried over to meet the arrivals.

Victor got up with a sigh. "The fun never stops." He paused. "Jacinthe, can I talk to you for a second?"

The two cops conferred briefly in private, after which the detective sergeant headed for the interrogation room.

Victor was on his feet, circling the chair in which the young man sat. The young man seemed intimidated, and Victor was having trouble getting anything out of him.

"How can I be sure you're telling the truth, Wu? First you told the other officers that you were Mr. Lawson's son. When I mentioned that he had no children, you changed your story. Now you claim he's a friend of your parents and he's putting you up. But we can't get through on the phone number you gave us."

"Telephone lines not so good in China, sir."

Victor gazed into the black depths of the young man's eyes. Loïc, sitting at the end of the table, was following every word, his head swivelling like a spectator's at a tennis match.

"You have no passport. No identification. On top of all that, you say your wallet was stolen. Are you playing games with me?"

Loïc laughed. Victor gave him a sharp look.

"I tell the truth. Mister Lawson, he call me, say he is leaving for vacation. He say to me, please prepare overnight bag and passport."

"Which you gave to the doorman."

"Like Mister Lawson tell me to do."

"You didn't see him?"

The young man shook his head.

"And when did all this happen, Wu?"

"Like I say to you, Friday afternoon."

"Loïc, keep an eye on him. I'll be right back."

"Okay, Vic."

The detective sergeant looked at the young cop and raised a forefinger. "No screwing around, kid."

Victor left the room and filled a paper cup with water at the fountain. Then he stepped into the adjoining room, where Delaney was watching the interrogation from behind a two-way mirror.

"I think he's being truthful about what happened Friday," Victor said, crumpling the little paper cone and dropping it in the wastebasket. "But he's lying about his relationship with Lawson. He may be keeping quiet to protect someone, or he's scared to talk. Either way, he's hiding something from us."

His tie loosened and his shirtsleeves rolled up, Paul Delaney leaned back in his chair and put his feet up on the table. "What do you think he's hiding?"

"I could be wrong, but I get the feeling he's an illegal immigrant."

"What was he doing at Lawson's place?"

"Come on, Paul. You saw the note in the file. Lawson's gay."

"Yeah." Delaney sighed. "And the stolen wallet story?"

"That's getting to be a lot of stolen wallets, if you ask me."

They heard a loud voice in the hallway.

"I forgot to tell you," Delaney said, "the young man called a lawyer before the patrol cops brought him in. I suspect that's the lawyer we're hearing. We've got nothing on Wu for the moment. Let him go. I'll have him put under surveillance."

The moment Victor opened the door, he was accosted by a large individual with brush-cut blond hair, a square jaw, and a quarterback's build.

"Are you Lessard?" the individual demanded.

Crossing his arms, Victor placed himself in front of the interrogation room door, blocking access. He raised a hand to calm Delaney, who was getting ready to intervene.

"That's me. And you are ...?"

"Louis-Charles Rivard. I'm a lawyer at Baker Lawson Watkins." There was arrogance in his voice. "Where's Wu?"

"In there," Victor said, indicating the door with his chin.

"You have nothing on him. Is it a crime for a person to get his wallet stolen?"

"Absolutely not, Mr. Rivard," Victor said in a harsh tone.

Alerted by their voices, Taillon arrived to provide backup.

"But that leads me to wonder," the detective sergeant continued, "why does he need a lawyer?"

Rivard's face reddened. Victor stepped aside to let him enter the interrogation room.

"Get your things, Wu. We're leaving."

A loud *pop* broke the silence. Under Rivard's irritated gaze, Loïc Blouin-Dubois sucked in his deflated bubble and resumed chewing. For once, Victor couldn't suppress a smile.

The frightened young man rolled his weary eyes and put on his jacket.

"While you're here, I have a couple of questions concerning Mr. Lawson."

"Mr. Lawson is on vacation. There's nothing else to say."

"Oh, really? He went on vacation without his wallet?"

There was a momentary light in Rivard's eyes, then it went out.

"What if I wanted to reach him?" Victor asked.

"Out of the question. He's resting."

"In that case, I'll have to put out a missing person alert."

Louis-Charles Rivard darkened and advanced on the detective sergeant. Rivard was a very large man.

"You'll do no such thing," he growled, a threatening finger hovering inches from Victor's chest.

The atmosphere was getting tense. Delaney and Taillon stood by, ready to intervene.

"He has until tomorrow to get in touch," Victor said.

"Is he suspected of something?" Rivard demanded.

"Murder," Victor said without hesitation.

14

GOING HOME

The Gnome was the first to leave, after getting a distress call from his wife at 8:30 p.m.

"It's Sunday, after all," he had said, as though apologizing for walking out on the team.

He'd pulled on his boots, grabbed his coat, and rushed headlong toward the exit, pressing his phone to his ear. There were seven children in the Lemaire family, each as diminutive as their father. The ages of these youngsters, collectively dubbed "the Seven Dwarfs" by Jacinthe, ranged from a few months to thirteen years.

"No, Mathieu, you can't spend the night in the shed! ... Why? Because it's not heated and the weather's freezing! ... Yes, it does matter! Let me speak to your mother ..."

Looking worn out, with the Tupperware that had contained his lunch in a plastic bag under his arm, Paul Delaney had left an hour later. Knowing where his superior officer was headed, Victor had given him a look of heartfelt sympathy, but Delaney, caught up in his own thoughts, hadn't even noticed.

Loïc Blouin-Dubois had waited ten minutes after the boss's departure before leaving himself. Every evening since he'd been sidelined, the young detective had felt obligated to put in long, conspicuous hours at the office, but everyone knew he was spending those hours on Facebook.

Victor was peering through a magnifying glass at the unknown woman's face in the Polaroid pinned to the big board when Jacinthe approached.

"Did you call?" he asked, turning to look at her.

"A while ago. She should be here any minute. What do we want from her, exactly?"

"Have you read the incident report?"

"Skimmed it."

"What was Lortie talking about before he jumped?"

"I don't remember," she answered, unruffled, as she put her hand in her pocket to retrieve her ringing phone. "Hello? … Hang on, I'll come down and open the door for you."

"Speak of the devil," she said without turning.

Victor invited Constable Gonthier, a friendly young woman with laughing eyes, to sit down in the conference room. He gave her a cup of coffee, resisting the urge to have one himself. Between his reflux and the digestive problems that assailed him, he could permit himself only one or two decafs a day.

The detective sergeant regretfully poured himself a glass of hot water and sat down facing the policewoman. Jacinthe was pacing the room, drinking a Red Bull and looking at the big Plexiglas board.

"Sorry, we were on a call," Gonthier said. She smiled, displaying white teeth.

"We're grateful to you for coming so quickly. Listen, I read your incident report, and I have a few questions."

At Lessard's request, Gonthier gave him a general account of the intervention.

"So, Lortie was searching for a heart carved into the brick wall along with his initials and those of a woman," Lessard said.

"Yes."

"Do you remember the woman's name?"

The policewoman searched her memory before finally shaking her head.

"Could it be Sylvie, by any chance?"

"Sylvie! That's it!"

Victor asked a few more questions and confirmed some details, then accompanied the patrolwoman to the elevator.

Taillon questioned him when he got back to the conference room. "How did you know the woman's name?"

He picked up the magnifying glass from the table and handed it to her. "Look at the smudged letters on the Polaroid."

"You could be right," Taillon conceded, one eye closed, the other peering through the lens. "But a first name by itself doesn't get us very far."

"It's a start. We can bring in the experts. They may be able to tell us the model of camera that took the photograph. That could help us date it."

"Pfff. That'll take days and get us nowhere. I don't need an expert to tell me this picture was taken in the seventies. Look at the woman's clothes, her hairstyle."

"In any case, there's another detail that's more interesting."

"When the dude said he wished he could remember, or something like that."

"Exactly. We need to talk to his doctor at Louis-H."

"Maybe his medication left holes in his memory."

"We'll look into that."

Taillon opened the envelope that she'd been holding since Gonthier's departure and laid out a series of photographs. "These came in from forensics. Pictures of the cardboard sheets found at Lortie's place."

They looked at the images in a silence that was almost spiritual. The writing conveyed agitation; the letters and symbols had been drawn with urgency.

"It looks like a series of mementoes," Victor said at last.

"A series of what?"

"Memory aids. Look closely ... what do you see?"

"Well ... dates, street names, words without any logical connection. This part looks like a grocery list."

"Precisely. This is where Lortie wrote down his notes."

"So it was like an agenda?"

"More than that, Jacinthe. I'll bet Lortie was experiencing memory loss, and he wrote notes on the cardboard in an effort to stay on track. What you're seeing here is the inside of his brain."

Coming out of the Villa-Maria metro station, Victor texted Nadja to let her know he'd be home soon. His old, rusted-out Corolla, which had served him faithfully for nearly two decades, had given up the ghost in November. The day before it expired, the car had started without a hitch. But on that fateful morning, when he had put the key in the ignition, there had been no response. Flatline. He'd felt a twinge of heartache when the tow truck came to cart away the remains, but he'd consoled himself with the thought that his car had had the kind of death he dreamed of for himself: to lie down for the night and never wake up.

He hadn't bought a new one yet. Not that he couldn't afford it, but for the moment, he was making do with the metro, with taxis and occasional lifts from Jacinthe, and, now and then, with borrowed service vehicles. On weekends he could count on Nadja to drive him wherever he wanted to go.

Plugged into his iPod, Victor crossed the overpass bridging the Décarie Expressway, the long scar that disfigured the city. At the corner of Girouard, he stopped for a moment to admire the spectacle: windblown snow was swirling in the air, bathed in the greenish halo of the Monkland Tavern's neon sign. A few steps farther along, through the fogged-up window, he saw a press of people inside the Old Orchard Pub. The door opened and a

wave of noise spilled out, along with two girls who teetered away
through the snow, laughing.

Victor had quit drinking a long time ago, but he liked going to
the pub for breakfast now and then on weekends. At the corner of
Marcil, he almost stopped at the Provigo grocery store for milk and
bread. It was just an old habit: since Nadja had come into his life,
his refrigerator had never been so well stocked.

He checked his messages.

Usually she replied when he texted her, but not this time. With
the tip of his nose numb from the cold, he walked down Oxford
Avenue, watching the tree branches sway to the rhythm of The
Dears' "Tiny Man."

His son, Martin, had created the playlist he was listening to.
After several difficult years of flirting dangerously with drugs
and hanging around with friends who had criminal connections,
Martin had finally gotten a grip on his life. He was still working in
the music business as a sound engineer.

Lost in thought, Victor narrowly avoided being hit by a car as he
crossed Sherbrooke. He stepped into his apartment building to an
accompaniment of honks.

Moving through the semi-darkness, he pressed the light switch.

"Nadja?"

As he took off his jacket, he wondered where Martin was at this
moment. It had been several days since his son had called. Nothing
unusual about that; Martin would turn up again as soon as his girlfriend, Mélodie, threw him out after their next fight.

Victor walked into the living room, puzzled by Nadja's
absence. She had texted him earlier that she'd be there when he
got home.

"Nadja?"

He was about to turn on the TV to watch the news when he
heard a faint noise: a scraping sound in the bedroom. His dread
was irrational, but now that it was in his mind, he couldn't dislodge
it: there was someone in there.

His pulse accelerated. Fear released a rush of adrenalin into his veins.

"Nadja?"

Pistol unholstered, hands trembling, he advanced noiselessly, saw a light under the door, and, with a swift movement, kicked it open.

"Put away the popgun, cowboy. You won't be needing it. Not that one, anyway."

By the soft glow of a candle, his girlfriend's sweet features were shining. Her ebony hair fell in a wave over her shoulders. Her jade eyes held him transfixed. Her naked body was a coppery flame against the white sheet, whispering its invitation. The taut buds of her nipples teased him.

Victor shook his head, hands on his hips, and let the air out of his lungs in little bursts. Relaxing gradually, he put his weapon on the dresser and finally smiled. "That could have gone very wrong. Why didn't you answer when I called?"

"Sorry, handsome. It's no picnic trying to surprise a paranoid cop. Come on over here," she said, patting the mattress with her right hand.

Victor ran his fingers through his short, thick hair, then smiled and took off his T-shirt. The muscles and veins rippled under his skin. During the last few years, pumping iron had become a release for him.

He and Nadja had been together since the King of Flies case. They had met at Station 11, to which Victor had been demoted after a serious blunder. Still living with the mother of his children back then, the detective sergeant had gone through a terribly bleak time.

It was only later, in the aftermath of his painful relationship with his girlfriend, Véronique, that he had become aware of Nadja's interest in him. He still found it hard to understand that interest, mostly because of the difference in their ages. It had, in fact, become a source of humour in their relationship.

"Oooh, not bad for a man in his forties," Nadja breathed suggestively.

The young woman caught him before he could slide down next to her. She opened his zipper. Reaching in with her fingers, she pulled him out and began to fondle him.

"What were you thinking about when you came in?" she asked, feeling him harden in her hand. "Your investigation?"

She sped up her movements; he was having trouble focusing. "Just now? Mmm ... oh, that's good ... No, I was thinking about ..." The image of his son rose up before his eyes. "I was thinking about Martin."

"Oh, really? And now?" she asked in a wicked voice.

"Not so much ..."

When she took him in her mouth, Victor stopped thinking about Martin, or about the outside world that devoured a little more of him each day.

He was, at last, living in the infinite space of here and now.

15

THE THIRD MAN

On the northern flank of Mount Royal, the three masked men were advancing, the ice-encrusted snow fracturing under their feet. Dressed in white, economical in their movements, they progressed unhesitatingly with the precision of a military unit, avoiding the glare from the streetlights on De la Forêt Road.

The leader stopped in the middle of the graveyard and raised a hand. Without a word, one of the other men joined him. Working together, they started toppling gravestones methodically, one after another. As the monuments fell, they crashed noisily through the icy layer that covered the snow.

Armed with an aerosol can, the third man approached a gravestone topped by a Star of David. After shaking the can to mix the paint thoroughly, he began spraying red slogans on the monuments: *Muslim power, Death to the Jews, You will pay.*

He had just finished tagging his fifth grave when a hand touched his shoulder. "That's it. We're done." He glanced to his right and saw that his two accomplices had overturned a dozen monuments.

The third man tossed his aerosol can into the snow and followed his companions. They left the Shaar Hashomayim Cemetery, climbing over the iron fence that marked its perimeter. The entire operation had taken minutes. The plan had gone off without a hitch.

The group was on its way to the car when a light went on in the window of a nearby house. At this time of night, that was an ominous sign. They'd been spotted.

The front door opened. A man with unkempt grey hair, wearing a bathrobe, leaned out over the threshold. "Hey! What were you guys doing down there? The cops will be here any minute!"

The leader of the group thrust a hand under his coat and pulled out a pistol with a silencer attached. Still walking, he fired two shots in the direction of the homeowner. The bullets struck the door, which immediately swung shut.

The car was parked in a shadowy spot, its engine running. The group piled in quickly and sped away. They were already on Mount Royal Boulevard when a police cruiser shot past in the opposite direction.

Sitting in the front passenger seat, the shooter turned to the third man, who was in the back seat, and the only one still masked. "Take that thing off, Lessard. You're gonna get us all caught."

Martin did as he was told. Then he slid his hands under his legs so the others wouldn't see that they were shaking.

16

INTERROGATIONS

Monday, December 19th

Victor's gaze slid out the window of the Shäika Café and wandered through Notre-Dame-de-Grâce Park, pausing when it came upon a dog pissing on a tree. Beside the dog, its master was stiff with cold. On Sherbrooke, a ceaseless stream of cars flowed eastward, accumulating in a jam each time the traffic light at Girouard turned red.

"Earth to Victor."

His gaze returned along the snowy sidewalk and re-entered the restaurant, skating momentarily along the tabletop before rising to meet Nadja's eyes. It was barely 7:00 a.m. They had just finished breakfast.

"I was daydreaming. Sorry."

Nadja put her hand on his and gave him a heavenly smile. He'd willingly have died for another one.

"It's all good. When is Jacinthe coming to pick you up?"

"She should be here any minute. I'll get the bill."

They waited on the sidewalk with their arms around each other. The wind bit at their flesh. Victor was about to kiss his girlfriend when a high voice rang out behind them: Nadja's yoga partner came up, guiding a baby carriage through the slush.

There were delighted cries and hugs: the two friends hadn't seen each other since the baby's birth two months earlier. Nadja bent over the carriage and pulled back the blanket to show Victor the infant's face.

"What a little angel," she said, her eyes shining with a light he hadn't seen before.

"Mmm," he responded in a strangled grunt.

A car horn honked. Victor turned and saw Taillon on the other side of the street. He waved to Nadja and her friend before running across between the stopped cars.

Seizing the door handle of the Crown Victoria as though it were a life raft, he dived into the vehicle.

"You okay, Lessard? You don't look so great."

Jacinthe was weaving through traffic, but Victor didn't object. Their power struggle was unfolding at a different level, in a war of knobs. When he boosted the car heater, she lowered it. When she tuned the radio to one station, he switched to another.

"You know I can't stand western music, Jacinthe."

"That was country. Totally different. And don't even think about putting on your club music."

In the end, they settled on a jazz station that, when Victor tuned to it, was playing "So What" by Miles Davis.

"What's the age difference between you and Fernandez?"

"Twelve years."

"Does she want children?"

"Not sure. We've never really talked about it. Change of topic. What do we know about Judith Harper's boyfriend?"

"Bennett? Not much. He's a vice president at Pyatt & White, a company that makes aircraft parts. What about you? You ready to have more kids?"

"You don't think I messed up badly enough with the ones I've got? Where did he go on his business trip?"

"I think Gilles mentioned Boston." Jacinthe fell silent for a moment. "You may not have a choice, if you want to hang on to her. It's right over there."

The Gnome was waiting for them in the lobby of a high-rise near the Italian Consulate on Drummond, just south of Doctor Penfield Avenue. In the elevator, he explained that Will Bennett had gotten back to town during the night and had called Lemaire first thing in the morning.

"He knows?"

"He insisted on being told."

The three police officers wore appropriately sombre expressions as they offered their condolences to Will Bennett, who seemed more taken aback than overcome by grief.

At Bennett's request, the cops took off their shoes before heading up the passage to the living room. The space was decidedly masculine, expensively decorated but not ostentatious. Will Bennett asked the detectives if they'd like a cup of coffee. After a significant look from Victor to Jacinthe, the three declined.

As they sat on the couch, the detective sergeant studied their host. Trim and athletic, in his midfifties, with a sweater draped casually over the shoulders of his Lacoste polo shirt, Bennett projected the carefully crafted image of a prosperous man.

The standard introductory questions revealed that he was divorced and had a daughter in her twenties. He'd been at P & W for more than fifteen years. He'd met Judith Harper four years ago, at a Fangs fundraiser. They had become lovers shortly afterward.

"When did you last see Dr. Harper?" Victor asked him.

"We had dinner the night before I left." Bennett reflected for a long time. "That would have been Tuesday."

"Did you hear from her after that?"

"No," Bennett replied immediately.

"Take a moment to think it over. No emails or text messages?"

"None. Judith didn't own a computer or a cellphone."

"You weren't worried when you didn't hear from her?"

"Not at all. We had a very open relationship. We could go for weeks without seeing each other, and then not be apart for a dozen days in a row."

"Did she have any family?" the Gnome asked.

"Judith was a widow, an only child who never had children of her own. Her father died when she was in her teens. She lost her mother several years ago. She must have a few cousins, but nobody close enough for me to know about."

"There was a big age difference between you, wasn't there?" Taillon observed.

"That's right," Bennett said drily. "I'm fifty-eight and Judith was seventy-six. What's your point?"

"We apologize, Mr. Bennett," the detective sergeant said calmly. "This is a difficult time for you, and here we are, asking questions. Under other circumstances, you would have been a potential suspect, but since you were out of the country …"

"I have an alibi, is that what you're saying?" Bennett's face reddened with indignation.

"I can understand that you're upset," Victor said placatingly. "But give us ten more minutes and we'll be done."

The detectives asked a few more questions about the business trip. At Victor's request, Bennett gave them his boarding passes, his parking stub, the bill from the hotel where he had stayed, and contact details for the two colleagues who had accompanied him.

When they left, Will Bennett slammed the door behind them.

"Ten bucks says he drives a Range Rover," Taillon said, pressing the elevator button.

"My money's on Mercedes," Victor answered.

"You're both wrong. It's an Audi," the Gnome declared, not needing to recheck the report that had been drawn up the day before and was now tucked into a folder under his arm.

The conversation continued as they stepped outside to the building's parking area.

"Even so, follow up with his colleagues," Victor instructed Lemaire.

"Waste of time," Taillon said. "The guy's got a cast-iron alibi."

The wind was wailing between the buildings.

"What's on your mind, Vic?" the Gnome asked, shivering.

"It's probably nothing, but when I asked about the last time he saw Harper, he had to think before answering. When I asked if he'd heard from her since then, he answered right away. Like he didn't want to seem doubtful."

"Lessard and his hunches," Taillon said sarcastically, rolling her eyes.

From the living room of Judith Harper's apartment, Taillon stood with her hands behind her back, watching the bundled-up pedestrians trudging along Sherbrooke. Then she raised her eyes to admire the sheen of the river.

"Not exactly hard up, was she?" Taillon said as she joined Victor in the kitchen.

The detective sergeant was standing with his arms folded, seemingly lost in thought.

"Okay," Taillon said, "you wanted to see where she lived. Happy now?"

He'd looked into each room, examined every hiding place, but for some reason, it was the kitchen that drew him like a magnet.

"Have you found something?"

Silence.

"No? Can we leave?" Jacinthe was already walking up the hallway.

Before turning off the lights, Victor cast a final glance behind him, frowning.

* * *

On the sidewalk beside the car, he lit a cigarette and took a long drag. In the driver's seat, Jacinthe was on the phone, her muffled voice resounding in the cold air. Blowing out blue billows of smoke, he tapped on the passenger window.

She hung up and pressed a button to lower the window. "Finished your smoke?"

"What time are we meeting Lawson's secretary?"

"Eleven o'clock."

Victor tossed his cigarette in the snow and got into the car. "We have time. Let's go."

"Where?"

In operation since 1865, Joseph Ponton Costumes was located in a heritage building on Saint-François-Xavier.

"We're going to be late because of this, Lessard," Jacinthe muttered as she pushed open the door of the boutique.

"Two minutes, that's it," Victor answered. He was already scanning the shelves.

A sales clerk with a triple chin walked toward them, rubbing his hands. "Can I help you, sir?"

"Yeah, maybe. I'm looking for a Santa's elf costume."

"I don't have any in your size. What I've got in stock would only fit a child."

"Show me," Victor said, laughing.

Taillon frowned. She'd just figured out what he was up to. "You're a fucking idiot, Lessard!"

Adèle Thibault had agreed to meet them in the food court of the Stock Exchange Tower. The place was full of morose-looking professionals who, days before the Christmas holiday, were already dreaming of tropical beaches, or country places in the Laurentians, or the seasonal cheer of their own homes. Lawson's secretary was wearing a severe black dress with a yellow carnation above the left breast. Her grey hair was drawn into a bun, revealing her face and highlighting its imperfections. She drank her coffee in little sips, grimacing, as though she were swallowing bitter cough syrup.

"You seem surprised by Mr. Lawson's departure," Victor remarked.

"He's taken a handful of vacations in twenty-six years. This is the first time he's ever left without dictating memos in his active files. And he delegated the bulk of his work to Mr. Rivard, who isn't ... I mean ..."

"Not the best legal mind?" Victor suggested.

She closed her eyes, nodded, and opened them again with a confidential look. "You didn't hear that from me."

"Were you aware of Mr. Lawson's relationship with a young man named Wu?"

The secretary allowed herself a half smile. "Not with that young man in particular, but I'm sure you already know he was a confirmed bachelor."

Victor and Jacinthe exchanged a look. The reference to Lawson's sexual orientation couldn't have been clearer. Adèle Thibault was from a generation that still used euphemisms to describe gay men.

"How did he spend his time on the day in question?" the detective sergeant asked.

"He had an important meeting with clients at seven a.m., which he walked out of before it was over. He asked to have a file brought up from the archives."

"And then?"

"He appeared at my desk ten minutes later, told me to hold his calls, and shut himself in his office. When the file arrived, he asked the mail boy, Lucian, to take it down to his car. Then he left."

"I'm guessing it was unusual for him to behave that way?"

"It had never happened before."

"And this file ... what was it?"

It was an old, inactive file whose exact name she couldn't remember. "North Industries, something like that," was all Victor could get from her. She promised to email him the details.

"Did he seem different as he was leaving? Perturbed?"

"Perturbed? Oh, yes! But that was how he always looked."

Victor couldn't help but smile. Having finished her coffee, the woman pulled a packet of mints from her purse and slipped one into her mouth. She held out the packet to the detectives. Jacinthe, who hadn't said a word so far, couldn't resist.

"You don't think he's gone on vacation?" Victor resumed.

"Not for a second."

"So where is he? Did anything else happen that was out of the ordinary? Think back … a strange phone call? A visitor?"

Taillon touched Victor's shoulder. "Look out. We've got a problem."

The detective sergeant turned and glanced in the direction Jacinthe was pointing: a smiling Louis-Charles Rivard was strutting in front of an attractive young articling student whose shapely legs shimmered through sheer black stockings. The lawyer's smile died on his lips when he saw Lawson's assistant with the officers.

He rushed over, red-faced. "How dare you question our employees without permission?" he demanded in a low voice, trying to keep a lid on his indignation.

Taking Adèle by the arm, he pulled her to her feet and started to lead her away.

For the second time in twenty-four hours, Victor blocked his path. This time, he was deadly serious. "I don't need your permission. What can you tell me about the file that Mr. Lawson took with him on his 'vacation'?" Victor asked, using his fingers to frame the last word in air quotes.

"Nothing. It's covered by lawyer-client privilege. Step aside."

Suppressing an urge to insult the man, Victor stood watching Rivard in silence. Jacinthe knew that look. Victor wouldn't retreat. Suddenly he seemed as impenetrable as a wall. She rose to her feet and placed a thick hand on her partner's chest.

"Let him go, Vic. Before he shits his pants."

●   ●   ●

From the Stock Exchange Tower, they went straight back to Versailles and had a quick bite in the atrium before sitting down at their desks to carry out routine tasks: analyzing evidence, cross-checking facts, organizing information, and doing paper-work. At one point, still preoccupied by her list, Jacinthe went to the hospital to see Horowitz. She returned two hours later wearing a scowl, and shut herself in the conference room.

As for Victor, he blackened his notebook despondently as he scratched out details that had been checked: the documents expert, the medical examiner, and the forensics team were continuing their evaluations; the divers had found nothing after dragging the canal; and the Polaroid woman hadn't turned up in any of their photo databases.

Apart from the information on file, Victor wasn't able to learn much more about Lortie's movements during the days that had preceded his suicide. After being told that the chief of psychiatry at Louis-H. wouldn't be in his office until tomorrow, Victor went out for a smoke in the damp air. With the winter solstice hours away, darkness was already descending on the city.

The parking lot was emptying out little by little. Victor was in a foul humour, feeling as though every opening in the case led nowhere. When he got back to his desk, a Post-it on his computer screen informed him that the boss wanted to talk.

The office was as quiet as a coffin's interior. Leaning back in his chair with his feet propped up on the windowsill, Paul Delaney seemed to be asleep.

"Hello, Chief."

"Have a seat, Victor."

Sighing, Delaney sat forward. With his purple-ringed eyes, hag-gard features, and grey complexion, the head of the Major Crimes Unit had grown old before his time.

"How is she?"

"Stable. She has another test later in the week."

"And how about you, Paul?"

With one finger, Delaney swept dust particles from the surface of his desk. He was silent for a moment. "Madeleine is well treated. The doctors are really good. What I find hard is being shut out. No one tells me anything. The doctors have joined with her, they're fighting the illness as a team, and I'm not part of the process." Delaney's eyes brimmed.

Victor lowered his gaze. "If there's anything I can do ..."

Delaney wiped away a tear and coughed, trying to give the impression that his allergies were acting up. "I read your email. You want me to authorize a missing person alert for Lawson."

"He may be dying somewhere, Chief."

"Or he may be the killer. You don't need to convince me, but the answer's still no."

"Are they putting pressure on you?"

"They're threatening legal action."

"Rivard?"

Delaney nodded.

Victor told him about the confrontation with the lawyer that morning. "I can understand that he'd prevent us from questioning Wu to protect Lawson's reputation. But trying to stop me from talking to his assistant? They're covering something up."

"You're reading too much into it. They want to avoid negative publicity. Do I really need to spell it out? Think how it'll play in the media when it comes out that a principal partner in one of the city's biggest law firms has disappeared. We're not talking about some nobody; the guy's name is on the firm's letterhead. Now throw in the fact that we want to talk to him in connection with a murder, and imagine their reaction."

"Tough luck for them."

"Give me a little time, okay? The higher-ups are feeling the heat. If Lawson doesn't turn up in twenty-four hours, you'll get your missing person alert."

Victor made a face. He didn't like the idea, but he trusted Delaney's judgment and knew the top brass were making his life difficult. Besides, although the chief didn't owe him any explanations, he was still keeping him in the loop — for which Victor was grateful. Delaney's work methods showed him to be the polar opposite of Victor's former boss, Tanguay.

"Okay, Paul."

The detective sergeant was already on his feet, ready to leave, but Delaney detained him.

"Hey, Vic … Gilles was telling me you've put Loïc back out in the field."

"Yeah."

"You sure that's a good idea?" Delaney was glad the initiative had come from Victor, but he didn't want him feeling obligated to take Blouin-Dubois under his wing. A few weeks previously, while examining photographs of a crime scene where Loïc had assisted them, Jacinthe and Victor had noticed that the young man had stepped with both feet onto a bloodstained carpet. It was clearly inadvertent, but his contamination of an important element of the crime scene had provoked anger among his colleagues.

"The kid knows nothing about homicide, but he knows the street. In any case, it's time we gave him another chance …"

In the conference room, with crime-scene photos arrayed in a semicircle in front of her, Jacinthe was eating the contents of a box of brownies and feeling miserable. Though she hated to admit it, Lessard had been right: going back to see Horowitz had been a waste of time. The interrogation of Bennett had also proven useless.

It was past 5:00 p.m. Another day had been wasted following leads that went nowhere. Jacinthe had hoped that looking at the photographs would yield a flash of insight — but there was nothing. Nothing but emptiness, piling up on itself.

She finally tore her gaze away from Judith Harper's bluish face, stood up, and turned off the light. The show was over. She was going home.

Lessard still lingered at his desk. He was usually the last to leave the office. She was about to make a wisecrack when she realized that he was whispering into his phone. Silently edging closer, she caught snatches of his conversation.

"I'm sending them to you ... but you've got to keep this to yourself. If anyone finds out, I'm going to be in hot water." With that, the detective sergeant hung up.

"Who you talking to, Lessard?" she asked, walking up to him.

Victor reacted with surprise. He hadn't noticed her approaching. "Jacinthe! You startled me," he stammered. His heart was pounding.

Taillon was gazing at him sus piciously. "Who was that on the phone?" she insisted.

"Huh? Uhh ... it was Nadja," he said, looking her in the eye.

Victor left around 8:00 p.m., completely drained, with a single thought in his head: to eat something and go to bed. He stopped to pick up butter chicken at D.A.D.'s Bagels on Sherbrooke, a 24-7 curry place where he'd spent Christmas Eve the year after his separation.

After dumping his things on the couch, he turned on the TV and resumed watching *Casablanca*. He and Nadja had started the film the night before, but he'd fallen asleep before the end. And while Humphrey Bogart, his face bleak, promised Ingrid Bergman that they'd always have Paris, he ate the meal he'd heated up in the microwave. In a daze, he watched the end credits without seeing them, then abandoned his dirty dishes in the sink. He was in his undershirt, brushing his teeth before bed, when he heard the front door creak open.

Nadja, on night duty at Station 11, had come by during her break to say hello. Victor was about to kiss her and ask how the evening was going when she bit his lip and pressed him against the tiled wall. "Fuck me."

He took her there, among their hastily discarded clothes, from behind, against the bathroom sink. Nadja's panting breath fogged the mirror each time he pressed into her; her shining lips brushed against the glass. Gripping her by the hips, Victor watched her spine dancing to the rhythm of his thrusts. He didn't take his eyes off the perfect curve of her haunches until he exploded into them.

Nadja had come and gone; she'd evaporated, evanescent as a ghost. Now that she was sharing his bed almost every night, he had trouble falling asleep without her. He'd gotten up several times to go to the bathroom, he'd rearranged his pillows repeatedly, and he'd been unable to make up his mind whether to leave one leg outside the covers.

His mind strayed idly in a half-conscious doze, mixing up details of the case with old memories: his mother and his brother Raymond, both murdered, were walking barefoot over shards of glass, leading Judith Harper into a dark and sinister forest. He dreamed that Nadja, pregnant by him, had given birth to triplets in the kitchen; when he got home from the office, he found the infants sitting in a puddle of blood in front of the refrigerator, playing with magnetic letters and numbers. Nadja was seated in a corner, weeping, her face buried in her wrinkled hands.

He cried out and sat up abruptly in bed. After catching his breath, he checked his watch. Too bad. He got up, pulled on his jeans, and opened the window. After a few drags on a cigarette, he picked up his phone from the bedside table.

"Hello?" a sleepy female voice said.

"Jacinthe?"

"No. Just a second, Victor, I'll put her on …"

The whispers he heard at first soon gave way to loud exhortations. Clearly, Taillon was a heavy sleeper.

"What the fuck, Lessard!" she roared when she finally came on the line.

"Judith Harper didn't have children."

"You woke me up at two in the morning to tell me that?"

"We need to go back to her apartment with the forensics team."

"You're wasting my time, Lessard. I'm hanging up now."

"There were number magnets on the fridge, Jacinthe. Coloured plastic numbers — for kids. Think about it. The killer was there!"

17

COLLAR

The car window descended, revealing the sinister features of the huge man behind the wheel. Wearing sunglasses at night, he looked like a Corey Hart wannabe.

Will Bennett handed him the envelope.

As the driver counted the wad of bills, he smiled, revealing immaculate teeth. "Room 38," the man said, giving him a key.

The window was rising when Bennett put out a hand to stop it. "I hope the merchandise is top quality. Because last time ..."

The driver took off his glasses, narrowed his eyes, and gave Bennett a long look. He seemed to be hesitating between laughter and black rage. "It is," he said. "But no bruises this time. Or it'll be the last."

Will Bennett entered through a door that opened onto the parking area, thus avoiding any contact with the motel receptionist. The drab room was lit by a lamp on the nightstand.

The girl was stretched out on the unmade bed with a collar around her neck, her hands tied behind her back, her legs bound by duct tape. A rope attached to the collar was fastened to the bedposts, immobilizing her head, while a rubber ball, held in place by a leather strap, gagged her.

Will Bennett saw fear in the girl's eyes as he advanced toward the bed. He pulled on his gloves, in no hurry.

18

EVIL

Evil creeps. Evil prowls. It insinuates itself into the soul's blank spaces. And sometimes, for no apparent reason, when you're sure it's busy elsewhere, it catches your scent of ashes on the cold air, turns from its path and follows you. From that moment onward, every fibre of your body knows there will be no truce. The husk that carries you is doomed. But the brain, up to the very last second, manages to create the illusion that there's a way out, some possible avenue of escape.

While he drifted between half-conscious states, Nathan Lawson had been untied from the bed. A collar had been attached to his neck with a metal rod whose sharp points penetrated the flesh on his breastbone and under his chin, forcing his head back at a forty-five-degree angle, making it an agony to swallow and preventing him from breathing normally.

Behind Lawson's back, a complicated mechanism linked the collar to the metal shackles encasing his hands. At its other end, a sort of metal spider armed with a black dart loomed threateningly over the back of his neck. Before Lawson had fully woken up, his eyes and mouth had been covered with duct tape.

A yellow brilliance had scalded his retinas when the tape was pulled off, but it had taken him only an instant to assess the danger of his situation.

Lawson was in the storeroom, in the basement. He had recognized the space when he saw the jars of preserves on the shelves and the butcher's table standing in the corner.

The tiny space was sealed by a metal door. The glow from the ceiling bulb licked the grey concrete. Lawson could walk, but he was unable to bend his knees; he had strained his eyes in a vain effort to understand why.

He was shaking with cold. As far as he could tell, only his underwear remained on his body.

Each time his alertness waned and his head sagged, the sharp points dug into the flesh of his sternum and his chin. They didn't touch any vital organs, but the searing pain forced him to stay awake. A rivulet of blood flowed from his wounds, drying in layers on his throat and chest.

How long had he been here? Two hours? Twenty?

The second answer seemed more likely: the odour of his own excrement hung in the air, and his soiled legs were trembling with fatigue. He had briefly contemplated letting himself fall to the floor to rest, but he was stopped by fear of the points penetrating his soft flesh. He couldn't stand any more pain.

At first, he had convinced himself that he wanted to die.

At his age, he had no regrets. He had lived the life he'd dreamed of: he had seen what he wanted to see in the world, acquired the objects he coveted, treated himself to all the sex he desired. On a human level, now that his mother was gone, he had no attachments left, no one to miss, no one to be missed by. There was his work. He could have continued for a few more years. But he knew the end was drawing near.

Then he started to think about the situation in which he found himself. He hadn't seen his executioner; they hadn't exchanged a word. But he knew it could only be André Lortie. Once again, without being able to formulate an answer, he wondered why the affair was resurfacing now.

Then fear had engulfed him, and all his attention had turned to the key he'd seen out of the corner of his eye, lying on the table. For hours it had occupied his thoughts. For hours his brain had tried unremittingly to convince him that the key held the promise of escape, that if he succeeded in getting his hands on it, he could open the shackles that bound his wrists and free himself from this trap.

Ready to die?

On the contrary, Nathan Lawson felt ready to do anything just to savour one more Christmas Eve, which he'd spend alone, continuing the ritual that he and his mother had observed for so many years: watching *The Phantom of the Opera* — the classic silent version — while consuming large amounts of champagne and foie gras.

And yet, for hours, his body had refused to obey him and pick up the key.

All because of the red line.

Indeed, there was a strip of red tape in front of the table. Each time he approached it, his body would contract and he'd retreat a few paces, convinced that it was a trap or a signal; that if he crossed the line, he would die.

Hobbling to the metallic accompaniment of his restraints, Lawson advanced to the table in a stiff-legged penguin walk. He had finally convinced himself that he had to do something; that he'd soon die anyway if he didn't take a chance. His strength was ebbing fast. He was losing blood and wouldn't be able to endure the pain much longer before lapsing into madness. His entire body was racked by suffering. His neck felt like it was about to snap; his arms and back were at the breaking point.

Lawson paused to think. He must, at all costs, see what was under the butcher's table. Because of the yoke that immobilized his head and impeded any movement, it was the only place he'd been unable to look. It was the only place where a threat might still be hiding.

Eyes bulging, short of breath, his nostrils greedily sucking in every molecule of air, Lawson forced his head forward. The sharp points drove farther into his breastbone and his chin; blood spurted; the pain became unbearable.

A scream died in his throat. Tears rose to his eyes.

But he had seen! There was nothing under the table. Nothing!

He took superstitious care not to touch the red line with his feet.

With his back to the table, he groped along the surface until the key was in his hand. With a twisting effort, he managed to insert the key into the lock of his shackles. When he turned it, he felt relief as the hold on his wrists loosened.

His brain rejoiced. All the time he had lost was compressed, passing before his eyes like a promise.

At the same moment, the turn of the key triggered a mechanism: latches were unbarred, springs were released. The dart flew with blinding speed into the back of his neck and came out his throat, perforating the carotid artery and severing the jugular vein.

Face down on the floor, Lawson was soon lying in a pool of blood. Until the last second, he had believed there was a possibility of escape. If he had listened to his instincts instead of his mind, he would no doubt have lived longer.

But just a little longer.

NOVEMBER 1981
THE NIGHT OF THE LONG KNIVES

That night, in a kitchen of the Château Laurier Hotel in Ottawa, while René Lévesque and his delegation slept in Hull, Attorney General Jean Chrétien was negotiating in secret with the premiers of Canada's other provinces.

The shock was brutal: a deal to patriate Canada's Constitution was struck by Prime Minister Trudeau and agreed to by ten of the country's eleven governments, without the assent of the government of Quebec.

Obviously, Lévesque refused to sign. On television, there was a romantic quality to his sad expression. It was justified. He felt betrayed, stabbed in the back by the other provincial premiers.

I wish I could take him in my arms and whisper to him that we'll overcome the rage of being held captive in our own land. Just as I have overcome the rage of being held captive in my body and mind.

Living in the pain of exclusion, Quebec is a different being, a unique entity, a space to be shaped and defined.

I believe exactly the same thing could be said of me.

READ-ONLY MEMORY

19

LOUIS-H. LAFONTAINE

Tuesday, December 20th

It was 6:25 a.m., and the plastic plants at Chez la Mère were swaying to the rhythm of the plow's rumble as it pushed the previous night's snowfall to the edge of the sidewalk. Nearby, at the corner of Pie-IX Boulevard, a tow truck siren ululated, commanding those who hadn't yet moved their cars to do so now. Taillon was about to dig into a poutine, while Victor's ill temper swirled at the surface of his coffee. They had been in the restaurant for a few minutes, having spent most of the night exploring Judith Harper's apartment with the forensics team.

"Watching your cholesterol, are you?" he asked ironically.

"It's this or cigarettes. Gotta die of something, right?"

Reaching for the condiments, she turned her food into a sodden mush. The detective sergeant shrugged and went on: "It's pretty frustrating …"

"What?" Jacinthe asked, before stuffing a quarter of the poutine into her face on the first bite.

"0 blue, 1 red, 2 orange, 3 yellow, 4 purple, 6 green," Victor recited, his eyes on his notebook as he reviewed the colours of the magnetic numbers found on Judith Harper's refrigerator. "We worked through the night, and this is all we've got."

"Unless the forensics people come up with prints."

"Don't count on it. That wasn't an oversight. The killer wanted us to find the numbers."

"Why? To give us a lead?" she asked between bites.

Victor blew on his steaming drink before taking a sip.

"Did you notice that there were six digits? One less than for a phone number, but it could be a date …"

Jacinthe's fork hung in the air, then her fist banged the table. "Maybe he's trying to direct our attention to something that happened!"

"Or to some significant date for Judith Harper."

"Okay! So why were you bitching just now, like we had nothing to go on?" She scratched her forehead. "But if he was trying to give us a lead, why leave the numbers all mixed up?"

"No idea." He was silent for a moment. "You've got sauce on your chin," he said, yawning.

"Six digits … that's a lot of possibilities." She wiped her face with the back of her hand. "What time are we seeing the psychiatrist again?"

"Eight o'clock. Give me the keys. I want to take a nap in the car. I'm fried."

Jacinthe handed him the keys and said something about dessert, but Victor had already hoisted himself from his seat and was moving between the tables, where a few customers sat reading the *Journal de Montréal*.

He opened the restaurant door and his eyes were bathed in whiteness. The cottony sky hung so low that he wanted to lie down in it and fall asleep.

Taillon had woken him up after parking the car in the lot of the Louis-H. Lafontaine psychiatric hospital. With a stiff lower back, Victor had smoked a cigarette in front of the hospital entrance, his teeth chattering.

They had expected to find a sparsely decorated workspace, with diplomas on the walls and piles of dusty files, but Dr. Mark McNeil's office surprised them: white walls, dark wood floors,

minimalist furniture, nothing visible on the desk but the clean
lines of an iMac and an agenda.

The chief of psychiatry was a well-built man with a gravelly
voice and a luxuriant moustache reminiscent of *Magnum, P.I.*

The detectives started out by settling legalities with McNeil,
specifically the issue of doctor-patient confidentiality. Though
he wasn't obliged to answer their questions in the absence of a
warrant, McNeil assured them that since Lortie had died without
known next of kin, and since this was a murder case, he would
be flexible.

Taillon and Victor then got down to business, asking the psychiatrist to tell them about André Lortie. Looking through his notes,
McNeil told them that Lortie had first come under the hospital's
care in 1969. At the time, he had arrived at the emergency ward
in crisis, suffering from psychotic delusions. After being examined
and put under observation, he had been diagnosed with severe
bipolar disorder — the term back then was *manic depression* —
accompanied by typical delusions of grandeur and persecution.

McNeil explained that Lortie's file contained few details about
his past. Had he, like so many others, once had a house, a job,
a social life, a wife? What events had tipped him into a life of
vagrancy? The doctors who had worked on his case over the years
didn't seem to know. But McNeil was able to confirm that the man
had spent the past several years living in the streets of downtown
Montreal or staying at homeless shelters.

The psychiatrist also informed them that Lortie had been an
in-patient at the Louis-H. Lafontaine Hospital numerous times
since his first admission. Depending on the seriousness of his condition, these hospital stays had lasted from a few days to several
months. Each time, he had presented symptoms of psychotic delusion. Nevertheless, over the past few years, thanks to an increasingly
effective drug regimen and more structured treatment, his condition had been "stabilized." More recently, he'd been able to move
into the rooming house that the two detectives had visited.

"When you say Lortie was in a state of psychotic delusion, what does that mean, exactly?" Jacinthe asked, seeming for once to actually be interested in the conversation.

McNeil sat up straight, his hands lying flat on the armrests of his chair. "An intense manic phase can lead to psychotic symptoms like delusions and hallucinations. There's often an element of truth in the delusions, but the person suffering from them loses touch with reality and becomes convinced of the veracity of something that is objectively false. Manic phases often involve dangerous behaviour on the part of the patient, or even depressive episodes marked by suicidal thoughts."

"At which point hospitalization is in order," Victor suggested.

"That's right. Hospitalization happens voluntarily or at the request of a third party. In Lortie's case, it was usually the police who brought him here when he stopped taking his medications."

"And generally, what are the delusions about?" Victor asked.

"My goodness … the mentally ill can be delusional in a variety of ways. For example, there are delusions of persecution. That's what happens when a person thinks he's the object of a scheme or conspiracy."

Jacinthe told the psychiatrist about the writing on the cardboard sheets found in Lortie's room.

"We also found a newspaper article he'd hidden away," Victor said. "It was about the kidnapping of Pierre Laporte."

The psychiatrist's expression became animated. "I wasn't one of his treating physicians, but from what I remember of my conversations with colleagues, Laporte was one of Lortie's obsessions. He claimed that he'd participated in the kidnapping. Which is false, obviously. The names of the FLQ members involved have been known for a long time. You see, this is a good example of megalomaniacal delusion: an overestimation of the self that is at odds with reality. The writing you saw on the cardboard sheets is most likely the product of his delusions."

"Is it a sickness?" the detective sergeant asked.

"We refer to it as a psychiatric disorder. In itself, delusion is a symptom that shows us that the patient's thoughts are disturbed."

Victor lifted his gaze from his notebook; he had already filled several pages. "Are the causes known?"

"They can be numerous." McNeil sighed. "Ingestion of toxic substances, disease of the central nervous system, trauma, inherited traits, stress. We try to identify precipitating factors, but often we don't find any."

"And Lortie?" Jacinthe asked.

The psychiatrist frowned doubtfully. "From what I recall, we never really identified a precise cause. Except that in his case, the symptoms finally evolved into chronic hallucinatory psychosis."

"In words I can understand?" Jacinthe demanded.

"The patient hears voices. His condition fluctuates between periods of greater and lesser severity."

"How is it treated? Is there any cure?" Victor asked.

"Antipsychotics allow for a reduction of symptoms in some cases. But no, there's no cure. From the moment the defences crumble, the problem will come back repeatedly in the form of breakdowns. The sick person is condemned to extreme solitude. The social impact is terrible."

Victor stood up and took a few steps around the office to restore circulation in his legs. "In your opinion, could Lortie have killed anyone?"

"Short answer: definitely. A person affected by bipolar disorder can have homicidal and suicidal tendencies."

"And the long answer?" the detective sergeant ventured.

McNeil launched into a veritable dissertation, offering explanations that the two investigators didn't altogether follow.

The conversation went on for a little while before Jacinthe changed the subject. "Did you know the people Lortie hung out with?"

The psychiatrist shook his head. "As I said, the impact of this illness makes it hard to sustain social relationships. Lortie probably didn't have many friends."

"I understand," Victor said, nodding. "But I'll try my luck one last time: did he ever mention a Sylvie?"

For a moment, McNeil studied the documents spread out before him, smoothing his moustache. "I don't see anything in the file," he said, lifting his eyes. "But maybe you could talk to Ms. Couture."

"Who's that?" Jacinthe asked.

"She's an orderly who often looked after Lortie. I'll have my assistant take you to her."

The two cops thanked the psychiatrist. They were about to walk out when McNeil put a hand on the detective sergeant's shoulder, studying his face. "Forgive me, Detective, but something's been bothering me since you walked in. Do we know each other? Your face seems familiar."

Victor lowered his eyes. Taillon looked over in surprise.

"We saw each other at the psychiatric emergency ward in July." Victor smiled awkwardly. "You prescribed Paxil for me."

Victor had gone into a serious depression after the King of Flies case. One night, with dark ideas slithering like worms inside his head, he'd voluntarily checked himself into Louis-H. after coming within a hair's breadth of losing his sobriety at a bar in the Hochelaga-Maisonneuve district. The detective sergeant had spent a few days at the hospital on a voluntary basis.

"Of course! Forgive my indiscretion," McNeil said, looking sincerely sorry.

Self-effacing and anonymous, Dr. McNeil's secretary walked noiselessly as she guided them through a maze of corridors. Jacinthe glanced suspiciously in all directions, half expecting the characters from *One Flew Over the Cuckoo's Nest* to jump out at her. When they came to a waiting room, the secretary asked them to take a seat and excused herself to search for the orderly. Wringing her hands, Jacinthe wondered how to dispel the awkwardness and break the wall of silence — but Victor spoke first.

"Did you know that Émile Nelligan lived here from 1925 until his death?"

"The poet? Was he crazy?"

"That's the official story. But he was probably just somewhat asocial. So you see, it isn't just insane people who end up in an asylum."

"Why didn't you say anything?"

The detective sergeant's eyes dimmed. He shrugged.

Jacinthe put a hand on his forearm. She knew how sensitive the moment was. "For a long time, Lessard, you were the only person on the team who knew about my private life. You never judged me. I say plenty of dumb things, but I never would have joked about this."

Victor said nothing.

"Anyway, that explains the 'Tylenol' you've been taking on the sly. You should have talked to me. I was scared you were getting hooked again."

"I haven't had a drink in seven years," Victor said, turning his head slowly toward his partner with a dark expression. "Get over it."

He went to AA meetings four times a year, more to see old friends in the group than out of necessity.

"I'm not just talking about alcohol, Lessard. With all the medication you had to take for your leg, you could've gotten hooked. They say dependency is genetic. It's not your fault. There's a fragility in you."

A fleeting image arose in Victor's memory: his drunken father, mouth foaming, had just given his mother another beating before Victor's eyes.

"Whatever," he muttered, shaking his head.

"You never know, my friend."

Jacinthe's remarks had stirred dark, painful emotions in him, but he held his temper in check and didn't react.

They waited in silence for a few minutes, neither one saying a word, until a woman entered. Dressed in a powder-blue uniform, she had touches of pink in her cheeks, and her ash-blond hair was held back with an elastic.

"Hello," she said in a calm voice. "I was told you wanted to see me."

"Yes," Victor said. "Dr. McNeil thinks you may be able to help us with a case."

"I have to look after a patient. If you don't mind, we'll talk on the way."

Victor began to ask questions about Lortie, trying to learn more about the people he had spent time with. As McNeil had already indicated, Lortie had led a marginal life, with limited social interaction. Making an effort to remember, the orderly eventually told them about a young man with whom Lortie had occasionally played chess, but the memory was too vague for her to remember his name. As for the places he'd frequented, her memory was even less clear.

They came to a room in which an obese male patient lay on his side. The orderly approached him, speaking softly. He emitted a few guttural growls. Victor and Jacinthe understood that it was a matter of going to the bathroom, and the man was expressing strong reluctance. With manifest empathy, the orderly helped him roll over and get on his feet. She supported him all the way to the bathroom, then came out once he was safely installed.

"How do you do it?" Victor asked. "It must take incredible patience and strength to do your job."

"I have my father to thank for the strength," the woman said, chuckling. "He always wished I'd been a boy."

"Did André Lortie ever mention the names of people close to him? Sylvie, for example?"

"Not to my knowledge," the woman said after thinking for a moment. "But if you don't mind my asking, what's prompted all these questions? Did something happen to Mr. Lortie?"

"Oh. I'm sorry. I thought you knew."

Victor described the circumstances of the homeless man's death.

A frown creased the woman's brow. "Maybe Dr. McNeil already told you, but what you've described sounds a lot like a story that Mr. Lortie often told."

"What was it?"

"He was convinced that he'd had blackouts in the past. And after one of those episodes, he'd woken up in a panic, believing he had killed somebody."

"Why do you see a link with our story?" Victor asked, intrigued.

"Because he said that when he woke up, his clothes were bloodstained."

The orderly raised her head and looked at the two cops with piercing eyes before continuing. "And according to him, he had the victims' wallets in his possession."

20

BAD SON

"You'll never take me alive! Never!"

Martin turned and saw them on the other side of the chain-link fence, running toward the adult, their strident yells filling the air.

Grabbing the YMCA teacher's legs, the children wrestled him to the ground. Overwhelmed by their weight and their laughter, he died in a flurry of theatrical convulsions on the snow.

Leaving the daycare behind him, Martin continued on his way. As he looked at a line of crows perched on a wire, he tried to recall the moment in his imaginative progress through childhood when he had tilted into the dismal reality of adult life. A distant memory came back to him, bringing a smile to his lips. His father had woken him up early one morning. They had tiptoed out into the silver glow of dawn. At the park, in silence, they had flown a red kite.

The smile faded. Each return of that reminiscence brought its share of melancholy. Why couldn't he shed the impression that his childhood had been stolen from him? That he had wasted his time? Why did only fragments remain? After all, Martin hadn't had a particularly difficult childhood. He'd always been able to count on his loving parents.

There had been times when he tried to follow the thread of memory back in time to figure out what had caused the change in his trajectory. One certainty emerged: it wasn't a single decisive event, but rather a series of factors that had all seemed trivial in the moment.

Martin crossed Notre-Dame-de-Grâce Avenue and continued south on Hampton.

It was 8:53 a.m. The temperature was minus eight degrees Celsius, and he was walking unhurriedly, with his hoodie pulled low over his eyes.

He was a few blocks from his father's apartment, hoping not to run into him. But if he did happen to see him, he would say that he'd spent the night at Mélodie's place in Côte-Saint-Luc and was on his way to have a cup of coffee with some friends.

Which wasn't too far from the truth …

As he cautiously neared his mother's house, Martin keyed a number into his phone and waited for the voice mail before hanging up. He repeated the procedure twice. When he was certain that the coast was clear, he went around the side of the house and, calf deep in snow, crossed the yard to the deck. The key was hidden in the usual place.

He entered through the French doors and left his shoes on the rubber mat. Listening to be sure no one was home, he hurried up the stairs to the second floor. He hesitated for a few seconds, then opened his bedroom door, stopping on the threshold. His mother hadn't touched anything since his departure. Everything was as it had been: his hockey cards were still stacked on the chest of draw-ers, his Guitar Hero instruments were piled in the corner, and his old Canadiens' jersey was rolled in a ball on the carpet. Kurt Cobain, crucified on the wall, looked down at him.

His parents' divorce had happened a few years ago. Martin had seen them both struggle with the messiness of being single. His mother had coped more successfully at first, while Victor had sunk into depression. Marie's return to unmarried life had been pret-ty painless; still in her early forties, she had turned into a cougar, going out with men much younger than she was.

Funnily, his relationship with her had never been so close and harmonious as it was during that period, when she'd seemed to understand him better, and rules were more relaxed. One evening, she had even confided to him that she'd taken ecstasy at a rave.

Then, after a few wild years, she had settled down with Derek, an accountant whose pleasant personality Martin hated, believing it to be insincere.

Marie, on the other hand, was utterly smitten: "Derek says …"; "Derek thinks …"; "Derek believes …"

There had been no quarrels with Marie. Martin hadn't slammed the door. He had simply found refuge at Victor's place, his arrivals and departures dictated by the ups and downs of his relationship with Mélodie.

The young man stepped into the room. He pulled out the bottom drawer of the chest and turned it over on the bed. The object he had come for was wrapped in a white cloth and taped to the external surface of the back of the drawer. Martin hadn't touched the weapon since his father had saved his ass, getting him out of a dangerous situation a few years ago. He removed the cloth and felt the object's weight in his hand for a moment before sliding it into his belt.

This time, he would see it through.

And he wouldn't need anyone's help to get him out of trouble.

Martin restored the drawer to its place. Shaking off his nostalgia, he glanced around the room one last time, then closed the door.

He went down the stairs, holding the handrail. The pistol bumped against the small of his back.

21
FORTUNE·TELLER

Jacinthe and Victor stood facing a diminutive elderly woman. Dressed in a flowing ochre robe, her head encased in a rainbow-coloured turban, she looked like a fortune teller in some cheesy sitcom from the 1960s. Mona Vézina had left a message on Victor's voice mail an hour earlier, but he had listened to it only as they were leaving Louis-H. The detective sergeant had called back, and they had agreed to meet right away. The woman occupied a small, nondescript space in a commercial building not far from Place Versailles that contained several professional offices.

"Come in, sit down," the documents expert said, gesturing to her guest chairs, making the dozens of bracelets on her wrists jangle.

For a second or two, they half expected her to pull a crystal ball out of a drawer and start reading their fortunes.

"Thanks for seeing us," the detective sergeant mumbled as he sat down.

A framed photograph of Pope John Paul II hung on the wall behind the documents expert.

"It's a pleasure," she said, putting down the rosary she'd been fingering when the officers had walked in. She smiled for the first time, revealing small, closely packed teeth that overlapped a little in front. Bathed in the office's humid warmth, she seemed to move slowly through the thick air.

Jacinthe sat down. With her cheeks already flushed, she picked up an envelope from the desk and began fanning herself.

Mona Vézina started out with the usual disclaimers, telling the officers what they already knew: that her opinion was based on her examination of the Polaroid photo and the cardboard found in Lortie's room, the sheets on which the tangle of writing that she called "the mosaic" had been inscribed. She added that her opinion was provisional and subject to change if new facts were subsequently brought to her attention. Then she opened a file folder, withdrew a sheet of paper, and consulted it.

"What I can tell you straight off is that the mosaic was laid down in numerous stages, using different kinds of ink. If you want to date them and find out when they were created, you'll have to talk to a chemist. I can recommend one who works with the Montreal Police."

"That won't be necessary," Jacinthe said.

"Good. Also, I've gone over the materials carefully with a magnifying glass and microscope, and I have no reason to believe any parts of the mosaic have been falsified or simulated. Which leads me to conclude that the mosaic is the work of a single person. However, I'm not in a position to identify Mr. Lortie as the author of the mosaic. If you want me to go further, you'll have to provide me with a sample of his handwriting for comparison. A letter, for example …"

"At the moment," the detective sergeant said, "the only other writing sample we have is the word on the Polaroid: 'Sylvie.'"

"And for that matter," Taillon added, "we can't connect the photo to Lortie with certainty."

"Lortie is the writer, Jacinthe," Victor said. "I think we can take it for granted that the contents of his room belonged to him." He turned to Mona Vézina. "Does the handwriting match?"

"You have to understand, a single word isn't a representative sample, so I can't give you a definite conclusion," the woman answered. "But I'd say there's a better than seventy-five percent chance that the writing on the Polaroid and the mosaic came from the same person."

"Anyway, it's a man's writing, that's for sure," Jacinthe declared.

"I don't like to contradict you, Detective," the documents expert said, "but contrary to popular belief, there are three things that can't be categorically determined from handwriting analysis: whether the person is left- or right-handed, the person's sex, and the person's age."

In her surprise, Jacinthe fell briefly silent. Then, thinking about it, she came at the problem from another angle. "What can you tell us about the writer's personality?"

"I'm a documents expert, not a graphologist."

Still fanning herself with the envelope, Taillon refused to be dissuaded. "You must have an opinion. What was your first impression as you examined the mosaic?"

Mona Vézina looked at Victor, as though asking for permission. He nodded.

"Well, I don't imagine you'll be surprised to hear that I think the writer was disturbed. This may sound odd, but he seems to be simultaneously confused and methodical. All handwriting contains natural variations. In this case, the writing comes from a single person, but in certain respects, there are clear, radical breaks. If I had to bet, I'd say the writer was affected by some kind of personality disorder."

Something in the body language of the documents expert caught Victor's attention — perhaps it was the way she lowered her eyes when she spoke. He had a vague sense that she didn't dare express herself unreservedly.

"Did you notice anything else, Ms. Vézina?"

The woman hesitated, twisting her hands nervously. There was an awkward silence.

"Listen … how can I say this?" She paused, gathering her thoughts, choosing her words with care. "As you know, I'm a police consultant. I have a specific mandate, and that's to analyze handwriting. As a rule, I examine the container and ignore the contents. You understand? But in this case, because it's a murder and I was intrigued, I allowed myself to do an analysis that went beyond my usual area of competency. I just want you to understand that I have no desire to tread on the specialists' toes …"

Victor understood perfectly. Ever since popular TV shows like *CSI* had started glorifying their work, some of the bigger egos on the forensics team had come to see themselves as intellectually superior to lesser mortals. The documents expert, being curious by nature, had been told more than once, with some condescension, to stick to her job description.

Still, it would cost them nothing to hear her out. The forensics unit was analyzing the mosaic as well, but had come up with nothing so far.

"Don't worry, Ms. Vézina, this stays between us."

Reassured, she gave Victor a grateful smile. She appreciated this indication of his faith in her.

"Most of the writing on the mosaic consists of isolated words or word sequences without apparent meaning, often repeated many times. For several hours, I looked for some kind of pattern or underlying logic, but without success. So I changed my approach. I tried to isolate sentences. There aren't many, but in the end I found a few."

Mona Vézina placed a photograph on the table in front of them.

"I got this from forensics. It's a segment of the mosaic measuring about ten by eighteen centimetres."

The documents expert withdrew another sheet of paper from the folder and handed it to the detective sergeant before continuing.

"I identified the four sentences that appear most often and retranscribed them. By the way, I had fun counting the appearances. And I don't know if it's a coincidence, but if you look carefully at the photo, you'll see the four sentences in close proximity to each other. This is the only section of the mosaic where they're grouped like that."

Victor examined the sheet for a moment, then handed it to Jacinthe:

Meeting with Mr. McGregor at Federated Laymen of Quebec, May 1st 1965 (3)

Richard Crosses The Door (7)
My ketchup uncle Larry Truman relishes apples (9)
Watermelon man is watching (13)

"My ketchup uncle?" Taillon erupted. "What a fucking whack job!"

"Do you have any insights?" Victor asked.

"You see the crosses here and there? Religion seems to be a preoccupation. I note a possible opposition between the crosses and the term 'Federated Laymen of Quebec.' Are we looking at some kind of split between religious and secular values? A conflict of some sort? In any case, I did an internet search. As far as I can tell, no organization called the Federated Laymen of Quebec has ever existed."

"Don't tell me we've got another religious case on our hands!"

Victor gave Jacinthe a scolding look.

"Go on, Mona," he said.

"While we're on the subject, look at the second sentence. Does the word *Crosses* have any special value in this context? Also, there are three references to food: two to fruit — apples and watermelon — and the third to a condiment, ketchup. Don't ask me whether that means anything. I have no idea."

Jacinthe's forehead was bathed in sweat; she looked ready to faint. The detective sergeant was also starting to wilt in the heat. But Mona Vézina was on a roll.

"The black dots seem to be eyes, which may suggest that Lortie thought he was under surveillance," she said. "Especially in light of the last sentence, 'Watermelon man is watching.' Is that a reference to a man with a large head? To someone who eats a lot of melon? Who knows?" she concluded with a theatrical shrug.

"Do you have any opinions?" Victor asked.

Of course she did. Mona Vézina allowed herself a small smile, like someone who knew more than she'd been letting on.

"Since you ask, I think we could be looking at coded messages of some kind," she said, only too pleased to be contributing to the solution of the mystery. "But that's all I'm going to say." She mimed zipping her mouth shut. "I've gone far beyond the limits of my expertise."

For the twentieth time, Victor pushed aside a leaf from a plant that was creeping along his shoulder and tickling the back of his neck.

"Well," he said to Jacinthe, "at least we have a date and names that we can run through the databases: Larry Truman and Mr. McGregor. It's a starting point. We can also do some research on the Federated Laymen of Quebec."

"Send that to Gilles," Jacinthe said. "He loves crosswords. He should be able to help."

"Good idea," Victor said. He turned to the documents expert. "Can you fax a copy of this to Gilles Lemaire at the Major Crimes Unit?"

"Unfortunately, I don't have a fax machine."

Jacinthe stood up suddenly and squashed Mona Vézina's hand in her own. "I'm sorry, but I can't take this heat anymore. Thanks, ma'am." Charging out into the corridor, she called over her shoulder. "I'll be downstairs, Lessard."

Victor stood up and took a deep breath. His partner's bad manners exasperated him, but he tried not to let it show. "We're very grateful to you, Mona. You've been most helpful."

The documents expert blushed with pleasure.

"May I keep this?" he asked, pointing to the sheet.

"Of course. It's your copy."

On the ground floor, Victor bent over a water fountain to take a drink. Jacinthe was approaching as he straightened up.

"Here's a thought," he remarked, wiping his mouth. "If you take the initials of Federated Laymen of Quebec, you get FLQ. And 'Richard Crosses the Door' could be a reference to the kidnapping of Pierre Laporte."

"Just because 'the Door' in French is *la porte*?" Jacinthe exclaimed. "Why not add an S and make it a reference to Jim

Morrison?" She was about to have a good laugh when she saw the look on her partner's face and suppressed the urge. "Uhh ... so what about the Richard Crosses part?"

"You've never heard of James Richard Cross?" Victor asked with a faint note of disdain in his voice.

"Is he a singer, too?" Jacinthe asked, without irony.

Victor zipped up his jacket and they stepped outside into the parking area. The cold air revived him. "Cross was a British diplomat. I don't remember the precise date, but he was kidnapped by the FLQ in 1970, a few days before they got Pierre Laporte."

Victor was floating in an alternate reality: his lips were moving in slow motion; his words were distended; his voice plunged so low that it was inaudible. The woman in the front row kept crossing and uncrossing her legs — did she want him to notice? He finished reading the statement in a monotone, then seized his glass of water. The continuous flashing of cameras blinded him.

When they returned to Versailles, they had briefed Paul Delaney. In light of the most recent developments, he had authorized them to draw up a warrant to obtain André Lortie's psychiatric file. Jacinthe was sending off the paperwork as the detective sergeant faced the reporters.

Squinting, Victor looked at his notes to make sure he'd covered everything. Then he grabbed the pitcher and refilled his glass. "I'll take your questions now," he said, sighing.

The room, which was oppressively hot from the camera lights, erupted in a clamour of voices. A reporter with a sparse beard stood up. A jumble of papers overflowed from his jacket pocket.

"Yes, sir?" the detective sergeant said, wiping his forehead.

"Jacques-Yves Brodeur, Radio-Canada. If I understand correctly, you don't think Mr. Lawson's disappearance is linked to another case ..."

"That's correct," Victor answered after taking several gulps of water.

"So, why the press conference? Why not a simple missing person alert?"

Victor had expected this question, but not so soon. In his discussion with Delaney, they had concluded that, considering Lawson's high profile, regardless of how they put out the news, the media would jump on the story. They might as well maximize their return by putting it out as widely as possible.

"Because Mr. Lawson is an important member of Montreal's business community."

"Do you think his disappearance is linked to the death of Judith Harper? Is Lawson considered a suspect?"

Victor took another gulp of water before answering. Either Brodeur was sharp, or someone had been feeding him information. "For the moment, we're treating the two cases separately."

The woman with the crossed legs raised her hand.

Victor pointed to her immediately. "Yes, ma'am?"

"Virginie Tousignant, *La Presse*. You know that Lawson said he was going on vacation, but you have no information confirming that he left Montreal, is that it?"

"Yes. We know he has his passport, but as of now, he hasn't been spotted at any border crossing."

Victor watched her as she held her iPhone at arm's length, recording their exchange. She had long, dark hair, thick-rimmed rectangular glasses behind which large green eyes shone, an Angelina Jolie mouth, and something indefinable in her expression that made his pulse quicken.

"Do you think Lawson has been kidnapped, Detective? Or worse, murdered?"

Victor drained his glass. "We're not ruling out any theories, but for the moment, nothing points conclusively in that direction."

The detective sergeant answered a few more questions before the public relations officer at his side called an end to the press conference and the reporters filed out in controlled disarray.

●   ●   ●

With too many water molecules in his system, Victor made straight for the men's room to relieve his bursting bladder. The floor tiles in the washroom showed traces of mildew in several places, and the joints in the pipes that ran along the walls were covered in black slime. There were two stalls with crooked doors and three urinals lined up along the back wall. Victor walked past the yellow-ringed sinks, glanced at himself briefly in one of the mirrors, then walked to the middle urinal, unzipping his pants.

The detective sergeant didn't turn around when the door opened. For a few seconds, he was caught up in the sensation of relieving himself.

When he returned to reality, the sound of footsteps had ceased. Victor suddenly became uneasy; someone had stopped behind him. He was aware of being watched, and his peripheral vision was no help because the watcher was standing directly behind him. A tingle went up his spine. He couldn't help remembering John Travolta's character in *Pulp Fiction*, ambushed in the bathroom. With his cock in his hand, Victor was equally vulnerable. In a fraction of a second he made his move, closing his pants and spinning around, loaded Glock in his upraised fist.

The terrified Radio-Canada reporter waved his hands in front of his face, ducking his head between his shoulders. "Whoa, whoa! I just had one last question for you."

Victor holstered the pistol, his heart pounding, and released the air from his lungs, shaking his head.

After escorting the reporter to the exit, Victor joined his colleagues in the conference room. It was nearly 3:00 p.m. Seated at one end of the table, Delaney was quartering an apple with a knife. He offered a section to Victor and congratulated him on his performance in front of the reporters. Victor sank into a chair and put the piece of fruit in his mouth. As he chewed, he realized that he had skipped lunch.

Jacinthe announced that the request for access to Lortie's psychiatric file had been submitted, and she was waiting to hear from the legal department before sending it to Dr. McNeil. The detectives then discussed certain aspects of the investigation: the discovery of the plastic fridge-magnet numbers, the statements made by the orderly at Louis-H., and the documents expert's theories.

So far, forensics hadn't found anything of interest in the apartments of Lortie and Judith Harper. For now, Nathan Lawson and Lortie were considered the two main suspects.

The possible involvement of Harper's lover, Will Bennett, was also raised, but since it was the Gnome who was following up on that point, and he wasn't present at the moment, the matter went no further.

"We can come at it from any direction we like," Taillon grumbled. "The fact remains: we have no link between Harper, Lawson, and Lortie."

The comment threw a damper on the conversation. Everyone was quiet until Delaney broke the silence. "Have you heard from Loïc?"

Just then, the Gnome rushed into the room, out of breath. He immediately switched on the television and tuned it to a twenty-four-hour news station. "Take a look," he said, turning up the volume.

On the screen, they saw Louis-Charles Rivard, who was holding a semi-improvised press conference on the subject of Lawson's disappearance. Answering questions in front of the Radio-Canada building, he declared that his firm was prepared to pay a large reward to anyone who could provide information regarding the case. Then Rivard gave a number at which he could be reached.

"I'm addressing the person who kidnapped Nathan Lawson," he said. "No matter what happened, we can find common ground. Get in touch. I have what you're looking for."

Delaney, whose face had darkened, said, "If they think they can obstruct our investigation, they're sorely mistaken."

"They sure are acting like they've got something to hide," the Gnome observed.

"The guy's a jackass," Jacinthe summed up.

Victor's phone, which was lying on the table, came alive and started to hum. When he saw the number on the caller ID, he left the conference room to take the call in the privacy of the kitchenette.

With one foot on a chair, his elbow resting on his knee and his chin in his hand, he looked out the window as he talked. In the parking lot, a woman was scraping her ice-encrusted windshield. "Do you have anything for me?" he asked the caller.

"Maybe. But you'll need to give me access to the forensics file."

"Not online, it's too risky," Victor said, slightly irritated. "I can make a copy for you. But I'm counting on your discretion."

"Don't worry. I'll keep it to myself."

The photocopy area was next to the kitchenette, but it had a separate entrance.

As he re-entered the conference room, the detective sergeant was unaware that Jacinthe had slipped into that area to keep tabs on him.

A few minutes after Rivard's impromptu statement to the press, Victor dialed the lawyer's number in the presence of the other investigators.

"Don't play games, Rivard. It's dangerous!"

"Let the grown-ups handle this, Lessard. I deal with multi-million-dollar transactions all the time. And if someone comes forward, I may even get some payback before calling you."

"This isn't just another legal file you're sticking your nose into, Rivard. Your colleague's life could be at stake. Yours too, if you become a target." Victor reddened with anger and put down the handset.

"What did he say?" Delaney asked.

Closing his eyes, the detective sergeant shook his head in disgust. "The son of a bitch hung up."

SEPTEMBER 1964

HONOUR

The first thing Mom does is run a bath. With her customary gentleness and her tender, healing gaze, she uses a washcloth and soap to clean scraped elbows and skinned knees. Afterward, Charlie soaks in the hot water long enough to get pruney fingertips.

Then, after putting on pyjamas, Charlie sits down at the table, where Léonard and Dad have already taken their places. Under the crucifix, they say grace together and eat the chicken that Mom has cooked. Léonard never stops swaying on his chair. Bits of food are scattered all around his plate.

Dad asks Charlie how school was, but he doesn't ask for details of the altercation that caused the scrapes. Dad also refrains from making any mention whatsoever of the scene that Léonard and Charlie witnessed when they got home.

After the meal, while Mom is doing the dishes, Dad helps out with Charlie's homework. Then he gives Charlie a dictation: a story about horses running free in the orchards, plucking apples straight from the branches.

Later, while Charlie is watching television with Lennie, Dad and Mom have a heated discussion. Scraps of the conversation reach the kids' ears. Dad thinks the money should be returned, but Mom says it would be better to keep it and forget the whole thing.

With a noisy sigh, Charlie goes into the kitchen and, frowning, hands on hips, sharply puts an end to the debate. "Stop fighting, you two! We can't hear the TV."

Mom smiles and gives Charlie a hug, while Dad hurriedly slips a big envelope into a drawer, out of sight.

Now the house is silent. Mom pulls up the sheet and places a kiss on Charlie's forehead. Before leaving the bedroom, she smiles, restoring balance to the world. Then she goes downstairs, most likely to delve back into her history books. For years, Mom has spent every evening working hard on her thesis. She never quits, never stops repeating that women are just as capable as men. Charlie knows that after coming in to say goodnight, Dad will spend the rest of the evening adding up columns of numbers.

Through the open window, Charlie hears nothing but the crickets chirping. It's a warm night for this time of year; summer has lingered.

Dad opens the door and sits on the side of the bed, near Charlie's pillow.

"What happened after school today, Charlie?"

"René Desharnais started it. He called Lennie a retard!"

"So you fought with him."

"He insulted us, Dad! You're always saying that we may be poor, but we have our honour."

Dad bites his lip, not wanting Charlie to see his emotions. "You're right, Charlie. But sometimes you have to pick your battles."

Charlie sits up on the bed. "I picked mine. I wasn't going to let them say mean things about my brother."

Charlie reaches up and, with one finger, brushes a tear from Dad's cheek, then touches the bruise under his eye. "What happened to you?"

With a love so great it could pull the moon down from the sky, Dad strokes Charlie's hair. "Nothing. Sometimes, Charlie, honour costs a lot."

23

SLEEPLESS

Victor started the service vehicle and cranked the heater to maximum. Then, grumbling, he got out of the car and went to work on the windshield with an ice scraper. It was dark out. His fingers and toes were freezing. He looked down at his Converse high-tops. "You really need to get a pair of boots," Nadja was constantly saying. With the cold biting his face, he had never been so ready to concede that she was right. And while he was at it, a pair of gloves wouldn't hurt, either.

"Fucking winter," he muttered, and kept scraping.

As he drove west along Sherbrooke toward downtown Montreal, Victor turned on the radio. Sports commentator Ron Fournier, a man who defined the word *colourful*, was in the midst of one of his trademark musical numbers. Before taking listeners' calls, Fournier was performing an improvised song in which he pleaded with Canadiens' management to do something about the team's power play. It took only a few seconds for a smile to appear on Victor's face. He surprised himself by laughing out loud. Listening to Ron Fournier hold forth on the air was always a pleasure. The man didn't always get the credit he deserved, but in Victor's opinion, he was a brilliant communicator.

The car was starting to warm up. His toes stung as they thawed. The rectangle he had scraped out on the icy windshield was growing, its edges becoming blurry, melting gradually into a shape resembling the wings of a butterfly.

Victor slowed down when he came to Amherst Street. The car ahead of him slid on a patch of ice. While Fournier was dressing down a listener, the detective sergeant activated the windshield wipers. Big, soggy flakes were falling from the sky.

Victor parked on Viger Street.

With his hands in the pockets of his leather jacket and a large yellow envelope tucked under one arm, he walked quickly up Saint-Laurent. He'd just passed the Hong Kong Restaurant when he heard the blare of a car horn to his left. He looked toward the source of the sound, immediately spotted the vehicle, and ran across the street. He slipped the envelope through the half-open window and exchanged a few words with the driver.

The car rolled away and Victor walked onward to De La Gauchetière Street, in the heart of Chinatown.

Jacinthe waited for a few seconds before following him. As far as she could tell, Lessard hadn't spotted her.

Coming around the corner, she let out a frustrated "Fuck!"

She peered through the shop windows and scanned the alleys but saw no sign of her partner. The car had been a Ford Escape, but she hadn't been close enough to see the driver's face or the licence plate.

It was another one of those nights when Victor woke up at 3:00 a.m. and couldn't get back to sleep. He lay staring at the ceiling for a while. He was sweating. The mattress was damp beneath him. To his left, Nadja was asleep, her head resting on his arm.

They'd had dinner together around nine, after she'd gotten off work. Victor had brought home fresh pasta from Pasta Casareccia on Sherbrooke, just a few steps from his apartment.

Over the meal, they'd talked about their experiences at work that day, and Nadja had offered her perspective on certain aspects of Victor's investigation. As she was getting ready to do the dishes, he had pulled her toward the bedroom. Nadja hadn't resisted. Watching her clothes come off, listening to the fabric whisper on her dusky skin, Victor had felt as though the air itself had rarefied and flowed from the room.

Afterward, they'd fallen asleep, their limbs entwined.

With infinite care, Victor liberated his arm, which had begun to go numb, and got out of bed. He picked up his clothes from the floor and tiptoed out of the room, closing the door softly behind him.

He dressed in front of the living room window. The room was bathed in the orange glow of a streetlight. With a shake of his head, he grabbed his jacket and pulled on his high-tops.

The air outside was dry; the snow crunched under his feet. City workers hadn't yet cleared the sidewalk. Reaching Sherbrooke Street, the detective sergeant stopped for a moment and lit a cigarette before continuing on.

He passed D.A.D.'s Bagels. Since he was awake anyway, Victor considered stopping for a bite to eat, but thought better of it. He could hear the laughter of a group of young people inside, no doubt on their way home after a night of clubbing downtown. What he needed right now was solitude. Following his usual route, he went up Wilson Avenue to Côte-Saint-Antoine.

As he walked through Notre-Dame-de-Grâce Park, he passed a man and woman carrying a Christmas tree tightly wrapped in plastic webbing. He gave them a nod. His years as a resident of Montreal had taught him not to be surprised by anything.

His phone vibrated. He pulled it out of his pocket and read the text.

Jacinthe Taillon rolled over in bed. She couldn't sleep.

The apartment had been filled with the aroma of stew when she got home. She'd kissed Lucie and taken a shower, then they'd eaten dinner together.

Lucie and Jacinthe were yin and yang: two inseparable opposites, two stray pieces from an improbable jigsaw puzzle, fitting perfectly into each other. Lucie moderated her, calmed her, talked her down when she went ballistic, picked up the pieces when she fought with her family or took out her rage on the furniture. Slight, delicate, soft-voiced, Lucie looked a little like Jane Birkin. In a few weeks, they would celebrate their twentieth anniversary as a couple.

They had met through Jacinthe's mother, who was a friend of Lucie's. Now in her early sixties, Lucie had filled her life with books, both at home and at the library where she worked.

She'd suffered from health problems earlier in the year, but she was better now. Jacinthe often said that on the day Lucie died, she herself would have no reason to live. Lucie was gentleness incarnate. An angel. She was Jacinthe's balance, the four points of her life's compass.

During Lucie's convalescence, Jacinthe, who had never finished a book in her life, had given in and agreed to read a novel to her beloved. It was the story of a young boy who was learning to fly.

Jacinthe tried to untangle herself from the covers clinging to her body.

Her mind had begun to race the moment she lay down, and she'd made the mistake of giving in to it. Fucking Lessard. This was his fault.

Had he concealed himself because he'd spotted her, or had he gone into a shop in Chinatown to meet someone? To whom had he given the envelope? What was in it?

Jacinthe nearly picked up her cellphone from the bedside table to call him and put an end to the mystery. Honesty was always the best policy.

She glanced at the alarm clock; it could wait until tomorrow.

Besides, she trusted Lessard.

Up to a point.

◆   ◆   ◆

Sitting on the side of the bed, his head in his hands, Paul Delaney wept in silence.

He couldn't remember how he'd gotten home from the hospital, couldn't remember the doctor's exact words. His mind had retained only one thing: Madeleine's cancer had spread.

In the early days of her illness, he had felt emptiness. The kids had taken shifts keeping him company. But the treatments had gone on longer than expected, and, little by little, everyone had gone back to the old routines.

Delaney lifted his head. He wanted to scream.

Madeleine's side of the bed was vacant. The house through which he moved like a living corpse had become a prison. Each passing day failed to fill the void left by the day before. He felt the emptiness in his flesh, saw it everywhere he looked, was aware of it wherever he went.

The emptiness was devouring him.

Berger's text asked Victor to call him back as soon as possible, which Victor did as soon as he had lit a fresh cigarette.

"I thought you might be awake."

"Hello, Jacob. Apparently I'm not alone in my insomnia."

"You know how it goes. I'm trying to get everything done before the holidays, but it seems like the more I do, the more I still have left to do."

Victor sighed, discouraged. The holidays … What he feared most of all was the moment when he'd have to inform Nadja that the way things were going, he wouldn't be able to join her at the chalet they'd rented in the Laurentians. She'd been overjoyed at the prospect of spending the week there between Christmas and New Year's Day … "If it makes you feel any better," he said, "I'm in the same boat."

"Sorry, but it really doesn't."

They both laughed. Then Victor turned serious. The medical examiner's text had intrigued him. "So, to what do I owe the honour, Jacob?"

"I just looked at the lab results that came in today." Victor heard a rustle of papers. "It may not be important, but I thought you might be interested to know that Judith Harper had chlamydia."

24

FIVE ROSES

Wednesday, December 21st

Old Montreal was still asleep, its streets deserted.

Holding a Thermos of coffee and a bag of bagels purchased at D.A.D.'s, Victor arrived at the agreed-upon location — the corner of Smith and De la Commune. The wind whistled against the graffiti-covered railway bridge, beside which two human forms were stretched out under a mountain of blankets and rags. In front of them, the Five Roses Flour sign loomed over the city.

A fetid odour of sweat and urine wafted up to Victor's nose. Having seen him arrive, one of the two figures wriggled out of his sleeping bag and came to greet him.

"You okay, Loïc?" the detective sergeant asked a little anxiously, seeing his young colleague's sunken eyes and waxy skin.

"Yeah, just a little chilly," the kid responded, taking the coffee offered to him. Blouin-Dubois clearly hadn't slept at all.

During Victor's teens, when he had run away each time he was placed with a new foster family, he'd lived on the streets now and then himself. "You spent the night here?" he asked.

Loïc nodded, shivering. "We're not looking at the usual pattern with this guy. He's totally brilliant. A doctoral candidate at the University of Montreal. He's been in bad shape lately, doing heroin. He says it happens now and then, but I get the feeling this time it's worse."

"I can't believe it. A Ph.D. student living on the streets? Does he have a criminal record?"

"I wasn't able to check. He wouldn't tell me his real name. He goes by Nash."

"How'd you find him?"

"I visited all the homeless shelters and refuges, like you told me. I was starting to get discouraged, but I decided to give it one last shot. Went and hung out in front of the Accueil Bonneau shelter. Nash was there. He asked me for a cigarette. I don't know why, maybe because we're the same age, but he opened up to me. It didn't take him long to figure out I was a cop. When I showed him the picture of Lortie, he recognized him right away."

"What else did you get from him?"

"Nothing so far. But we made a deal."

"What kind of deal?" the detective sergeant asked.

The kid waved a hand evasively. "You know … a deal. Nothing serious."

Victor gazed at Loïc with an expression that contained no judgment, but made it clear that he wasn't going to let himself be played for a fool.

"Okay. Fine. He wanted me to score a fix for him. And spend the night out here. He wanted company, someone to talk to. In exchange, he said he'd meet you and answer your questions." He looked Victor in the eye. "Seriously, what was I supposed to do?"

The detective sergeant nodded. He wasn't about to scold the kid: he'd have done the same thing. Truth was, he'd done plenty worse. More than once. But that was no reason to praise the kid's behaviour.

"I understand. But the fix stays between us. Not a word to Paul or anyone else."

Blouin-Dubois nodded.

A train bound for Central Station rolled noisily over their heads. It didn't seem to wake up Nash, whose loud, regular snoring became audible again after the last railcar had gone by.

"Does he know why we're interested in Lortie?"

"I told him the guy's family was looking for him."

Victor took out his cigarettes and offered one to Loïc. Shielding the flame with his hand, he lit the two smokes.

They'd barely taken their first puff when a cavernous voice rang out: "Hey! Gimme one of those!"

Nash's bearded face poked out of his sleeping bag. His feverish eyes looked Victor up and down.

The three men sheltered from the wind behind one of the pillars of the rail bridge. Nash had a greenish complexion, dark circles under his eyes, and terrible teeth. He made quick work of two bagels before attacking the Thermos of coffee.

The detective sergeant guessed he was between twenty-five and thirty-five.

The effects of the fix Loïc had bought him had worn off, but the young vagrant was showing none of the classic signs of withdrawal, which suggested that he was keeping his drug use under control.

Victor knew from experience that, while very few people can actually pull it off, it is, in fact, possible to be a heroin addict and remain functional, for a while.

At first, they talked about the weather and the difficulties of living on the streets in winter. Then, little by little, the questions became more specific.

"Loïc tells me you're studying at the University of Montreal ..."

"I'm doing a doctorate in mathematics. The department's given me a scholarship to work on number theory." Nash was blinking constantly.

"What exactly is number theory?"

The homeless man lifted his head and gave Victor a wry smile. "You really want me to get into it?"

"On second thought, maybe not." The detective sergeant sighed. The three men chuckled.

"How can you work on a doctorate if you're homeless?"

"I've been writing my thesis for the last eighteen months. On the streets for six. This isn't the first time it's happened."

"And you're making progress with the thesis?"

Nash looked up and saw that Victor wasn't judging him. "It's going okay. I have my laptop."

"That's gotta be tough." The police officer gave him a sympathetic nod. "Can you talk to me about Lortie? Where did you meet him?"

Nash plunged filth-encrusted fingers into the bag and grabbed another bagel.

"At Bonneau. André doesn't get along with people. Neither do I. There's a common room at the shelter where you can get some peace, sit by yourself. Not too many people go in there. He and I would see each other. I usually brought a chess set and played against myself. One night, he asked if I felt like a game."

Nash was shoving pieces of bagel into his mouth and chewing while he talked, as though he feared someone might snatch the food away.

"Is he a decent chess player?"

"Hopeless." Nash laughed, revealing scurvy-ravaged teeth. "But he's one hell of a storyteller. I can listen to him for hours. You know, like your specialty is police work. Mine's numbers. His is telling stories."

Victor lit two cigarettes and gave one to Nash. Loïc had opened his mouth several times to participate in the conversation, but hadn't actually spoken.

"What kind of stories does he tell? What do you talk about?" asked Victor.

"Oh!" Nash exclaimed, coughing as he took a drag. "You name it. André has opinions about everything. He knows a lot about politics and economics."

"He must have said some things that struck you …"

"When he gets going, he says all kinds of things."

"Such as?"

"He claims he was part of the FLQ. Says he was in on the kidnapping of James Cross and Pierre Laporte. I don't know if it's true, but he also says they planted bombs near some consulate. I forget which one. Funny thing is, he's pretty convincing. When he talks, he throws out so many details that you end up believing him."

"What kind of details?"

"Well, for instance, the technical aspects of making bombs. He seems to know all about that stuff." Nash put a hand to his chest and hiccuped. Then he burped and let out a satisfied sigh.

"Did Lortie ever talk to you about wallets?" Victor asked casually.

Nash laughed. "He tried that blackout story on you, too, huh? He told me that when he was younger, he killed some people he didn't know. When he woke up, he had their wallets."

Victor turned to Loïc, inviting him to ask the question that was eating at him.

"Did Lortie ever mention the names of his victims?" Blouin-Dubois asked.

Nash searched his memory for a few seconds, then said, "If he did talk about them, I've forgotten."

"What's he like?" Victor asked.

"André? Super suspicious. I've never seen him talk to anyone apart from me. And he's pretty weird. Always watching, like a hunted animal. One time, we were sitting in the common room and he said we had to get up and sit in a different part of the room. He said you should never sit with your back to the door, and never be too far from the exit. Like, you've got to know who comes in and be ready to react. When we're outside, he's always looking behind him, saying he needs to make sure no one's following us."

Nash took a long swig of coffee.

Victor thought for a few seconds before continuing. "Do you remember anything else about him?"

"He can handle himself in a fight," Nash said, taking another bite of his bagel.

"What do you mean?"

"One night, we were sleeping here and three squeegee kids came up. Punks. They were getting in our faces, saying they wanted smokes, drugs, food. Finally, André got fed up and told them to leave. The three guys just laughed. They called him grandpa. He went straight at them, started pounding on one of them. Fucked the guy up so bad the other two had to carry him away."

"Apart from playing chess and talking, what do you do together? Where do you go?"

"We don't do anything else. Sometimes we'll sleep here for a couple of days. Then he's gone for weeks."

"Did you know he has a room in a rooming house?"

"Yeah, but he's more comfortable on the street."

"Does he take drugs?"

"No."

"Medications?"

"Don't know."

Victor saw that Nash was eyeing his pack of cigarettes. He handed it to him.

"Keep it."

"Thanks," the young vagrant said, and put a cigarette in the corner of his mouth.

"When was the last time you saw Lortie?"

"A couple of days ago. I'd have to check." He pointed to a camouflage-pattern rucksack lying beside his sleeping bag. "I note everything down in a journal. I'm thinking I might write a book about my experiences someday." He was silent for a moment. "Can I ask you a question?"

"Go ahead," Victor said.

"Is André dead?"

"Why do you ask that?"

"I don't know, but I'm thinking the cops wouldn't send two detectives to ask questions unless something bad had happened to him." Nash's eyelids blinked for the ten-thousandth time since the start of their conversation.

The detective sergeant couldn't think of any reason to conceal the truth. "He killed himself Saturday night. We have reason to believe he was implicated in a murder that was committed Thursday night."

Silence fell over the trio. At first, Victor thought Nash was too emotional to speak, but then he realized he was thinking.

"I'd be surprised if André had anything to do with the murder," the young man said.

"Why?" Victor asked, surprised at his certainty.

Nash had already gone over to his rucksack and was pulling out a weathered notebook. "Because he was here," he said, turning the pages agitatedly. "He showed up Thursday afternoon and didn't leave until Saturday morning."

25

CORPSES IN THE CLOSET

His eyelashes fluttered; the image of the ceiling wavered for a moment on his retinas, then steadied itself.

The mattress was soaked, swamp-like.

Shuddering, Will Bennett raised a hand to his jaw: a dull pain coursed through his gums. He stared for a moment at his wet fingertips. Droplets of sweat were running down his rough cheeks. It had happened again. The fever had returned. It was crawling under his skin, devouring him.

He had wanted to silence the voice in his head, the loathsome music that maddened him. Since Judith's death, he could no longer hold back the urges. He gave in to them without restraint. Because nothing mattered anymore. It was just a question of time before the inevitable end.

Bennett got up and, in the half light, looked around the disordered room. Twisted clothing was strewn across the arm of the couch. Liquor bottles littered the coffee table. On the frayed carpet, pieces of chicken and limp French fries swam in a puddle of congealed sauce beside an overturned plate.

Bennett stiffened at the sight of the bedspread, covered with brownish stains, rolled into a ball in one corner. He didn't need to wonder whether those were bloodstains. What would he tell Daman this time? He shook his head to chase away the thought. What did it matter? There was nothing to say, nothing to do. He had looked into himself, tried to understand how all this had started, but he couldn't locate the root of the evil. Yet, even if he was unable to locate its origin, he knew that his descent into the abyss was coming to an end; that he was very close to hitting bottom. And, after all, perhaps it was better this way. Perhaps now he'd be compelled to stop. Perhaps, in truth, it was what he wanted.

An image of Judith flashed before his eyes. For a fatalistic instant, he grasped the irony of the situation: she would surely have spoken of satisfying unconscious urges.

Staggering, leaning on the nightstand, he took a few tentative steps. He swallowed to produce a little saliva; his throat felt like he was ingesting pearls of fire. He licked his index finger and ran it along the table to pick up the powdery white residue, which he rubbed on his gums.

The cocaine numbed the membrane and anesthetized his tongue.

Bennett crossed the wasteland of the room, went to the closet and found his phone in the breast pocket of his jacket: 6:32 a.m. He'd been out of circulation for nearly forty-eight hours. The number of messages in his voice mail confirmed the extent of the damage. He put the phone back without even listening to the messages. At this point, there was nothing to gain from trying to make amends.

What difference did a few missed meetings and appointments make?

Soon he would be delivered; soon he would atone for his sins.

Will Bennett walked to the bathroom sink and turned on the tap. Head bent forward, he stood for a moment with his hands on the cold porcelain. Then he leaned down and drank at length from the stream of water. He splashed his face until the skin no longer felt the cold water's bite, then pressed the switch, steeling himself to confront his reflection in the harsh light.

His cracked lips and inflamed nostrils paled in contrast to his bloodshot eyes. He turned his head. To his right, a turd floated in the toilet.

Suddenly, he reacted with a start as memories of the last forty-eight hours crowded back into his head.

The girl lay curled in the bathtub, her flesh drained of colour. With her head thrown back, mouth open, and the collar around her neck, she looked like a dead fish.

He put his hands to his temples. Daman mustn't find him here.

Silent laughter seized him. *When you have corpses in the closet, everything comes out sooner or later.*

He looked at the girl again. One breast glimmered, hanging out of her bra. A pathetic swelling took shape in his pants. Because nothing mattered. Because it was all just a question of time. They might as well hang him, or spit on his grave.

Bennett unzipped himself, drew closer to the tub, and began to masturbate.

26

NORTHERN INDUSTRIAL TEXTILES

Loïc hit the switch and the neon tubes started to crackle.

The light directly above Victor's desk flickered at the rhythm of his heartbeat for a moment before igniting. The detective sergeant looked at his watch: 7:00 a.m. Aware that the office would soon be a hive of activity, he let himself savour this brief moment of peace.

In the washroom, Victor used his fingernails and some hand soap to wash out the mug he'd retrieved from his desk. Once he'd scrubbed out all the crust that clung to the bottom, he filled it with water, returned to his chair, and watered the plant he'd rescued from Lortie's room.

Loïc was sprawled at his workspace, feet up on the desk, his gaze blank as he waited for his PC to start up.

Victor had found the solution to that problem: he never shut down his computer. He simply turned off the screen each evening to avoid scoldings from the ayatollahs of secrecy who got upset whenever they found a computer running after hours. The detective sergeant pushed a button; within seconds, his screen lit up.

Looking through his emails, he answered the urgent ones and sorted through the ones that could wait. He was about to log out when he noticed that he'd received a message the previous evening that had gone straight to spam. He didn't recognize the sender's address: adth1952@hotmail.com.

Assuming it was an advertisement for a miracle treatment to lengthen his penis or increase his IQ — one measurement often being, he thought, the corollary of the other — Victor almost deleted the email without reading it. But he decided he'd better click on it, just in case.

He was glad he did. It was from Adèle Thibault, Nathan Lawson's assistant, who had written to give him further details about the file that Lawson had taken from the archives before disappearing. She mentioned that she was writing from her personal email address because she was under orders not to talk to the police.

Her message was short. The database to which she had access contained only fragmentary information about the contents of the folders in question. That information included the name of the client — a provincially incorporated company specializing in the production and distribution of work uniforms — and the fact that the file had been opened in 1971 and closed in 1972.

Thibault ended the message by noting that further digging on her part would risk alerting her employers, which would mean trouble for her.

Victor logged in to the website of the Quebec Enterprise Register, intending to call up a CIDREQ, a digital file that contained essential information on every company in the province, such as date of incorporation; head office address; names and addresses of principal shareholders, board members, and officers; sphere of activity; and so on. The detective sergeant made sure he had the spelling right and repeatedly re-entered the corporate name the secretary had given him, but the same message came back each time:

> Northern Industrial Textiles Ltd.
> No files found under that name.

Having done many such searches in the past, he knew he wasn't using the web service incorrectly. This problem was beyond his capability. He'd have to ask the legal experts at the provincial Justice Ministry for help.

Victor wrote an email, copied in the relevant information, and sent it to the expert with whom he regularly collaborated, asking her to find available details on the company.

Then he waved his mug in the air. "Coffee, kid?"

The two cops went to the kitchen. Allowing himself to break his usual rule, Victor gave the decaf a pass. A little caffeine would help him get through the day.

Nash had become agitated when Victor asked him to come with them to the station. The detective sergeant had seen terror in Nash's eyes. Obviously, Victor could have forced Nash to come, but he'd decided that wouldn't be helpful.

In exchange for a promise not to get him in trouble, Victor had obtained Nash's real name. He was sure the young man had a criminal record. But, as he'd told Nash, his past crimes were of no concern: this was a murder investigation. Nash had promised to make himself available if the police needed him, and to drop by the Accueil Bonneau shelter now and then. If investigators were looking for him, they could leave word there.

Before leaving, Victor had also given him Pearson's contact details at Station 21, and a little money. "If you go over there," he'd said to the young vagrant, "tell him I sent you. There's a multi-disciplinary team called EMRII. They offer help and advice to homeless people. There are two social workers on the team, as well as a nurse."

Nash's account gave Lortie an alibi for the day of the murder. But could they consider him totally reliable? He might have gotten his dates mixed up. Yes, he kept a journal, but he wasn't exactly a personal assistant. And time of death was another issue that had to be considered. A discrepancy of a few hours would be enough to invalidate the alibi.

On that score, until they had definitive results from Berger's autopsy, they'd have to go with the medical examiner's preliminary findings. The final report wouldn't be available for another few days, at least.

Victor searched his notebook, turning pages without finding what he sought. "What's his real name again?"

"Eugène Corriveau," Loïc said, blowing on his coffee. "Do you think we can believe him?"

"I hope I haven't made a mistake trusting him," Victor muttered. He was silent for a moment. "Run his name through the system, confirm his identity. Then go get some rest."

"Okay." Loïc hesitated. "Nash's story raises doubts about Lortie's guilt, huh?" Blouin-Dubois got to his feet, slipped his thumbs into the waistband of his jeans, and pulled them up. "You know, it could be the other dude, the one who's missing …"

"Lawson? I don't know, Loïc. But one thing's for sure. Until we find him, we won't have the whole picture."

"Maybe it's nothing, but I'm thinking there's a possible connection between the warehouse where Harper's body was found and the rail bridge where Lortie and Nash camped out."

"Oh, yeah? What connection?" Victor asked, clearing his throat. He spat voluminously into the sink, then ran the water for a few seconds.

"The bike path … it runs between the two locations."

Just then, a string of obscenities erupted in the reception area.

"You better get out of here, kid. I get the feeling that Jacinthe and I are about to have a little discussion."

Before leaving, Loïc turned toward the detective sergeant. "Hey, Vic," he said, wringing his hands, "thanks for giving me a break."

"Don't mention it, Loïc. You did some damn fine work."

A smile lit up the young man's face. He stepped out just in time to avoid Taillon, who, with spittle-flecked lips, rolled into the room like an unpinned hand grenade.

"Well, well, look who's here! You might've called so I could go with you, instead of leaving me a message after!"

"Good morning, Jacinthe," Victor said in a low, soft voice. "I didn't want to wake you up for nothing."

"Wake me up for nothing? Oh, that's a good one. Wake me up for nothing! Go fuck yourself, Lessard. Your idea of *nothing* seems pretty damn flexible to me. You were just fine with waking me up for *nothing* in the middle of the night when you wanted to go check out the Harper woman's apartment!"

"Sit down, Jacinthe. Let's have some coffee. I'll tell you what I found out."

Taillon kicked the table, sending several chairs flying. "You can stick your coffee where the sun don't shine!" she yelled, stomping out of the room.

Victor kept busy, giving the storm time to pass. The office was coming to life, the worker ants arriving one by one, shedding their outerwear. Sounds of conversation began to fill the room.

Delaney came in wearing headphones. Looking disconsolate, he crossed the detectives' area without greeting anyone and shut himself in his office. Victor watched him go. The boss didn't have to say anything for his distress to be apparent. The detective sergeant would check in on him later.

After looking at his emails, he answered a text message from Nadja, sent two hours earlier, asking where he'd gone.

Then he got up and walked over to Jacinthe. Her body language made it clear that she didn't want to talk, but he stood in front of her desk anyway, wearing his best look of contrition.

"I was going downstairs. Can I treat you to a couple of honey-glazed donuts?"

She gave him a dark glare that gradually brightened. "Manipulative son of a bitch." She shook her head theatrically to convey her disapproval. "You know I can't resist when you play on my heartstrings." Jacinthe stood up, wrapped her massive hands around his throat, and mimed strangling him.

They both laughed, then descended to the Place Versailles food court, where they sat down.

Store employees were rolling back the metal shutters from the storefronts. The regulars were starting to come in — mostly seniors who whiled away their days on the benches of the shopping mall.

"I'm sorry, Jacinthe. I should have called you."

"Fucking idiot," she said for form's sake, but she was smiling.

Victor recounted in detail the circumstances in which Loïc had made contact with Nash, as well as the information the young vagrant had given them.

"Lortie talked to him about the Laporte and Cross kidnappings? How about that …" She was silent for a moment, then she asked, "You sure there isn't anything you're forgetting to tell me?"

The detective sergeant held her gaze. Telling her that Loïc had bought heroin for Nash wouldn't have been the end of the world, but he preferred, if possible, to keep that to himself.

He was about to say something evasive when his face lit up. "Yes! I talked to Berger. Judith Harper had chlamydia."

Surprise was apparent on Jacinthe's heavy features. "At her age? That's pretty weird."

Victor had to concede that it was unusual, to say the least.

"She wasn't raped, was she?" Jacinthe asked.

"No, no. Berger's categorical about that."

"Good." She gave him a searching look. "Are you hiding anything else from me?"

"I don't understand," he said, shrugging. "Like what, for instance?"

"Like, for instance, what you were doing yesterday with —"

Victor had bent over to pick up a napkin from the floor when the miniature shoes and impeccably creased pantlegs of Gilles Lemaire entered his field of vision.

"I knew I'd find you here," Lemaire said, cutting Jacinthe off.

The detective sergeant pulled out a chair for him. "Have a seat, Gilles. What's up?"

"I'd rather stand. For once, I don't have to crane my neck when I talk to you two." With Lemaire standing and Victor sitting, Lemaire was indeed the taller of the two, by a slight margin. "I finally managed to get in touch with Will Bennett's co-workers yesterday."

"Bennett? Judith Harper's lover?" Jacinthe asked. "What did you find out?"

"I'd been trying to reach them for two days. I was starting to wonder if they were avoiding me. The first one wouldn't talk, but I turned up the heat on the second one, and he finally opened up."

"Come on, Gilles, spit it out," Jacinthe said impatiently. "Stop beating around the bush."

"You ready?" The Gnome leaned forward, like he was about to divulge a state secret. "Bennett went AWOL during their business trip." Lemaire stepped back, as though assessing the effect of his words.

"Long enough to come here, commit the murder, and get back?" Victor asked.

"His co-workers lost track of him for twenty-four hours."

"Do they know what happened to him?" the detective sergeant asked.

"Bennett offered no explanation, which may be due to the fact that he's above them on the corporate ladder. Apparently it wasn't the first time he'd disappeared, but he'd never been gone so long before."

"They have no idea what he was doing?"

"I didn't squeeze as hard as I could have, but they say they don't."

"This is worth looking into. If he crossed the border, he'll have left a trail. Did you check with customs?"

"I know he wasn't on any flights. As for everything else, I'll need a little time."

"Did you ask for a financial profile?" Victor asked.

"I should have it this afternoon."

"It won't show a thing," Jacinthe declared. "There's no way Bennett would be dumb enough to rent a car or buy a train ticket on his credit card," she said, biting into her donut. "We don't have time to mess around. We need to go back and question him right away."

"That's where things get interesting," the Gnome said with an enigmatic smile.

"What do you mean?" she asked, her mouth full.

"Bennett is nowhere to be found."

27

VETERINARIAN

Victor stopped in front of his reflection in the mirror and examined himself for a moment. With his fingertips, he palpated the sagging, purple-tinged flesh encircling his eyes. This whole aging thing was starting to get on his nerves.

For some years now, he'd been working to maximize what nature had given him. He ate vegetarian as often as possible, and strenuous training had enabled him to gain in muscle what he'd lost in flab.

Though he sometimes tried to convince himself otherwise, the age difference with Nadja troubled him. Feeling mildly downcast, he walked away from his image and continued his search of Nathan Lawson's bedroom, opening drawers, picking up items, examining a pile of old invoices. From the living room, he heard Taillon's voice as she grilled Wu.

When they'd returned to the office after their break, they received confirmation that Wu's visa had expired. Since his status was now illegal, they had decided to use that fact as the basis for talking to him. In the car, they'd worked out their strategy. With her usual talent for subtlety, Jacinthe would threaten Wu with deportation if he refused to talk, while Victor promised to leave him alone if he collaborated.

Just before their departure, Lemaire had informed them that database searches of Larry Truman and the other phrases highlighted by the documents expert had yielded nothing so far, except for the meeting with a certain Mr. McGregor.

On that subject, Lemaire had confirmed what Victor already suspected: "Federated Laymen of Quebec" was a reference to the FLQ. Lemaire had discovered that on May 1st, 1965, the FLQ had detonated a bomb in front of the U.S. consulate on McGregor Street.

Victor had also received an update from Loïc on the subject of Eugène Corriveau, a.k.a. Nash. His intuition had been right: the young man had several convictions to his name, including one for possession of narcotics, but overall it was small-time stuff. In addition, the kid's digging had revealed that Nash had lied to them about one detail: he was no longer a Ph.D. student in mathematics at the University of Montreal. The department chair had confirmed to Loïc that Nash had been expelled from the math program the previous year, after failing repeatedly to complete the required coursework, despite several warnings. In addition, his thesis adviser had noted that Corriveau's drug problem was a matter of public knowledge, and that he'd made use of the counselling services that were available to students.

So, the question remained: could they trust Nash's word when he declared that Lortie had been in his company between Thursday afternoon and Saturday morning?

Loïc had also pointed out to Victor, significantly, that the distance between the railway bridge where the two men had spent the night and the warehouse where Judith Harper's body had been found could be covered on foot in less than an hour along the bicycle path, which was still quite passable despite the snow. It was thus conceivable that Lortie had made the trip without Nash's knowledge, while Nash was out cold after a heroin fix.

Victor was about to search under Lawson's bed when Taillon came in. From the look on her face, it was clear that her conversation with Wu hadn't yielded the results she was hoping for.

"The guy's only been in Quebec for a few months. I don't think he knows Lawson very well, but he did finally admit that they met at a sauna in the gay village a couple of months ago. Lawson had been putting him up since then, in return for sexual favours. Otherwise, he's sticking with the story he gave us the other day. He repeated to me that on the night he went missing, Lawson called and told him to put some clothes and his passport in an overnight bag. Wu went down to the front desk and gave the bag to the door-man, as Lawson asked."

"That's it?"

Jacinthe took the question as a criticism. "Feel free to talk to him yourself, smart guy." A sadistic smile appeared on her lips. "Unless you'd like me to …"

"No! I'll handle it."

With Jacinthe at his heels, Victor walked to the couch where Wu was sitting. Looking wary, clasping his hands, his head sunk down between his shoulders, Wu was clearly afraid. Even without the use of force, Jacinthe was an intimidating presence, and her threats of deportation had clearly had an effect.

Victor felt immediate sympathy for the young man, who seemed lost in a world whose rituals he was unfamiliar with.

"Hello, Wu. I have a few questions for you as well. Then we'll leave you in peace, I promise." As he spoke, he crouched down to put himself at the young man's level.

Wu raised frightened black eyes and nodded.

"From what I understand, you didn't see Mr. Lawson on the evening he went missing. Is that right?"

"That right," the young man murmured.

"Okay. Now take your time before answering. Try to remember. When he asked for his passport, did he tell you where he was going?"

"No," Wu replied without hesitation.

"Repeat to me in your own words what he said."

"He say he going away for a few days, and I can stay here."

"Did he say anything else?"

"He say nothing else."

"How did he sound over the phone?"

The young man frowned as he thought about it. "He upset. Very upset, yes."

Behind Victor, Taillon was becoming impatient, rocking from one leg to the other. Knowing that she might blow up at any moment, and that her presence was making it hard to create an atmosphere of trust with the young man, the detective sergeant asked her to go search Lawson's office. She walked to the far end of the apartment, unleashing a torrent of profanity.

Turning back to Wu, Victor saw relief on his face.

"During the last few weeks, had you and Mr. Lawson talked about a vacation, a trip, someplace he wanted to take you?"

The young man shook his head. "I think no."

"Do you have any idea where he's gone, Wu? Can you think of any place you and he went together?"

The young man thought it over, then shook his head, but just as Victor was about to ask another question, he saw a light in Wu's eyes.

"Did you just remember something?"

Nathan Lawson's companion reddened. "He take me one night for sex. To a house."

"Where?"

"I don't know city so good. Can't say. It happen at night. Big house, two floors. Nobody inside, just Nathan and me."

Victor made a face. They were groping in the dark. "Did you go by car?"

"Yes. Maybe twenty minutes."

So Lawson and the young man had stayed in town. That was a start.

"Close your eyes, Wu. Describe the house, what was around it, what you saw through the windows."

"I see mountain through window!" he exclaimed. "Mountain covered in snow."

Mount Royal. The house overlooked Mount Royal!

"Would you know the place if I brought you there?"

"Yes."

Victor went down to the lobby and spoke to the doorman on duty. It was the same man who had given Lawson the overnight bag prepared by Wu. The doorman said Lawson had insisted that the handover take place in the adjacent alley, and he hadn't gotten out of the car, which suggested that he was nervous. Besides that, the detective sergeant learned nothing new, except that Lawson was disagreeable and haughty, that he rarely spoke to the building staff, and that when he did, it was always to complain about the quality of their service.

Victor stepped outside to smoke a cigarette on the sidewalk.

They knew Lawson hadn't used his passport. The more Victor thought about it, the more convinced he became that the lawyer had been trying to cover his tracks; that he'd never intended to leave the country. But he'd wanted someone to think he intended to leave. He was hidden away someplace close. Victor was prepared to bet on it.

Could he be at the house Wu had mentioned? If the house was on the mountain, that limited the number of possibilities, but not enough to waste precious time roaming the streets of Westmount and Outremont with Wu, hoping for a flash of recognition.

The gathering darkness signalled the end of the afternoon. The wind had risen. Snow was falling. According to news reports, the impending snowstorm would bury Quebec.

The detective sergeant shivered as he puffed on his cigarette; he had stepped out without his jacket.

His phone vibrated. For the first time all day, a smile lit up his face. It was Nadja:

thinking of you xxx

Although Victor wasn't overly worried about having left Wu with Taillon, he didn't linger outside. When he returned to the apartment, he noticed that Jacinthe had found a bag of chips in Lawson's pantry. She was sprawled on the living room couch with her feet up on a glass table. From the satisfied look on her face, Victor knew immediately that she'd found something.

"Did Lawson have any pets?" she asked, bringing the bag to her lips and tilting her head back to scarf down the last crumbs.

"No idea. Did you ask Wu?"

"He says he didn't."

The detective sergeant looked around, seeking the young man.

"Don't worry. He went to lie down in his bedroom. I didn't touch him."

"Why ask the question if you already know the answer?" he said, sinking into an armchair.

Wearing an enigmatic expression, she held out a sheet of paper. Victor leaned forward to take it.

"A vet's bill," he said, after glancing at it.

It was dated the previous month. Jacinthe had found it among Lawson's papers.

"Kind of strange for a guy who doesn't own a pet, wouldn't you agree?"

"Did you call?"

"Pfff. Do I look like a maid to you?" She was clearly pleased with her discovery. "You can do the honours, my friend."

After being placed on hold for several minutes while the receptionist checked the files, the detective sergeant learned that the bill in question related to a dog that had been euthanized.

"Mr. Lawson's dog?"

"No, it belonged to a friend of his. Mr. Lawson brought the animal in to be put down a few days after the owner died."

Victor's heart started to race. "Do you know the friend's name?"

"Yes, it's Frost. Peter Frost."

"You wouldn't happen to have his address on file, would you?"

28

SUMMIT WOODS

"Look out!" Taillon yelled.

Jaw clenched, muscles tensed to the breaking point, Victor wrenched the steering wheel. The Crown Victoria's rear slid and the car fishtailed, threatening to skid off the road, but the detective sergeant hit the accelerator and managed to straighten the car out at the last moment. They were racing along Summit Circle. Snow was falling hard through the headlight beams; they couldn't see a metre in front of them. Nestled into the flank of the mountain, Peter Frost's house appeared as they emerged from a hairpin turn.

"There it is … Stop. Stop!"

They left the car in front of the driveway with the doors open and the emergency lights on.

Victor made a mental note of the FOR SALE sign near the entrance.

"It's unlocked," Jacinthe said, panting.

The detective sergeant pushed the door with his metal flashlight.

"We're going in," he murmured, unholstering his Glock.

The flashlight beam swept over a living room stuffed with Victorian furniture and thick, red-velvet drapes, then a dining room with a crystal chandelier and a table that could seat fourteen. Victor hit the light switch. Nothing. There was no power. Next, they discovered a kitchen, its walls lined with solid oak cupboards, and a cluttered office.

The two partners moved silently, methodically, each securing a position before the other advanced. Victor signalled to Taillon, pointing to the upper floor. Several stairs creaked under Jacinthe's weight. The detective sergeant felt an oppressive mix of fear and adrenalin gripping him. Cold sweat ran down his temples. They found five bedrooms with outdated furnishings and wallpaper. In one of the rooms, the bed was unmade. Victor touched the rumpled sheet with his fingertips: it was cold.

They went through every room. No signs of a struggle. Nobody.

In the basement, ceramic recesses containing hundreds of wine bottles covered an entire wall. Old furniture was piled in a corner next to skis and a golf bag with fuzzy yellow covers on the clubs. The other side of the space was occupied by shelves laden with items Frost hadn't been able to get rid of over the years. Moving forward, the detectives entered a workshop with tools neatly arranged on the wall.

They were startled by a noise resembling the striking of a matchstick: the burner on the gas furnace had just lit up. Victor released his breath, wiped his forehead with the back of his hand, and opened the door at the far end of the workshop.

The beam of his flashlight slid across the room, and a cry froze in his throat. An odour of death and offal hung in the air. The body of a man in his underwear lay in a puddle of blood and excrement.

The detective sergeant snapped a mental image of the scene: the corpse was lying face up, arms crossed. Brownish wounds were visible on the diaphanous skin of the throat and chest. The wrists bore purple bruises, and the cracked, dry lips had split open in several places.

The walls began to spin. Victor's grip loosened, and his Glock and flashlight both clattered to the floor.

Suppressing the urge to vomit, he barrelled past Jacinthe as he rushed through the darkness toward the stairs.

        ·   ·   ·

The detective sergeant made it out onto the back deck in time to avoid throwing up. His nausea gradually dissipated in the cold air. He smoked a cigarette and gazed down at the winding road below the house, which had been freshly plowed.

Beyond Mount Royal, the lights of the city sparkled.

Recovering his cigarette stub to throw away, Victor went back inside. Through the living room window, he saw that the emergency lights were still flashing and the car doors were open. He stepped outside to radio for backup from the Crown Victoria. In front of the house, the wind was screaming through the treetops of Summit Woods. A light appeared in the forest, then went out.

Intrigued, the detective sergeant advanced a few paces, squinting. At first he couldn't make out anything. Then he thought he saw movement behind a spruce tree. As his gaze swept over the area where he had spotted the movement, he reacted with a start: in the distance, a dark silhouette was watching him.

"Hey!" he yelled, waving. He knew lots of people went for walks along the wooded paths.

A halo of light began to dance away through the trees.

It took him a moment to realize that the silhouette had turned on a flashlight and was fleeing. Victor rushed forward in pursuit. "Taillon!" he shouted as loudly as he could, hoping she'd hear him.

Instead of circling around to the start of the path, he went straight up the two-metre escarpment that fronted the street. His high-tops skidded in the snow, but he managed to grab a branch and hoist himself up. He was now on rising ground among the trees, but the vegetation wasn't thick enough to prevent him from reaching the path, which opened before him.

Reflexively, he touched his holster. Empty. His Glock and flashlight were still in the basement. Knee deep in snow, with branches slapping his face, he advanced as fast as he could in the darkness. He stopped for a second on the path to locate the halo; he'd momentarily lost sight of it. Then he set off again after the point of light, which he spotted about a hundred metres to his right.

Victor was gaining ground fast, ignoring the growing pain in his leg — the leg that had almost been torn off by a vicious criminal during a previous investigation. He could see the fugitive moving through the shadows. Another few steps and he'd be on him. Now he understood why he'd been able to catch up so quickly; the fugitive was wearing cross-country skis, which were slowing him down on the uphill path. But they were coming to the crest of the rise. Victor accelerated, putting all he had into the pursuit. If he didn't catch the fugitive now, he'd have no chance once they started downhill.

"Stop!" the detective sergeant shouted, regretting that he didn't have his pistol.

And then, even though he hadn't made a false move, his leg gave out just as he was reaching desperately for the fugitive's jacket. For an instant, he seemed to float, suspended in the air; then he fell, his head slamming into the ground. With a hood pulled low over his eyes, the shadowy figure returned and leaned over him. A powerful light blinded him. For a fraction of a second, the detective sergeant thought he saw a pistol pointed at his face. Or was it an illusion?

Everything began to spin.

He passed out.

29

SOUNDTRACK

The room was filled with tumbling words that his brain was struggling to grasp and arrange into sentences, whose meanings he couldn't quite discern.

"You're lucky I heard you yell …"

Sitting on the kitchen counter, Victor lowered the bag of ice that Jacinthe had given him and touched the bump on the side of his skull.

"You should have waited for me, instead of acting like an idiot!"

The detective sergeant remembered that when he had come to, Jacinthe was bending over him, and he was chilled to the bone. How they'd managed to make it back to Peter Frost's house remained blurry in his memory.

"Good thing you've got a hard head …"

The sequence of events was starting to come back to him. The halo in the woods, the desperate pursuit, the skis. His fall. Then blackness.

"Are you feeling dizzy? You should probably go to the hospital. You may have a concussion …"

Victor waved his hands. "No, no, I'm okay," he said in a low voice, as though to convince himself.

"How's the leg?"

He bent and straightened the limb a few times, wincing. His leg would never regain its former strength. As far as the doctors were concerned, the fact that he could walk at all was an achievement.

While he was in rehab, they'd stressed that he would have to take care from now on. Precisely the opposite of what he'd just done.

"It's fine," he lied.

"Here, pop a few of these," Jacinthe ordered, handing him some acetaminophen tablets that she'd found in the medicine cabinet upstairs.

Victor washed them down with a gulp of water. Then he noticed that the lights were on in the house. Jacinthe confirmed that she'd restored the electricity herself. Someone had turned off the main switch on the breaker panel.

"What about the body downstairs?" Victor asked.

"It's Lawson, all right. The forensics team is on its way."

The detective sergeant had more questions for his partner, but Jacinthe wanted to discuss what had just happened in Summit Woods. She suggested that the skier might simply have misunderstood Victor's intentions, becoming frightened when Victor had charged at him.

"You're forgetting the gun," he said.

"You're not even sure he had one," Taillon replied.

On the way back to the house, Victor had indeed admitted his uncertainty. Had his disoriented mind imagined what he'd seen? Despite his doubts, he couldn't help thinking of the old cliché: the killer returning to the scene of his crime. Was that what had happened? He didn't have to ask out loud. He knew the question was already on Jacinthe's mind.

The two detectives quickly went to work when the forensics team arrived.

While Jacinthe coordinated with the crime-scene technicians, Victor called the Gnome and enlisted his aid. They needed a profile on Peter Frost. Then the detective sergeant went down to the basement, where he found several old pairs of cross-country skis, along with footprints in the snow outside the garden door. Under his thoughtful gaze, one of the techs made casts of several prints that led out to the street.

Had the killer been in the house when they arrived? Had he seized his opportunity, while they were searching the upstairs rooms, to grab a pair of skis from the basement and flee?

Victor went back out into the forest with the technician. The ski tracks ended at the edge of the road on the far side of the woods, near the lookout.

Had a car been waiting for the skier there? If so, any tire marks in the snow had been obliterated by the plow that had cleared the street before they arrived.

Victor lit a cigarette and propped an elbow on the parapet. His gaze plunged down toward the luxurious houses of Westmount, the lights of Montreal, and the river.

Victor had finished searching the ground floor of the house when the Gnome called back. Peter Frost was the owner of several pharmacies. He had died a month earlier following a lengthy illness. According to his sister, Frost had named his old friend Lawson as his executor. The woman had also confided to Lemaire that Frost and Lawson had once been lovers.

The detective sergeant thanked Lemaire and called the real estate broker whose name and number were on the FOR SALE sign in front of the house. The broker told him that the property had gone on the market two weeks previously, on Lawson's orders as executor, and that all communications with Lawson had been by telephone.

The agent also said that the steep asking price and the seasonal slowdown in activity explained why the house hadn't yet been visited by any prospective buyers.

The place was full of crime-scene spotlights, with technicians in jumpsuits moving around, taking care not to trip over the wires that snaked across the floor. Victor and Jacinthe had been working together so long that they could operate in the midst of this silent ballet without a word to each other.

While Taillon helped the technicians in their preliminary examination of the body, the detective sergeant searched the room with the unmade bed, where he found clothes and a leather overnight bag containing additional garments, as well as a passport and papers in the name of Nathan R. Lawson. A glass that had contained alcohol stood on the nightstand. Victor sniffed it: whisky. He also found a loaded hunting rifle under the bed. The weapon had come from Frost's personal collection, which was kept in a locked cabinet in his office.

Victor outlined his findings to Jacinthe when she came up from the basement and found him in the dining room, examining papers that he had laid out on the table. "He was never planning to go abroad," Victor said. "He was in hiding, afraid for his life. Judging from the dirty dishes in the sink and the contents of the wastebasket, I'd say he'd had a few meals. My guess is he's been here since the day he went missing."

"I don't know when he arrived, or how," Jacinthe said, "but he has the same wounds as Judith Harper. I'm sure you realize what that implies."

"Please, fill me in," Victor challenged her.

"You're the expert on serial killers, my friend."

Jacinthe was provoking him, referring to a previous investigation that had made Victor the reluctant object of extensive media coverage, giving him a public profile that he disliked and would gladly have done without.

"Don't start with me," he said, scowling.

"Relax, I'm kidding. But still —"

Victor didn't let her finish. "You're getting ahead of yourself! The wounds may look identical, but you and I aren't medical examiners. And even if both murders were committed by the same person, that doesn't mean we have any basis for talking about a serial killer!" Victor wiped his mouth. He'd been spitting as he spoke.

"Whoa, settle down there, big guy," Jacinthe said, raising her hands in a humorous attempt to shield her face from the flying spittle.

He shook his head and sighed deeply. Then he spoke again in a low voice. "Change of topic. I looked everywhere for the file but didn't find it."

Jacinthe frowned, puzzled. "What file?" she asked.

"Lawson's secretary told us that on the day he disappeared, he left with a couple of boxes of documents in the trunk of his car."

"Right, I forgot," she conceded.

Suddenly they looked at each other, both struck by the same thought.

"The car!" Jacinthe exclaimed.

The garage was a brick structure that stood apart from the house at the end of the driveway. Through the layer of frost covering the window, the two officers saw a Mercedes parked in the shadowy interior. Victor went back into the house and retrieved the set of keys he'd found upstairs in one of the dead man's pants pockets.

Despite a careful search of the car and the garage, they found nothing but a pair of empty cardboard boxes in the trunk. No sign of the file.

"We'll have a forensics tech dust for prints," Victor said at last.

He looked at his watch: 5:12 p.m. In his notebook, he found Adèle Thibault's number and dialed it. With a little luck, she'd still be at the office.

When she answered, Victor put his phone on speaker so Jacinthe could listen in. Without telling Lawson's assistant that they'd just found her boss's body, Victor asked again about the file. Was she sure it had been in Lawson's possession when he left the office? She repeated her version of the facts: that it was Lucian the mail boy who had helped the lawyer stow the boxes in his car. Victor asked to speak to him. The secretary put him on hold while she checked to see if the mail boy was still in the office.

Several clicks later, he was talking to Lucian, who confirmed that he had transported the boxes to Lawson's car in the underground parking garage.

"A metallic-grey Mercedes," Victor said.

"That's right," Lucian answered, specifying the model number. "I put the two boxes in the trunk. Mr. Lawson kept looking around. He seemed nervous."

Victor glanced significantly at Jacinthe, who remained impassive, her face illuminated by the harsh glow of the ceiling light. "Do you know what was in the boxes? Did he say anything about a file?"

"No. He was more interested in the message."

"What message?"

"I'm not sure … a sheet of paper he said someone sent him."

Victor's follow-up inquiries didn't yield any additional information about the sheet. Lucian had no memory of that particular message. His job involved putting hundreds of documents into hundreds of pigeonholes every day.

Lucian said he'd given the same answer to Lawson on the way down to the parking garage when the lawyer had asked him where the sheet of paper had come from.

The call was transferred again. There was a long silence on the line. More clicks. After giving it some thought, Lawson's secretary told the detective sergeant that she couldn't remember discussing a specific message with her boss on the day of his disappearance. Or maybe, yes, now that she thought about it, he had stood in her doorway, holding a piece of paper.

But she couldn't remember anything more than that. She hadn't been paying attention.

Baffled, Victor ended the call. Beside him, Jacinthe was leaning into the Mercedes's interior, her large, latex-gloved hand probing the space between the passenger seat and the transmission console.

"What are you doing?" he asked impatiently.

"Hang on, there's something stuck in here," she grunted.

When she withdrew her hand, she was holding a CD between her fingers. "Start the car," she suggested.

Victor complied, and she slid the disc into the CD player.

A voice neither of them recognized started repeating a single sentence in a loop: "*I emphatically deny these charges ... I emphatically deny these charges ... I emphatic ...*"

30

LAURENTIANS

The minivan tore along the icy highway. Now and then, the lights of a house would break the dark monotony of the evergreens. Through the speakers, Eminem and Pink were chanting that they wouldn't back down. In the back seat, fear was gnawing at his entrails. The time for doubt had passed. It was useless to ask questions or seek answers.

The gears were turning. He was caught in the machinery. There would be no turning back now.

The man in the passenger seat looked hard at him. "Almost there ... You ready, Lessard?"

Martin nodded. His hand closed on the butt of his gun.

"Remember what we said. It's closing time. Just a couple of employees in the place. No cameras, no armed guards, no security system ..."

"Fuck, they don't even have a fence, Boris!" the driver said, laughing.

"In and out," Boris continued, ignoring the interruption. "We put what we need in the bag, not one stick more, then we're gone. No problem."

The driver downshifted to slow the vehicle and turned onto a secondary road. He drove along for a few minutes, then, extinguishing the headlights, entered a gravel drive that led to a concrete warehouse. The minivan stopped a hundred metres from the parking area. Two trucks were parked next to the building.

"Let's go," Boris said, quietly opening the passenger door.

Martin pulled the ski mask down over his face. "No problem," he murmured, as though trying to convince himself.

The two silhouettes advanced as far as they could in the shadow of the building, nearly invisible in their black jumpsuits. Beating against the windowpanes, the wind howled and wept frozen tears. Brandishing pistols, the pair burst in on an employee seated at the reception desk reading a newspaper. His soft belly sagged under a distended T-shirt that must have been the right size in another life.

Before the man could react, Boris approached and pressed a gun barrel to his head.

"Here's the deal, lard-ass. Do what I say and there won't be any problems. Try to be a hero and they'll take you away in a body bag. Are we clear?"

"Y-y-yes," the man stammered, terrified.

Martin looked around the warehouse: dead calm. No one else in sight. No movement.

"How many others are on duty?" Boris asked.

"Ap-ap-apart from me, one guy. He's in the b-back."

"Call him," Boris said, unlatching the safety on his gun. "And don't try anything stupid."

The man swallowed, shaking with fear. Martin saw a puddle on the concrete floor. The poor guy had wet himself.

"Mar-Marcel?" he called out in a weak voice. "Marcel?"

Like his co-worker, Marcel was dumbstruck by the two steel barrels aimed at his face. He put up no resistance.

Martin did a quick recount of the dynamite sticks he'd carefully slipped into the compartments of the bag. The number was right. He nodded to his partner, whose gun was pointed at the demolition company's two employees. The operation had taken less than two minutes.

"We're good to go," Boris said, leaving the two men on their knees in a corner, hands duct-taped behind their backs.

They sprinted to the minivan. The driver had positioned the vehicle to be ready for a quick departure. They were rolling before the doors had closed. Boris and Martin settled into their seats. Martin took off his ski mask and wiped the sweat from his forehead. Removing the magazine from his pistol, he felt the tension finally begin to ease. Little by little, the knot in the pit of his stomach dissipated.

As the driver swung onto the main highway and it became clear that no one was following them, Boris broke the silence. "Hell of a good job, guys! You were perfect, Lessard!"

Yells and high-fives filled the minivan.

While Boris and the driver were talking and passing a joint back and forth, Martin pretended to doze. He discreetly typed a text into his iPhone, which was hidden in his coat pocket, and sent it. He was about to delete the message from the call log when Boris put a hand on his knee and shook him. Pretending to wake up with a start, Martin stretched.

"Take a hit, Lessard. It'll do you good."

The minivan driver let them off in front of an unremarkable residential building in Hochelaga-Maisonneuve.

"Store the goods, then come back and join us," Boris ordered the driver.

The vehicle rolled away. Boris put an arm around Martin's shoulders and led him toward the building.

"What's the matter, bro? You're a million miles away."

Martin pulled himself together and laughed. "I'm fine. Just coming down from the rush."

"Hah! Seems like maybe you were a little nervous back there, Marty-boy."

Never show weakness. Never be vulnerable. Never.

"Me?" Martin scoffed. "Nervous? Not a chance."

"Oh, man … was that awesome or what?"

"Totally. Did you see those two clowns when we walked in?" Martin opened and closed his mouth repeatedly, imitating the first employee's reaction.

Boris guffawed. "It's gonna be a great night. Roxanne'll be there. Lolita and Muriel are coming over. Maybe Amélie."

Martin forced himself to look excited.

"Muriel likes you, bro," Boris went on. "She is *hot*. Woo-hoo, that girl is hot! Play your cards right, Amélie'll join in. They're into three-ways."

I wanna fuck you like an animal.

The brutal music of Nine Inch Nails shook the apartment. The synthetic bass hammered inside Martin's chest like his own heart. Bodies were everywhere, writhing against each other in the smoke, blending sweat and saliva.

Muriel led him to a corner. The strobe light slid over her large breasts; her nipples were already hard. He tried to lick them, but Muriel evaded him. His zipper opened. A hand pulled him out, and a sudden spasm of pleasure shook him: Muriel's mouth was burning his flesh.

I wanna feel you from the inside.

His gaze locked with Boris, who, on the far side of the room, was spreading his tentacles over Roxanne's sculptured form. Was he paranoid, or was his friend looking at him strangely? Earlier in the evening, Martin had gone to the washroom, forgetting his iPhone on the table from which they'd snorted several runways of powder. When he'd returned, Boris had handed him the phone, suggesting with an enigmatic smile that he be more careful where he left it.

You get me closer to God.

Martin shuddered and clutched at Muriel's hair as she drove her mouth down on him with mounting intensity. Had Boris read the text message he'd sent from the minivan? Or were the alcohol and drugs affecting his perception?

Fuck. How could he have forgotten to delete the message?

Amélie approached, her slender legs glistening in the light. She bit her lower lip. Then, caressing Muriel's hair, she flicked her tongue in Martin's ear. Freeing one hand, he seized her buttocks and pulled her to him.

Martin closed his eyes. Images of Boris pointing a gun at his head were jumbled with the sight of Muriel eating him. He let himself be swept into the maelstrom. There was no point in resisting.

31

LOOKING-GLASS GAMES

With Win Butler and the other members of Arcade Fire filling his ears, Louis-Charles Rivard was doing his best to make it seem like his only reason for watching himself in the mirror was to monitor his final set of curls. But in truth, he was admiring his biceps, his athletic build, and his classically handsome face.

He turned his head imperceptibly to one side. The tall redhead walking his way fully met his high standards of beauty: slender legs, a compact bust, and a flawlessly rounded little ass in tight-fitting shorts. To top it off, she had a perfect beauty mark, and the smooth contours of her thighs were untouched by cellulite. Rivard had noticed her when she came over to use the rowing machine near his. He had also noticed that this was her third trip to the water fountain. She passed behind him and, once again, glanced in his direction.

Apart from the thrill of self-admiration, this was the thing he liked best about working out at the gym: locking eyes in the mirror. He had always known that true communication was achieved with looks, not with words. Everything could be read in the gaze: attraction, repulsion, love, truth, falsehood. Yet most people tended to neglect this fact. He was well aware of it. He'd told countless lies in his life and gotten away scot free.

The only person he couldn't fool was his mother. They were too similar.

Louis-Charles looked at the redhead again. Bent over the water fountain, she was knowingly offering him a clear view of her endowments. He guessed she was in her midtwenties, a resident of the Plateau area, or perhaps the Mile End district. She wasn't a regular at the upscale Sanctuaire club. She had come here with the intention of attracting the right kind of man; she was ripe for the picking.

Louis-Charles would provide satisfaction.

When she went by again, he gave her his best untamed look, his king-of-the-jungle stare, the one that said *I want to fuck you, right here, right now.*

She made a show of ignoring him, but their eyes met in the mirror for a second. A second too long. He knew. She was caught. Her gaze had betrayed her: *I'm acting like I'm not attracted to you, but I'd be more than willing.*

In Rivard's experience, most women, especially the really beautiful ones, played this game. They showed a degree of interest initially, then acted like they weren't really into it. After that, they waited for the man to make the first move.

A woman in her fifties walked past, her face flushed after her workout. Then a man went by — bearded, with a shaved head, a swaying walk, and a tattoo on his right bicep. He and Louis-Charles looked at each other in the mirror. With gay men, it was entirely different. They had mastered the art of the direct approach.

Louis-Charles received all kinds of offers, whether it was at the club, or at the gym on Bélanger Street where he took boxing lessons, or on Facebook. Though he was resolutely straight, he had no qualms about exciting a man's desire or playing seductive games with a male counterpart. He found it as satisfying to attract a gay man as to attract a woman. He was comfortable either way, and he took advantage of that ambiguity at the office with Lawson. Nothing had ever actually happened between them, but Louis-Charles had always sustained the fantasy, using his charm on the old man, deliberately preserving a grey zone in which Lawson kept hoping that someday, maybe …

Standing up, Rivard returned the barbells to their places on the rack and walked straight toward the redhead.

When a woman had shown her interest but was feigning indifference, you had to be audacious — you had to take the initiative and use the element of surprise. And you had to lie. Most definitely. Never tell the truth. You had to act like you were ready for lifelong love, though the truth was that you just wanted to hook up and spill some seed, after which she wouldn't hear from you again.

"Hi, I'm Louis-Charles," he said, extending a hand and offering the redhead a sexy flutter of the eyelids, which, depending on the context, might mean *Vote for me*, or *I'm a whore*, or *You can put your faith in me*.

Louis-Charles headed for the locker room with the girl's email address stored in his iPhone. It had been almost too easy. Two minutes of idle chatter and he'd gotten what he wanted.

As always, he had told her that he was going on a business trip for a few days, but he'd be in touch when he got back. This permitted him to identify short-term opportunities and avoid missing any because of scheduling conflicts.

Thereafter, the mathematical equation was pretty straightforward: *nice restaurant + good dinner + free-flowing alcohol = your place or mine?* All he had to do was drop a few references to his Porsche Cayenne, his loft in Old Montreal, and his sailboat moored at the marina off René Lévesque Park in Lachine, and the equation would produce results as predictable as a Fibonacci sequence.

And after? After, he wouldn't call back. He'd move on to the next file.

He thought only about himself, about his career and the money it generated for him.

His Adidas T-shirt was soaked with sweat. He removed it and rippled his abs in the mirror for a few seconds. Satisfied with what he saw, Louis-Charles opened his locker and drank his protein shake. He would take creatine with his post-workout snack when he got home.

Or maybe he'd have dinner on Saint-Laurent before going home to bed. There was that waitress at the trendy restaurant who was just waiting for a snap of his fingers.

Placing his iPhone on the shelf inside the locker, he reached into his pants pocket and pulled out a second phone, a generic model that he'd bought at the suggestion of the man who had called following his impromptu statement to the press. The mailbox was empty.

As he put down the phone, he saw it: someone had slipped a piece of paper into his locker. Folded in two, it had fallen onto his personal effects. Louis-Charles saw a row of digits and his face lit up.

Lawson's disappearance had become a profitable enterprise for him. The partners had agreed with his arguments and were trusting him to handle the crisis. Everyone wanted to avoid a scandal that might damage the firm. Pressing the auto callback, Louis-Charles reached a voice mail and left a message with his counter-offer.

After tearing the paper into small pieces, he dropped them in the locker-room toilet, flushing several times to make sure they were gone.

He noticed the man with the shaved head whose gaze he had met in the mirror earlier. The man had a towel around his waist and was looking at him with a puzzled expression, having seen him flush the paper. Louis-Charles shrugged, gave the man his brightest smile, and stepped into the shower, where he washed himself unhurriedly, using two separate shower gels, one for his body and the other for his face. Then Rivard applied a variety of creams and lotions to his skin. Like Patrick Bateman in *American Psycho*, he believed in taking care of himself.

Walking to his car, he checked the voice mail again. The call he was expecting had come through while he was in the shower. His counter-offer had been accepted. A sensation of power washed over him.

Rivard made up his mind to have dinner on Saint-Laurent. That waitress was hot. But first, he would recover an item that now appeared to be his passport to freedom.

In the parking lot, he opened the hatch of the Cayenne. Balancing on one leg at a time, he removed his running shoes and put on hiking boots. Then he donned a cap, bundled himself into a parka, and grabbed a pair of Gore-Tex mittens.

As he touched the handle on the driver's door, he froze. The reflection of a face had appeared in the window for an instant. Heart pounding, he spun around.

Then he relaxed and smiled.

No one was there.

32

DEBRIEFING

Lost in thought, Paul Delaney had spent the evening gazing out his office window, watching but not seeing the colourful crowd. All those people hurrying to buy last-minute gifts as though the fate of the world depended on it.

The parking lot had emptied out hours ago, but his reddened eyes were still staring into the slush.

Madeleine would be undergoing another operation on the evening of the 24th.

The doctor had refused to say anything about the chances of success. The surgical team would open her up first and offer opinions later. If the cancer had metastasized to the liver, there would be nothing they could do.

The head of the Major Crimes Unit had spent the night at the hospital and would be there over Christmas. He had to tell the kids. But tell them what?

There was a knock at the door.

Delaney mumbled something along the lines of "Come in" and watched Victor struggle with the door while holding two cups of steaming coffee.

"Mind if I sit down, Chief?" Victor asked, indicating one of the guest chairs with his chin.

"Go ahead," Delaney said, picking up a ballpoint for the sake of appearances.

Victor gave one cup to his superior and placed the other on the desk in front of him. "Good thing we're both in AA," Victor said wryly, "or you'd be pulling a bottle out of your drawer right about now."

"Believe me, I'd like to," Delaney answered bleakly.

"What's the news?" the detective sergeant ventured, blowing on his coffee.

"Not good. Surgery in three days. Make or break."

Victor shook his head, stunned. "Fuck." He wanted to say something more, something helpful, but nothing came. Neither man spoke for a moment. "Do you want me to come back later?"

Delaney took a breath and sat up a little straighter. "No, no, I'd rather you stayed. I need the distraction." After a long silence, he said, "How's the head? And the leg?"

Victor took a sip and made a face. The coffee was too hot. "I've got a fair-sized bump," he said, running his fingers across the swelling on his scalp, "but no concussion. And the leg's okay."

"Good. Have forensics found anything that might help identify your skier?"

Victor picked up a paper clip from the desk and unbent it. "No. Still nothing."

"Don't worry. Whether he's connected to the case or not, we'll find him eventually." Delaney rubbed his bald spot. "Anyway, now that Lawson's dead, that takes him off the list of suspects. Lortie too, surely."

"Let's wait for Berger to give us an exact time of death for Lawson before ruling out Lortie as a suspect. We still don't know why he had the wallets in his possession, or how he was connected to the victims."

"Maybe it's just a coincidence. Lortie was homeless. He might very well have found them in a garbage can, or stolen them."

"You're forgetting what we learned at Louis-H. about his wallet fixation."

Delaney put his face in his hands, then looked at the floor, seeming overwhelmed. "That's right. I'm sorry. I forgot."

Victor put a hand on his superior's arm. "Hang in there, Paul. We're all here for you."

The moment Victor had stepped into the office, Delaney had understood that his visit was more about showing sympathy and support than discussing the case. This was Victor's way of communicating his respect and his friendship. The chief smiled and cleared his throat, eyes glistening. "Did anything turn up when the house was searched?" he asked.

Victor shrugged and shook his head. "So far, all we've got is the CD, Lawson's body, and his personal effects. We didn't find his cellphone, but we checked his call log. Nothing suspicious there." He paused. "Going by what the secretary and the mail boy told me, we should have found a file in the trunk of the car."

"Concerning a company called ..." Delaney rummaged among a stack of papers on his desk. "Where the hell is it? I was sure I'd printed your email."

"Northern Industrial Textiles," Victor said, scratching his cheek. "All we found was a couple of empty boxes in the trunk of his car. Either the killer took the papers, or Lawson got rid of them before going to Peter Frost's house. Either way, we have to consider the possibility that the file had something to do with the murders." He took a sip of coffee. "I'm waiting for a research report from the Justice Ministry concerning the company. I'll send it to you."

"Okay, thanks." Paul was silent for a moment. "This Northern thing could be a court case that went wrong."

"Could be. But if so, it's ancient history."

"Has Berger confirmed that the two murders were committed with the same weapon?"

"Not yet. But Jacinthe is convinced they were. Sometimes I think she gets ahead of herself, but in this case, I'd be surprised if she was wrong."

"What about the recording that you found in Lawson's car?"

"The CD? You heard it?"

"Jacinthe played it for me earlier."

"*I emphatically deny these charges.*" He paused briefly. "At first, we had no idea what it was. But Gilles pointed out that those were the exact words spoken by Lee Harvey Oswald after his arrest. It seems to be a copy of one of the clips that were broadcast at the time. It would be easy enough to get. There are plenty of links on YouTube."

"What's the connection between our case and the Kennedy assassination?"

"I don't think there is one. I talked it over with Gilles and Jacinthe, and we agree: you shouldn't take the message literally. You've got to look at it symbolically. One possibility is that the killer's pointing us toward a case where someone denies guilt, someone who's been caught by the system but still claims to be innocent."

Delaney resumed his favourite sport: hunting for specks of dust on the surface of his desk. He spotted one next to Victor's elbow, trapped it under his middle finger, and released it into the air by rubbing his fingers together. "An individual who was treated unjustly," he suggested.

"Something like that." Victor sat for a moment, idly inspecting his high-tops. "But you know what I find weird? This is the second time the killer's left a clue. First the numbers on Judith Harper's fridge, and now the CD …"

"As though he were showing us where to look."

"That's what worries me. He may be sending us down the wrong path while he continues with his plan."

"You believe there'll be more deaths?"

"I fear there may be."

"Serial?"

"Did Jacinthe mention that? It's too early to talk about serial killings, Paul. Though their victims have common traits, serial killers usually choose them at random. This is too organized, too structured to be the work of a serial killer. I don't think that's what's going on."

"Serial killers tend to be methodical …"

"Up to a point, yes. But not like this. And then there's the message Lawson received."

"Another message, besides the CD?"

Victor told Delaney about his discussions with Adèle Thibault and the mail boy. Both had mentioned a sheet of paper. The two cops talked briefly about the possibility that the lawyer had received an envelope containing both a letter and the CD.

Then the chief spoke. "So, he received threats?"

"Seems that way. Which would explain why Lawson left the office so fast. He was in a big hurry, Paul. He received a message, took the Northern file, and went into hiding." Victor drained his coffee cup. "In the Judith Harper case, we found magnetic numbers on her fridge." He fell silent for a few seconds. "If you ask me, the victims were chosen with care. It's like the killer was after specific targets. Lawson was on the run, and the killer still got him."

Without seeming to notice, Delaney was rhythmically pressing the button on his ballpoint, causing an incessant clicking noise that irritated Victor.

"I agree with you," Delaney said. "When I mentioned serial killings, I was playing devil's advocate." He seemed to lose his train of thought for an instant. "Either way, Lortie's suicide doesn't fit. Then there's the writing on the carboard, and the skier," he murmured to himself. Delaney sighed, seemingly lost, before gathering himself. "Hey, I know I'm not being logical here, but when you see Berger, tell him to get his ass in gear. It would be damn helpful to know what the murder weapon was."

The detective sergeant raised his arms helplessly. "You know Berger. Let's not piss him off. Anyway, with what we've learned already, it's not hard to guess that it'll be something unusual."

Victor looked at his watch and stood up. "I'd better call that lawyer, Rivard. I want to notify him of Lawson's death and ask him a few questions about the Northern file. I'm also curious to find out whether anyone came forward after the statement he made to the media."

Victor dialed Rivard's number as he returned to his desk, but the call went to voice mail. He left a message. Then he turned around and hurried back to Delaney. "Hey, Paul?"

Bent over his keyboard, Delaney had started to type in his password. He looked up.

"About Madeleine … hang in there."

33

THE PHANTOM OF
THE OPERA

The night was inky black. The gates of the Mount Royal Cemetery were locked, but Louis-Charles Rivard slipped in without difficulty. Covering his flashlight beam, he found the Mordecai Richler monument in minutes. Carefully, with the back of one hand, he brushed the accumulated snow off the top of the gravestone. As Lawson had indicated, the key was hidden under one of the rocks placed there in honour of the writer.

The damp pierced him to the bone. The wind moaned in the trees; the twisted branches came to life, as though wanting to touch him. Was it the lugubrious surroundings or his own imagination that made him shiver? Rivard pulled up his hood, tugged his hat low over his eyes, and set off again, leaving the Richler monument behind.

A family vault came into view a hundred metres away, at the end of the path. The lock wasn't a problem. The metal door swung open on well-oiled hinges.

There was no coffin inside, only an altar topped with votive candles, a congealed puddle of wax, and a book wrapped in protective plastic. Rivard pointed his flashlight at the cover: the book was a vintage edition of Gaston Leroux's novel *The Phantom of the Opera*. On the altar's stone surface, the flashlight beam found a weathered inscription: *In Loving Memory of Jane Margaret Sophia Lawson 1912–1986.*

Rivard gave himself a shake. He had work to do.

The two garbage bags were lying in a corner. Louis-Charles went to them, opened one, and saw that it contained documents. He closed it immediately. Lawson had spoken to him about the file without telling him what it contained — but the less Rivard knew about it, the better off he would be.

Lawson had called him from a confidential number the day of his disappearance. The old man hadn't said where he was hiding; he had simply given the necessary instructions for locating the file.

His directives had been clear: he would call each evening around 6:00 p.m. If he failed to call, that would mean he was dead. In which case Louis-Charles was to retrieve the file, convene a press conference, and make its contents public.

By way of compensation, Lawson had suggested that he check his bank balance. Rivard couldn't believe his eyes when he saw that the old man had transferred fifty thousand dollars into his account. Lawson had also made it clear that he would get twice that much after the press conference.

But Rivard was smart enough to read between the lines.

Believing the file was his insurance policy, the old man had threatened to reveal its contents, hoping that would be enough to discourage attempts on his life. Now that he'd failed, more than once, to call at the appointed time, Rivard was forced to draw the obvious conclusion: Lawson had played for keeps and lost.

At the time, Rivard hadn't known the identity of the man who wanted the file, but he knew that if the man was ready to kill for it, he must value it very highly.

The lawyer had consequently seized the opportunity that presented itself. He had applied the most basic of economic principles: the law of supply and demand. Lawson was dead. There was no reason to have qualms about getting rid of the file. Rivard knew the value of money. He stood to gain far more from breaking his promise to Lawson than from keeping it and making the file's contents public.

And so, in his statement to the media, he had sent a clear message to the person who wanted the file: it was in his possession, and it was for sale. The message had been received. Initial contact had been made by phone after the press conference.

The man who had contacted him at the office hadn't raised the issue directly. He had simply offered assistance in searching for Lawson. But the subtext had been clear to Louis-Charles.

After delaying for a few hours, Rivard had called the man from home. "I can get what you're looking for," he had said flat out.

The man had responded by suggesting that he purchase a prepaid cellphone, so they could "communicate more freely."

Rivard regretted not having brought the assault pack that he'd kept after his stint in the army. The garbage bags were heavy. He couldn't carry them both by hand over such a long distance.

Besides, although Lawson had doubled the bags, the plastic might tear.

Tough luck. He'd make two trips.

After twenty metres, Louis-Charles realized that the cargo was more awkward than he'd anticipated. He was struggling to make progress, sinking into the snow. Getting the bags to the car wasn't going to be easy. But he gritted his teeth and redoubled his efforts. This little challenge was nothing compared with the rigours he and his fellow recruits had faced, long ago, at the hands of Drill Sergeant Deschenaux.

His trained eye glimpsed movement on his right. He advanced, then stopped. Senses alert, he tried to make out the silhouette in the darkness. Was he seeing things? Was that a tree or a human form on the high ground?

Rivard waited. The cemetery was still, the trees motionless. The lawyer was about to set out again when the shadow moved. Fear seized him. A shudder ran through his body. Someone was on the hill.

The shadow extended one arm, pulling the other back before opening its hand. The shaft sliced through the air. Rivard's stomach exploded with pain. Horrified, he lowered his gaze to the arrow that had impaled him.

He dropped the bag, which slid on the snow. Then the pain came. It was blinding. He tried to get away between the gravestones, but fell to his knees.

The shadow skied down the slope.

Rivard hiccuped, fighting for air, and spat up blood. Behind him, the shadow stopped and pulled down his hood. Rivard turned. His eyes widened — he knew that face.

The shadow pulled back the bowstring once more. A second arrow flew past Rivard's ear and was lost in the snow. A flood of images passed before his eyes, then another projectile hit him in the solar plexus.

Darkness enveloped him.

34

BURGERS

Thursday, December 22nd

Jacob Berger's face was barely visible over the stack of papers on his desk. It was stiflingly hot in his windowless room on the twelfth floor of the building on Parthenais Street, where the offices of the Forensic Science and Legal Medicine Laboratory were located.

"Kinda warm in here." With her fingers in her collar, Jacinthe was tugging at her sweater for ventilation. "And take that thing off your face, you damn nitwit," she growled. "I can't understand a word you're saying."

Victor did as he was told, reddening like a schoolboy busted mid-prank.

Every time he visited Berger's office, he would put on the goalie mask that the medical examiner had kept after performing an autopsy on a rapist dubbed "Jason" by the media — the man had spread terror through suburban Laval for three years before being stabbed to death by the last woman he tried to attack.

"So, Jacob," Victor said, "what you're telling us is that Lortie couldn't have killed Lawson."

"Correct," Berger replied, pushing his glasses up the bridge of his nose. "His suicide occurred too soon. Lortie died on Saturday. I'd say Lawson was murdered on Monday, or shortly afterward. I'll be able to give you a more precise window after I finish the autopsy. But I can tell you now that he was suffering from dehydration."

"And the wounds are the same, right, Burgers?"

Despite numerous attempts by the medical examiner to make her stop using that nickname, Taillon had persisted. After years of trying, the doctor had finally given up. Taillon wasn't malicious, but some of her bad habits were beyond correction.

"Right, Jacinthe. For the moment, I can't tell you anything more about the murder weapon, but it's the same projectile path, entering the back of the neck and exiting the throat. Lawson has similar punctures on the chin and sternum, which are deeper than the ones on Judith Harper."

"And the abrasions on the neck and wrists?"

"Same on both victims. And Lawson also has the same adhesive residue on his ankles and thighs. I'll be able to supply more details in a few days."

"Okay, well, that confirms what we suspected. The two murders were committed with the same weapon, using the same modus operandi. Which means, logically, that Lortie didn't kill Harper either. Anyway, he had an alibi. The homeless guy you spoke to, Nash, says he was with him that night."

"This is what we expected." Victor sighed, discouraged. "But it's still frustrating as hell. The only link we had connecting the two murders was Lortie and the wallets."

"Yep," Jacinthe said, also sounding disappointed. "We've officially lost our prime suspect. Back to scare one, my friend."

"That's *square one*, Jacinthe," Victor snapped. "Got it? Square one."

Jacinthe rolled her eyes. "Settle down there, big guy. No need to get snippy just because I put a little poetry in your life."

The detective sergeant felt his phone vibrating in his pocket. "We've still got Will Bennett and the skier," he called over his shoulder as he left the room to take the call.

"You're not even sure the skier had a gun," Taillon retorted.

Too late. He was gone.

35

MIDDLE AGES

Victor was walking with difficulty along Ontario Street as a savage wind did its best to knock him off his feet. He looked around, trying to spot a Ford Escape parked near the café entrance. No luck.

Inside the establishment, two customers sitting near the window were deep in conversation. Having arrived first, Victor took a table at the back of the shabby room. A jowly waiter approached. Though the detective sergeant had already had a cup at Berger's office, he ordered a coffee.

What with the discovery of Lawson's body, the examination of the crime scene, and the animated discussion in which he, Jacinthe, and the Gnome had engaged until the small hours of the morning, Victor was running on very little sleep.

For breakfast, he and Nadja had eaten a couple of croissants in the kitchen while talking about their plans for the day. Walking on eggshells, Victor had brought up the subject of the holidays. He had learned with relief that she was neither surprised nor offended to hear he might not make it to the cottage between Christmas and New Year's Day.

The Major Crimes Unit office party was already scheduled for the next day. Then, accompanied by Victor's kids, they'd be spending Christmas Eve with Victor's surrogate father, Ted Rutherford, and his partner Albert Corneau ...

"So, you see, I've already got a lot on my plate."

"Of course. You'll come up when you can. If you can."

Nadja was so perfect that it sometimes put a knot in the pit of his stomach. The fact that he hadn't even started his Christmas shopping did nothing to reduce his stress level. As usual, he had no idea what he'd buy for Martin and Charlotte. Whenever he asked for suggestions, they said they wanted money. So he had become a regular issuer of holiday cheques, but he felt guilty for not being able to recapture the magic of their childhood Christmases. With Nadja, the challenge was just as great. He could always fall back on jewellery, but she hardly ever wore it.

And what about Ted? And Albert?

Victor sighed. Just thinking about it wore him out.

He looked at his watch. What was keeping the guy? They'd met in Chinatown last time because it was midway between them and Victor had had other engagements in the area. Now he was starting to have doubts. Had he misunderstood the instructions he'd received about the meeting place? He was checking the messages on his phone when a small, spare man wearing unfashionable glasses came in and walked straight toward him.

"Hey, Doug," Victor said, standing up and extending a hand. "How's it going?"

The man placed a yellow envelope on the table before shaking his hand vigorously. "Not bad, Vic. Not bad. Sorry, I couldn't find a parking space."

Doug Adams was the crime-scene technician Victor had worked with regularly while he was at Station 11. He was a quiet, solitary man, difficult to approach. Like Victor, he'd done some suffering in his life.

Their working relationship had started out with frequent disputes, but over time, Victor had come to trust Adams completely. And the trust was reciprocated.

Though he wasn't normally given to paying compliments, the detective sergeant hadn't hesitated to proclaim to the world that he considered Adams to be the best in the business.

For that reason, and because he hadn't yet forged a similar relationship with the crime-scene people he now worked with, Victor occasionally made a discreet call to the retired forensic technician, asking him to apply his talent and intuition to a case.

Because Adams no longer worked for the Montreal Police, consulting him was risky, especially as a matter of confidentiality. Victor knew he'd be in trouble if the practice were ever revealed. Which was why he did it in secret, without his colleagues' knowledge.

"How was China, Doug?"

Adams had turned in his badge a few months previously and was living in quiet retirement with his wife and their cats in a condo on Nuns' Island.

"Ahh … incredible! I'll be able to show you, one of these days. I'm in the process of editing a video."

They went on talking amiably for a little while, then Adams ordered a coffee. When it came, the retired expert, true to his old form, got straight to the point.

"I looked over the forensics file," he said, placing a hand on the yellow envelope. "I did a good deal of digging, and I think I have a lead."

Adams leaned forward, looking Victor straight in the eye.

The detective sergeant felt his heart beat faster. Adams's leads were always based on meticulous research and analysis. "Did you figure out what the murder weapon was?"

"In part, maybe." The little man cleared his throat and took a sip of coffee. "What I discovered doesn't explain the fatal injury, but it could have caused the wounds on the chin and sternum."

Victor took out his notebook and, with his teeth, pulled the cap off his ballpoint. "Go ahead, Doug," he said, spitting the cap into his palm. "I'm all ears."

Adams removed his glasses, breathed on each of the lenses, and wiped off the fog with his paper napkin. "I warn you, we're talking about a nasty little contraption that dates back to the Middle Ages."

36

HERETIC'S FORK

The steel-rimmed glasses of the former forensics technician had returned to their perch at the end of his nose.

"Does the term *heretic's fork* mean anything to you?"

Victor's expression registered puzzlement. "Not a thing. What is it?"

"It's an instrument of torture that was used in medieval times to extract confessions by depriving subjects of sleep. I've printed up an article that I found online." Adams took a sheet from his jacket pocket, unfolded it, and placed it on the table in front of Victor. "The device was an iron bar with a two-pronged fork at either end." Adams gestured to a drawing of a man harnessed to a heretic's fork, his face twisted with pain. "As you can see, two points pressed down on the sternum, while the other two points pressed up on the raised chin, with the iron bar parallel to the distended neck. A strap or collar around the neck would hold the instrument in place."

"You say this fork could have caused the wounds on the chin and sternum?"

"I believe so, yes."

"And that would also explain the marks on the neck? Berger talked about a large collar ..."

"Definitely," Adams replied. "The strap had to be very tight." He took a sip of coffee, made a face, and returned his attention to the drawing. "You see, for the device to work, the victim's hands had to be tied behind his back, or he'd be able to remove it. Typically, the victim would be suspended from the ceiling to prevent stretching out. Then, whenever the head sagged from fatigue, the four iron points would puncture the chin and pierce the breastbone. Besides causing terrible pain, the points made it impossible to move the head or speak clearly."

Victor's expression darkened. He'd seen plenty of horrors, but this still made him shiver.

"Pure sadism," he said.

"Maybe, but also very effective. The fork was used to extract confessions or prevent those who'd confessed from saying anything else, and also to make subjects abjure."

"Abjure?"

"To renounce their religion. The fork was widely used during the Inquisition to make heretics abandon their faith. The Latin word *abiuro*, which means *I abjure*, was engraved on the metal. You can imagine the effect. After days without sleep, in horrendous pain, many victims were ready to say anything."

Victor's mind had strayed far away, to another world. He hoped with all his heart that the investigation wouldn't hinge, once again, on a question of religion.

"But to pierce the neck and throat, the killer would need something besides the fork, right?"

"Correct. Another mechanism, or else a modification to the original device."

"Where does one get an item like this, Doug? Are there any for sale?"

"I'd start by checking out shops that specialize in armour and medieval items. I know there are clubs where people get together for role-playing. They might be able to give you some leads. You can also try collectors of medieval objects. There may be an online resale market, an eBay type of thing."

The detective sergeant scribbled in his notebook. He would have Loïc follow up on these suggestions.

"There's another possibility," Adams added.

"What's that?"

"A skilled craftsman could make a fork from scratch."

The coffee dregs had dried out in their cups by the time Victor had exhausted his supply of questions. After paying the bill, he thanked Adams, shaking his hand warmly before the two parted on the sidewalk.

Finding his car windows covered with frost, he took out the scraper. Then he sat behind the wheel and tossed the envelope that Adams had given him onto the passenger seat. The motor coughed, and the detective sergeant dialed the heater up to max.

"About time you got back. I was cold as hell …"

The surprise was absolute: Victor's blood froze and his ass jumped from the car seat.

"Ahhhh!"

Jacinthe had materialized in the back seat. Her expression was blank.

"What were you doing with Doug Adams?"

"Are you out of your damn mind? You could've given me a heart attack!"

"What were you doing with Adams?" Taillon asked again, her voice unyielding.

Placing a hand on his chest, Victor took a few seconds to catch his breath. In an ill-tempered mumble, he answered that they got together for a cup of coffee every so often now that Adams was retired …

"Do *not* fuck with me!"

The two partners traded glares, each trying to gauge the other's reaction. For an instant, they were like two wild animals, poised to attack.

"What'll I find if I look through that envelope? Cute little butterfly stickers, or the autopsy report you handed over to Adams when you met him in Chinatown?" Victor's eyes widened. "Or is it the forensics report? Don't treat me like an idiot, Lessard!"

The detective sergeant finally lowered his gaze and sighed. "The murder weapon may be a collar mounted with iron points placed below the chin and over the breastbone," he grumbled. "It's called a heretic's fork."

Jacinthe roused herself from the back seat, got out of the car, then re-entered on the passenger side. Victor gave her a summary of his conversation with Adams.

"So the murderer wanted to get confessions from the victims before killing them?" Jacinthe asked, after listening attentively to her partner's monologue.

"Get confessions, extract information … put it any way you like."

Their breath formed wisps of vapour in the cold air as they spoke.

"Pfff. Sounds awfully complicated. Make me listen to Lionel Ritchie for ten minutes and I'll do anything to make it stop!"

Ignoring the joke, Victor finished updating Jacinthe on what he'd learned.

"Okay, fine," she said, "but we already know the wounds on the chin and sternum weren't fatal. And you say the victims were usually suspended from the ceiling? We can have forensics double check, but they'd have found indications if one of the victims had been strung up. In any case, the ceiling wasn't high enough in the cold room where Lawson died."

"I know." Victor shrugged. "Look," he said irritably, "it's only a starting point …"

The lines on Jacinthe's brow began to wiggle. Something was on her mind.

"What?" he asked.

"I've just had an idea. You may think it's a bit much, but I'm wondering if we've been too quick to rule out Lortie as a suspect."

"Why?"

"This fork of yours," Taillon said, pursuing her train of thought. "If it keeps the victim awake for days, that opens up another possibility. Maybe Lawson's death was preprogrammed. Burgers said he was dehydrated. What if Lortie put the gizmo around the lawyer's neck just before killing himself?"

"So Lawson would have been trapped for several days until a second mechanism was triggered, killing him?"

"Exactly. It would have been like a countdown."

"A timer, you mean ... Yeah, that could work, in theory." Victor seemed unconvinced. "But why go to all the trouble? I'd understand if Lortie wanted to be on the other side of town at the moment Harper died, giving him an alibi. But the guy jumped off a building. It makes no sense ..."

Jacinthe waved a hand. "It was just a thought. Okay, get your ass out of there. I'm driving."

"How did you follow me?"

"By car."

The detective sergeant looked at her, puzzled. "You're leaving it here?"

"I'm having it towed," she growled. "Don't ask!"

A smirk appeared on Victor's lips as he got out of the driver's seat. "Get into a little fender-bender, Jacinthe?"

As she slid into the driver's seat, she gave him a murderous look.

"Okay, okay, forget it," he said, ducking his head submissively.

He barely had time to close the passenger door before she floored the accelerator.

"Where are we going?" he asked.

"Versailles. I spoke to Gilles while your lordship was having his coffee break. André Lortie's psychiatric file just came in. It may give us a link with the two victims."

"Great." The detective sergeant ran his hand over several days' growth on his chin. "By the way, did the Gnome find Bennett?"

Jacinthe frowned. She was driving cowboy-style, one hand on the wheel at twelve o'clock, her arm fully extended, the seatback fully reclined.

"Don't know. Probably not, or he'd have told me."

Victor buckled his seat belt, watching the building facades fly by. He was starting to feel a little queasy. "About Adams ..." he began, and hesitated. "I'd appreciate it if we could keep that between us."

"You would? Okay. Here's the deal. *I'd* appreciate it if you kept me in the loop next time. Either we're partners or we're not."

Victor nodded emphatically. He was ready to promise whatever she wanted in return for her discretion. "You have my word. We're partners."

"In that case," Jacinthe said coolly, "you can tell me what you got up to in Chinatown after giving the envelope to Adams."

Victor lost his temper instantly. "Fuck off! That's none of your business."

"Oh, really?" she asked mockingly. "For a guy who just said we're partners, you sure are tight lipped."

"Give it a rest, Taillon," he said, pointing an angry finger in her direction. "You want to know what I was doing? Smoking opium. Excellent shit, by the way. I'll bring you along next time. We can get wasted together, like good partners do."

Taillon couldn't hold back her mirth. "You're a barrel of laughs, big guy. But don't worry, Auntie Jacinthe will figure out what you were up to."

Slumped in his seat, Victor kept his mouth firmly shut. He opened it only once, to yell at Taillon to slow down before she rammed the car ahead of them.

37

FOR JUDITH, WITH LOVE AND SQUALOR

In the bathroom of his apartment, Will Bennett looked at himself in the mirror.

A naked worm. His thoughts were jostling each other, oscillating between lucidity and confusion. The older one gets, he'd read somewhere, the more forgiving one becomes of one's appearance. A bitter smile contorted his face.

Banal insights like that, aimed at reassuring ordinary people, made him want to puke his guts out. He had never reconciled himself to aging, never tolerated the sight of his wilting body. He couldn't stand being called handsome "for a man in his fifties," being told by wizened hags in their forties that he looked ten years younger than his age. He detested his wrinkles, his grey hair, his softening muscles and dimming complexion, the coarse strands he had to remove more and more often from his nose and ears.

Cosmetic surgery had helped, more or less, to slow time's ravages, but the cruel years had caught up to him at last. He couldn't bear the fact that women in their twenties weren't noticing him anymore. His eye had become a radar screen tuned to their wavelength, a deforming prism through which he filtered reality. The street was his battlefield. He admired the breasts bouncing in their snug camisoles, the buttocks undulating beneath their skirts; he was moved to ecstasy by this one's saliva-moistened lips, shining like a vulva, or that one's nipples, erect in the chilly air, dazzling his eyes.

Little bitches.

Bennett never overlooked a single one. He wanted to fuck them all. He wanted to see them die. In his dreams he cut them into pieces and re-created a perfect body from the fragments.

Judith had liberated the animal. She had encouraged him to become his truest self, surrendering to his urges. At first, he had thought things were better this way. He'd felt powerful, god-like, freed from the cloying petty morality of his Judeo-Christian upbringing. Then, little by little, he had lost his footing. He had slid out of control. The prostitutes no longer sufficed. He'd had to go ever further to feed the beast.

Judith was the only woman he had ever loved. He grieved for her.

Will Bennett looked away from the mirror.

The reflection of the mollusc dangling between his legs sickened him. He had masturbated one last time an hour ago, giving depraved instructions via webcam to a Ukrainian girl who'd clearly been down that road before.

Bennett laughed out loud.

Getting older and more forgiving … what bullshit.

He'd never looked his age as much as he did right now.

Suddenly he heard yelling. The apartment door shook under repeated powerful blows, and then there was an immense crash of wood splitting. Daman's men had found the whore in the bathtub yesterday, and now they were coming for him. They would show no mercy.

Trying to summon the courage to make an end of it before they reached him, Bennett pressed the cold knife blade against his carotid artery, holding his breath. Adrenalin rushed into his veins.

One motion and it would all be over.

The man in the mirror finally appeared to him as he really was: an evil being, abject and perverted. A cry rose up in his throat, resonating against his vocal cords. The cry of a dying animal.

This was the end. It had to be. His fingers tightened around the handle.

At that moment, police officers armed with pistols burst into the room, shouting orders he could no longer hear.

38

REVOLVING DOOR
SYNDROME

Victor opened the discoloured file folder and took a yellowed sheet off the top of the pile. Contemplating the document, lost in his memories, he couldn't help smiling: carbon paper had disappeared from use a long time ago.

Before starting to read, he took a sip of water.

The first time André Lortie had come under psychiatric care was in the late 1960s, following an incident at Montreal's Old Port. Victor noticed that, at the time, the hospital hadn't yet borne the name of Louis-H. Lafontaine.

Montreal
Saint-Jean-de-Dieu Hospital
February 3, 1969

Male patient was brought in at 11:50 a.m. by Montreal Police Constables Tremblay and O'Connor. The individual had no identification when arrested for vagrancy and disorderly conduct. He says his name is André Lortie and he is 31 years old. According to the officers, he has no known address.

Constable O'Connor states that Mr. Lortie was apprehended while urinating on the wall of a restaurant on Saint-Paul Street. According

to the officer, Lortie seemed disoriented and
smelled of alcohol. Lortie told the officers
he had been beaten, mistreated, and injected
with drugs. Officer Tremblay notes that Lortie
could not specify where the mistreatment had
occurred; nor could he name his assailant(s).
He also notes that Lortie shows no physical
signs of violence.

On examination, I found no marks or injuries. Generally speaking, the patient is in
good health. He has an appendectomy scar that,
judging from its appearance, dates back to his
teens. Patient states that he consumes between
six and twelve large bottles of beer per day.

The physician then proceeded to an analysis of Lortie's psychiatric condition. Victor skipped the technical part and went straight
to the conclusions:

To sum up, my psychiatric examination leads
me to believe the patient is in a manic phase,
and that he suffers from manic-depressive psychosis. I am keeping him under observation
for 90 days. I will withhold a definitive
diagnosis until the end of that period. I
have prescribed lithium and Haldol for the
duration. Depending on the course of the illness, the patient may be a candidate for
electroconvulsive therapy.

Dr. Robert Thériault
Psychiatrist
#1215
(Dictated but not read)

Transcribed by: PK

July 3, 1969

Patient brought in by police officers during
the night. No fixed address. Found walking
naked through Parc Maisonneuve, disturbing
other citizens. Had ceased taking his medication. Heavy alcohol consumption. Patient
estimates that he drinks one 40 oz. bottle of De Kuyper per day. I have increased
the dosage of Haldol. Electroshock treatments
are scheduled for this morning and tomorrow.
Patient is in a manic phase. Says CIA killers
are after him.

July 8, 1969

Patient still in manic phase. Symptoms of
alcoholic withdrawal. Now claims he detonated
bombs for the FLQ. Electroshock treatments
calm him. Additional treatment scheduled for
tomorrow morning.

July 31, 1969

Patient decompensating. Depressed but lucid.
No delusions. I have determined an effective
dosage for his medication. Patient often
crosses himself before taking pills.

Looking over the doctor's handwritten notes in the margins of
the typed document, Victor saw that during André Lortie's first
stay at the institution, the psychiatrist had tried repeatedly but
unsuccessfully to locate a family member, friend, or acquaintance.

Lortie seemed to have no past.

After being discharged in mid-November, Lortie hadn't been readmitted during 1969. Which didn't mean he hadn't been interned at another mental institution, such as the Pinel Institute or the Douglas Hospital.

After getting out of hospital, people like Lortie often ended up in rundown apartments or on the streets. For the vast majority, their discharge would be followed by numerous readmissions to psychiatric institutions, a phenomenon that Victor's former partner Ted Rutherford called "revolving door syndrome."

The detective sergeant had seen the phenomenon firsthand. During his days as a beat cop, he had worked in the poorest and most unsavoury areas of downtown Montreal. The street was a teeming jungle in which no one could be trusted, where yesterday's gentle, likeable vagrant was transformed overnight into an animal who would rush at you, eyes bulging, in the grip of madness.

A distant memory came to the surface: the image of a frozen body. Frank.

Victor shook his head to chase the vision away.

Lortie's case didn't surprise him; he'd seen many others. But the portrait drawn by Dr. Thériault still touched him. The detective sergeant felt great empathy when he thought about the misery this man had been forced to endure.

The next entry represented a jump of nearly three years in Lortie's psychiatric history:

March 13, 1972

Patient brought in by police. Arrested in a drunken condition near the offices of the Liberal Party. Currently lives in a rooming house in the Hochelaga district. Was found in a psychotic state. Wanted to speak to Quebec Premier Robert Bourassa about his participation

```
in the kidnapping of James Richard Cross and
the murder of Pierre Laporte. Resumption of
medication. Electroshock treatments.


March 14, 1972

Patient   in   complete   psychotic   breakdown.
Violent. Restraints needed. Fresh delusions.
Convinced he participated in deadly crimes.
```

Victor entered the date in his notebook, then shook his head, suddenly discouraged. What could he hope to find in the psychiatric file of a patient who had been delusional for more than forty years?

He picked up the stack and ran his thumb over the sheets. The file went on for hundreds of pages. He had neither the time nor the patience to look at every entry. Rather than try to analyze and understand all the details, he decided to look at the big picture.

The first thing he noticed was that there were significant gaps in the timeline. Lortie hadn't received psychiatric treatment between 1974 and 1979. What had happened to him during that period? Had he taken his medication regularly and stabilized his condition? Had he found work? Had he experienced moments of respite? Or had he swirled deeper into the vortex of his unbalanced mind and continued to deteriorate? Lortie had received treatment at Louis-H. once in 1980. Then, between 1981 and 1987, the revolving doors had begun to spin at a frenzied rate:

```
August 12, 1981

Patient arrested after a brawl among homeless
individuals. Facial bruises. Manic phase.
Delusions of grandeur and persecution. Bit a
nurse who was trying to give him medication.
```

```
August 16, 1981

Patient decompensating. Deeply depressed.
Lithium, Haldol.

August 18, 1981

Patient very distressed after learning about
his behaviour toward the nurse. Intense
despair, self-reproach, feelings of worth-
lessness. Suicidal ideation. I have requested
24-hour surveillance. Important that he not
be left alone.
```

Victor interrupted his reading to take the vibrating phone out of his pocket. Nadja's name appeared on the caller ID. "Hello," he said in a weary voice, but with a smile on his lips.

"Detective Sergeant Lessard," a mischievous voice said, "this is Mrs. Claus. I'm calling to remind you that Christmas is right around the corner. Have you bought presents for your kids?"

An anxious sensation constricted him. Picking up his ballpoint, he wrote *Presents* on his hand. "Mrs. Claus, the number you have dialed is not in service. I repeat, the number you have dialed is not in service."

They both laughed.

"No," he said, in a more serious tone. "I haven't bought anything yet. I still have time to rack my brain for ideas."

"Oh, come on, it's super easy. Martin's always talking about the Second World War. Buy him the box set of *Band of Brothers*. And Charlotte keeps borrowing my earrings. You know, the gold hoops."

Tears came to Victor's eyes. What had he done to deserve such a woman? For a giddy moment, he thought of asking her to marry him then and there, but immediately he thought better of it. Marriages don't last. He knew from experience. What they had right now felt like perfection — or close to it.

But his pessimistic nature reasserted itself; the fear of losing everything rose up in him, followed by the conviction that he would wake up one day to find all his blessings destroyed and their love gone in a puff of smoke.

"Vic?"

"Sorry," he said, shaking off his despondency.

"How's the investigation going?"

Nadja knew all about the case. Or just about. In a few sentences, he brought her up to speed on the latest developments, describing his discussions with Berger and Adams.

"Heretic's fork, huh? Sounds interesting. I'll look it up online."

"I'm not sure Adams is on the right track, though. For the device to work, the victims would have had to be suspended above the ground. But I just checked with forensics and Berger. That wasn't the case." He paused. "How about you? How's it going?"

"Tanguay's on my ass." She sighed. "Other than that, I'm okay."

Nadja was investigating a series of home invasions targeting upscale homes in Notre-Dame-de-Grâce. As always, Commander Tanguay wanted immediate results. He wasn't giving the detectives at Station 11 time to do their jobs properly.

"The guy's an idiot," Victor said, then added, laughing, "Mind you, considering the ass in question, I can hardly blame him." He turned serious. "Still, you're too talented to be stuck over there … Have you given any more thought to your talk with Delaney?"

"I haven't made up my mind yet."

They'd looked at the matter from every angle. Though the idea of joining the Major Crimes Unit excited the young detective, the sacrifices that came with the job made her hesitate. Nadja felt that her career had progressed to a stage where she had a certain level of comfort in her work. If she went to Major Crimes, she'd have to start fresh and prove her value all over again.

Whenever the subject came up, Victor said he understood. But in his heart, he believed she was making excuses. In truth, he suspected that Nadja wanted to get pregnant. And the thought made his head spin.

They talked for another couple of minutes.

Before hanging up, she said she loved him.

Victor went out for a smoke, then returned to his desk and went back to work. After a moment, he noticed that from the early 1980s onward, the notes in the file weren't typed on carbon paper anymore. They were handwritten on simple sheets of lined paper.

A few pages later, he found another gap in the timeline, this one between 1988 and 1995. Lortie had once again dropped off the radar for several years. The detective sergeant recorded the gap in his notebook and resumed his progress through the file.

The infernal round of psychiatric treatments picked up again in late 1996 and continued until the early 2000s. Lortie's hospitalizations varied in duration from a few days to several weeks:

October 8, 1996

Former patient of Dr. Thériault. Long history of bipolar disorder. Alcohol abuse. Agoraphobia. No psychiatric treatment since 1987. Was brought in by police. Psychotic delusions. Confused. Claims he knows important secrets about a conspiracy related to the 1995 referendum on Quebec independence. Says he has information concerning the victims of the mass shooting at the Polytechnique and the multiple murders committed by Valery Fabrikant. I have decided to put him on Divalproex and Seroquel.

Dr. Marina Lacasse, psychiatrist

October 12, 1996

Patient still delusional. Frequent references to ethnic plots and
money. I am increasing the Seroquel dosage.

Victor shook his head in disbelief.

The referendum. The Polytechnique shooting. The Fabrikant
murders.

The only thing missing was an alien mothership at Roswell. If
Ted Rutherford had been present, he would have laughed and trot-
ted out his favourite saying: "Go any lower, you'll strike oil."

39

INVOLUNTARY COMMITMENT

Victor sighed and elbowed a pile of papers to one side. The painstaking exercise he was engaged in had ended up depressing him. He searched in his pocket, found the prescription bottle, popped an anti-anxiety pill into his mouth and washed it down, grimacing, with cold coffee. After crushing the disposable cup, he tossed it at the wastebasket and missed. Rather than get up to correct the stray shot, he plunged back into his reading. There were entries in the file for the period from 2001 to 2010, including an eight-week stay that had started last April:

```
April 5, 2010

Former patient of Dr. Lacasse. Set a fire
in the garbage cans across the street from
his building. Manic phase. Profoundly delu-
sional. Highly intoxicated. Alcohol and other
substances? Confirms that he has not taken his
medication in several years. Divalproex and
Topamax.

Dr. Marco Giroux, psychiatrist
```

After that, the only other entries concerned the present year, covering the period from June to November. His hospitalization had lasted six months, Lortie's longest stay at Louis-H. since the early 1970s.

June 12, 2010

Severe breakdown. Suicidal thoughts. Brought
in by police. Wanted to throw himself off
an overpass onto the Décarie Expressway.
Psychosis. Manic phase. Convinced someone
is trying to kill him. Hallucinations. He
sees the ghosts of people he believes he
killed. Claims he woke up in possession of
bloodstained clothes and wallets. Episodes of
terror. Recurrent delusions. I am seeking a
court order. Involuntary commitment and isolation. Divalproex and Lamictal.

Dr. Marco Giroux, psychiatrist

June 27, 2010

Not responding to treatment. Persistent hallucinations and suicidal thoughts. Dosage
increased.

Victor wrote a reference to the wallets in his notebook, but he
didn't learn much else, apart from the fact that the attending physician had sought a court order to keep Lortie in the hospital for
an extended period — a request that the court had granted on the
basis of Lortie's suicidal thoughts and failure to respond to treatment. His medication had been adjusted numerous times by Dr.
Giroux before a satisfactory dosage was found:

November 12, 2010

Patient's condition has been stable for several weeks. Responding well to medication.

Court order will soon run out. Patient wants
to leave. Recommend transitional housing.

Dr. Marco Giroux, psychiatrist

Lortie had finally been released two weeks later. Looking
through the file, Victor realized that Lortie had been kept against
his will for a brief additional period because he had nowhere to go.
In fact, as a result of his past episodes of misbehaviour, none of the
regular community shelters would take him.

They had considered him too hard to deal with, and feared that
he'd upset the other residents. When the court order lapsed, the
hospital had had no choice but to let him leave. Finally, with the
help of the head nurse, Lortie got a space at the rooming house that
Victor and his colleagues had searched.

What had happened in the interval between his release and his
death on December 17th?

A shadow passed through Victor's field of vision. He raised his
eyes and nearly rubbed them to be sure he wasn't seeing things.
Jacinthe was standing in front of his workspace, looking almost
friendly, holding out a Styrofoam cup.

"My turn to make a peace offering." She laughed. "It's decaf."

The detective sergeant accepted the offering and took a sip. "We
already buried the hatchet. But thanks."

"So?" she asked. "Have you found anything?"

The two detectives briefly discussed Lortie's psychiatric file. Victor
went over the main points of what he'd read, but Jacinthe, moving
toward the big Plexiglas board, wasn't listening. Looking at the cardboard sheet bearing the four sentences that Mona Vézina had brought
to their attention, Jacinthe shook her head and sighed loudly. "Gilles
usually works magic when he searches the database. But this time,
running those sentences through the system has turned up nothing."
Jacinthe looked at her partner. "Lortie was crazy. We need to stop trying to interpret what he wrote like it was holy fucking scripture."

Victor looked at the ceiling. "Where is Gilles, anyway?" he asked.

"Don't know. He left with Loïc, and he's not answering his phone." She shook her head, disgusted. "My ketchup uncle," she muttered. "That shit won't get us anywhere."

Jacinthe had just returned from a meeting with the legal expert at the Justice Ministry, a meeting that Victor had originally requested for himself, hoping to obtain information on Northern Industrial Textiles. Caught up in his examination of Lortie's psychiatric file, he had asked his partner to fill in for him.

"I know your friend over at Justice is a sweet person, but she's totally useless. She doesn't explain things in a normal way. She started out by saying there was nothing she could do if we didn't have the date of … uhh" — she looked at the scrap of paper she'd taken notes on — "the date of incorporation or dissolution of the company. I mean, what the fuck?"

"Jacinthe, don't tell me you yelled at her," Victor said, horrified.

She made a gesture that was meant to be reassuring. "No, no. Let's just say she and I had a constructive discussion. We're not the Gestapo here, but at some point, you've gotta put your foot down!"

Victor buried his face in his hands. When Jacinthe put her foot down, it was generally on someone's throat.

Questioning his partner in detail, Victor learned that the legal expert had indeed found an entry corresponding to Northern Industrial Textiles Ltd., a company incorporated on March 11th, 1959, and dissolved on December 17th, 1974, with a reference number.

But in the information boxes reserved for the corporate address, names of board members and executives, nothing was written. Swamped with work and uncertain whether the entry she had found was the right company, the expert had opted to suspend her research until she received further instructions. She surely hadn't anticipated having to answer to Taillon.

"There must be a way to dig deeper," Victor suggested.

"That's exactly what I said to her," his partner bellowed.

The detective sergeant hardly dared imagine what tone of voice she had said it in.

From Jacinthe's convoluted explanation, Victor understood that two options presented themselves: consult the archivists at the Central Enterprise Database, a sloth-like operation whose personnel didn't even answer the telephone; or search directly in the collections of the Revised Statutes of Quebec, a task that might take hours of effort and would yield information only if the lawyer or accountant who'd been responsible for the publication of the statutes at the time had done their job properly.

"So Little Miss Legal Eagle is going to figure out which option is fastest. She'll get back to us when she finds something," Jacinthe proclaimed triumphantly. "It's a long shot, but you never know."

Preserving good relations with the staffers at Justice was crucial. It had been a mistake, Victor now realized, to send Taillon in his place. He would ask Gilles Lemaire to step in and handle the follow-up.

Hearing voices in the corridor, he and Jacinthe both turned. The door opened, and Victor saw Lemaire come in. He was wearing a hard expression. Then Victor noticed that Lemaire's suit and shirt were splattered with blood. Lemaire walked past without seeming to notice them.

A few paces behind him, Loïc stopped chewing his gum long enough to bring Victor and Jacinthe up to speed. "We reached Bennett too late. He's in a coma. He tried to kill himself ..."

OCTOBER 26TH, 1992
MEECH LAKE AND CHARLOTTETOWN

The game of musical chairs goes on. Only the players are different.

On the federal side, Pierre Elliott Trudeau has been replaced by Brian Mulroney. Now that René is gone, Robert Bourassa represents Quebec.

But the delusions … the delusions never change.

The Meech Lake Accord, the Charlottetown Accord.

In the end, we agree to disagree. The supporters of one side become the enemies of the other, a laughable masquerade pitting good guys against bad guys in a manner sadly reminiscent of All-Star Wrestling.

Federalist conspiracies? Strike up the band, toss the confetti — I don't believe a word of it!

After the failure of the Meech Lake deal, Robert Bourassa declared, "English Canada must clearly understand that whatever people may say, whatever they may do, Quebec is and will always be a distinct society, with the freedom and capacity to determine its own fate and future development."

With these declarations, we try to convince ourselves that we have the ability to move forward.

Someday, we'll have to sweep away the past, stop talking, and act.

• • •

That is what I aspire to do.

MEMORY THIEVES

40

MY KETCHUP UNCLE LARRY TRUMAN RELISHES APPLES

The sink's blackened enamel resembled a decaying tooth. The stream of water bounced off it and ran down the drain. With reddened features, Gilles Lemaire didn't flinch when Victor pushed open the washroom door and approached him.

The little man broke the silence. "There was blood everywhere. Bennett slit his throat …" His gaze drifted emptily for a moment before returning to his hands, which, though immaculate, he couldn't stop washing. "When I see someone do that in a movie, I think, *What a cliché …*"

Victor touched his shoulder. "It's a cliché until it actually happens. You should take the rest of the day off."

Jacinthe got up and turned the knob on the thermostat.

If she'd been able to lower the temperature in the conference room below the freezing point, she'd have done it. Her family doctor had already warned her: these hot flashes were quite possibly a precursor to menopause. Which did nothing to improve her humour.

Loïc explained to his fellow detectives that the doorman of Will Bennett's building had advised them of Bennett's presence in his apartment, as requested by Gilles Lemaire. The kid then summarized the intervention that he and the Gnome had carried out at the home of Judith Harper's lover, and he noted that the forensics team was now going over the place. Blouin-Dubois also mentioned that among the man's possessions, they had seen a wide variety of sex toys, including a rawhide collar.

By now, the collar would have been delivered to Berger, who, after examining it, should be able to determine whether it had left the marks found on the necks of Harper and Lawson. The kid concluded by pointing out that Lemaire had saved Bennett's life by maintaining a constant pressure on his throat until the ambulance attendants arrived.

As soon as Loïc finished speaking, he resumed chewing.

"He seemed pretty shaken up," Taillon observed. "Did he go home?"

Just then, the door opened, revealing the Gnome's diminutive form. Despite his waxy complexion, he managed a smile. "You won't get rid of me that easily, Jacinthe."

Lemaire informed the team that he'd just called in Bennett's two colleagues for further questioning. Despite investigative efforts over the past few days, it wasn't possible to say for sure whether Bennett had returned from Boston incognito. His bank cards hadn't been used in any transactions. There had been no car rentals; nor was there any sign that he'd been at the airport.

None of which proved anything, as far as the Gnome was concerned.

Bennett was highly intelligent. He could have paid in cash, or hitchhiked, or caught a ride with a trucker. Crossing the border illegally wasn't easy, but it could be done, if you were smart. The area to cover was vast, the possibilities endless. Bennett could have slipped through a gap somewhere.

Jacinthe wasn't buying it. She shook her head.

Why would Bennett have gone to all that trouble to give himself an alibi that wasn't even solid? His own colleagues had known of his absence and had finally admitted as much to Lemaire.

But the Gnome wasn't giving up. He clung to the fact that there was a gap in Bennett's timeline and that, during the period in question, Bennett would have been able to kill Harper and make it back to Boston.

Lemaire argued that Bennett had surely expected his colleagues to stay quiet out of fear of reprisal. Bennett was their superior in the company hierarchy, which meant he could do them harm.

And indeed, Lemaire added, he'd had to grill the subordinates for a long time before one of them finally admitted the truth. Bennett's suicide attempt was the final piece of evidence confirming that he was right.

"Let's say he killed Harper," Jacinthe replied. "And let's say he went back to his business meetings in Boston afterward. How do you explain the Lawson murder? Huh?"

"Lawson went missing last Friday. According to Berger, he died on Monday. That could suggest someone held him captive during that time. Bennett flew back to town Sunday night. Which means, in theory, he could have killed Lawson. And then there's your timer theory, which opens up other possibilities."

Loïc was listening quietly to the discussion, working his jaw muscles while he typed on his BlackBerry.

"What do you think, Lessard?" Jacinthe asked.

Victor, who'd been gazing fixedly at his high-tops, now found himself in the midst of what was starting to feel like a family dispute. He got up. "I don't know," he said dismissively. "I'm going for a smoke. And while Bennett's in the hospital, let's get him tested for chlamydia."

Putting on his jacket, he went downstairs and walked through the shopping mall. As he stepped out into the parking lot, a guy with bulging arms and a suntan followed him.

"Hey, jumbo, got a light?" the guy asked. Wearing only a T-shirt, he seemed unaware of the cold. There were tattoos on his arms.

Douchebag, Victor thought, and sparked his lighter.

The guy thanked him and stepped away to smoke in peace.

Victor had answered Jacinthe's question honestly.

The investigation was frustrating him. He didn't know what to think anymore. At first, Lortie had seemed like an obvious potential suspect, but the detective sergeant had ruled him out after Berger's confirmation that Lortie had died before Lawson. Nor did the detective sergeant set any store by Jacinthe's timer idea.

As for Will Bennett, he didn't know what to make of his suicide attempt.

The Gnome seemed convinced that Bennett had somehow been involved in the violent death of Judith Harper, but he couldn't point to any proof, nor any motive, in support of his contention. The absence of evidence didn't mean Bennett was innocent, but Victor was hesitant. He felt conflicted. He wanted to believe the Gnome's theory, but his intuition told him that they were barking up the wrong tree, that Bennett had nothing to do with this case.

He took a final drag, filling his lungs with the seventy carcinogenic substances contained in cigarette smoke. His gaze drifted idly for a moment, then he tossed the butt into the soiled snow at his feet.

Chilled, the detective sergeant went back upstairs, sat at his desk, and answered a few emails before returning to the conference room. He found Gilles Lemaire by himself, immersed in André Lortie's psychiatric file.

Gilles looked up when he heard Victor come in.

"Where are Taillon and Loïc?" the detective sergeant asked, glancing at their empty chairs.

"They went down to the cafeteria," the Gnome said. His voice was higher than usual.

Victor saw that Lemaire was agitated. "You okay?"

"I think I've found something," he said.

"Oh yeah? What?"

"This …" The Gnome pointed at the cardboard tab on the first file Victor had consulted. There was writing on it, in pencil. The detective sergeant squinted. He hadn't noticed the writing while going over the reports.

"Ref. Dr. Ewen Cameron, 1964," he read, puzzled. "What's the problem?"

"There are two. First, what do those words mean, exactly? That Lortie was referred by Cameron in 1964? If so, then we have only part of his file."

"That would surprise me," Victor said thoughtfully. "The chief of psychiatry at Louis-H. told me Lortie was admitted for the first time in 1969, after being brought in by police."

Victor leafed through the pages and showed him the relevant passage.

"I'm not denying it," Lemaire protested. "I'm just asking."

"I'll take your word for it. And the second problem?"

"I did a bachelor's degree in psychology before going to police college. If this is the same Ewen Cameron, we studied some of his experiments. He was well known for his research, and not in a good way."

"What do you mean?"

"He did experiments at McGill University in the sixties. His work was in behaviour modification through brainwashing. Dozens of patients drawn from the population of Montreal had their minds manipulated, specifically by injection of psychotropic substances."

"I've never heard about this before," Victor admitted. "You think Lortie might have been one of his patients?"

"Hang on, I haven't told you the best part," the Gnome said in an excited voice. "Do you know who was financing Dr. Cameron's work?"

"I hate guessing games, Gilles."

"The United States intelligence services. Specifically, the CIA."

Victor frowned, intrigued.

"And do you know what code name was given to the project?" Lemaire continued.

"No idea."

"MK-ULTRA."

The Gnome had clearly expected a strong reaction to this information, but, despite his best efforts, Victor couldn't see where his colleague was going with this.

"Should that mean something to me, Gilles?"

The Gnome turned and pointed at the cardboard sheet stuck to the big board.

"You've found a link to Larry Truman," Victor persisted. "Is that it?"

"You really don't see it?" The Gnome sighed, shaking his head in disappointment.

Lemaire read one of the sentences in a loud voice, overenunciating, taking his time with each syllable, in a style one might expect of a teacher addressing a class of halfwits.

"My Ketchup Uncle Larry Truman Relishes Apples." Silence. "What do you get if you take the first letter of each word and string them together?"

"You get MK-ULTRA," the detective sergeant said, stunned.

SEPTEMBER 1964
TWO DAYS

Mom hasn't slept in two days.

Two days in which her spectre has haunted the house. Two days in which, at any moment, her eyes might flicker briefly in the emptiness, then darken once again. Two days in which she's listened to every tiny noise, in which she's run to the window at the faintest creak, her gaze losing itself in the infinity of heaven.

Two days in which Léonard, despite his man's body, has sniffled back his snot and walked in circles, crying like a child who must learn to do hard things.

Two days in which Charlie's jaw and fist have never unclenched.

Two days in which Dad has been missing.

Charlie gets up decisively, putting on a baseball cap. "I'm going to look for him."

Mom puts a hand on Charlie's forearm. "No. You're staying right here." She stifles a sob and adds, "We don't even know where he is."

At the far end of the room, nestled on the couch, Léonard is staring in wonder at the fuzzy black-and-white images. Charlie, who would normally be delighted to join him, has no desire to watch TV.

Charlie pulls away from Mom, slamming an angry fist onto the table. "We have to call the police."

Mom bites her lower lip. Her anxiety is palpable. "Out of the question," she says firmly, but her voice is weak. "That would be the worst thing we could do."

Mom finally gets them to bed, despite their protests. In their shared bedroom, Léonard quickly falls asleep. Charlie waits to hear the change in Léonard's breathing before throwing back the covers and getting out of bed. After crawling along the floor, Charlie takes up position at the top of the stairs. From that vantage point, it's possible to observe everything that happens down below. Some evenings, Charlie has seen ill-tempered discussions between Mom and Dad. On other occasions, certain happenings have prompted Charlie to return to bed with a funny smile.

This time, head lowered, Charlie feels the pain of an anguished heart.

Mom is curled up on the living room carpet, weeping, moaning, begging heaven to return her husband safe and sound, repeating over and over again that something's happened to him, that he must surely be dead.

That noise …

Charlie wakes with a start, sore necked as a result of the hours spent leaning headfirst against the railing. Charlie gets up and rushes to the window. In the country, at night, depending on the speed and direction of the wind, sound travels fast and far. The engine's growl has been audible for several seconds by the time the headlight beams swing into view.

Charlie is motionless for an instant, then breaks into a run.

"Mom! Mom! A car!"

On the road, a '57 Chevy slows down but doesn't stop. A door opens. A body rolls out onto the gravel.

Out of breath, the three of them reach the road at the same time. Dad is alive. He doesn't appear to be seriously injured. But he seems weak, confused, disoriented. He murmurs a stream of garbled words.

"What have they done to you?" Mom keeps repeating, rocking him in her arms. "What have they done to you, my love?"

Léonard emits little yelps, crying into his legs.

With a dark expression, and holding a large rock, Charlie watches the Chevy speed away until the two bobbing yellow eyes vanish into the night.

Two days. Enough time to turn their lives upside down.

41

CO-AUTHORS

Victor had stood up and was pacing the room, constantly running his fingers through his hair. Wearing a slight smile, the Gnome was watching him struggle to get his thoughts in order. Having returned from their break, Loïc and Jacinthe had joined the conversation. If it hadn't been for the sound of Jacinthe's munching, they might almost have heard the detective sergeant's mind at work.

"Is the hamster wheel turning?" Lemaire asked jokingly.

Victor stopped pacing, put his hands on the table, and leaned toward his fellow cop. "If I'm understanding you, Gilles, you're saying Lortie was used as a guinea pig in a secret CIA research project — a series of psychiatric experiments carried out at McGill in the 1960s. Is that it?"

Lemaire nodded.

While Victor searched feverishly through a stack of papers, Jacinthe put another handful of Smarties into her mouth.

"I would have liked to have memories," the detective sergeant quoted at last, holding up the report on the homeless man's suicide, which contained a verbatim account of his exchange with the police officers.

He looked around at his colleagues. "That's what Lortie said to the two patrol cops before jumping to his death."

Those seemingly harmless words now took on a new significance.

Loïc stopped blowing bubbles for a moment to consider the Gnome's idea. "If that's the case," he said at last, "and Lortie was lucid enough to write a coded sentence to identify a super-secret project, then maybe he wasn't so delusional after all."

"Oh, come on, kid," Jacinthe blurted out. "The CIA? Get real. Gilles learned about this secret project, MK-whatever, in school. Can we agree that it stopped being secret a long time ago? Lortie probably heard it mentioned somewhere and began having delusions about it, like he did about everything else. Whether he wrote sentences or drew pictures, that doesn't get us any further than if he was knitting granny slippers. And it all just proves what I've been saying since the beginning: the guy was a fucking whack job!"

The conversation turned into an argument. Loïc suggested that the treatments Lortie had undergone might have affected his memory, and that he wrote on the cardboard sheets to preserve information about his past — information he didn't want to forget.

The Gnome had his doubts, wondering why Lortie would have needed to code the information, but he conceded that a more detailed analysis of the writing might be helpful.

Her colleagues' theories cracked like so many roaches under Jacinthe's heel. She accused her fellow cops of jumping to conclusions. For starters, they had no proof that Lortie had been used as a guinea pig in the MK-ULTRA program. All they had was a note on a file tab.

While the others argued, Victor was tapping on his keyboard. "Anyway, the two of them knew each other. They co-authored a couple of papers."

Everyone looked at him.

"Who?" Taillon asked.

"Ewen Cameron and Judith Harper."

The detective sergeant turned his screen around so they could see. On the website of McGill's psychiatry department, he'd found a page devoted to Judith Harper's research. There, in her list of publications, two titles had caught his attention:

CAMERON, E., and J. HARPER, "The Use of Electroconvulsive Therapy and Sleep Deprivation Drugs to Eliminate Past Behavioural Habits," *North American Journal of Psychiatry*, McGill University, Allan Memorial Institute of Psychiatry, 1960.

CAMERON, E., and J. HARPER, "A Case Study on Depatterning to Eliminate Past Behavioural Habits," *North American Journal of Psychiatry*, McGill University, Allan Memorial Institute of Psychiatry, 1961.

"There's our connection," Loïc said eagerly. "Judith Harper was a psychiatrist, too. Let's assume Lortie was treated by Cameron and Harper. He could have killed her in revenge for the mistreatment he went through."

"You're way out in left field, kid," Jacinthe proclaimed. "Think for a second. We've got two murders committed with the same weapon, which means a single killer. Lortie was already dead when Lawson was killed. Burgers confirmed as much. For the Harper murder, he had an alibi. What else do you want? You gonna tell us Lawson was Lortie's attorney and the whack job decided to get back at him for overbilling?"

Loïc hung his head.

"Jacinthe, please," Victor intervened. "Weren't you talking about a timer not so long ago?"

The argument continued, with all the cops vigorously defending their viewpoints.

The chair of McGill's psychiatry department, Richard Blaikie, had white hair and a goatee, and wore a bow tie and browline glasses. For a moment, Victor searched his memory — Blaikie vaguely reminded him of someone. But who? An immense oil portrait, its surface finely fissured, hung on the wall behind him.

In the portrait, an austere man with a regal head and scornful lips contemplated the horizon. The detective sergeant tried unsuccessfully to read the name on the brass plate. It was surely one of Blaikie's predecessors, perhaps even the department's first head.

Jacinthe, caring little about decorum, was drumming her fingers on her armrest. Despite the fact that it was nearly 5:00 p.m., Blaikie had agreed to see them right away after a brief phone conversation in which Victor explained that they were investigating the murder of Judith Harper.

Blaikie had begun by expressing his sincere sadness at the death of his former colleague, saying he preserved excellent memories of her.

But when they began to discuss details, his attitude changed markedly.

Victor saw irritation on the department head's face when he was told that the detectives had obtained access to the psychiatric file of a certain André Lortie and were trying to determine whether he had been one of Ewen Cameron's patients. When Victor mentioned the MK-ULTRA program, Blaikie's irritation turned into outright annoyance.

"Listen, I have no way of checking whether this man was treated under the program. While it's true that the MK-ULTRA experiments were carried out at McGill, they were never under the authority of this institution."

"There must be files somewhere," Victor suggested.

"It's been more than forty-five years! I wasn't in the psychiatry department back then. In any case, the files were kept by Cameron. If I remember correctly, they were destroyed during the 1970s on the orders of the CIA director at the time."

Blaikie's assistant, who had been in a corner of the room preparing beverages on a metal trolley, now placed a steaming cup in front of her boss. She poured glasses of water for the police officers and left the pitcher on a tray close at hand.

"Since they co-wrote papers, is it possible that Judith Harper participated in Cameron's experiments?" Victor asked.

Blaikie dismissed the suggestion out of hand.

"You're going up a blind alley. Judith was a researcher, not a practitioner. She co-wrote those papers at the start of her career. She later dissociated herself from the work when she realized the true nature of Cameron's clinical experiments."

The assistant put a plate of assorted cookies in front of them before leaving. Blaikie thanked her with a stiff smile as Jacinthe reached forward.

"In any case, the MK-ULTRA program has given rise to all kinds of baseless legends."

Victor asked a few more questions, but he ended the discussion when it became clear that he'd get nothing out of Blaikie. Even so, he understood the man's reticence. For years, the events in question had tarnished the reputation of the department he now chaired.

After the usual thank yous and handshakes, Victor turned to go to the door. As he did so, he saw that a single cookie remained on the plate.

He gave Jacinthe a dark look. She responded with a shrug, as though wondering what he was upset about.

The two detectives didn't exchange a word as they walked to the car, which they'd left in the parking area off Pine Avenue. Deep in thought, Victor turned up his collar and lit a cigarette. As he smoked, he looked up at the outline of Mount Royal looming in the darkness.

Taillon was on her phone, telling Lucie she'd be home soon.

"That guy made me hungry," she said, hanging up. "Didn't you find he looked like Colonel Sanders?"

The reaction was impossible to suppress. Victor spluttered and coughed out his smoke. Colonel Sanders! That was the resemblance he'd noticed in the department head. For once, Taillon had him laughing heartily.

"Ha ha! It's true!" The laughter faded. "But seriously, Jacinthe, do you ever think about anything except food?"

"Now and then," she replied without hesitation. "On the other hand, I never think about smoking."

42

ICE RING

As soon as they arrived at Versailles, Taillon got into her car and left. Though he was tired and eager to get home, Victor went up to the office. In the corridor, he ran into the Gnome, who was on his way out. Bennett's condition was critical but stable. The doctors would alert the detectives as soon as he was out of his coma.

Next, Victor went to check up on Paul Delaney, but his office was empty. Victor hoped his boss hadn't received any more bad news.

He found Loïc at his desk.

Searching the web, the young detective had discovered a portal for medieval resources in Quebec. After more than a dozen calls, he still hadn't found a shop that sold heretic's forks. Nor had his luck been any better with online sellers. If there was a market for such things, it was marginal at best.

"Go on home. You can keep trying tomorrow."

The kid nodded. He looked downcast. Victor sat on the edge of the desk. Something had been bothering him since the team meeting that afternoon, and he wasn't going to pass up this opportunity to clarify some things.

"You know, Loïc, Jacinthe doesn't pussyfoot around. Not with me, not with Gilles, not with anyone. She's a warrior. She won't hesitate to put her life on the line to save yours. But she's short on tact and sensitivity. And chances are, that'll never change." Loïc was watching Victor, clearly wondering what would come next. "I'm telling you this because you need to know who you're dealing with, and, above all, because you mustn't let yourself be hurt by the things she says. You were right to defend your opinions today. Even if she makes fun of them, that's no reason to back down. Keep your head up, kid. You've been doing good work lately."

Victor knew right away that his instinct had been right. Loïc's face brightened. The detective sergeant gave the young man a pat on the shoulder, grabbed his jacket, and left. Before getting on the metro, not having heard from his son in a while, Victor texted him with a reminder that they were spending Christmas Eve at Ted's place. A reply was waiting in his inbox when he stepped out of the Villa-Maria station: Martin confirmed that he'd be there.

Nadja had made a beef-and-vegetable stir fry, and Victor had washed the dishes. He was about to make himself comfortable on the couch and watch a documentary on Muhammad Ali (which he had downloaded more or less legally) when Nadja approached, holding an old pair of white skates and wearing a broad smile.

"Say yes," she pleaded.

First, he claimed not to know where his own skates were, but she'd foreseen the objection. They were waiting in the closet by the front door. For form's sake, he invoked all the half-hearted excuses in his repertoire: he'd eaten too much, it was cold out, his blades weren't sharp, he was sleepy, his back hurt.

Nadja gracefully overcame every excuse: a little exercise would help him digest; he could wear his new coat, the one he usually found too warm; since he'd played hockey in his younger days and she was a beginner, his unsharpened blades would put them on an equal footing; he'd sleep better after getting some fresh air; and she'd give him a back rub when they got home.

There was never really any doubt. Victor couldn't resist. He'd have followed her to hell if she'd asked.

"Okay, fine."

She whooped joyfully, put her arms around his neck, and smothered him in kisses.

He savoured the moment with a smile.

There were a couple of dozen skaters circling the ice ring at Beaver Lake in Mount Royal Park. The air was frigid. Victor didn't notice the cold. This outing was doing him a world of good, allowing him to clear his head and think about nothing.

They skated arm in arm. The sky was cloudless. Nadja's lips shone in the glow of the overhead lights.

"I've been thinking about the weapon used in the murders. Did you talk to local role-play organizers? I know there are groups that do that kind of thing."

Victor said Adams had already raised that possibility, and he described Loïc's ongoing efforts to find a lead. In a few sentences, he summarized the day's developments. Nadja's questions helped reassure him that he hadn't overlooked any angles so far.

"The thing that doesn't fit with your murders is the suicide. I'd make that my starting point. There has to be a connection somewhere."

"I agree. Lortie baffles me. The psychiatrist said there's often an element of truth in a bipolar individual's delusions. I looked through his file. The problem is, his delusions are so extreme that it's hard to get a clear sense of what's real and what isn't. Was he a patient in the MK-ULTRA program? Was he in the FLQ? Did he have other wallets in his possession, apart from the ones belonging to the victims?" Victor sighed. "I don't know what to think. I feel like I'm missing something …"

"So you'll go back and see the psychiatrist at Louis-H. tomorrow?"

"Yes. I want to find out what he knows about MK-ULTRA. I also want to ask if it's possible that Lortie was treated somewhere else before being admitted to Louis-H."

Next, they discussed their plan to move into a new apartment together. They agreed to resume looking at condos after the holidays. And they kept skating until their faces froze.

All of a sudden, Victor felt happy and optimistic. Nothing would disturb their happiness, not even a maniac who killed people with instruments of torture straight out of the Middle Ages.

Nadja was laughing wildly as she did an awkward pirouette. Catching her before she fell, Victor murmured the words in her ear for the very first time.

"I love you."

43

NEVER DO ANYTHING AGAINST YOUR CONSCIENCE, EVEN IF YOUR CONSCIENCE DEMANDS IT

Martin woke up sweating in the midafternoon. Harsh light from the street was coming in through the curtains. Dry-mouthed, he staggered to the bathroom.

Luckily, Boris kept acetaminophen in his medicine cabinet. Martin drank from the bathroom tap, then, nauseated, he knelt beside the toilet bowl.

The will to live returned when the tablets started to ease the excruciating pain in his temples.

Going up the hallway was an ordeal. Empty bottles littered the living room floor. Memories of the previous evening flooded back when he stepped into the kitchen. Sitting there with a cup of coffee, reading a newspaper, Boris answered the question that Martin lacked the strength to ask.

"Hello, sleepyhead. Muriel left last night. Roxanne an hour ago."

Before going back to his paper, Boris added with a yawn, "There's coffee on the counter."

Martin ate a couple of croissants and gazed out the window. The winter day was grey and dirty. Taking out a pair of scissors, Boris began clipping articles in silence. Waiting for him to say something, Martin felt his worries returning.

Had Boris seen his text?

•   •   •

After showering, Martin dropped onto the couch and turned on the TV. While channel surfing, he landed on a twenty-four-hour news channel. A reporter was talking about a robbery committed the night before "in the Laurentians, at an explosives-storage warehouse."

Martin raised the volume and called out to Boris.

The reporter said that authorities were "declining to reveal the exact number of explosives taken by the two armed, masked men," and described the operation as "carefully planned." He wrapped up his report by noting that the investigation had been handed over to the organized crime unit of the Quebec Provincial Police, suggesting that the robbery was probably linked to "the turf war between motorcycle gangs that has been heating up in recent months."

"You hear that?" he said to Boris, muting the TV.

Boris had barely raised his head to watch the report. "Yeah, I saw the news this morning. They think it's the bikers. Perfect. That means they don't have any leads. Take a look." Boris handed the newspaper clippings to Martin.

The articles were a few days old, taken from Montreal's main dailies. They all dealt with the same subject: the desecration of a Jewish cemetery attributed to "a radical Islamist group that has been increasingly active on the island of Montreal over the past three months."

Acts of vandalism against two synagogues had also been blamed on the group, which was said to operate "in the shadows, with no clear motive other than hatred toward Jews."

Though the group was dismissed as a "marginal phenomenon" by a professor of ethnic studies at the University of Montreal, it was becoming a source of concern. Especially in "a city where peaceful multiculturalism prevails, despite recent tensions arising from the debate over reasonable accommodation for religious minorities."

Barely suppressing his anger, Martin looked over the articles. Then, concealing his emotions, he forced himself to smile as he turned to Boris.

"What did I tell you?" Boris said. "It's working."

They spent the rest of the day playing video games and drinking beer. Boris gave Martin a couple of chances to recount the details of his wild night with Muriel and Roxanne, but Martin's answer was brief and truthful: he hardly remembered a thing. Afterward, they talked about hockey and smoked a joint. Then Boris stood up and grabbed his jacket.

"Come on."

It was more of an order than a suggestion. Martin stretched his limbs before hoisting himself upright and putting on his coat. "Where are we going?"

"For a drive. Now that we have explosives, we're going to be needing some detonators." Boris turned and gave him an inscrutable look. "If you're looking for your phone, I put it on top of the fridge."

Martin swallowed with difficulty, terrified.

44

IN FRONT OF THE ALLAN MEMORIAL INSTITUTE, IN THE SUNSHINE

Friday, December 23rd

Victor walked painfully to the Villa-Maria metro station, his face contorting as he went down the stairs. The previous evening, without a warm-up, he had foolishly gone all out and done a few high-speed laps of the ice ring to impress Nadja.

On the drive home, he had felt a twinge in his lower back. When they arrived at the apartment, rather than use his head, he had given in to the urges of his lower anatomy and invited Nadja to join him in the shower.

After a couple of acrobatic moves, he had found himself on the cold tiles with his manhood shrivelled and his back immovable. Unable to stop laughing, Nadja had done her best to provide relief with a massage. Victor had finally fallen asleep around one in the morning. The pain radiating down to his buttock had woken him up at five. He had left at dawn, before Nadja was awake. In a homicidal mood, he had no desire to talk to anyone.

In the elevator, feeling the buzz of the muscle relaxants he'd taken on his way out of the apartment, Victor promised himself that he'd resume his healthy habits as soon as this investigation was over. He wanted to get back into regular cardiovascular training. Forced to give up jogging because of his leg, he had turned to swimming. It was a full-body workout and much easier on the joints. But, little by little, he had let it slide.

For one thing, his swimming technique was hopeless; he couldn't master the front crawl. After a few lengths of breaststroke, he was ready to drown himself.

But more fundamentally, he hated the environment. The chlorine smell of the YMCA pool gave him a headache, and the sight of other swimmers, with their flabby bodies and loud bathing suits, made him sick to his stomach.

Expecting to be the first to arrive at the office, Victor was surprised, as he walked through the main entrance, to see that the place was a hive of activity. The whole team, or just about, was already at work. Delaney's door was closed, indicating that the chief himself was there.

Gilles Lemaire gave him a smile and a hearty "Good morning."

"What's going on?" Victor growled. "Why is everyone here at this hour?"

"The Christmas party's tonight. We're getting off early, remember?"

Victor smacked his forehead. He had completely forgotten. His Secret Santa gift was at the apartment. And it wasn't wrapped. Muttering to himself, he sat down at his computer and sent an email to Nadja, asking her to bring the gift when she came to join him. Pretending to consult his messages, he sat staring at the screen for several minutes. Feeling hollowed out, a hair's breadth from catatonia, he struggled to beat back the depression that was assailing him.

With an effort, he roused himself from his reverie and dialed the number of the chief of psychiatry at Louis-H. When he asked for an appointment with Dr. McNeil, the assistant answered that the doctor would be in a meeting all day long. Victor almost insisted, wanting to say that he was a police officer and it was an emergency, but he didn't have the strength — and anyway, it wouldn't have been true. He wrote down the time of their appointment the next day and hung up.

Taillon's massive form appeared at the end of the corridor. She came directly toward Victor. It was more than he could endure; he wasn't going to put up with another of her attacks. Not today. The detective sergeant prepared himself for battle, ready to go ballistic on her at the smallest unpleasant remark. Without bothering to say hello, she tossed a cardboard envelope on his desk.

"You've got mail."

Oblivious to his response, she walked on. Without slowing her pace, she took a notebook off her desk and headed for the conference room.

Victor's tension faded. He sighed, almost disappointed that no confrontation had occurred.

He held the envelope between his fingers, noting the absence of a stamp or postmark, or any return address. The only writing was his name in block letters in the centre of the envelope. Using the letter opener that lay on his desk, he unsealed it and was surprised to discover a photocopied black-and-white photograph of two men and a woman. They were standing in front of a building. From their squinting faces and the clarity of the image, it was clear that they were standing in bright sunshine.

Victor immediately recognized Judith Harper, though she was easily forty years younger in the picture. From the more recent photographs he'd seen, he'd formed a clear sense of her appearance and knew she'd once been what one would call an attractive woman. But until now, he hadn't realized just how attractive. Making an effort to detach his gaze from the goddess smiling at the camera, he looked at the caption under the photo:

> Dr. Ewen Cameron and colleagues posing in front of the Allan Memorial Institute, where MK-ULTRA experiments were conducted. Montreal, Canada, circa 1964.

Victor guessed that the older man must be Ewen Cameron. He turned his attention to the younger one. The detective sergeant needed a moment to make the connection in his head, but once it was made, he had no more doubts about the man's identity. Forgetting the pain in his back, he jumped to his feet and walked quickly to the conference room.

With her fingers deep in a bag of Cheetos, Jacinthe was looking at the photos that the forensics team had made of the cardboard in André Lortie's room.

"Don't start getting ideas, Lessard. I'm still convinced this'll lead nowhere. Lortie's just a fucking whack job. But I thought I'd look over the puzzle anyway, just in case ..."

Victor made a face and put a hand to his lower back. The stabbing pain that ran through his buttock now descended as far as his knee.

"You gonna pull through, big guy?"

"Sciatic trouble. Where'd this envelope come from?"

"No idea. It was at the reception desk this morning. Why?"

Victor put the photograph down in front of her. "Take a look."

Jacinthe wiped her orange fingers on her pants and picked up the picture.

"Fuck! That's Harper and Cameron."

"Recognize the second man?"

Taillon examined the snapshot for another moment, then gave up.

Victor got Dr. McNeil's assistant on the line once again, and once again she told him her boss was in an all-day meeting, and —

Cutting her off, the detective sergeant informed her peremptorily that if she didn't clear a space in the agenda right now, he would get an arrest warrant against the doctor.

"We'll be there at nine o'clock," he said drily.

"Nine-thirty," the assistant replied, panic stricken.

Jacinthe nodded approvingly. She liked it when Victor got tough.

"I'm going down to the food court. I'm hungry."

"And I want a smoke."

The two detectives walked down the corridor without exchanging a word. Victor nodded a greeting to a fellow cop in another section, whom Jacinthe ignored.

"Who sent us the picture?" she asked at last. "It wasn't the murderer, that's for sure."

Victor looked at her enigmatically. "I have a fair idea who it was."

Neither the detectives' hard expressions nor the fact that they'd threatened to arrest him if he didn't see them immediately seemed to intimidate Dr. Mark McNeil. Whether feigned or genuine, his anger was plain to see.

"This had better be important. Do you understand that this is the only time in the month when the service chiefs get together, and I'm the one who's supposed to be chairing the meeting?"

Jacinthe sprang from her chair, ready to return the doctor's hostility. But Victor put a hand on her arm, and she sat down. In the car, they had discussed her hot temper and agreed that she'd let Victor lead the conversation. In return, he had promised not to waste time. He would be as direct as possible.

"Did you know Judith Harper?" the detective sergeant asked without preamble.

Cracks appeared in McNeil's mask. Incomprehension was followed by surprise on his wavering features. "Uhh … yes. Everyone knew her by reputation."

"Did you ever spend time with her?"

"As a matter of fact, she was one of my medical professors," he said, smoothing his moustache, visibly nervous.

"You didn't think to mention that the last time we met?"

"You didn't ask. How is this relevant?"

McNeil pulled a handkerchief from his pocket and dabbed his brow, on which a line of droplets had appeared.

"You tell me," Victor said, and tossed the photograph onto the desk.

The psychiatrist picked it up and looked at it. McNeil's mouth opened to object, but no sound came out.

"You can start by explaining your involvement in Project MK-ULTRA," Victor said.

The words seemed to take their time reaching McNeil's brain.

"What? My involvement in ..." The psychiatrist was affronted. Reddening, he shook his head vigorously in denial. "This is ridiculous. It's just a coincidence that I'm in this picture."

"Oh, really?" Victor asked coldly. "How so?"

"I was doing my master's studies at the time. Judith had hired me to write up abstracts, summaries of psychiatric research papers. I worked in a windowless cubbyhole. I had no contact with patients."

The detective sergeant got up, took a few paces around the room, then came back to the desk, placing his hands flat on its surface and looming over the psychiatrist. "So why are you in the photograph?"

The doctor sighed, clearly distressed by the direction the conversation had taken. "Because Judith liked me. She took me everywhere that summer."

"The summer of 1964."

"I don't remember exactly. If you say so ..."

"Did you fuck her?"

McNeil's eyes had shrunk to tiny slits. "Judith was married. I was her plaything ... her hobby, if you like."

"You had a relationship ..."

"You don't think about it in those terms when you're young. My hormones were white hot, and I was having sex with a married woman a decade older than I was. Our affair lasted three or four months, until Judith put a stop to it. End of story."

"Really?" Victor asked in an innocent voice.

The detective sergeant was watching the psychiatrist's reaction. McNeil held his gaze without flinching.

"If you're wondering whether I slept with Judith after 1964, the answer is no."

Jacinthe and Victor had spent the hour before the meeting looking into the psychiatrist's past and gathering all available information about him. The research report they'd obtained was still incomplete, but they'd found out that a few years previously, McNeil had married a young woman of Thai origin, thirty years his junior, with whom he had a daughter.

"Not even recently?" Taillon asked. "Apparently, some women lose their interest in sex after giving birth. A man your age has needs. Judith wasn't young anymore, but once the dentures came out …"

"You're disgusting," the doctor said.

Victor tried to intervene, urging tact on Jacinthe, but the idea of showing any trace of restraint never crossed her mind.

"Then when she threatened to reveal the affair to your wife, you lost your head and …"

The psychiatrist rose from his chair, his face scarlet. "You suspect me of killing Judith? Seriously?"

"By the way, have you had a case of chlamydia lately?" Jacinthe asked, leering malignantly.

With a roar, McNeil rushed forward. Victor had to step between his partner, who hadn't retreated an inch, and the doctor, who, with flecks of saliva at his lips, was intent on attacking her. Insults began to fly. Trying to calm them both down, struggling to hold them apart, the detective sergeant finally had to raise his voice. After a brief negotiation, he prevailed on Jacinthe to wait outside.

The psychiatrist took a moment to compose himself and sit back down.

Then McNeil apologized to Victor, repeating several times that he wasn't in the habit of behaving this way. Victor said he understood and managed to get the conversation more or less back on track.

"It's completely absurd. I'd run into Judith now and then at a cocktail party or a conference. But that's it. You've got to believe me!"

"Did you take part in Dr. Cameron's work?"

"Of course not."

"And Judith Harper? Did she participate in his experiments?"

McNeil loosened his tie and unbuttoned his collar before answering.

"They had a professional relationship. But Judith was a researcher, not a practitioner. Her collaboration with Cameron was limited to exchanging information. Since she specialized in memory disorders, Cameron would consult her sometimes to validate his hypotheses. That was as far as it went."

"So, she wasn't involved in the abuses inflicted on some of the patients?"

"No."

Either McNeil wasn't sure of what he was saying, or he was lying. Victor's gaze fell on the psychiatrist's folded hands, noted his manicured fingers, his monogrammed shirt cuffs, and his gold cufflinks adorned with a black cloverleaf.

"Nice cufflinks," the detective said, raising his eyebrows.

"They were a gift," the psychiatrist said distractedly.

Victor got up and drifted to the bookshelf, where he saw several framed photographs of McNeil with his wife and child.

One picture caught his attention. A small detail brought him up short, but he composed himself, making an effort to hide his reaction. Readjusting his pants, he stood directly in front of the psychiatrist.

"Was André Lortie one of Dr. Cameron's patients?"

McNeil hesitated slightly, avoiding Victor's gaze. "How would I know? I wasn't involved in the work. And why are you asking me all these questions about Cameron?"

Victor described the handwritten note that the Gnome had spotted on the file tab. A light seemed to appear in the psychiatrist's eyes, then it went out. As far as the detective sergeant could judge, McNeil's surprise was genuine. "What about his file? If he was treated by Cameron, the file should be obtainable."

"Lortie's psychiatric file before he arrived at Louis-H.? If it existed, no one here ever saw it. I've given you all the documentation we have."

Victor continued to grill McNeil until his store of questions was exhausted.

"Are you going to arrest me?" the psychiatrist couldn't help asking.

The detective sergeant's gaze strayed back to the photographs on the shelf.

"No. But I'm going to ask that you stay in town and be available at all times."

After leaving McNeil's office, Victor spent a minute looking for Jacinthe in the corridor. When the head nurse told him Taillon had gotten into the elevator, he couldn't resist a smile. He went down to the cafeteria, expecting to find her seated in front of a heaping plate.

To his surprise, she wasn't there, either. Puzzled, the detective sergeant stepped outside to the parking lot. In the fierce cold, shielding his eyes with one hand, he saw that the car was no longer in its space. Pulling out his phone, he was about to call her when he was startled by a honk behind him.

The Crown Victoria pulled up. The passenger door swung open violently. "Been waiting long?"

Victor climbed in and said no. A Christmas tree, still covered in snow, was dripping on the back seat. The odour of sap filled the car's interior.

"It'll brighten up the room. Not bad, huh? I've asked Gilles to go buy some ornaments and tinsel at the dollar store."

The detective sergeant gave voice to the thought that had been dogging him since the previous day: wouldn't it be preferable to cancel the celebration, given the illness of Paul Delaney's wife? Jacinthe assured him that the answer was no. She had spoken to the boss, who swore the party would do him a world of good.

And before Victor could say a word, she debriefed him. One: Loïc had made barely any progress in his research on the heretic's fork. Two: the Gnome had received the names of the Northern Industrial Textiles directors from the legal expert at the Justice Ministry, and was now digging to learn more. Three: Bennett was still in a coma. And four: the forensics team hadn't found anything that might constitute a lead.

When they came to a red light, Victor had a sudden thought. He turned, looked at the tree, then at Taillon, then back at the tree, back at Taillon, and ... no! She wouldn't have dared.

"Jacinthe, tell me you didn't cut that tree down on someone's property."

She gave him a mischievous look. "Oh, come on! Do you think I carry a hacksaw in my bag?"

"I wouldn't be surprised."

Jacinthe laughed heartily. Then she questioned him about McNeil. Victor described the part of the conversation that she'd missed.

"He's lying about some details, but I don't know which ones," Victor said. "We'll need to get a warrant to see his call log and to put his cellphone under surveillance."

"Oh, yeah?" Jacinthe asked, surprised. "For a guy who doesn't know which details McNeil's lying about, you're awfully motivated. Is there something I'm missing here?"

The light turned green. She put the car in motion over the ice-covered asphalt.

"In his office, I saw a framed picture of his daughter."

"So?"

The detective sergeant looked over at his partner. "She was in front of the fridge ... which was covered in plastic number magnets."

The Crown Victoria swerved, but Taillon managed to keep it under control.

45

BLACKJACK

It was 11:25 a.m. The buses and shuttles full of gamblers had already begun to arrive at the Casino de Montréal. Looking up at the building, Victor couldn't help thinking it looked like a spaceship. Two old ladies in sweatsuits bustled past him and Taillon. Seeing their haste, Victor knew they were headed for the slots.

He took a drag on his cigarette.

For several weeks now, he'd been in a program to help him quit smoking. But the demands of the last few days had prevented him from going. In any case, with the stress levels he was facing, the timing was less than optimal. He promised himself that he'd go back when the investigation was over. He'd make it his New Year's resolution, though he never made such resolutions. Nadja hadn't asked, but he knew it would make her happy.

After one last puff, he stubbed out the butt in the wall-mounted ashtray. Taillon had just ended her phone call.

"The wiretap warrant is in the works. Paul spoke to his friend the judge. It shouldn't take long. Gilles is putting together a financial profile. He was surprised when I told him about the picture in McNeil's office."

The detective sergeant shrugged as they walked toward the entrance.

"You're always saying we shouldn't jump to conclusions. The McNeils aren't the only people with number magnets on their fridge."

"You're right. But it's quite a coincidence."

Victor opened the door for Jacinthe.

"Did you talk to Colonel Sanders's assistant?" she asked. "Was she the one who sent us the picture of Judith Harper with Cameron and McNeil?"

"Yes, ma'am."

While his partner was bringing the Gnome up to speed on recent developments, the detective sergeant had called McGill's psychiatry department and spoken to the chair's assistant. At first, the woman hadn't wanted to talk, but she'd finally admitted that, yes, having overheard the detectives' conversation with Richard Blaikie, she had sent Victor the photograph of the trio. Reluctantly, she had described the rumours that circulated about Judith Harper's involvement in Cameron's experiments. But she had no information that might confirm McNeil's participation in the research.

"Why did Dr. Blaikie hide this from us?" Victor asked.

"They all cover for each other. And most importantly, they all protect the university's holy name."

"So, what prompted you to send me the picture?"

After a long silence, the assistant said, "For years, Richard has been promising me that he'll leave his wife. But he never will."

The two detectives had been waiting in the carpeted outer room for eight minutes when the door opened. An immense man stood in the doorway. Guillaume Dionne wore a tailored suit. His head was shaved and he had a few days' worth of stubble on his chin. When he saw the detective sergeant, his hard features broke into a broad grin.

"Victor Lessard! What brings you here, my man?"

They exchanged a warm handshake, and Victor introduced Jacinthe. Dionne brought them into his office, which commanded a superb view of the river, Île Notre-Dame, and the Port of Montreal.

"Oooh, yeah." Victor chuckled as he settled into a luxurious armchair. "You've got it good, Guillaume. I don't imagine you spend a lot of time missing the force."

The two men had become friends while working together as patrol cops. Since then, their paths had crossed occasionally on their new assignments. But they hadn't really gotten back in touch until a few years ago, when Chris Pearson, Victor's former protégé at Station 11, had married Dionne's sister, Corinne. Since then, the three men had made a point of having lunch together now and then.

"Don't miss it one bit. Oh, I know, some folks might say running casino security is no match for police work, but we get our share of action. And I don't need to tell you the working conditions are way better. We could always use someone like you, Victor. But I'm guessing you didn't come to talk about career opportunities. Hey, before we get started, can I offer you something? You name it, we've got it!" Dionne grinned, revealing nicotine-yellowed teeth.

"I'll have a —" Jacinthe began.

Victor cut her off. "Thanks, Guillaume, but we're in a hurry."

Dionne leaned back in his chair, clasping his hands behind his head, while Jacinthe scowled. "I've gotta admit, your call intrigued me. What's up?"

"Do you still have your cufflinks?"

Dionne looked at him blankly, then laughed.

"Lessard, you'll never stop surprising me! Cufflinks? You didn't really come out here to ask about that, did you?"

When Victor didn't join in the mirth, Dionne glanced over at Jacinthe, looking for a sign to confirm that this was some kind of joke.

But Jacinthe was expressionless.

"This is important, Guillaume. I'm talking about the cufflinks you were wearing the last time we had lunch with Pearson at the Vietnamese place. Gold, with a cloverleaf."

"Yeah, I remember. You were both razzing me about them. Pearson asked if you could buy them for men. I don't see what this has to do with anything."

"As I recall, you said there were only a limited number in circulation."

"Right. The casino's VIP service handed out forty pairs to our highest rollers. But that was chump change. They just brought over a Chinese group from Macao. The VIP service covered airfare, hotel rooms, meals, and promised to refund ten percent of their losses."

"I don't give a damn about the Chinese, Guillaume. At the moment, I'm interested in the players who got cufflinks. You must have a list of names."

Guillaume Dionne had lost his good humour. "I should've known you'd give me headaches, Lessard."

46

PAY PHONE

Mark McNeil descended to the basement, where there was a secluded pay phone. It was in one of the quietest, most isolated sectors of the hospital, where he could be sure he wouldn't be bothered by the incessant comings and goings of patients and nurses.

Footsteps rang out on the polished floor. McNeil looked up, his heart racing. A maintenance man went by without a glance in his direction, pushing a garbage trolley and muttering to himself.

The psychiatrist waited for the man to disappear at the end of the corridor, then took a slip of paper from his pocket. Feeding coins into the slot, he dialed the number on the paper.

While the ringback tone trilled in his ear, he went over the events of the last few hours in his mind. The meeting with the police officers had shaken him badly. His nerves were a jangling mess.

Taillon was loathsome, certainly, but she was just an ignorant minion. It was her colleague, Lessard, whom McNeil feared. Had the officer believed him, or had he suspected something? Hard to say. The detective knew how to hide his emotions, which made him difficult to read.

McNeil's thoughts turned to himself. How could he have lost his temper? Had he given himself away? Somehow, he'd returned to his meeting and managed to keep up appearances. Now he would have to take the necessary steps.

On the fourth ring, someone picked up. He heard the familiar guttural voice at the other end of the line.

Always the same.

"It's McNeil. Uhh … No. Not yet. I need more time." He rolled his eyes, exasperated. "I understand. Yes. I'm well aware that there won't be any more extensions … Yes. I'll pick up the money in the same place as usu— Perfect. This is the last time. I promise."

After hanging up, he rubbed his right hand, which was trembling slightly.

McNeil exhaled, puffing out his cheeks, ruffling his moustache. How had he let himself get into this mess? Shaking his head, he walked toward the elevator. There was something else he had to look into. Right away.

It might turn out to be a new opportunity.

47

CELEBRATION

Through the bay window overlooking the entrance, Victor watched her take off her coat. Nadja smiled at the Gnome's wife, who was holding the youngest of the Seven Dwarfs in her arms. Her glistening lips revealed dazzling white teeth. Nadja bent over Number 7, stroked his pink cheek, and gazed at him tenderly. Victor saw the light reflected in her jet-black hair, and the shine of her olive skin.

She entered the corridor.

Watching her every gesture, the detective sergeant was aware of his good fortune. Her black dress hinted at the outline of her bust and opened onto her endless legs. Her high heels made her hips sway as she moved. Nadja hadn't seen him. Over one arm she held a garment bag containing fresh clothes for Victor, who hadn't had time to get home and change. The smaller bag in her hand no doubt held his gift for the Gnome, which she had promised to bring. And she had wrapped it because, as always, she knew what he needed. She completed him.

He felt his heart swell. A tear crept down his cheek.

Had he ever loved someone as he loved her? Would he do the right thing this time? A chill seized him; he felt exposed and helpless. What was the right thing?

Victor had never really known. He wouldn't figure it out.

Nadja raised her head and their eyes met. A smile lit up the face of the woman he loved.

Yes, he would figure it out.

*   *   *

The conference room was unrecognizable. Holiday classics were playing on a borrowed sound system. The big board had been covered by a black sheet. The Christmas tree that Jacinthe had found was sparkling in the corner, gifts lying all around its base. It had been decorated by Loïc and the Gnome, who had also strung tinsel across the room.

Lemaire had been a good sport and put on the elf costume that Victor had given him as a joke. Now he was handing out presents. The detective sergeant had also bought a second gift for his diminutive colleague: a biography of Winston Churchill. The Gnome was fascinated by the great British statesman and regularly quoted him to liven up conversations. Victor planned to give him the book later.

Lemaire's children were everywhere. Numbers 1 and 2 had red noses and were passing a tissue box back and forth. As soon as Numbers 3, 4, and 5 — two girls and a boy — had received their presents, they started running around in the corridor, encircling Loïc, who was pretending to be a zombie.

Number 7 was now in Nadja's arms. She was stroking his hair as she talked with Lucie, Jacinthe's partner. As for Taillon herself, she had volunteered to serve the food. Which, in practical terms, amounted to little more than removing the plastic wrap from the platters that the caterer had laid out on the table an hour earlier. But it allowed Jacinthe to dip into the goodies and tell herself no one had noticed.

Crouched in a corner, Paul Delaney was helping Number 6 put together a LEGO Bionicle figure.

Standing off to one side, Victor was taking pictures and shooting video with the digital camera that Nadja had bought a few weeks ago. The results would no doubt be singular. Having ignored the recommended muscle relaxant dosage, Victor was now floating in a pleasantly altered state. The pain in his back had gone away.

"Victor Lessard!" Lemaire called out. "It's time to get your present. Come on over here and sit on the lap of Santa's coolest, smartest, hottest elf."

The detective sergeant handed the camera to Loïc and did as he was told. All the adults turned their heads simultaneously to watch the proceedings.

"Give him a big, wet kiss, Vic!" Jacinthe urged, cramming a crustless egg sandwich into her mouth.

It was a moment of laughter, shining faces, radiant smiles.

Everyone was enjoying the punch concocted by Lemaire's wife. Given the personal histories of Victor and Delaney, the drink was alcohol free.

The detective sergeant unwrapped the present the Gnome had handed to him. It was a novel: *Mr. Vertigo* by Paul Auster. Victor sat theatrically on the elf's lap for another moment, then, when Lemaire called out Delaney's name, he went over to Jacinthe, scanning the book's jacket. Victor had never read Auster, but Véronique, his ex-girlfriend, had been an enthusiastic fan.

"This came from you, right?" he asked, holding up the book.

Perched on high heels, squeezed into a flowery dress, and wearing makeup for the occasion, Taillon nodded.

"Thank you," Victor said warmly. "Have you read it?"

"Yes," Jacinthe said. There was a shy note in her voice. "Actually, I read it to Lucie while she was getting better. It's the story of Walt the Wonder Boy and an old guy named Master Yehudi, who teaches him how to fly. Only, not really how to fly. Lucie says it's like an image, it's … it's …"

"A metaphor."

"Right! It sounds fucked up when I try to describe it, but you'll see, it's really good. You get used to the style …"

Laughter rang out to their right. Numbers 3, 4, and 5 had now surrounded Loïc and were jumping up and down in front of him, waving their arms, while he called out their names and pretended not to see them.

Smiling broadly, Taillon cupped her hands around her lips and called out teasingly, "Hey, Loïc! It's time you started having kids of your own. You sure look ready to be a dad!"

The joy fled from the young cop's face. A shadow fell over him. For an instant, he seemed on the verge of tears. Then he walked out.

Only Victor and Jacinthe had seen his reaction.

"Did I say something wrong?" she murmured, a hand over her mouth.

"You didn't know?" Victor asked.

"Know what?"

"Loïc has no experience in homicide, but when he got out of police college, he spent three years working undercover for the drug squad. He infiltrated a street gang in Montreal North. While he was on assignment, he got involved with a gang member's sister. She got pregnant. When the operation ended, they all went to prison for trafficking because of Loïc. Now his ex-girlfriend won't let him see his own daughter. The child must be two or three years old by now. It's very painful for him."

Taillon stared at him, stricken.

Victor put a hand on her shoulder. "Don't blame yourself. It wasn't common knowledge. Paul kept it quiet to spare the kid's feelings. I only found out when I tried to get him fired over the carpet thing."

"Fuck. If I'd known … but to look at him, you'd never guess. Always in a good mood, always upbeat. Too upbeat, sometimes!"

"You of all people should know that appearances can be deceiving." Silence. "A smile sometimes covers pain. I'll go talk to him."

He started to leave the room, then turned back, approached his partner and kissed her cheek. "Thank you for the book, Jacinthe. I appreciate it." He looked into her eyes. "Truly."

The detective sergeant had reached the doorway when Jacinthe called out to him. "Hey, Lessard … I just wanted to say …" She clasped her hands nervously. "I know I'm not always easy to put up with, but … I'm glad we're partners again."

*   *   *

Victor found the right words to comfort Loïc and bring him back to the celebration without anyone noticing his reddened eyes.

After the gifts were handed out, it was time to eat. Salad bowls went from hand to hand; paper plates bent under the weight of the food. Victor, Delaney, and Loïc were sitting in a corner, animatedly discussing the Canadiens.

The Gnome, who loved his gift, was eagerly looking through the Churchill biography. The women were deep in conversation. Jacinthe was holding Lucie's hand.

Victor raised his eyes and smiled. He was among family.

It was a good party.

While everyone was getting ready to dig into the Yule log cake that Lucie had prepared, the Gnome discreetly caught Victor's eye. They stepped away from the others. Still dressed in his elf costume, Lemaire sat on the corner of a desk and announced, pleased with himself, "I did a little digging this afternoon. I have two pieces of good news."

Lemaire was a methodical man. Victor would have preferred that Gilles simply tell him what he'd found out, but he knew his colleague needed to explain the process that had led to his discoveries. That was part of his personality, and the detective sergeant had learned to respect this way of doing things.

The Gnome started by explaining that the apparent connection between Judith Harper and Lortie through MK-ULTRA had led him to wonder about Lawson. Was there any way to link the lawyer to the project that Cameron had run for the CIA?

Lemaire had come up with a few ideas, one of which seemed more promising than the others. Sure enough, as he combed through public documents, he saw that lawsuits had been filed by former patients in the MK-ULTRA program and their families in the early 1970s. The Canadian and U.S. governments had hastily settled the cases out of court to avoid trials that might have revealed information that would "compromise national security."

Since the experiments had been conducted in McGill University facilities, the university had been named as a co-defendant in the court filings.

"And guess which law firm represented McGill?"

Victor felt a surge of adrenalin. "Lawson's?"

"Bingo. Baker Cooper Sirois — the predecessor to Baker Lawson Watkins — was engaged by McGill to defend it against the claims related to MK-ULTRA. And there's more. Lawson himself was the partner in charge of billing."

The detective sergeant took a few seconds before reacting.

His brain was making new connections, opening a range of possibilities. The MK-ULTRA code hidden in Lortie's writing on the cardboard sheets, the photograph of Judith Harper with Dr. Cameron, and now the involvement of Lawson's firm — for the first time since the investigation opened, they could, perhaps, establish a connection between the two murders and the suicide.

The ring of his cellphone alerted him to an incoming text. Victor glanced at the message. Guillaume Dionne, the head of casino security, was letting him know that he'd be sending a fax. Victor pocketed the phone and looked at his fellow cop. "This is big. Good work!"

The Gnome glowed at the compliment. Victor stood there for a moment, still processing the information.

"You said you had two pieces of good news."

"I was keeping the best for last ... I got my hands on the call log for Mark McNeil's cellphone. Guess who called him the day she died."

Victor thought for a moment. The name flashed in his mind. He shook his head in disbelief.

"Not Judith Harper?"

"The very same," the Gnome answered eagerly. "And you want to know the best part of all? McNeil turns out to be a pretty unusual psychiatrist. He was once charged with assault."

48

HOCHELAGA

Through the window of the Audi, Mark McNeil watched the tavern's shabby exterior, observing the customers as they came and went. The dive was located in a rundown area of Hochelaga, a pocket of resistance that hadn't yet fallen to hipster gentrification. It was 8:17 p.m. The dimly lit sidewalk was deserted.

Near the entrance, scraps of paper and detritus littered the dirty snow.

Two men in track suits staggered out the door. One of them relieved himself against the brick wall. Then the two drunks vanished into the lane.

Anxiously, McNeil took a deep breath and stepped out of the car. He hurried across the street to the tavern entrance.

Inside, he looked around at the clientele, which was made up of dubious-looking regulars. In his cashmere coat, McNeil definitely didn't fit in. He walked up to the bar and nervously ordered a cognac. The bartender, an immense man with grimy fingernails, put a glass in front of him and poured out a drink. The psychiatrist drained the glass. The alcohol burned its way down his throat, making his eyes water.

"My name is McNeil," he said, wincing. "I believe you have something for me." He made an effort to smile.

The bartender's gaze was expressionless. McNeil began to worry. Had they gone back on their decision? The big man reached under the bar. Sensing a threat, McNeil stepped back instinctively, his shoulders hunched with fear. The bartender laughed, revealing a mouth from which numerous teeth were missing. He held up a brown envelope wrapped in a thick elastic band and placed it in front of McNeil.

"One more," the psychiatrist said, relaxing a little.

After draining his glass a second time, McNeil tossed a twenty-dollar bill on the bar, picked up the envelope, and hurried out. Back in his car, he gunned the engine and sped along for several blocks. Then he slowed down and pulled over to the curb. Feverishly, he pulled the elastic band off the envelope. The wad of bills he saw inside prompted a sigh of relief.

With this initial step out of the way, the hardest task had been accomplished. All that remained now was to put the second phase in motion.

A nasty smile came to his lips. This unanticipated second phase gave him reason to believe the future would be bright.

49

ARREST WARRANT

Jacinthe and Loïc came over to join Victor and Lemaire. The cops continued their discussion, proposing various theories in light of the new facts that the Gnome had discovered. The detective sergeant knew he'd find it hard to get back into the festive spirit. His brain was teeming with questions and busily assembling new theories.

Suspecting that his colleagues were in the same state of mind, he proposed a strategy session in Delaney's office. The better halves weren't upset. They were in the midst of a lively conversation about the loss of traditional values in Quebec society, and anyway, they were used to sudden changes of plan.

Letting the others go ahead of him, Victor made a detour to the fax machine, where he picked up the document that Guillaume Dionne had sent. Arriving in the chief's office, he closed the door behind him.

The other cops were expecting him to lead the discussion, so he did.

"We'll tell you what we've got, Paul, and you can decide whether it's enough for an arrest warrant. Fact number one: McNeil knew Judith Harper. And not just because she was his professor in medical school."

Victor showed his boss the picture taken in front of the Allan Memorial Institute, linking McNeil to Harper and Cameron and, by extension, to Project MK-ULTRA. Then he briefly described the experiments that had been carried out under the program.

"Fact number two: Judith Harper called McNeil the day she died."

The Gnome handed Delaney a copy of the psychiatrist's call log.

Victor continued. "Fact number three: in McNeil's office, there's a photograph of his daughter playing with number magnets in front of the fridge. Those coloured plastic numbers are identical to the ones found in Harper's apartment."

To keep his hands busy, Delaney pulled out a notepad and started doodling.

"Fact number four: we can't say yet whether Lawson and McNeil knew each other, but Gilles has found out that Lawson's firm was engaged to defend McGill in the civil suits launched by the former subjects of the MK-ULTRA program."

Delaney looked over at the Gnome, who nodded.

"Fact number five: McNeil is a regular at the Casino de Montréal, where his name appears on the high rollers' list."

The detective sergeant produced the document that Guillaume Dionne had just faxed him.

"Fact number six: over the last three months, based on reports from the casino's VIP service and the financial profile that Gilles put together, we know McNeil has lost a pile of money. Something along the lines of …"

"Six hundred thousand dollars," Lemaire said. "His credit's been cut off everywhere."

"How did you know he was gambling at the casino?" Delaney asked, looking over the document.

"His cufflinks," Victor answered.

Delaney's puzzled expression cleared up; he remembered having been told about this detail earlier in the day. "You don't expect to see a psychiatrist fall into this kind of compulsion," he said, shaking his head and looking disillusioned.

"He wouldn't be the first, Chief. But that's a separate issue," Victor said. "Fact number seven: McNeil once faced an assault charge." The detective sergeant turned to the Gnome. "Gilles?"

"It dates back to 2003, a dispute between neighbours. Something to do with snow removal. McNeil claimed he was acting in self-defence after the other guy tried to run him over with his car. He hit the man in the face with a shovel three times. The victim had four broken teeth and significant bruising. McNeil got off with community service."

"Fact number eight," Victor continued. "I'll admit, it's purely circumstantial, but the secretary and the mail boy both told me that on the day Lawson disappeared, he received a message that worried him."

"I remember. A threat …"

"That's our guess."

Sticking a pinky finger in his ear, Delaney tilted his head to the right. "You think McNeil was blackmailing Harper and Lawson, is that it?" He turned to the kid. "Loïc, you're chewing like a cow."

Blouin-Dubois froze, red faced.

Victor continued. "McNeil has gambling debts, Paul. He needs money. He stumbles across an old case and discovers the buried secrets of MK-ULTRA. McNeil then threatens Nathan Lawson with a letter and a recording of Oswald's voice. He threatens Judith Harper with the fridge magnets. Pay up, or I'll reveal the truth."

"But what's the connection between the recording, the fridge numbers, and MK-ULTRA?"

"Do you remember when we were talking a couple of days ago about the symbolic value of the recording?"

"Sure, it was a reference to someone who'd been treated unjustly."

"That's kind of what happened to the MK-ULTRA patients, isn't it? For Harper, the symbolism was in the numbers. Maybe they referred to a significant date associated with the project."

"Which leaves Lawson," Delaney said. "What did he do wrong? It's hardly a crime to represent McGill in court."

"I'm just speculating, but maybe he helped hide or even destroy evidence. He wouldn't be the first lawyer to do some 'house-cleaning' in the files and 'inadvertently' dispose of key documents."

"Okay. It all makes sense. But why wouldn't McNeil just walk away with the money? Why kill Harper and Lawson?"

"That's the big question, Chief. For now, all we have is theories. But we know these things often go sour. Once a scheme is in motion, it's too late to back out. We know McNeil has a criminal record. We know he can be violent under the right conditions. Maybe Judith Harper talked to Lawson. Maybe they decided not to pay, or else threatened to go to the police. Who can say?"

Delaney picked up his ballpoint and resumed his doodling. There was a pregnant silence. "And the vagrant who killed himself?" the chief asked after a moment. "How does he fit into all this?"

"Lortie?" Taillon said. She'd stayed quiet until now. "He's the perfect fall guy. A former victim of MK-ULTRA — fragile, psychologically unstable. McNeil slips the wallets among his possessions to incriminate him. But Lortie finds them and, for reasons we don't understand, jumps off a building before we can follow the trail back to him."

"Everything hinges on MK-ULTRA, Chief," the Gnome said. "That's our key element. It's the common thread that links all the other details."

The head of the Major Crimes Unit didn't ponder long. "All right. Draw up the warrant application and I'll sign it. The connection with Lawson seems iffy to me, but whatever …" Silence. "Do you want to move on this tonight? I don't mind, but it'll mean the party's over."

Victor looked over at his teammates, who nodded. "The party was already over, Chief. Jacinthe's had her dessert."

There were smiles all around.

"I'll see what I can do," Delaney said, looking irritably at his watch. "I'm not promising anything. At this hour, sometimes even judges are in bed."

Victor shrugged. "Do what you can, Chief. At this point, whether it's tonight or in the morning won't make much difference."

Delaney tore the top page off his notepad and crumpled it into a ball. "When we get the warrant, you can bring McNeil in for questioning and search his home. But let's keep it quiet for now. If some reporter starts asking questions, you know the standard line ..."

"By heart, Chief." Victor nodded. "'Dr. McNeil isn't considered a suspect; he's simply an important witness.'"

OCTOBER 30TH, 1995
MONEY AND THE ETHNIC VOTE

Jacques Parizeau gave a stirring speech to the troops.

"We fought well.

"We were so close to being a country.

"Never forget: three-fifths of French-speaking Quebec voted YES. That wasn't quite enough, but soon it will be. We will have our country!"

But then I was startled to hear Monsieur Jacques blame money and the ethnic vote. I wish I could have put those words back in his mouth, for the sake of his reputation. I wish I could have hit the rewind button and scrolled back thirty seconds.

Because Monsieur Jacques did fight well, and respect is owed to those who have the courage to fight for their convictions.

This second NO hurts me, in my being, in my flesh.

From now on, my pain is an interior country.

WATERMELON MAN

50

I ALWAYS CALLED HIM "SIR"

The officers obtained their warrants quickly. At this hour, judges were sometimes in bed, but they were also sometimes partying with friends at a tapas bar in the Plateau-Mont-Royal. Despite his protests, Loïc didn't accompany the group. Paul Delaney wanted to be sure his experienced detectives were unimpeded as they undertook this delicate operation.

Outside, snow had begun to fall. With the wind rising, it was beginning to look like another blizzard was on its way.

They drove past an outdoor rink. Under the bright lights, a handful of players in Canadiens, Bruins, and Canucks colours were braving the bad weather for a game of shinny. Sitting in the back of the car, the Gnome turned his head to watch the game through the window until the players were no more than dots in the distance. He was lost in his memories for a moment.

"There was an old man in my neighbourhood, in Rosemont. In the wintertime, he used to water the rink and keep it clear of snow so we could play hockey. I never knew his name. I always called him 'sir.' He lived alone. When my mother did her holiday cooking, she always made a few extra meat pies and sugar tarts. On Christmas Eve, she'd tell me to bring them over to him. I remember how I hated having to do that, just like I hated asking for the paternal blessing on New Year's Day. The old man always insisted on making me a cup of hot chocolate and showing me pictures of his grandchildren. I never knew what to say. One day, I showed up at his doorstep with the bag my mother had prepared. I rang the bell a couple of times, but he didn't answer. So I tried the door. It swung open. I found him in his armchair in the living room. He had died there, by himself." Silence. "Whenever I go by an outdoor rink, I think of him."

Lemaire's eyes met Jacinthe's in the rear-view mirror. He lowered his gaze.

"I'm sorry. I don't know why I mentioned that."

Victor was unfamiliar with the wealthy suburb of Town of Mount Royal, with its winding avenues of spacious homes, opulent facades, and curving driveways. The psychiatrist's residence was one of the most imposing homes on his crescent. The detectives had to argue through the closed door, and Taillon was forced to hold up her badge before Mark McNeil's wife finally let them in.

Though he'd known she was thirty years younger than her husband, Victor hadn't expected her to be so pretty. Silken strands of black hair fell across her face, accentuating her almond eyes. She had a delicate complexion and wore a dark kimono-style robe that stopped mid-thigh, revealing slender legs and red-painted toenails.

"Did something happen to Mark?" she asked anxiously as they entered. "Has there been an accident?"

Realizing that McNeil wasn't home, the Gnome took the initiative and reassured her. There was no reason to worry about her husband's safety, but they had a warrant to question him and a second warrant to search the house.

When Lemaire asked where her husband was, she answered warily, "He told me he had a few errands to run after work, and he'd be home later."

Once the initial surprise had passed, the young woman was admirably self-possessed. She tried without success to reach McNeil on his cellphone, left him a message, looked over the warrant with Lemaire, inquired about the possibility of consulting a lawyer — adding that she had nothing to hide. Then, with her head in her hands, she became anxious about logistics. During the search, would she be allowed to stay in the house with her child, who was sleeping upstairs?

The Gnome, who had long since exchanged his elf costume for street clothes, nodded to his two fellow cops. He'd handle the formalities with the young woman, whom he was already guiding toward the living room.

"Don't worry," he said, offering her his arm, "my colleagues will be careful not to wake up your little girl."

Victor and Jacinthe headed straight for the kitchen. The colourful magnets were still on the fridge door. The two detectives tallied them. The letters of the alphabet were all there, but, assuming there was only one of each digit between 0 and 9, six were missing: 0, 1, 2, 3, 4, and 6.

Victor leafed backward through his notebook until he found the entry he'd made days before, while looking through Judith Harper's apartment.

"0 blue, 1 red, 2 orange, 3 yellow, 4 purple, 6 green," he said, showing the page to Jacinthe. "The numbers and their respective colours correspond."

Jacinthe nodded. They bagged the remaining numbers, then did a thorough search of McNeil's office.

The effort was painstaking and unproductive. McNeil's computer was password protected, and his wife didn't know the password. So she claimed, anyway — but they had no reason to doubt her word. Apart from that, there were very few files in the office. The documents that were present turned out to be routine paperwork.

Jacinthe went down to the basement while Victor scoured the bedroom.

Here, too, there was nothing of interest, unless you counted the twin sinks in the bathroom and the his-and-hers walk-in closets.

Victor couldn't help noting that the square footage of the bedroom and ensuite bath exceeded that of his entire apartment.

Standing in the doorway of the child's room, seeing her steady breathing, Victor hesitated. But he couldn't run the risk that McNeil was hiding in the room. The detective sergeant entered and searched the room noiselessly. Everything was in order.

Before leaving, he stopped for a few seconds and looked with a tender smile at the curly-haired angel sleeping peacefully in the bed.

Coming back down to the ground floor, he saw the Gnome sitting beside McNeil's wife on the couch. The detective was handing her a glass of water as they spoke in low voices. Gilles Lemaire was a perfect gentleman with an undeniable human touch, which the detective sergeant envied. Gilles knew how to talk to people, how to listen, and how to show empathy.

Not that Victor was entirely incapable of these things, but sometimes he found it hard to communicate. Still, like a good wine, he was improving with age.

Or, as Jacinthe might say, he was getting softer. It all depended on your point of view.

Victor advanced without making a sound, his feet sinking into the thick rug.

When he was just a few steps away, Lemaire and the young woman turned toward him. Gilles barely had time to confirm, in response to Victor's question, that there was no news of McNeil, when a low roar came up from the basement.

"Lessard!" Jacinthe bellowed. "Lessard! Get down here!"

Victor excused himself and headed for the basement stairs. As he descended, he heard a clatter of metal striking metal.

What was she up to?

It was only after crossing the family room and stepping into the garage that he saw her from behind, bent over a plastic ski case.

"Check it out," she said excitedly, straightening up.

She was holding cross-country skis in one hand and poles in the other.

51

PARC MAISONNEUVE

Mark McNeil was walking along the deserted path, his head bowed against the biting wind. The tower of the Olympic Stadium glowed vividly white in the darkness. A line of trees stood to his right. Behind him, the blowing snow swept away his footprints.

The masks had come off earlier that day.

"I know it's you," he'd said into the telephone.

The answer hadn't come right away over the crackling line. The psychiatrist had expected protests, vigorous denials, or attempts at explanation, but no, there had been none of that.

"What do you want?" The voice was calm, but icy.

He had specified what he wanted, and the voice had given him this nocturnal rendezvous in Parc Maisonneuve. And then: nothing. The line had gone dead.

The psychiatrist had left his car on Rosemont Boulevard. Entering the park from that thoroughfare, he had a better view of the entire area. Convinced that he was in control of the situation, he felt no fear. But he wasn't about to get careless. With his fingertips, he touched the handle of the knife in his pocket.

Coming around a turn in the path, he saw the hill.

Nobody in sight.

Was he in the wrong place? The snow was falling hard. McNeil squinted and looked around. He closed his eyes to dislodge the frost from his eyelashes. To his left, with a cap pulled low over the eyes, a shadow emerged from the line of conifers and stopped ten metres away from him.

"Did you really think you could go on lying and duping the world forever?" the psychiatrist crowed.

Was that a smile? He wasn't sure. He could barely see.

"I'm pleased with our arrangement," he said. "You pay, I keep quiet. And the police go on searching in all the wrong places. It happened so long ago, they'll never find their way back to the truth. Do you have the money?"

The shadow held up a plastic bag and put it down on the snow. "It's all here." Without another word, the shadow turned and walked away into the night.

Savouring the moment, McNeil walked unhurriedly to where his reward lay. He picked it up and plunged his fingers into the bag to seize the bills, then froze — his fist was full of matchbooks.

Furiously dumping out the contents of the bag, he roared in anger. He was about to set off in pursuit of the shadow when he heard a noise behind him: a hiss on the snow.

With the knife in his hand, he turned sharply. A skier was approaching at high speed.

The skier stopped and McNeil relaxed. He was about to walk away when he realized that the skier was watching him. A shudder raced up his spine — the skier was drawing back a bowstring, aiming at him.

The psychiatrist knew that if he wanted to survive, he'd have to make it to the cover of the trees. He started to run as fast as he could. A whistling sound near his ear alerted him; he dived to his left and rolled.

The arrow hadn't missed by much.

McNeil jumped to his feet and started running again. He glanced over his shoulder and saw that his pursuer was in motion, gaining fast.

The line of trees was getting closer. No more than a hundred metres, he estimated. He could make it.

Once he was among the trees, anything could happen. For one thing, the trunks and boughs would deflect arrows; for another, speed would no longer be a factor. The skis might even be a disadvantage. And at close quarters, with his knife, he could do some damage.

At that moment, Mark McNeil was cursing himself for having left his phone in the car. But he was glad of the rigorous training program that he'd followed in recent years.

Just a few more metres …

The trees were close. He could practically touch their branches.

Panting, he took refuge behind the trunk of a large spruce. The knife was trembling in his hand. Had his attacker followed him into the trees? He had to get his breathing under control, so as not to give away his position.

Little by little, his auditory awareness became sharper. He heard the wind's shriek, the swaying of the boughs, and, farther off, the street traffic.

No sound of footsteps. No cracking of snow or rustling of branches. McNeil risked a look toward the spot where the skier should be.

Nobody. He was alone.

With infinite caution, the psychiatrist turned and began to walk, bent low. He paused every ten metres to listen before continuing his progress. Suddenly he stopped. His eye had glimpsed something, ahead and to the right.

The skier appeared in front of him, features concealed by a hood, fingers poised near his mouth, drawing back the bowstring, ready to let fly. The psychiatrist began to shake. Where had he come from?

McNeil wanted to run, to dive into the sheltering vegetation, but fear had frozen his limbs. He couldn't take his eyes off the bow.

His heart was pounding. His lips were twisted in a bitter rictus. "Please," he heard himself murmur, "not like this."

An image imprinted itself on his retinas: his assailant's thumb and forefinger releasing their hold. The arrow left the bow, whispering.

Thoughts flashed through his mind. His desire to live had never been as intense as it was at this moment. All the years he'd believed he had left were vanishing, slipping from his grasp, flying away among the trees. He thought of his wife, of his daughter.

The little girl loved him. He would never see her grow up, and he had only himself to blame. He thought of the gambling demon that he'd allowed to crawl into his life — into their lives.

Knowing all the mental processes by which people became pathological gamblers, he had imagined himself stronger than the disease, protected from it.

McNeil's eyes widened. His brain knew it was too late; he couldn't escape the projectile hurtling toward him. His thoughts sped up as the arrow whistled through the air. Only nanoseconds remained before impact. The whirling of his mind ended in questions.

What would have happened if he'd been honest with Marsha from the start? He was convinced that she loved him. But what did that even mean? Did she love him genuinely, or merely for what he represented? McNeil had never reflected on this. Now he would never know the truth.

The arrow reached its destination, shattering the breastbone, piercing the heart. His mouth half opened. His fingers tensed, then released their grip on the knife. A second arrow entered his throat. His lifeless body collapsed to its knees and toppled backward.

His staring eyes no longer saw the outline of the trees.

52

VIDEO CLIP

Saturday, December 24th

The ringing of his cellphone roused Victor from a deep sleep. Stretching out his arm, he groped along the bedside table for the phone. His elbow knocked over the bottle of sleeping pills, then bumped a glass, which teetered for a moment, hanging between solidity and empty space, then tipped over and fell to the floor. Sitting up in a tangle of damp sheets, Victor opened his eyes and was blinded by daylight.

Rubbing his eyes, he glanced at his watch.

Why had Nadja let him sleep so late? Their arrangement was crystal clear: she was supposed to wake him up before leaving. Period. Silence reigned in the apartment. Where was she?

The echo of her name bounced off the walls.

Victor squeezed the bridge of his nose; the pain was harsh and throbbing. No surprise there. Both his nostrils were completely blocked. He remained immobile for a long moment. Then, straightening his back, he got off the bed.

His feet came down into a viscous substance.

He looked at his toes — the crumpled tissues beside the bed were now floating in water. Luckily, the glass hadn't broken. When he bent over to pick it up, Victor realized that the pain in his lower back and buttock had returned.

Feeling a cold coming on, he found decongestants in the medicine cabinet and swallowed them in a cocktail consisting of his antacid, an antidepressant, and some anti-inflammatories.

In an effort to chase away his depression, he broke his usual habit and took out the package of regular coffee that he kept in the refrigerator for emergencies.

After fetching his cellphone, he opened the kitchen window and lit a cigarette. Someone had left him a message while he was in the bathroom. Confidential number.

Victor recognized the nasal voice of Lawson's assistant.

"Detective Lessard, it's Adèle Thibault. I'm not sure this is the right thing to do, but I'm calling to let you know that Mr. Rivard left a message on my voice mail late Wednesday, cancelling all his appointments for the next day. Then, yesterday, without contacting anyone, he failed to show up at the office, even though he had several important meetings scheduled. Nobody here has been able to reach him. I thought you might want to know."

Victor shook his head, blew smoke out his nostrils, and saved the message.

Given the tension that had existed between the police and Baker Lawson Watkins since the investigation opened, the detective sergeant knew that Paul Delaney would want to speak personally to one of the firm's partners to get information about Louis-Charles Rivard's absences.

The chief answered on the first ring and listened without interruption as Victor told him about Thibault's call. Victor went on to describe the previous night's operation in a few flat sentences: they'd stayed at McNeil's house until 5:00 a.m. and had found a pair of skis, which they'd sent to forensics to see if they matched the tracks found in Summit Woods. Patrol officers had also been posted in front of the suspect's house with instructions to call if McNeil turned up.

"Do you think McNeil's on the run?" Delaney asked.

Victor blew out a cloud of smoke as he pulled on a pair of jeans. "No idea, Paul. But it definitely isn't a good sign that he's gone missing at the same time as Rivard. We can talk about it shortly. I'm just getting dressed, then I'll come to the office."

"Did you try to triangulate McNeil's phone?"

"It didn't work. Either the phone was off, or it was in a location where there was no signal."

"That's just great." Delaney coughed and took a minute before continuing. "Listen, there's no rush. It's Saturday. Jacinthe and Gilles haven't come in yet, and you're going on less than three hours' sleep. Let me see what I can find out about Rivard. I'll keep you posted."

Victor threw his cigarette butt in the toilet, then went to the kitchen to make some breakfast and have a cup of coffee. He saw a note on the counter that he hadn't noticed before. It made him smile for the first time:

You got in late (or early), and you looked so peaceful, I didn't have the heart to wake you up! Have a good day, my love.

See you tonight :)

N xx

Victor dragged himself down to Versailles. The elevator, bouncing from one floor to another without ever descending to ground level, was testing his patience. The Gnome arrived, freshly shaven, wearing a sharp grey suit and looking decidedly chipper.

At the sight of Lemaire, a sudden thought darted through the detective sergeant's mind. But he was unable to concentrate, and the thought slipped away. It was as though someone had removed his brain during the night and replaced it with mush.

Victor ran his hand over his days-old stubble. Looking down at his leather jacket, his frayed jeans, and his high-tops, he sighed wearily. "Hey, Gilles."

"Morning, Vic," Lemaire replied cheerfully. "Short night, eh?"

Victor nodded and closed his eyes, discouraged. "Tell me about it."

After a brief silence, the neural connections were re-established. "Hey, Gilles, before I forget … did I dream this, or did Jacinthe tell me yesterday that you'd found the names of the managers of Northern Industrial Textiles?"

The Gnome smiled. "No, you didn't dream it. With everything that was going on, I forgot to mention it to you."

"You ran the names through the Police Information Centre database?"

The ground-floor indicator finally lit up and the metal doors opened. The two detectives stepped onto the elevator and their conversation continued.

"That didn't turn up anything, but Loïc helped me find the three managers. One of them died of cancer in 2005. Another one is in a long-term care facility — Alzheimer's. The third one is the former president of the company, which was dissolved in 1974. I spoke to him yesterday. He doesn't know Harper, and it took him a while to remember Lawson. He says it's been at least thirty years since they spoke. He only dealt with Lawson's firm on a few occasions, and he doesn't remember any particular files that might have sparked his interest." Silence. "That's why I forgot to mention it. Unless I'm very much mistaken, those three managers have nothing to do with our murders."

"Strange," the detective sergeant murmured, gazing vacantly into space.

With bags under her eyes, Taillon shuffled into the conference room at 10:54 a.m. holding two Red Bulls in one hand and a box of donuts in the other. She placed her cargo on the table, seemed to consider saying something, then contented herself with a yawn. After cracking her knuckles one by one, she popped the first can and brought it to her lips. She emptied it in a few gulps and put it back on the table. She burped loudly, with a satisfied smile. "When did you get here, Lessard?"

Frowning, Victor hit the remote control to freeze the video image on the screen. "About an hour ago," he said, turning to his partner.

"Want one?" Jacinthe asked, biting into a raspberry jelly donut that left a residue of icing sugar at the corners of her mouth.

Bothered by Adèle Thibault's phone message about Rivard's absences, Victor had spent the last few minutes viewing the same video clip repeatedly.

"Later, maybe. Take a look at this."

The clip showed Louis-Charles Rivard speaking to journalists at the unscheduled scrum he'd held with reporters after the police press conference:

"If, for any reason, you're afraid to speak to the police, call me directly. No matter what happened, we can find common ground. Get in touch. I have what you're looking for."

Taillon took a sip from her second can of Red Bull, which she seemed determined to savour this time. She shrugged. "Yeah, so?"

"Come on. Aren't you struck by anything?"

Victor replayed the end of the clip. "Listen closely …"

Rivard's face appeared in close-up. "Get in touch. I have what you're looking for."

"What's the big deal?"

"You don't find that odd? What does he mean by 'I have what you're looking for'?"

"Come on, Lessard, it's as plain as the eyes on your face. He's willing to pay a ransom. He has money. That's all he's saying."

Victor sighed and rolled his eyes. His partner's lack of imagination irritated him. "As plain as the *nose* on my face, Jacinthe," he said through clenched teeth. "And no, I don't think that's all he's saying. At a time when we were simply publicizing Lawson's disappearance, he was already talking about a kidnapping. It's just hit me. He's sending a message to someone. He's speaking to the person who killed Lawson and Harper. He's saying he has something the killer wants."

Jacinthe's brow furrowed in puzzlement.

Victor's gaze strayed vacantly over the wall behind her. "We were wrong about Rivard and McNeil. They're both dead."

The Red Bull came out Jacinthe's nose, and she started coughing for all she was worth.

53

A QUESTION OF PROFILE

After wiping her face with a hastily grabbed paper towel, Jacinthe had voiced her opposition to Victor's theory about Louis-Charles Rivard's remarks to the cameras, and she'd thrown in a mean crack about Victor jumping to conclusions. The detective sergeant had leaped to his feet, pointed a finger at his partner, and opened his mouth to spew out invective. Then, changing his mind, he'd walked away without a word.

Striding quickly through the detectives' room, he was heading for the exit when Jacinthe, almost at a run, caught him in the corridor. Seizing his arm, she forced him to turn around. "What? What did I say?"

For a long time, they glared at each other in silence. One wrong word and they'd both go thermonuclear. A light that Jacinthe hadn't seen in a long time burned in Victor's eyes, then went out.

"Everything I say, you contradict," he said at last, through clenched teeth.

"I didn't know I had to agree with whatever came out of your mouth."

"It all depends on how you go about it, Jacinthe! Do you really need to be so unpleasant all the time?"

Taillon lowered her eyes. He had a point. "Where are you going?"

Victor took a deep breath and unclenched his fists. His anger was back under control. "To Rivard's apartment. He hasn't shown up at the office in two days."

"Another disappearance! In case you hadn't noticed, we don't have a warrant."

"Since when do we need a warrant to visit someone? Move your ass, we've wasted enough time."

An evil little smile appeared on Jacinthe's lips. She had no idea what had stung her partner, but she liked this Lessard 2.0 just fine.

In the car, Victor took two donuts out of the box that his partner had brought along and ate them in silence, chewing each bite with care. Jacinthe tried to make peace by asking why he thought Rivard and McNeil were dead. Victor answered that it was more a matter of intuition than certainty. He was convinced, he said again, that Rivard had sent a message to the murderer. With the lawyer now missing, it was logical to conclude that the killer had eliminated him.

"As far as I'm concerned," Jacinthe said, "McNeil is the killer."

Victor shook his head. "I'd have said the same thing yesterday, but now I doubt it. Look how easily the puzzle pieces fell into place. And when you think about it, Jacinthe, some of the elements we're working with are questionable."

"Which ones?"

"The fridge magnets, for instance. Why would a brilliant, educated man like McNeil use magnets taken from his own refrigerator?"

Taillon remarked that murderers often gave themselves away in stupid ways, through errors of judgment no sensible person would commit.

Victor conceded the point, but observed that that was generally true of what they referred to as "little murders," those involving alcoholism, addiction, domestic violence, etc.

"This isn't one of those cases," the detective sergeant said. "And I can give you other reasons. Think about the sophistication of the murder weapon. Think about the level of planning that went into these killings. After going to all that trouble, would McNeil really drop the ball on a stupid detail like fridge magnets? I don't think so, Jacinthe. He's too smart to leave such an obvious piece of evidence in his wake. It doesn't fit the profile."

"What about the skis?" Taillon asked.

"We haven't heard back from forensics, but I'll be surprised if the snow tracks in Summit Woods match McNeil's skis." Silence. "We were blinded by the prospect of making a quick arrest. McNeil isn't our killer, Jacinthe. Maybe he's indirectly involved in the case, or maybe someone set him up so we'd suspect him, but something doesn't fit. We've got to figure out what, and soon, or we're going to find more bodies in our path."

Jacinthe's heels clicked on the brick pavement. The calcium flakes that had been put down to melt the ice were crackling under her soles. The entrance to Rivard's apartment building was located on Cours Le Royer, a pedestrian street in the heart of Old Montreal. After a knock at the door of the unit at the end of the hallway went unanswered, Jacinthe screened Victor from view as he bent over to pick the lock.

Concealed by her bulk, he was practically invisible. Beads of sweat appeared on his forehead. The lock was proving trickier than he'd expected.

"Yes, Your Honour," Jacinthe whispered, chuckling, "we just came to pay Mr. Rivard a visit. When we saw the door ajar, we decided to step inside."

The lock finally turned.

Victor released his breath and wiped the sweat from his brow.

"Just a quick look, okay?" he said, handing a pair of latex gloves to his partner. "If anyone catches us here ..."

The loft was spacious and light filled, with designer furniture and a minimalist décor that featured two paintings by the same artist — portraits of distorted, agonized faces — as well as a flat-screen TV that took up the better part of one wall and a Swedish sound system.

Or was it Finnish? Véronique, his ex, had bought the same system, but he couldn't remember where it was made. He'd never forgotten the price she paid, though. It was nearly half his annual income.

Jacinthe went straight to the glass-topped desk, on which there was a telephone, a computer, a fax machine, and a few papers. She poked through them with a fingertip, then emptied the contents of the recycling basket onto the bed. Victor did a quick search of the kitchen before heading to the bathroom.

Looking over the bottles and tubes carefully arrayed on the glass shelf, he couldn't help smiling. What would Taillon have said about Rivard's panoply of toiletries, if she was prepared to call Victor a metrosexual just because he made an effort to stay in shape?

Finding nothing of interest, he went back into the main space and looked around, allowing his brain to process what he was seeing.

He was searching for something incongruous, something that might seem like it was in the right place, but wasn't. A feeling of urgency and frustration took hold of him: they had to work fast. Yet, at first glance, everything seemed to be in order.

"Did you try the computer?" he asked.

His partner had sat down on the leather office chair and was tapping the telephone keypad with one hand; with the other, she scribbled on a slip of paper.

"I can't get into the computer; it's password protected. I'm taking down his calls. The last one dates back to Tuesday."

The detective sergeant pointed at the papers spread out over the bed. Jacinthe shook her head to indicate that she hadn't found anything noteworthy.

With the stress forming a knot in his stomach, Victor examined the bookshelf for a moment. Apart from some automotive magazines, there were only a few law books. Rivard clearly wasn't much of a reader.

A pile of DVDs lay on a coffee table: *Platoon*, *Saving Private Ryan*, *The Thin Red Line*. Nothing but war movies. How sad.

Victor looked anxiously at his watch. This was taking too long.

"We should look at the fax machine, too," he said, while rummaging through the contents of several drawers. "Some models store recent messages in memory."

Without looking up from her work, Taillon laughed loudly. "Get real, Lessard! Do I look like a computer geek to you?"

Having seen Adams execute the manoeuvre on several occasions, Victor thought he might be able to pull it off himself. Examining the device, he pressed a few buttons. The interior purred. A sheet slid into the feeder and the rollers began to turn.

"Some machines print the newest messages first," the detective sergeant observed. "Others start with the oldest."

The ring of his cellphone made him jump. The caller ID showed that it was the Gnome. Before answering, Victor took a deep breath to calm himself.

"Hello, Gilles …" His expression darkened. "What?! Where? … Yes, she's with me. Hmm? … No, nothing important … I'll explain later. We'll meet you there, okay?"

Victor ended the call. Jacinthe frowned. She could see that the news wasn't good.

"What's going on?"

"They've found another body in Parc Maisonneuve."

"Who is it? McNeil or Rivard?"

"They're not sure yet, but they think it's McNeil." The two cops looked at each other in silence. "What have you got?"

Jacinthe handed him the slip of paper on which she had noted the numbers of the ten calls recorded on Rivard's land line. Four of the calls were from the same number. The fax machine spat out a sheet. Jacinthe picked it up and saw that it was the first page of a ten-page contract.

"Shit! We're not finished here. I'll go down to the car and send this to the office," she said, referring to the numbers she'd jotted down, "so we can find out who we're dealing with. Come down when you're done."

After Jacinthe left, Victor paced back and forth as the fax machine's steady rumble filled the room. Anxiety levels were rising inside him. He had taken this initiative without considering its consequences. Now he was coming to the realization that entering Rivard's apartment illegally hadn't been a brilliant move. It might even get them into serious trouble.

The fax machine hiccuped. Victor went over to it, supposing that it had regurgitated all its contents. But a light was flashing: another printout was on its way.

"Damn machine," he muttered.

Back in the Crown Victoria, Taillon used the onboard computer to send the phone numbers to the office. Then she tried to reach Lucie. Not getting an answer, she left a message on the voice mail at home. She looked at her watch. Where was Lucie?

Even after all these years, Jacinthe's insecurity hadn't loosened its grip. She was still convinced that without her loving companion, everything would crumble, nothing would have meaning. Lucie was the invisible thread that kept her connected to the world. If the thread broke, she'd be a broken marionette, lifeless, useless.

Jacinthe's gaze got lost in the snowbank. The previous day's snowfall had left several centimetres on the ground. Losing patience, she was reaching into her pocket for her phone when Lessard came out of the building with a sheaf of papers under his arm.

He walked quickly to the Crown Vic and got in.

"Well?" Jacinthe demanded, activating the emergency lights.

In his eagerness to leave Rivard's apartment as soon as possible, the detective sergeant hadn't yet looked at the documents he'd scooped out of the fax machine's tray. After buckling his seat belt, he put the pile on his knees and started leafing through the pages.

"Contract … legal opinion … contract …" he said, licking his forefinger.

The Crown Vic was already racing along Notre-Dame East.

"We'll take Pie-IX," Jacinthe said to herself, working out the fastest route to Parc Maisonneuve.

Victor froze.

Carefully singling out one of the sheets, he removed it from the pile and examined it, holding his breath with an intensity that seemed almost religious.

"What is it? Talk to me, Lessard! Have you found something?"

"I think so." He nodded, angling the paper toward her so she could see it.

On the sheet, a hanged man was sticking his tongue out, accompanied by an invitation to Lawson:

```
Good morning, Nathan. Let's play hangman:
```

Next to the hanged man was a handwritten note that looked as if it had been scribbled in a hurry:

L–C, where are you?
I left a message on your cell
Will call back tonight
Need your help
This is fucking urgent
Nathan

54

GROUND SEARCH

The line was advancing in synchronized order. The movements of each officer were measured, precise, regular.

Ahead of the officers, the dogs were eagerly sniffing the ground, their snouts grazing the snow, stirring it. Having begun at the park entrance, the ground search was progressing toward the trees and the location where the body had been discovered.

Jacinthe and Victor went around the line, passing it on the right side. Constable Giguère, a few paces ahead of them on the marked-out path, spoke without turning. "This is their second pass. The first time around, they found ski tracks and matchbooks. Nothing else."

The constable's ears had taken on an ugly purple hue and looked like they might imminently disintegrate into powder. At the foot of the rise, he pointed to four red stakes that the forensics team had strung together with yellow plastic tape.

Those stakes, Giguère explained, marked the spot where the dogs had found the matchbooks, which had been partially covered by the previous night's snowfall.

Despite the fact that Jacinthe, like the other cops, had put on boots adapted for conditions in the park, she was having trouble keeping her balance and following them. Reaching the top of the rise, she leaned on Victor to catch her breath. A few metres farther on, Constable Giguère held back a fir branch to let them through. The three officers stepped into a little clearing surrounded by a circle of trees. A flashbulb flared, capturing the body and the red-stained snow.

Two forensics technicians were using shovels to dig out the corpse. They were working in silence, each gesture methodical and painstaking.

While Giguère rejoined his team, the Gnome, who'd been crouching beside the dead man, stood up and came over to Victor and Jacinthe. Wearing a knitted Canadiens hat that he'd borrowed from one of his children, he looked like a twelve-year-old.

"It's McNeil," he said, anticipating their question. "His heart and throat have been pierced. Berger will have to confirm this, but one of the techs says the marks look like arrow wounds. He was killed a short distance away, then his body was dragged here. He was found by a man walking in the park. Or, rather, by the man's dog."

The psychiatrist was lying on his back. Ice crystals had accumulated on his face, shrouding his features in a translucent film.

"What's with the matchbooks?" the detective sergeant asked. "Do they mean something?"

The Gnome shrugged. "No idea. We just found McNeil's car parked on Rosemont Boulevard. He'd hidden a bag of cash under the driver's seat — fifteen thousand in small bills. His cellphone was on the passenger seat. Now we know why he couldn't be located. He'd turned it off. I went through the call log. Nothing."

"What about the ski tracks?" Jacinthe asked. "Do they match the ones in Summit Woods?"

"They do," Lemaire said. "One of the forensics people just gave me the confirmation. They also determined that McNeil's skis are wider than the tracks here and in Summit Woods."

"We kinda figured that, Gilles," Jacinthe snapped. "Otherwise I wouldn't be standing here freezing my tits off."

Victor couldn't take his eyes off the body. He was thinking of McNeil's wife, whom they had met the evening before, and his daughter, who would grow up without him. The little girl would bear the scars all her life, just as his own DNA had been marked, decades ago, by the death of his family. Leaving the cover of the trees, he walked a few paces.

The line of police searchers had passed the red stakes and was now approaching the base of the hill. Victor closed his eyes and tried to visualize the scene, to get a mental picture of what had happened. He imagined the psychiatrist and the skier meeting at the base of the slope.

In his head, he re-enacted McNeil's movements. At one point, fearing for his life, McNeil had fled up the rise, trying to find safety among the trees.

The detective sergeant pictured the killer drawing his bowstring, coldly, methodically, his arrow flashing through the air under the psychiatrist's horrified gaze. When Victor reopened his eyes, an idea had fixed itself firmly in his mind, dominating all others — an intuition he couldn't have explained.

He was roused from his reverie by the sound of Jacinthe's breathing as she came up behind him with the grace of a dump truck.

"McNeil and the killer knew each other," he said without turning. "He wasn't scared."

While Jacinthe drove at breakneck speed through traffic, Victor, gripping the dashboard, reached Paul Delaney by phone and communicated his initial impressions on the subject of McNeil's death. First: the ski tracks eliminated all doubts; the skier in Summit Woods was definitely linked to the case. And second: the fact that the murderer had used a different weapon from the one that had killed the first two victims was particularly intriguing to the two cops. What had motivated this change in modus operandi? The possibility of a serial killer was raised once again. Changes of method were frequent in such cases.

Then the conversation turned to the psychiatrist himself.

"The fridge-magnet numbers, the call from Harper the day she disappeared, the fact that Lawson's firm had defended McGill ... it all added up to make Mark McNeil the perfect suspect. It was too good to be true, Paul." Annoyance and frustration filled the detective sergeant's voice.

"Let's not throw out the baby with the bathwater," Delaney said prudently. "His death proves he was involved. We just don't know how. Lab analysis will tell us whether the fridge magnets at McNeil's house are from the same set as the ones found in Harper's apartment." Silence. "And there was surely a reason why he had fifteen grand under his car seat."

When they finished discussing the subject, Victor decided it was time to confess. "There's something I need to tell you, Chief. You won't be happy about what we did, but you'll like what we found."

Without hesitating, Victor told his commanding officer about the illegal entry into Rivard's apartment.

The admission was met with silence.

"What did you find?" Delaney finally said with a sigh, clearly irritated by his team members' irregular methods.

Victor gave him a detailed description of the hangman drawing that had come out of Rivard's fax machine.

Delaney erupted in a prolonged fit of coughing. "Sorry. I just choked on my own spit." He coughed again. "Okay. This is the proof we were looking for: Lawson really did receive a threatening message. But there's something I don't get. Why did he turn to Rivard for help?"

Victor took some time to ponder the question before answering.

"What do we know, Paul? In response to the threat conveyed by the drawing of the hanged man, Lawson left the office with a file in his possession."

"The Northern file."

"Right. Now, as though by coincidence, that same file is nowhere to be found, and Rivard seems to have gone missing. I could be wrong, but it sure seems like the two men were in communication." Silence. "So, what can we conclude?"

"That Lawson had Rivard recover the file," Delaney said.

"I don't see any other explanation. I'd say our top priority is to figure out what Rivard did with it."

Victor then explained his theory about the message that Rivard had sent out during his press conference.

Get in touch. I have what you're looking for.

"So, if I'm understanding you right," Delaney said, "since Lawson's dead, Rivard must be trying to get the Northern file into someone else's hands."

"That's what I believe. That file is the heart of the case, Paul. The text beside the drawing of the hanged man talks about a company filled with corpses." Silence. "But there are two details I don't understand. One: Gilles talked to the former president of Northern Industrial Textiles. Based on what he learned, that company has nothing to do with our case. And two: I tried every way I could think of, but the name 'Northern Industrial' doesn't fit the spaces for the secret word."

There was a pregnant silence as each man reflected on all this. Finally, Victor spoke.

"We should get Baker Lawson Watkins to help us, Paul. We really need information about that company file."

"I left a message with the managing partner. Trust me, with Rivard missing, they'll collaborate."

"Okay. Should we hold a press conference to announce that he's disappeared?"

"It's too soon. Let's put out a press release for now, and make sure it goes out to every police force."

"I have a feeling Rivard is dead, Paul."

"I'll grant you, his disappearance is suspicious. All the more so now that McNeil's body has been found. But I'd say it's premature to conclude that Rivard is dead. In fact, I'm wondering whether we should view him as a possible suspect. Especially if we believe the Northern file is in his possession."

"That makes no sense, Paul. If Rivard were the killer, do you really think Lawson would have faxed him the drawing of the hanged man and asked for his help?"

"It wouldn't be the first time a victim trusted his killer," Delaney replied.

Victor decided for diplomacy's sake not to press the point. He changed the subject. "Any word from Berger?"

"He's on his way to the park. By the way, I don't know if you've checked your emails, but he finished Lawson's autopsy. He confirms that death occurred Monday night, Tuesday morning at the latest."

"The nineteenth," Victor said, counting on his fingers.

"Right. Toxicology results won't come in for another week."

Before hanging up, Delaney promised to call as soon as he heard from the law firm's managing partner. As Victor pocketed his phone, Jacinthe's idea about a timer resurfaced in his mind. Could Lawson have gone for days without food or drink, unable to sit or lie down, with the heretic's fork piercing his chin and breastbone? Victor put his face in his hands and sighed. The churning of his brain cells made his head feel like it was about to explode.

The hangman picture had been received by Rivard's fax machine on Friday, December 16th, at 1:40 p.m., as indicated by the time stamp at the top of the document. The name and number of the originating fax machine were also indicated. Jacinthe and Victor had tracked it down to a business centre in the Côte-des-Neiges district.

They parked the Crown Victoria in front of the premises and went in. The place was empty, except for a clerk eating his lunch at the counter.

Putting down his sandwich, with traces of mustard clinging to his lips, the clerk looked at the photograph Victor showed him, then began bobbing his head and gesticulating so animatedly that the detective sergeant was sure he'd start talking instantly. But the clerk took an eternity to chew his mouthful.

"I remember him," he said at last, swallowing his food. He was confirming that he'd seen Nathan Lawson.

He reached for a Thermos on the counter, poured himself a cup of coffee, and drained it in a gulp without flinching. "He came in last Friday afternoon. Had me send a fax, then left. I remember, because you're not the first ones to ask about him."

After looking at each other in surprise, the two detectives bombarded the clerk with questions, but all they could get from him was a vague description: a young man in his thirties had come in the day after Lawson. He'd been wearing a toque and a black coat. No accent or distinguishing features. A thoroughly ordinary guy.

"He wanted to know who the old man had sent a fax to. He also asked what was in the fax. When I told him it was none of his business, he didn't argue."

"Then what?" Victor asked.

"Then nothing," the clerk said. "He walked out."

"And you didn't find that weird?" Jacinthe demanded.

"Listen, lady," the clerk said, moving a forefinger in circles next to his temple, "if I started getting upset every time some oddball wandered in here ..."

The clerk picked up his sandwich and bit into it. A fragment of ham and a shred of lettuce hung from his lip, but he sucked them into his mouth. With a sigh and a shake of her head, Jacinthe went to the door. She wasn't about to wait an hour while he finished chewing.

Victor thanked the clerk and handed him a business card, asking him to call if he remembered anything else. Then he joined Jacinthe on the sidewalk. The detective sergeant gazed along the street, where the tree branches were sagging under their cotton-ball burden.

A mechanical clatter made the two cops turn. They stepped aside to let a sidewalk plow go by and watched it disappear around the corner, leaving a low furrow of snow on the curb.

"No news from the documents expert?" Taillon growled.

Victor coughed out the smoke from the cigarette he'd just lit.

Less than an hour had gone by since they'd sent her a copy of the hanged man. "Mona Vézina? How about we calm down and give her time to examine the thing."

Jacinthe was venting her ill temper, kicking away the ice that had accumulated on the Crown Vic's wheel wells, when "Who Let the Dogs Out" began to play. Her ringtone. She answered and had a brief, monosyllabic conversation.

Victor looked for a more suitable place than the snowbank to toss his cigarette, but failed to find one. He flicked it away.

Jacinthe's expression had darkened.

"Something wrong?"

"It's about the phone calls made from Rivard's land line."

"The four calls to the same number?"

"No. Those were to some chick he's fucking. The others were to his dentist, his mother, and various other lawyers in the firm. None of them raise any flags. Except the last one. The one he made last Tuesday."

"And who was that special someone?"

"Senator Daniel Tousignant."

55

PURSE CALL

Victor took a drag on his cigarette as he watched the ice floes drifting in the current. His gaze rose to the Mercier Bridge, where a few motorists were crossing the rusted-out ruin, taking their lives in their hands.

Built on a rise overlooking the river in the district of LaSalle, Daniel Tousignant's Tudor-style house stood a short distance from the historic Fleming windmill. In another life, Victor had accompanied his kids for rides on the bike path that ran along LaSalle Boulevard.

Senator Tousignant's reputation preceded him. He was a distinguished lawyer who had amassed a considerable fortune through real estate investments. After liquidating his assets, he had begun the philanthropic activities that made him one of the most respected men in Quebec.

His foundation, which promoted environmental causes, was often compared to David Suzuki's organization. Despite having no known political ties, he had been named to the Senate a few years previously.

A charismatic man renowned for his affability, Tousignant was one of those rare individuals capable of assembling diametrically opposed personalities in support of a project. He had a gift for getting sworn enemies to work together for a common cause.

Considering the man's public image, the detectives weren't happy to see his phone number linked to Rivard, who was now being sought by every police force in the province because of his possible involvement in three murders.

Questioning a man like Tousignant wasn't something Victor and Jacinthe could attempt without first consulting their boss. Paul Delaney hadn't opposed the idea, and he'd assuaged their worries by informing them that Lawson and Tousignant had been colleagues in the past. The senator was a founding partner in one of the firms that had merged to form Baker Lawson Watkins.

With that in mind, Delaney had put forward a hypothesis: maybe Rivard had simply contacted Tousignant to update him on the subject of Lawson's disappearance, and later regarding his death.

Victor had assumed that he'd have to deal with a succession of assistants, but the senator had answered his phone personally. He'd shown no unease when Victor identified himself as a police detective, and he'd made no inquiry as to why the police wanted to talk to him. He spoke with the calm assurance of a man whose conscience was clear.

Despite the senator's openness, Victor had been taken aback when Tousignant, whose schedule must surely be as busy as a prime minister's, had agreed to talk to the detectives at his home right away. Though Victor wasn't expecting to be greeted by a butler or a liveried footman, he was nonetheless surprised when Tousignant himself opened the front door.

Straight-backed despite his seventy-nine years, with a ruddy complexion and silky white hair, Senator Tousignant had the natural charm of a good-looking man. His alert grey-eyed gaze was direct and disarming.

It was hard not to like the man from the moment you met him.

Even before he spoke, something about him inspired an eagerness to earn his approval. The effect became only more powerful when he opened his mouth. He had a warm, deep voice, with a subtle hint of vulnerability; a voice that could convince anyone of anything.

Tousignant greeted the detectives with courtesy, offering them a cup of coffee so cordially that neither of them was able to refuse. As the senator prepared the beverages in the kitchen, Victor was tempted to pinch himself. He couldn't remember the last time he'd seen Taillon drink coffee in the afternoon.

Carrying the tray, Tousignant led them through a succession of beautiful rooms. After the fifth crystal chandelier, Victor stopped counting. As they walked, the senator offered detailed accounts of how this eighteenth-century cabinet had been assembled, or how that painting showcased the artist's genius for colour composition.

And it was all done simply, without vanity or pretension, for the pure pleasure of sharing with his guests the depth of knowledge that he had acquired over the years.

They stepped into his private study, the door of which was covered in red leather. The walls of the room were entirely taken up by floor-to-ceiling bookshelves.

On every shelf, leather-bound books stood in tight ranks. A solid oak desk faced the big bay window, offering a view of the river. A stream of light licked the hardwood floor at their feet.

The senator set the tray down on a low table, handed cups to the detectives, then settled into a velvet armchair and gestured for the officers to sit down on the wide couch.

"Well," Victor said, a little intimidated, "your study certainly is an inspiring space."

He glanced sidelong at Jacinthe. She was sitting on the couch in a stiff posture that was at odds with her usual style.

"You're right, Detective Lessard. I never grow tired of looking at the river."

Victor's eyes drifted downward. He and Jacinthe had removed their footwear at the door. He suddenly felt ridiculous asking questions in his socks. He coughed and cleared his throat.

"I know you're very busy, Senator, so we won't take up too much of your time."

Tousignant waved a hand dismissively. "People think I'm busier than I really am. I still attend quarterly board meetings, but I've withdrawn from active management of my foundation. It's true that I sit in the Senate. But we all know what critics say about the workload senators have to carry." Tousignant winked and leaned forward in his chair, speaking in a confidential tone. "Between you and me, I sometimes think the critics are right."

His shoulders shook as he laughed.

"I'm sorry," the old man said, straightening up again. "I'm the one who should be careful not to take up *your* time. I imagine you've come to talk about Nathan." He turned pensive. "When you reach my age, friends pass away more and more often, but I have to admit, the news of Nathan's death, under those circumstances, came as a shock. What an awful way to go ..." He cast his gaze downward for a moment, as though in prayer. "You're aware that I'm the one who gave him his first job as a lawyer?"

Victor confirmed their knowledge of that fact. The senator, no doubt feeling nostalgic, spoke of "shining, faraway youth," of his generation's idealism in an age when all of Quebec society was being redefined. But he wasn't long winded or tediously sentimental. He spoke with the sincerity of a man sharing memories with good friends.

A dialogue got underway between the detective sergeant and the senator, with Jacinthe looking on in silence. Tousignant asked many of the questions himself before answering them, while Victor nodded in encouragement or intervened to request further details.

Unfortunately, the senator said, he and Lawson had followed divergent paths. Little by little, they had lost touch over the years. But he had great admiration for Nathan, who had become one of Montreal's most influential lawyers. Tousignant couldn't remember the last time they had seen each other, but it was a few years ago, at least. He regretted that he hadn't had the chance to see Lawson again before ...

In short, his death had been a great loss to the legal and business communities.

"Do you know Louis-Charles Rivard? He's a lawyer who worked closely with Mr. Lawson."

"I'd never heard of him until I saw him give that press conference after Nathan's disappearance was made public. I called him at the office to offer my help, and to assure him that he could count on my financial support for the payment of a ransom, if the need arose. It was the least I could do. Even if we no longer spent time together, Nathan was an old friend."

"Did you speak to him again?"

"To Rivard? No. Not after Nathan's body was found. But talking to you, I realize that I should call him, if only to offer my condolences." He lifted his cup and saucer with both hands and took a sip of coffee. "He's a smart young man, that Rivard. A bit rigid, though. Tell me, has your investigation made any progress?"

Without divulging sensitive information, Victor briefly summarized recent developments in the case. He watched Tousignant's face for a reaction, but all he saw was surprise and sympathy when he mentioned the psychiatrist's name. The detective sergeant didn't generally talk to civilians about active investigations, but he made an exception to his own rule out of respect for the man and because he wanted to prepare the ground for his next question.

"Listen, what I'm about to reveal to you is still confidential, but we have reason to believe Mr. Rivard has gone missing." A look of astonishment appeared on the senator's face. "We know he called you on the evening of the press conference." Victor told him about the call log. "I was hoping maybe you could give us some insight, that you might have information which would help us find a lead."

Tousignant held Victor's gaze. "You're right, Detective. The communication you're referring to did take place. It only lasted a couple of seconds. I could hear noises at the other end of the line. I tried to speak to him, but he didn't answer ... That kind of thing used to happen to my wife all the time. She'd be trying to find something in her purse. Her fingers would accidentally touch her phone keys, and she'd end up speed-dialing someone without realizing what she'd done. She even had a name for it," Tousignant said, smiling. "Purse call."

"That's strange," Victor said, frowning. "The call was placed from Mr. Rivard's home phone, not his cell." Silence. "You didn't call him back?"

"I had guests at the time. I told myself Rivard would dial again if it was important. Afterward, to tell you the truth, I forgot all about it."

"Have you ever heard of a company called Northern Industrial Textiles?" Victor asked.

Tousignant shook his head, putting a forefinger to his lips. "I don't think so. Is it a corporate client of Rivard's?"

Victor continued with a series of questions about the links that the senator had formerly had with Nathan Lawson. Tousignant answered willingly, making an effort to remember, going into detail whenever Victor asked him to. The exchange continued for several long minutes. The detective sergeant's questions were so rapid and aggressive that at last Jacinthe cleared her throat pointedly. Victor turned toward her, and there was a moment of awkward silence before he grasped the unspoken message.

"Senator," he said, getting up, "we'll stop annoying you with our questions. We've already taken up too much of your time."

Tousignant placed his cup and saucer on the desk and rose to his feet. "You haven't annoyed me in the least, Detective. On the contrary. I hope you won't hesitate to come back if there's any way I can help. My door is always open."

The old man stepped aside to let the cops pass, then, with silent strides, guided them back through the labyrinth to the front hall. He fetched their coats while they were putting on their footwear. Jacinthe had to sit down on a little bench, panting, as she pulled her boots on.

"One last question," Victor said as he slipped into his jacket. "Have you ever heard of Project MK-ULTRA?"

"The CIA experiments that were done at McGill? Of course. Everyone in my generation remembers MK-ULTRA. It was a huge scandal when it came out decades ago. Why do you ask?"

"We think there may be a connection between that program and some of our victims, including Nathan Lawson. Did you know that his firm was engaged to defend the university against certain civil suits?"

The senator scratched his head, looking like he was trying to remember. "That could very well be, but honestly, I don't remember. I can look in my archives, if you'd like ..."

Victor waved a hand.

"No, no, that won't be necessary. Thank you for your hospitality, Senator. And for your time."

The two men shook hands while Jacinthe, still struggling to zip up a boot, swore under her breath. Victor gave the senator an embarrassed smile.

The old man responded with a wink. "The pleasure was all mine, Detective."

Descending the driveway, they stepped out onto LaSalle Boulevard. Victor looked at the Crown Victoria and noticed that it was badly corroded by salt.

"Super-nice guy, eh?" Taillon said, visibly charmed by the old man.

Victor didn't answer.

Although he shared his partner's instinctive liking for Tousignant, a little voice in his head was counselling caution. The senator had answered all his questions without hesitation, clearly and coherently. The problem, Victor realized, lay with the abortive phone call: the purse call. Rivard hadn't dialed the number by mistake. Why had he made the call?

Victor reached into his pocket for his cigarettes.

A gust of wind swept through his hair, and he shivered. The humidity was chilling him to the bone.

Why had the senator shown so much concern over a former colleague with whom he was no longer in touch?

For that matter, what was the real reason behind the fact that the two men hadn't seen each other in years? Was it just happenstance, or had some ancient conflict driven them apart?

Victor made an effort to focus on the primary question: why would Rivard have contacted a man like the senator, if it wasn't to give him the Northern file?

Another possibility presented itself. An obvious one: was Rivard blackmailing Tousignant?

Taillon unlocked the doors of the Crown Vic.

Exhaling a final billow of smoke before getting into the car, Victor turned abruptly toward the house and thought he saw a curtain move on the upper floor.

56

LAST-MINUTE GIFTS

The entire world seemed to be conspiring to prevent their forward progress. Jacinthe growled and brought a fist down on the dashboard. Activating the siren and emergency lights, she got the car's two left wheels up onto the median.

After passing the traffic jam, she floored the accelerator. The Crown Vic shuddered, reared back, and leaped ahead in a clashing of gears. Gripping his seat as he was thrown left and right like a pinball, Victor fought off motion sickness by drawing hangmen in the frost on the window. Looking at her watch, Jacinthe had realized what a monumental bind they were in.

"Two hours left before the stores close," she declared amid a stream of profanity.

"Fuck," Victor said, clenching his jaw.

Their return to the office was a death-defying ride that would remain forever engraved on Victor's memory. More than once, he imagined himself embalmed, his waxen features at rest in a polished black coffin, hands folded across his chest. They entered the Place Versailles parking lot in a controlled skid, and Jacinthe left the car in an area reserved for emergency vehicles.

During the drive, Victor had called Lemaire to have him obtain call logs for the cellphones of Rivard and Tousignant. The detective sergeant wanted to know whether, despite the senator's claims, they had spoken more than once.

After that, Jacinthe and Victor had done their best to suggest gift ideas to each other, but neither of them had any inspirations that generated enthusiasm or sparked delight. They had both failed to do their Christmas shopping despite working above a shopping mall. Did that reveal a morbid appetite for risk, or was it just sheer negligence? Whatever the cause, the desperate state in which they rushed through the retail aisles was a sight to behold.

To hell with Christmas money for the kids. Victor decided to swing for the fences. With his credit card still sizzling in his back pocket and an electronics store bag under his arm, he couldn't resist imagining the surprise and joy that Martin and Charlotte would experience as they unwrapped their iPads.

Nadja was a thornier problem.

Failing to come up with a flash of brilliance, he finally decided to give her a getaway package at a spa in the Eastern Townships, which he would book online later. But having waited until the last minute, and knowing the certificate wouldn't arrive in the mail for a few days, he felt he should buy her something else, so as not to be empty handed.

Time was short and no other ideas were coming to him. So, feeling slightly intimidated, he entered the La Senza lingerie boutique. Checking the time on his phone, he was gripped by panic. With the shops due to close in thirty minutes, he still had to go to the liquor store to pick up a bottle for Ted, and he had to visit the flower shop for Albert, who loved roses. It was the very least he could do, considering that Ted and Albert were hosting dinner that evening. With a little luck, Victor would also have time to get his presents wrapped by the grey-haired ladies at the central kiosk.

"Can I help you?"

He must have seemed in distress, because, despite the fact that the store was full of women, a youthful salesgirl had come to his aid.

Awkwardly, he said he was looking for something for his girlfriend. When he was unable to be more specific, the salesgirl smiled and led him away among the displays.

Fortunately, she clearly had experience with customers like him. The operation went smoothly. A few minutes later, he was at the cash register, where the salesgirl rang up a black tulle baby-doll with pink cups and matching panties, a nightgown, and a pair of slippers.

Victor had paid for the purchase and was about to leave when he heard an all-too-familiar voice: "What did you buy, Lessard?"

Victor turned, reddening. Jacinthe was dawdling in the corset section.

Judging from the dimensions of the bustier in her hands, she was clearly shopping for Lucie. Even so, a mental image came to him of his partner wearing the lacy undergarment, flesh spilling out on all sides. He chased away the image and muttered something vague, then agreed to meet her upstairs after the shopping was done.

While he was waiting in the flower shop, he saw a reflection in the window.

The little boy, whose mother was behind Victor in line, must have been six years old. A zebra over one of the boy's hands was talking to a frog over the other hand. The child was entertaining himself with a pair of cloth puppets. The frog spoke:

"Mom says you're a cheater, Zo-Zo."

"No! Stop lying, Ping-Pong."

"Cheater, cheater, cheater!" the amphibian chanted.

The zebra opened its mouth and, with a roar, chomped the frog on the head.

"I'm not a zebra, Ping-Pong. I'm a wolf."

Emerging from the elevator with his arms full, Victor zigzagged among his fellow cops along the corridor. Some of his gifts had been encased in shining metallic paper. Others were in a cream-coloured wrapping adorned with red and green patterns.

Arriving at his desk, the detective sergeant put down his packages.

"Jesus, Lessard," a voice behind him exclaimed, "you sure didn't hold back, did you?"

"How about you?" he answered. "Find everything you wanted?"

Jacinthe said she had. Turning, Victor saw that she wasn't alone.

"Ah. Hello, Ms. Vézina," he said, greeting the documents expert.

Her presence in the office surprised him. She wouldn't have come if she hadn't found something important.

Jacinthe took a handful of cashews from a can and shoved them in her mouth. She always had a stash of snacks in her lower drawer. "We've been waiting for you," she said. She turned to the expert. "Show him what you showed me earlier, Mona."

On the desk, the documents expert laid a copy of the drawing Victor had sent her a few hours earlier. Three elements of the hanged man had been circled. Those three elements formed initials that no one had noticed in earlier examinations of the drawing, but that were now glaringly obvious:

JFK

57

CHRISTMAS EVE

Nadja was holding the steering wheel with one hand. With the other, she was squeezing his hand. At the red light, she gave him a languorous look that brought the world to a standstill. Time stopped in its tracks. Victor sighed and closed his eyes, then re-opened them, as though to be sure he wasn't dreaming.

He lowered the volume on Nat King Cole and turned with a loving expression to admire his children in the back seat: Martin and Charlotte were already young adults. They were arguing, as usual, but in a friendly, joking way.

"Oh yeah, great song. I just threw up a little bit in my mouth."

As far as Victor could tell, the song in question was by Avril Lavigne. Charlotte loved it, so naturally Martin was trashing it for the pleasure of making his sister indignant. Victor's fingers touched the volume button.

The music and the growl of the accelerating engine washed over the conversation, and he stopped listening. His smile widened.

It was 8:34 p.m. on December 24th.

Cottony clouds were sprinkling the city with snow.

Nadja found a parking space in front of the apartment building on Sir George-Étienne Cartier Square, where Albert Corneau and Ted Rutherford had lived forever. The two men had become a surrogate family for Victor after he had lost his own family under appalling circumstances. Since adoption by a same-sex couple would have been unheard of in the 1970s, Ted had convinced his secretary and her husband to adopt the lanky orphan.

Later, having inspired Victor to go to police college, Rutherford became his mentor during the early years of his career. They had even worked as partners briefly, before Ted's retirement.

The front door opened and Albert appeared on the threshold, wearing his trademark collarless white shirt. He was in his sixties, tall and trim, unaffected by age. Ted, in his wheelchair, was watching through the living room window.

He and Victor gazed at each other for a moment.

The older man nodded his head, eyes shining, happy to be welcoming them into his home. Victor smiled and waved. Ted had been the first officer on the scene of the crime that had wiped out Victor's family.

On that day, a lifetime ago, Ted had become his father figure.

The detective sergeant was in a kind of daze as Martin opened the trunk and helped him carry up the bags full of presents. Charlotte and Nadja were already hugging Albert.

As he crossed the threshold, Victor felt that familiar sensation, the one he always felt when he entered the apartment: nostalgia, mixed with melancholy, tightening his throat. The characteristic smell of the place filled his nostrils and carried him far into the past. He closed his eyes. An image of Raymond, his murdered younger brother, rose up in his mind.

For a moment, he wanted to scream. He felt like he was unravelling. Then the moment passed.

Nadja put a hand on the back of his neck and kissed him. "You all right, honey?"

Yes. He was all right. Everything was perfect. He put his arms around Albert. There were kisses and a few tears. This was the apartment of his youth. The place where he'd found shelter countless times after running away from the group home. Albert was already going up the hallway, his arms full of gifts, while Nadja and the kids trailed after him. At the end of the hallway, the sparkle of Christmas tree lights was visible.

Victor thought of Valérie, the sister he had gained through adoption at the age of sixteen. She had planned to join them this evening, but had decided at the last minute to spend the holidays at a sunshine resort with her kids and her new boyfriend. Victor's adoptive parents had died a few years ago. He felt their absence keenly during these family celebrations.

Taking a deep breath, Victor went to the dining room, where Ted was waiting to greet him. It was a time for renewing old ties. At this moment, Victor regretted not coming to visit more often.

Turkey, meat pies, mashed potatoes, sugar tart: once again, Albert had prepared a mouthwatering meal. The gifts were unwrapped with delight.

Charlotte threw her arms around her father when she opened her present. Even Martin, normally so hard to impress, seemed genuinely grateful.

Victor had decided to give Nadja her lingerie from La Senza in a more intimate setting, but he'd printed up the spa getaway package that he'd booked online and inserted it into a card, adding a hand-written message of love.

Opening the card, Nadja laughed out loud.

Half amused, half insulted, Victor swore to himself that he'd never risk writing romantic poetry again. But then, when he opened the card that Nadja had handed to him, he understood the reason for her laughter. She had booked a getaway package for two at a Scandinavian spa in the Laurentians.

"We're going to be super relaxed," she chuckled.

Her card also contained a gift certificate from La Cordée, an outdoor equipment store.

"Now you can get yourself some boots," Nadja said, kissing him.

•   •   •

Sunk into the couch in the den, Charlotte and Martin were tapping away on their iPads while everyone else sipped decaf cappuccinos. In reply to a question from Ted, Victor made the mistake of starting to talk in general terms about the investigation he was working on. This led to an energetic discussion about the role played by the police in a society where homeless people were ever more numerous. Once Ted got going on the subject, he couldn't be stopped.

"The problem is the law," he declared. "How many homeless people have died of exposure or been shot by cops? The new legal regime has cost vulnerable people their lives. By deinstitutionaliz-ing the mentally ill, we've put all our eggs in one basket. We've gone from one extreme to the other. It's gotten to the point where the people who most need custodial care are now on the streets. Victor, this Lortie guy might still be alive if they'd kept him inside."

Albert wiped a thread of spittle from his partner's lips. After two strokes, Ted now suffered from mild paralysis on the right side of his mouth, which slightly affected his speech.

"But Ted," Nadja intervened, "there were abuses under the old system. People were locked up even when their conditions didn't warrant permanent hospitalization."

"Yes, Nadja, that was once true. But now, like I said, we've gone to the other extreme. You could make the same point about the labour unions, but that's a whole other conversation …"

When it came to politics and public affairs, Victor often dis-agreed with Ted, who was a man of strong views. Over the years, the detective sergeant had learned to avoid useless arguments by staying out of conversations like this one.

His cellphone signalled an incoming text. Discreetly pulling the phone from his pocket, Victor looked at the message. It was from Mona Vézina:

The handwriting isn't Lortie's … Merry Christmas … Mona :)

He and Jacinthe had asked the documents expert to compare the handwritten message on the hangman sheet with the writing on the mosaic.

"Believe me, Nadja," Ted was saying, "we'd be doing a lot of homeless people a favour if we locked them up. A perfect example: I'm sure Victor has spoken to you about his friend Frank …"

Nadja turned to her lover and shook him from his idle thoughts.

"You've never told me about Frank, honey."

Images from the distant past bubbled up into Victor's consciousness.

"No?" Silence. "He was my best friend at the group home. We'd run away together. After a few days on the streets, I'd generally end up here. One time, he made up his mind to stay on the streets for good. That was how he lived until his early thirties."

After a few seconds' silence, Nadja put a hand on Victor's leg. "And then?"

"And then …" Victor said, his gaze drifting emptily. There was a long pause. "And then he died."

Rutherford looked at Victor, hesitating for a moment before picking up the narrative. He was a tough old man, but he had sensitivity enough to see that his former protégé was reliving that painful time in his head. Some ghosts never stopped haunting you.

"One night in January, it was bitterly cold," Ted finally said. "We went looking for him under his highway overpass and brought him to a shelter. He waited until we'd left, then he went back out. Frank was schizophrenic. It was Victor who found him the next day, frozen to death in his sleeping bag."

After a vocal group countdown to the stroke of midnight, there were hugs all around, and warm Christmas wishes were exchanged. For many families, it was the moment when the real festivities began. But for this group, it marked the end.

Ted's condition wasn't equal to the demands of a late-night celebration. He simply lacked the strength for it. By a quarter past twelve, Victor and his troops had said goodnight and were bound for home.

.   .   .

In the back of the car, Martin and Charlotte had put on head-phones and were lost in their own worlds. A smile glowed on Nadja's features.

"That was wonderful. Thank you for a lovely evening."

Victor pressed her hand to his lips. "Thank *you*."

"You haven't forgotten that I'm spending the day with my brother tomorrow?"

The detective sergeant stiffened. Diego thought his sister deserved better. He detested Victor. The feeling was mutual.

Nadja saw Victor look at his watch for the second time since getting in the car.

"Listen, would you mind ..."

She put a finger to his lips. "Shh. I know what you're going to ask, babe. I'll drop you off on the way."

58

OPERATING TABLE

Sunday, December 25th

The hospital was Paul Delaney's new world. Spending hours in the stifled silence of the corridors, watching the nurses' unobtrusive ballet, had become as natural to him as breathing. In this waking nightmare, he saw death lurking near the rooms, hiding under the patients' beds and dancing around the wheels of the gurneys. When daylight entered through the windows, it came to illuminate the sickness that dripped from the walls.

Victor found him where the nurse had indicated, slumped on an old vinyl bench, his head in his hands.

"Hey, Chief."

Startled, Delaney jumped to his feet. His features were drawn, his eyes bloodshot. The two men's handshake lasted longer than usual. Delaney clapped Victor on the shoulder several times.

"Did you guys plan this? Jacinthe came by earlier in the evening."

Nadja had dropped Victor off at the hospital entrance. She had offered to wait for him, but he'd insisted on taking a taxi home. While Victor's kids heckled and looked on mockingly, he and Nadja had shared a lingering kiss.

The woman transported him. She compelled him to be a better man.

The detective sergeant gave Delaney one of the two cans of Coca-Cola that he'd bought from a vending machine on the ground floor. The two aluminum tabs were pulled back, releasing near-simultaneous hisses. The open cans were clinked together.

"Merry Christmas, Chief."

"Same to you, Victor."

They were in an area of the hospital reserved for families. The place was deserted, but they whispered as they walked along the dark corridor. A long, festive banner, clearly made by children, had been hung on the wall, but it had come unstuck at one end. The last three letters of *Happy Holidays* were hanging in empty space.

Delaney's kids had left an hour ago. His daughter would arrive to take his place in the morning. The news regarding Madeleine seemed encouraging.

The doctors had ablated three localized tumours, and there were no metastases on nearby organs. Delaney had seen Madeleine for a few minutes after she regained consciousness. She was keeping up her spirits, refusing to concede defeat.

She would never surrender.

When Victor asked how he was holding up, Paul Delaney's eyes filled with tears. He had to pause in the middle of a sentence to fight back a sob.

Without really thinking about it, they had taken the elevator down to the ground floor. Victor left his empty soda can on top of a trash receptacle.

"I'm losing my mind in here," Delaney said.

With Victor following him, the head of the Major Crimes Unit went to the door, pushed it open, and stepped into the cold air.

"This feels good," he said, inhaling deeply.

Their breath came out in billows as they spoke. The chief looked at the pack of cigarettes that appeared in Victor's hand. "Gimme one."

"You sure, Paul? It would be dumb to fall back into the habit."

"That's an order," Delaney said with a wink. He fished a cigarette from the pack and leaned toward the flame that Victor was shielding with one hand.

"What the hell's going on with your case?" He blew smoke out his nose and coughed. "First it's Oswald's voice on a CD, then a hangman drawing, and now the three letters … Are we looking at a coincidence, or is that really a reference to JFK?"

"It could be a coincidence," Victor admitted, "but the documents expert thinks it's too explicit to be unintentional."

Victor was gesturing with his hands, making the ember on his cigarette glow red. Delaney kicked a chunk of ice with his shoe.

"Am I imagining things, or is someone doing everything possible to convince us that our investigation also has something to do with President Kennedy?"

Victor didn't answer right away, as he tried to put his thoughts in order.

"Project MK-ULTRA could have been authorized by the Kennedy administration. I did some searching online, but I don't know enough about American politics. I'm going to ask Gilles for some input."

Delaney cleared his throat and spat into the snow. "Anyway," he said pensively, "the hangman rattled Lawson so badly that he pulled the Northern file from the archives and went on the run." He took a drag on his cigarette. The smoke stung one eye. "What do you think scared him? The *JFK* in the drawing, or the secret word?"

"Honestly, I have no idea. But there's one thing about Kennedy that I keep going back to …" Victor looked Delaney in the eye. "I get the feeling that someone wanted to turn McNeil into a scapegoat, Paul. Same as Oswald …"

The two cops considered this for a moment. The chief shrugged.

"Could be, I don't know … In any case, initial lab results confirm that the fridge magnets seized from McNeil's house come from the same set as the ones in Harper's apartment." Clearing his throat once again, the chief spat into a snowbank. "And our mystery man, the one with the toque who visited the business centre … are we sure that wasn't Rivard?"

"Positive. The description doesn't match. And why would Rivard have bothered? He was the one Lawson sent the fax to."

Delaney took a last puff before stubbing out his cigarette in the ashtray on the wall.

The detective sergeant held the door for his superior officer. They went back inside and stood in the hospital lobby.

"There's one more thing that's bugging me, Paul — the calls between Rivard and Tousignant."

"You weren't convinced by the senator's explanation?"

Victor shrugged. "I don't know. I keep coming back to the idea that Rivard has the Northern file in his possession because he wants to hand it over to someone, or he's blackmailing someone, threatening to reveal it to the media …"

"And that someone could be Tousignant," Delaney said. "Let's wait until we have the call logs from their cellphones before we start tossing theories around." Silence. "I just wish we could question Rivard …"

"He'll have to be alive for us to do that." Victor was lost in thought for a moment. "By the way, did you speak to the managing partner about the Northern file?"

"Yeah, I took care of it. One of the firm's lawyers will email you the details. I think they've finally realized the seriousness of the situation."

The detective sergeant steered the conversation around to Madeleine. Delaney described the phases that lay ahead. The upshot was that the next forty-eight hours were likely to be critical.

When the time came for Delaney to go back upstairs, Victor sensed him retreating into a shell. The few minutes they'd spent together had offered the chief a brief escape from reality, but now it had caught up with him again.

Cold, hard, implacable.

As Victor pushed open the door, the reflection he saw in the glass made his heart ache. Delaney had sat down on a bench. He had put a hand over his eyes, and his shoulders were shaking.

59

MERRY CHRISTMAS

Christmas Day didn't unfold quite as planned. Victor had intended to lounge in bed with Nadja and then make breakfast for the kids — he'd thought he would surprise them with pancakes — but he was roused from sleep at 4:49 a.m. by his vibrating phone. Seeing Jacinthe's name on the caller ID, he was fairly certain that she wasn't calling to wish him a merry Christmas.

"I'll pick you up in twenty minutes. We're going for a little ride."

"Jesus," he whispered, "have you noticed what time it is?"

"Yeah, yeah, Lessard. You can shoot yourself later. Dress warmly, it's kinda nippy out there."

He sat motionless at the edge of the bed, dazed, staring at the depression in the pillow where, seconds ago, his head had lain.

Nadja was still sleeping peacefully.

Rummaging in his drawers as noiselessly as possible, trying not to step on creaky floorboards, Victor found his long underwear and put it on, then pulled on a pair of jeans and a fleece sweater over his T-shirt.

When the closet door squeaked, he froze. Nadja stirred and moaned softly, but didn't wake up. Letting himself breathe again, Victor picked up a canvas bag and shoved in a lined tracksuit jacket and extra socks. He tiptoed out of the room, taking an eternity to close the door without making a sound.

⋅　⋅　⋅

An aroma of fresh coffee reached his nostrils before he walked into the kitchen. Martin was eating breakfast, an old newspaper spread out before him on the table.

Victor put his bag on the floor. "You're up early."

"Mmm."

"What's wrong? You don't seem too happy."

"I couldn't sleep. Charlotte snores, and she keeps tossing and turning."

Since there was only one bedroom in Victor's apartment, the kids had to sleep on the sofa bed in the living room when they stayed over. Victor took bread and peanut butter out of the fridge and started making himself a couple of sandwiches.

"The set-up isn't great here, but there'll be a guest room in our condo. We'll make sure you're comfortable when you come to visit."

Martin looked up as he took a sip of coffee. "Have you checked out any new ones lately?"

"No. We'll get back to it after the holidays."

Victor searched a cupboard without finding what he sought, then opened another one. It was in the fourth cupboard that he finally spotted his stainless-steel Thermos.

"Mind if I help myself?" he asked, indicating the coffee maker with his chin.

Martin waved a hand. "Finish the pot. I'll make some more later." He took another sip. "It's pretty good, for decaf."

Victor poured the coffee into his Thermos, put the pot back on its stand, and wrapped his sandwiches in aluminum foil. Then he grabbed his keychain and unlocked the safe hidden under the broom closet, where he kept his service weapon. He put on his holster and slid in his Glock.

This didn't escape Martin's notice. He knew that if his father was going out with his pistol at five in the morning, it wasn't for a stroll.

"You're working today?"

"Just for a couple of hours, I hope. What have you got lined up?"

"I'm going to hang out here for a while. I have to go see Mrs. Espinosa later."

His son hadn't always behaved himself, but Victor knew he was a sensitive young man. At the end of his teenage years, Martin had accosted the old lady on the metro and grabbed her purse. Then, stricken with guilt, he had gone to see her the next day and returned the purse without touching the money inside. Instead of calling the police, she had invited him into her home. The relationship that began that day had deepened into a friendship, with Mrs. Espinosa becoming the young man's confidante, while Martin helped her with errands and odd jobs in her apartment.

Victor took the message pad off the fridge and scribbled a note to Nadja.

"Want a lift?"

"No, no, it's too early."

Was it something in Martin's voice, or his evasive gaze? Victor had a sudden feeling that his son was preoccupied.

"You sure you're okay, son?" he asked, pulling the blind aside with his fingers.

Martin opened his mouth, as though he wanted to speak.

"Shit. Jacinthe's already here."

Victor turned toward his son, determined not to leave without getting an answer.

Martin got up and approached his father. Uncharacteristically, he gave him a hug. "It's all good, Dad. Thanks again for the iPad."

Victor squeezed his son in his arms and patted him a few times on the back, which, in the emotional code of manhood, was roughly equivalent to saying, "I love you."

"That's fine, son. That's fine."

They wished each other a good day, and Victor left.

In the car, seething with impatience, Jacinthe was about to press the horn.

For her, there was no difference between five in the morning and five in the afternoon. She didn't give a damn about bothering the neighbours.

But when she saw her partner on the sidewalk, she held back from honking.

"Is it Rivard?" Victor asked, tossing his canvas bag onto the back seat.

This time, Jacinthe waited for her partner to close the door before hitting the gas.

"His body was found a little after midnight at the Mount Royal Cemetery. A man who'd gone to visit his sister's grave heard a phone ringing inside a locked vault."

Having activated the emergency lights, Jacinthe was taking corners at high speed and slamming on the brakes relentlessly. Victor was wrestling with his seat belt, which he couldn't fasten because the retractor kept locking.

"The poor guy must have been terrified."

"I'm not so sure. Apparently he's a bit of an oddball. I just talked to one of the techs at the scene. They found two cellphones on Rivard's body. His iPhone was turned off. That's why the Technological Crimes team couldn't triangulate or find it by GPS. The second phone was a prepaid burner."

"Any communications with Tousignant?"

"Nothing in the iPhone's call log. Same with the burner. That was the first thing I asked them to check. The only recorded call was the one that came in on the burner during the night. I looked up the number. It was one of Rivard's girlfriends."

As he listened to Jacinthe with a worried expression, Victor put a finger on his right eyelid, which wouldn't stop twitching. "The fact that the second phone was a burner confirms that Rivard was up to something and didn't want to leave a trail. If the burner's log is empty, that means he was clearing it as he went along." Silence. "Why did it take so long for forensics to contact us?"

"In case you hadn't noticed, big guy, it's Christmas. The 911 dispatcher had to send out a couple of patrol cops, who had to find a cemetery staffer, who had to get his hands on a key … and the only reason they got in touch with me is that I'd agreed to trade on-call shifts with Gilles. That'll teach me."

Jacinthe extracted a handful of gummies from a bag between her legs and scarfed them down, slurping as she chewed. "And the weirdest thing is, they found Rivard's body in the Lawson family vault."

60

R.I.P.

The forensics technicians at the scene were the same ones who had dealt with McNeil's body in Parc Maisonneuve. One of them remarked jokingly to Victor that all this work with frozen remains would come in handy if they ever went into the food business. Another tech had already left with Rivard's prepaid phone to see what could be extracted from it.

The technicians hadn't yet made any significant findings, apart from noting that Rivard's wounds were similar to those on the psychiatrist's body. Berger had confirmed to Jacinthe that McNeil had been struck by two arrows, one of which had hit him in the heart.

So the killer was using a bow, or a crossbow.

Because of the snow that had fallen, it was impossible to say whether the killer had been wearing skis in this case. Going by appearances, the forensics techs believed Rivard's body had been dragged a short distance before being locked in the vault, but there were no indications that allowed them to confirm the hypothesis definitively.

Clearly, the attack had taken place somewhere within the cemetery.

Powerful police lights inside the vault illuminated the corpse. Picking up the Leroux novel that lay on the altar, Victor leafed through it and found an inscription inside. Handwritten in ink that had faded over the years, the inscription was on the book's title page:

In memory of our lovely Christmas Eves
Forever, Mother
Nathan

While Jacinthe coordinated the ongoing operation — a ground search with canine units — Victor questioned the man who had called 911.

The man was a little eccentric, but his story moved Victor deeply. He spoke with a strong Russian accent, strong enough that the detective sergeant initially had trouble understanding him. But, with occasional requests that the man repeat details that weren't clear the first time around, Victor put the story together: the man's younger sister had died on Christmas Eve five years ago. Every year since, he had come to visit her grave. The man's anguish, the tears in his eyes as he remembered his dead sister, brought back the feelings of emptiness that still lingered in Victor's heart after the deaths of his mother and brothers.

Especially Raymond.

The interrogation confirmed what Victor had already suspected: apart from calling 911 when he heard the troubling sound of a phone ringing in a cemetery vault, the man didn't know anything that might help with the investigation.

Before letting him go, the detective sergeant assuaged the man's worries: he wouldn't get into any trouble for having entered the cemetery illegally.

A dog handler walked past Victor, his German shepherd sniffing the snow near the vault.

Jacinthe came over. She was bundled in the long red coat that she wore only in extreme cold. Uncharitable colleagues had suggested that the garment was sewn out of a boat sail. "I just spoke to Séguin," she said, adjusting the pompom on her toque. "They didn't find anything."

The detectives had asked Constable Séguin, who was among the first patrol cops on the scene, to examine Rivard's car with a forensics technician. On arriving in the cemetery parking lot, Jacinthe had noticed a snow-covered Porsche Cayenne. The vehicle was parked on the street, a hundred metres from the iron fence that blocked access to the cemetery at night.

A few swipes with a snow brush had been sufficient to clear off the windshield and reveal a parking ticket. The plate number had enabled them to confirm within minutes that the car was indeed registered in the lawyer's name.

With a search alert having been issued, the detectives should have been advised of the Porsche's presence much sooner. It was surprising, to say the least, that the parking officer who issued the ticket hadn't identified the vehicle as belonging to a missing person.

Victor had shrugged. He'd been in this job long enough to know that you can wish all you like; once a mistake is made, there's no going back to unmake it.

Victor shielded his eyes with one hand to block out the sun, which was playing hide and seek with the clouds. The dog handlers were following their animals as they sniffed around the gravestones.

The wind was blowing hard. His fingers were numb with cold. He pulled off his latex gloves, fished his mittens out of his pockets, and pulled them on.

"I'll be surprised if they find anything," he said. "There's been so much snow in the last few days ..."

Jacinthe had a finger in her mouth, probing between her teeth and gums. She finally succeeded in prying loose a fragment of gummy, which she examined momentarily before flicking into the snow.

"What was Rivard doing here?"

"I've been asking myself the same question. The only logical answer I can come up with is that he wanted to retrieve, or store, something in the vault."

"The Northern file?" Jacinthe guessed.

Victor's silence, as meaningful as any spoken answer, hung in the air like a snowflake dancing on the breeze.

It was nearly 11:00 a.m. The morning was dragging on, and Victor was frozen. The wait for the forensics people to complete their work was driving him crazy.

While Jacinthe was off buying food, he had drunk his Thermos of coffee, and the aluminum foil that had held his sandwiches now lay balled up at the bottom of his canvas bag. Victor roused himself; he had to move. He had to get up and do something.

Working from the assumption that Rivard had died near the vault, Victor tried to put himself in the killer's shoes and figure out the best vantage point from which to hit his target. After considering several options, he focused on the little hill to his right that rose behind the crypt in which Nathan Lawson's mother was buried.

Halfway up the slope, he regretted not having thought to bring snowshoes. Knee deep in the powdery snow, he was struggling to move forward. The climb turned out to be more arduous than expected. Catching his breath at the summit, he looked over the cemetery from the elevated vantage point, observing the choreographed movements of men and dogs on the snow.

As he had guessed, the top of the hill was an excellent observation point from which to track anyone approaching or leaving the vault. It also offered a view of the cemetery's main entrance. He saw Jacinthe talking to a patrol cop as she returned from her food-buying expedition. Victor had to smile: she was holding a pizza box.

The detective sergeant stayed on the hill for another moment, scanning the expanse, trying without success to spot ski tracks. As he began to descend, the sun emerged from behind a cloud for a couple of seconds before being covered up again. But a glint caught his eye. Something had sparkled in the snow fifteen metres behind the area where the dog handlers were working. Using a tall black-marble monument as his reference point, Victor descended the slope, never taking his eyes off the spot.

Jacinthe was waiting for him at the bottom of the hill. With one hand, she was holding a slice of pizza from which several bites had been taken. With the other, she was holding the box out to him. He guessed the pizza to be at least a large, but shook his head to decline the offer.

"I spoke to Gilles. He's received cellphone account statements for Rivard and Tousignant. No communications between them."

Jacinthe expected Victor to react, but his only response was to step around her, still staring at the black monolith. His lips were moving, but no sound was coming out.

"Come on, Lessard, I'm not asking you to jump up and down and sing hallelujah, but you could at least speak!"

She watched him walk away, then followed, grumbling, "Goddamn men!"

Victor gestured to her with one hand. He seemed to be searching for something in the snow. He squatted down near a gravestone. Removing his mittens, he put his latex gloves back on.

"What is it?"

Jacinthe had stepped closer as the detective sergeant used his pen to clear snow away from an object that lay just beneath the surface.

"Go get one of the forensics people," he said. "I think it's an arrowhead."

61
ANTI-TERRORISM UNIT

The sky had clouded over, making the temperature fall sharply. The wind was raising eddies of snow. Called over by Jacinthe, a forensics technician had carefully extracted the object that Victor had found — it was indeed an arrow. The steel tip, which didn't appear to be bloodstained, was attached to a black shaft with pink and grey fletching. For a moment, the police officers examined the projectile in silence.

"The killer probably missed his target," the technician explained, "and the arrow bounced off a gravestone, landing point up in the snow."

"He must have forgotten it," Jacinthe suggested.

"Or been unable to find it," Victor said.

After taking a series of photographs, the technician began noting measurements that would permit an exact reconstruction of where the arrow had been found, its angle, orientation, and any other useful information. Meanwhile, Victor was explaining how he had seen the metal tip glinting from the top of the hill. The technician seemed to agree with his theory that the killer had lain in wait at the summit. They heard a ringtone. The detective sergeant pulled his phone from his pocket.

"I bet it's your girlfriend," Jacinthe said.

A little smile appeared on Victor's lips when he looked at the caller ID. The smile widened as he turned to his partner. "What can I tell you? I'm a lovable guy …"

"You sound like a different person when it comes to her …"

"Different person? What are you talking about?"

Jacinthe batted her eyelids and raised her voice a couple of octaves. "Hello, my love ... yes, my love ... have a nice day, my love ..."

"Pfff. Whatever. I never call her that."

Victor had to make an effort not to laugh as he took the call. Not that he'd ever admit it, but Taillon was right. His voice softened when he spoke to Nadja.

"Hello, my love."

Holding his phone to his ear, Victor had said those words on purpose to confirm Jacinthe's comment and earn a hearty laugh from her. But his own smile quickly died on his lips.

"What's wrong?" Jacinthe asked, seeing his expression.

After another few seconds, Victor ended the call.

He stood there, staggered. Speechless.

"Lessard! What's the matter? Is there some kind of problem at home?"

His hand groped in his jacket and found his cigarettes and lighter. He lit up and took a long drag. His spirit was descending into a bottomless well of blackness; the surface was only visible as a tiny illuminated point, a fast-receding speck of light. Trying to stay afloat was futile; the abyss had caught him and was dragging him inexorably down.

Jacinthe's voice pulled him out of his torpor.

A sensation of dizziness was overwhelming him. Unable to breathe, Victor started to unzip his jacket, then lost his balance. Jacinthe caught him before he fell. Together with the technician, she lowered him onto the snow, leaning him against a gravestone.

"It's Martin," he whispered, his face pale. "He's been arrested by the anti-terrorism unit."

Jacinthe and Victor didn't exchange a word during the drive. With his head leaning against the window, the detective sergeant watched the landscape go by without managing to get his thoughts in order.

Nadja was waiting in the police station's reception area when they arrived. Victor saw her lips move, but her words fluttered in the air without reaching his brain.

She made another attempt to get through to him. He had an indefinite sense that she was saying things he needed to know, things they should talk about before going any further. But his capacity for absorption had reached its limit. This wasn't the time or place to try.

Nadja was standing in front of him, impeding his progress. Though Victor was aware of her emotions and her good will, he pushed her aside with his forearm, gently but firmly. Jacinthe, realizing there was nothing to gain from forcing the issue, didn't intervene.

Victor headed straight for the duty officer, a ginger-haired guy he recognized vaguely from the few weeks he'd spent on the Tactical Intervention Unit before realizing that SWAT work wasn't for him.

The two men greeted each other, and the officer responded to Victor's question by explaining that Martin and an accomplice had been arrested in possession of stolen dynamite sticks while trying to buy detonators for an apparent terrorist attack on a synagogue.

The light in Victor's field of perception was flickering like a light bulb about to burn out, and the opaque tunnel of his vision was shrinking. He knew his son. The claims being made about him were inconceivable.

He said so in a few dry phrases to his fellow cop, who shrugged and said the investigation had lasted several weeks, and the evidence was solid.

"Give me five minutes alone with him."

Victor wasn't asking for charity. He made the request in a peremptory tone. The officer met it with a flat refusal and began, calmly, to explain the reasons.

Victor reacted like a wounded animal, his survival instinct kicking in.

The man was standing in his way? If he wasn't on Victor's side, then he was his worst enemy. Without hesitating, Victor grabbed the ginger-haired guy by the shirt and shoved him against the wall. Jacinthe, Nadja, and two uniformed cops rushed forward to separate them, but despite his girlfriend's pleas and the shouted orders of the others, Victor didn't release his grip. The idea of shoving his gun in the officer's face crossed his mind, but numerous hands prevented him.

Shouts filled the room. The situation was becoming critical, threatening to spin out of control, when Jacinthe's roar pierced the din and, as if by magic, restored calm. "Listen! He's not asking for the moon. Five minutes with his son. That's it. Do you have kids? Put yourself in his damn shoes!"

Victor and the officer glared at each other for another moment. Then the ginger-haired guy lowered his eyes and nodded. He hadn't seen disrespect or malice in the detective sergeant's gaze, only distress. Who could blame a man for being ready to do anything for his son?

"Okay, let him through," he said to his subordinates.

Grips were loosened, clothing was straightened out. Nadja pushed a lock of hair out of her eyes. Fortunately, it was Christmas Day, so there was no one else in the police station to witness the event. Victor offered an apology to the officer, who accepted it with a nod of his head.

Then he reholstered his weapon. Ignoring Nadja's attempt to catch his eye to say something to him, he walked through the glass door that led to the cells.

His chest tightened when he saw Martin through the two-way mirror. The room was windowless, with concrete walls that had been painted a dull beige centuries ago. His boy was sitting at a dark wooden table, elbows resting on its surface, head in his hands, fingers in his hair. Victor stopped to gaze at him for a moment, frozen, gripping the door handle.

Suddenly, having fought tooth and nail to get here, he felt doubt take hold. What if they were right? What if the things they said they'd found out about Martin were true? For the first time, Victor contemplated the possibility that his son had become the kind of individual he had spent his life pursuing, cornering, and occasionally crushing underfoot.

The detective sergeant entered the room. The young man looked up.

Victor couldn't tell exactly what he was seeing in Martin's gaze. Fear, perhaps even terror; displeasure, but also relief.

The chair legs rasped on the floor as the cop pulled it toward him. Turning it around, he straddled it, leaning his arms on the backrest. "We have five minutes to get you out of this shit. Tell me it's not true."

Martin stared at his Doc Martens before raising his sad eyes to his father.

"It's not what you think. It's not what it looks like. Let me deal with it. Everything will be fine."

"Let you deal with it? Are you kidding? Do you have any idea what they're trying to pin on you? With the new anti-terrorism laws in place, they'll ask for the max. You being a cop's son means the judge will show zero leniency. You'll end up in prison with a bunch of guys I arrested — guys who'll enjoy nothing better than beating you to a pulp, then pissing on the pulp. And that'll be on good days." Victor looked at his watch. "We're down to three minutes. Talk."

"I can't, Dad. I can't talk."

Martin clearly wanted to open up, but … did he fear his father's reaction, or was there something else he was afraid of? Whatever the cause, Victor was on his feet in an instant, shoving the chair and table aside with a violent clatter.

"Quit fucking around!"

Eyes bulging, with froth on his lips, he slapped his son hard across the face. He regretted it instantly. Martin's head snapped back. He started to cry in silence.

Victor knelt beside the young man.

"Martin, if you don't want to rot in prison, you have to talk to me. Right now." He spoke these last words in a soft, calm tone.

There was a knock on the door. A voice called through. "One minute left."

Martin's chin trembled. He sniffled and wiped the tears from his eyes. "You're not going to believe me …" He took a deep breath. "I've been working as an RCMP informant. I infiltrated a neo-Nazi gang. They're fucked up, Dad. Hitting Jewish targets and making it look like Muslims did it. They're trying to stir up racial tensions so people will think multiculturalism's dangerous."

Victor's mind began to race. Neo-Nazis? Martin, an RCMP informant right under his nose? And he'd never guessed a thing?

In your face, Lessard.

Victor made an effort to block out any emotional reaction. "Have you contacted your RCMP handler?"

"Yeah. I'm waiting for him to get back to me."

"Do you have official status? Are you on the payroll?"

"It's more complicated than that, Dad." Martin hesitated, almost added something, then didn't. "I thought you'd be proud of me, for once," he said, looking his father in the eye.

There was the sound of a door being unlocked. Victor's neck began to tingle. The urgency of the situation provoked an adrenalin rush in his system. Time accelerated. "Give me your handler's name. I'll follow up."

"I can't."

"Don't be stupid. You've got to trust me, Martin. I can't help unless you talk to me." Victor leaned forward. Their faces were inches apart. "What's his name?"

The door opened. The ginger-haired cop was standing in the doorway. "Your five minutes are up, Lessard."

"His name is Diego Concha Fernandez," Martin murmured in his father's ear.

It took some time for the information to wend its way through Victor's synapses. Then the connections were made. Victor kissed his son's forehead, stood up, and backed toward the door. His eyes were asking Martin a question. Martin answered the question with a slow, deliberate nod.

With that nod came confirmation that Diego Concha Fernandez was the same man Victor was thinking of.

Nadja's brother.

62

CONFRONTATIONS

Sitting on a chair in the police station's reception area, Jacinthe raised a triumphant fist and yelled "Yes!" followed by a choice obscenity. She had just crushed her previous record on Angry Birds. Since downloading the game onto her BlackBerry, she'd been playing for an average of thirty minutes a day, usually on the toilet.

In the conference room to which Victor had led Nadja, gripping her arm, voices were raised. At the reception counter, the ginger-haired cop was ostensibly taking care of paperwork, but in reality, he was listening closely, doing his best to overhear what was going on. At one point, he almost opened the door to check that everything was all right, but Jacinthe dissuaded him with a look.

The door banged against the wall. Jacinthe felt a wash of air as Victor blew by. "Come on, Taillon. We're getting the fuck out of here." By the time she'd pocketed her phone, he was already outside.

Jacinthe poked her head in the door. Nadja's makeup was all streaked, which didn't lessen her beauty. She took a deep breath and said, in response to Jacinthe's question, that she was okay. Then she added desperately, "Please, Jacinthe, don't let him do anything stupid."

Nadja found the strength to put on her coat, leave the station, and walk to her car. Once she got behind the wheel, she began to cry. The memories flooded back.

Nadja and Martin had shared the duties of looking after Victor during his recovery, and a close bond had formed between them. She no longer remembered how the subject had come up, but Martin had confided to her that he wanted to become a police officer.

During the conversation, Martin had expressed a particular interest in the fight against terrorism. As Nadja's brother Diego led an RCMP section that specialized in that field, Nadja had put them in touch. Pleased that Martin was opening up to her, touched by his trust, she had foolishly promised not to tell Victor. Looking back, Nadja realized that was the moment she'd been taken in.

She should have been suspicious when Martin started asking detailed questions and evoking hypothetical scenarios: "What would happen if a civilian had information about a terrorist plot? ... How are informants recruited?"

She should have understood at that moment that Martin was talking about himself, that he had come into contact with some dangerous individuals and seen an opportunity to impress his father.

Above all, Nadja cursed herself for not following up more strenuously when, a few weeks later, she had asked Martin whether he'd spoken to Diego.

The young man had been evasive, suggesting that he'd started working on a new recording with an indie rock group called M-jeanne, and police work didn't interest him that much after all.

At the time, Nadja had thought the behaviour confirmed Victor's impression of Martin as a young man who was great at starting things, who loved to embark enthusiastically on new projects, only to abandon them soon after. She hadn't given any further thought to the matter, concentrating instead on caring for Victor. And since Martin had claimed never to have gotten in touch with Diego, she hadn't even brought up the subject with her brother.

Victor had every right to be furious with her. He had every right to say she'd shown a lack of judgment. And if Diego really had recruited Martin, Nadja was angry that he hadn't kept her in the loop.

But how could he have dared to do such a thing? She loved her brother and couldn't bring herself to believe he had done it purely out of spite for Victor.

Nadja looked hesitantly at her phone. Should she warn Diego?

The Crown Victoria was rolling at high speed along a quiet residential street in the south-shore suburb of Saint-Lambert. Victor was at the wheel of the car, his jaw clenched, veins standing out prominently on his temples.

"It's not her fault," Jacinthe said. "She couldn't have known."

"She *should* have known! And she sure as hell shouldn't have told Martin to go see that bastard. One, he's an asshole. And two, he hates my guts. I can't believe she hasn't figured that out!"

"He's her brother, Vic." Silence. "Slow down, will ya?"

"I'm telling you, she fucked up on this. She should have asked him if he'd spoken to Martin."

Jacinthe pointed at a car that was backing up the narrow street. Victor swerved, putting two wheels up on the sidewalk, and went around the vehicle without slowing down. "You're pissed off and you're worried about your son, but even so, I think you're being too harsh."

Jacinthe couldn't make out his muttered response in its entirety, but she clearly heard the words *son of a bitch*. She went on: "Listen, instead of barging in like a bull in a china shop, don't you think it might be a better idea to have Nadja talk to him first, so everyone can get a sense of where things stand?"

Victor wasn't ready to calm down. "Too late. We're going to settle this my way."

He looked down at his BlackBerry and saw that an email had just come in from a lawyer at Baker Lawson Watkins concerning Northern Industrial Textiles. The email would have to wait. There were more important matters to deal with.

Jacinthe shrugged. She was trying to make Victor listen to reason, but at the same time, she understood his impulse. In his shoes, she'd have done considerably worse. So she didn't feel entitled to moralize. "It's Christmas Day, buddy. You sure he'll be there?"

"He's supposed to meet Nadja at the restaurant at three-thirty."

He had just checked his watch and knew he had enough time to get there before Diego showed up. Even so, spurred by his anger, he activated the emergency lights and floored the accelerator. There was a malignant gleam in his eye. "He'd better not keep me waiting long."

Since their parents' deaths, Diego and Nadja had made it a Christmas tradition to get together at a restaurant in the old quarter of Saint-Lambert. Though they didn't see each other often, they were still close.

They would usually arrive early, have a drink, and talk about the wreckage of their respective love lives. All that had changed when Nadja had entered a long-term relationship. Maybe that was one of the sources of Diego's hostility toward Victor.

Whatever the reason, Nadja's brother never missed an opportunity to let her know in the strongest possible terms that an ex-alcoholic, twelve years her senior, with two kids, wasn't an ideal match for her.

As far as Diego was concerned, Victor was a loser.

Diego's SUV entered the parking lot and rolled through it in a wide arc.

Like many people who instinctively park near another car in a near-empty lot, he pulled up next to the Crown Victoria.

Whistling as he got out of the vehicle, Diego opened the rear hatch and took out a gift-wrapped present. He had just reclosed the hatch and was walking between the two vehicles when Victor opened the car door and got out, blocking his way.

"Hello, asshole."

Diego Concha Fernandez was built like a rugby player. He had a naturally menacing gaze, a flattened nose, a bull neck, and powerful hands. Startled at the sight of Victor, he retreated a couple of paces. Glancing past the detective sergeant, he tried to look into the Crown Vic, but the fogged windows prevented him from seeing anything.

"Hey, bro," he said with disdain. "Did you drive my sister over? Where is she?"

"It's just you and me, asshole."

Diego hadn't expected Victor to approach him so directly, but he didn't seem at all intimidated. His phone rang. He ignored it.

"What do you want?" he asked contemptuously.

Victor's eyes narrowed.

"You know what I want. You're going to get my son out of jail."

Motionless, arms at his sides, the detective sergeant was clenching and unclenching his fists. He seemed taller and broader than he had a few minutes ago. "I can't imagine what Nadja sees in you, Lessard," Fernandez said scornfully. "She deserves a lot better than the likes of you."

Victor ignored the comment.

"My son, asshole. You're going to take care of him."

"I have no idea what you're talking about. Now get out of my way."

"How'd you rope him in, scumbag? 'Want to make a little cash, Martin? Bring me information and you'll be paid for it. The more you bring, the more you'll make.' Something like that?"

Fernandez decided to stop playing games. "You're leaving out the most important part. 'If you get in trouble, we never met.' Forget it, Lessard. There's no contract. Martin's on his own. He knew that going in, and he accepted it. Your son doesn't have a lot of brains, but at least he's got balls. Clearly it's not genetic."

Fernandez stepped forward between the cars, heading for the restaurant, and tried to shove Victor out of his path. Victor's response, more instinctive than calculated, was a hard right hook that caught the RCMP officer with full force.

Bent forward, Fernandez brought his hands to his face. Blood began to pour from his nostrils. His fingers and coat were instantly stained.

"You broke my nose, motherfucker!"

With surprising speed and agility for a man of his build, Fernandez rushed at Victor. His elbow was up, aimed at Victor's head, which he was evidently determined to crack like a nut.

Victor dodged the blow, but Fernandez followed up with a punch that opened up Victor's eyebrow. Blood ran into Victor's left eye. He was momentarily disoriented, with his back against the SUV. As his adversary closed in, he shook off the cobwebs and caught him with a kick to the ribs.

Fernandez grimaced with pain, coming back with a kick that missed Victor and landed on the door of the SUV.

He threw another punch.

Victor managed to block it partially with a forearm, but the follow-up landed squarely on his chin. Pain exploded through his body. Instead of making him retreat, it magnified his rage tenfold.

He knew he wouldn't last long at close quarters with Fernandez, whose superior size and weight would quickly overwhelm him.

He had to go for broke.

He lunged at Fernandez. The two men grappled for an instant, their bodies leaning against the Crown Victoria. To Fernandez's surprise, Victor pivoted, ending up behind him. Grabbing him by the hair, Victor yanked his head back and hit him as hard as he could in the kidneys. With the air entirely knocked out of him, Fernandez sank to his knees and fell into the slush between the two cars.

Victor unclenched his hand. A tuft of hair had come away in his fist.

He kicked Fernandez, who cried out in pain. Inside the Crown Vic, Jacinthe, who had watched the entire confrontation, smiled in appreciation of her partner's technique. She had stopped playing Angry Birds and put away the phone some time ago, ready to intervene if necessary.

Victor grabbed Fernandez by the hair once again. The RCMP officer writhed in pain. "Now, you listen very carefully, asshole," he said, speaking deliberately, his voice lower and calmer than usual.

Victor was so focused on the pressure he was administering to Fernandez's neck with his fist that he didn't see Nadja's car come into the parking lot.

63

LE CONFESSIONNAL

Victor had been sober for seven years, five months, twelve days, eighteen hours, and twelve minutes when he walked into Le Confessionnal.

And he had plenty of sins to confess.

In an effort to settle himself, he had taken the metro to Place-d'Armes and walked through Old Montreal, which lay abandoned by local residents for the holidays. His gaze had strayed over the heritage buildings, stopping now and then at a light-filled window as he tried to imagine what was going on inside.

His wanderings had led him to the Alexandra Quay, where he had leaned against the railing for a long time, contemplating a moored freighter, imagining what it would be like to leave his nightmares behind and set sail for some hypothetical elsewhere. Though he had already taken several anti-anxiety pills, he still felt the need to smoke cigarette after cigarette, but nothing could quell the dark thing that was gnawing at him.

Then, hands in his pockets, ignoring the cold, he had followed the cobblestones of Saint-Paul Street, advancing into the depths of the darkness.

It was as he walked up McGill that he saw the poster on the door: *Our second annual "Christmas for Losers" starts at 9 p.m. at Le Confessionnal. You are not alone! After unwrapping your crappy presents, come party through the night with us.*

His watch showed 9:35 p.m. when he surrendered.

The door was at sidewalk level; there were no stairs to climb. Victor walked in without pausing to think about it. He made scant effort to appreciate the décor: the place was long and narrow, with exposed bricks on one wall, ceramic panelling on the other, and crystal light fixtures hanging from the ceiling. Walking to the back, he sat down at the illuminated, glass-topped bar. Moments later, with his cap pulled low over his eyes, he found himself alone with a glass of Scotch that he hadn't yet touched. It stared fixedly at him, murmuring dark incantations.

The place was gradually filling up with its trendy young clientele.

Nadja's arrival in the restaurant parking lot had been catastrophic.

Everything had gone against Victor, starting with appearances. She had found him between the two cars, brutalizing her brother. He hadn't heard her arrive, and — this was one of the disadvantages of having a cop for a girlfriend — she had put him in an armlock to make him release his victim.

Jacinthe had emerged from the Crown Victoria. Diego had gotten to his feet, and everyone had started shouting until Nadja ordered them to leave. Victor had tried to explain, to argue, to make her listen to reason, but Nadja was having none of it. Her angry glare had pierced his heart.

Victor had then shifted into Cro-Magnon mode, slamming the car door, then opening it and slamming it a second time to convey the extent of his anger. Seething, his face blood-streaked, he had roared away in the Crown Vic.

Jacinthe had dropped him off at his place. Despite all her efforts, she hadn't gotten him to open up. She had offered to stay and keep him company, but he'd shaken his head vehemently. He wanted to be alone with his bleak fate.

To top it off, entering the apartment, he had found a note from Charlotte on the dining room table — she had gone to spend the evening with her mother.

Victor had taken out his frustration on the kitchen wall. A series of punches had opened a hole in its surface.

The DJ's nasal voice roused Victor from his thoughts. The volume had risen on the electro beat.

Two young women in clingy, sleeveless tops, bare-shouldered, with plunging necklines, had sat down beside him. He turned and glanced at them briefly. They were in their thirties and might as well have had red labels on their foreheads: *Single and Desperate.*

One of them offered him an engaging smile. He responded with a compression of his lips, then looked back at the ice cubes in his glass.

The anger was a vortex from which he couldn't escape, a torrent he couldn't resist.

And it was a protection.

Running away had always been his first reflex. Putting some distance between himself and whatever was troubling him. Nadja had crossed a line she should never have crossed: she had sided with her brother. Everything was black and white. There was no reason for them to be together.

He knew the void would come. The void always followed anger. And he would start thinking about all the good qualities of this amazing woman he didn't deserve. He loved her …

Then the anger would return, reclaiming its ascendancy.

Victor knew it would fade eventually. And when it did, he'd be left in a state of indecision, not knowing what to do or how to behave.

He had no illusions about the future of his relationship with Nadja. He'd beaten up her brother. He'd lost his temper with her. He'd acted like a fool and thrown unjust accusations in her face.

Looking to his left, he saw a couple. The guy was laughing. The girl was rubbing his back, a tender gesture that hit him like a punch in the gut.

His fingers tightened around the glass.

.   .   .

Before entering Le Confessionnal, Victor had done some thinking as he walked through the streets of Old Montreal. He had put
in a call to Marc Lagacé, a criminal defence lawyer whom he'd
squared off against in the past when he was called as a witness for
the prosecution.

Lagacé was known for his relentlessly aggressive methods. He
was a fighter, a pit bull whose teeth were tearing at you almost
before the judge was seated on the bench. He was also exactly the
kind of lawyer you wanted on your side when the time came to go
to war.

The detective sergeant had left his phone number on the lawyer's answering service, hoping he was in town and not on some
Caribbean beach; and hoping, as well, that he'd call back promptly,
and … and fuck this! Summoning his courage, Victor had also
called his ex-wife, Martin's mother.

Having heard nothing about Martin's arrest, Marie was stunned
by the news. Sensing that she was too shaken to talk further, Victor
had asked to speak to her live-in boyfriend, Derek. The two men
had met a couple of times. Despite their differing personalities —
Derek was a soft-spoken accountant — they respected each other.

Victor had given Derek a quick summary of the situation,
describing the steps he had taken to secure a lawyer. Before ending
the call, he had promised to keep them informed. Then, unable
to remain inactive, he had contacted the ginger-haired officer who
had custody of Martin and asked for more details on the case.

The officer had initially been coldly reticent, but Victor finally
managed to learn from him that Martin and a co-conspirator
named Boris had been arrested as they tried to buy detonators
from an undercover RCMP operative.

Dynamite sticks stolen from a warehouse in the Laurentians
had been found during a search of a storage space leased by a third
member of the gang. When Victor hung up, his mind was teeming

with a thousand questions, one of which stood out: if his son was under surveillance, why had no one told him?

But he already knew the answer. Investigators couldn't take the chance of compromising an ongoing case.

Even so, he was surprised that he hadn't received a call from headquarters in advance of Martin's arrest. That was the informal practice generally observed in situations like this.

Maybe the new police chief didn't much care for him. Maybe the list of his detractors on the force had gotten longer without his realizing it. It was certainly true that Tanguay, his former boss, never hesitated to piss on Victor's good name whenever he got the chance.

Life on the force carried its share of risks if your methods were unorthodox. You needed someone influential on your side to offset your critics. Paul Delaney was a powerful man in the police hierarchy, and his support for Victor was unequivocal. But lately, with his wife's illness taking up all his energy, Paul had been a less assiduous defender than usual.

Victor swept these thoughts into a mental wastebasket. At the moment, he wasn't terribly worried about the repercussions that Martin's arrest might have on his career. In fact, he didn't give a damn.

The glass burned in his trembling hand. How much longer would he be able to hold it without bringing it to his lips and draining it? Doing so would be the end of everything; it would be the return to hell. The sad poetry of Fred Fortin's old song *Scotch* ran through his head.

Victor had an intuitive sense that someone was watching him. He looked up sharply.

Something moved in his field of vision. Was it an illusion, or had a guy in the depths of the bar, his face hidden by an old red, white, and blue Expos cap, lowered his head? Being the object of a gay man's interest didn't bother Victor, but right now he wanted to be ignored and forgotten. He longed to be transparent, invisible.

The crowd was thickening around him. Fingers were grazing hips, mouths were floating forward, speaking into ears, smiles were being exchanged, promises of sex were being measured out in glasses, in half truths, in lies and disappointments.

The barmaid's breasts jiggled beneath her sleeveless blouse each time she picked up a bottle or put down a glass, and Victor saw in a flash of alienated lucidity that the spectacle of those breasts was her stock in trade, as much as any drink the bar had on offer.

Returning to his thoughts, he remembered the ginger-haired officer telling him that Martin wouldn't appear in court until the 28th. That gave Victor time to seek more information and start to develop a defence strategy with the pit bull — assuming the pit bull agreed to take the case.

At the same time, Victor had no illusions about how the newspapers would handle the story. He could already see the headlines: MONTREAL COP'S SON CHARGED IN TERRORIST CONSPIRACY.

Let the media say what they liked; nothing could hurt him anymore.

Once again, the intense gaze of the guy in the baseball cap began to bother him. Victor put on his best back-off-if-you-don't-want-your-face-rearranged expression. The suture tape over his split eyebrow accentuated his menacing appearance. The guy lowered his eyes.

Whether this case cost Victor his job or his relationship with Nadja was secondary. All that mattered for the moment was making sure Martin didn't spend too much time behind bars.

Because if he did, Victor would never forgive himself.

The bar was packed by now. Young women were standing unsteadily behind him as they ordered their drinks, leaning on his shoulder and laughing, but he had withdrawn into himself. Nothing existed but the glass in front of him, which he was gazing at with due solemnity.

Self-Destruction for Dummies, by Victor Lessard. His fingers stiffened around the glass. He lifted it from the bar, brought it to his nose, and sniffed deeply. The malty odour made his nostrils tingle and his head spin. He felt as though he were greeting an old friend after a long absence, a friend he had missed terribly and wanted to take in his arms.

A shadow passed behind him. He didn't pay attention.

Suddenly, it was as though all the people in the bar were on their feet, possessed, clapping their hands as their bodies rubbed up against one another, limbs entwined, and every mouth chanted his name:

Victor, Victor, Victor …

Just as he was bringing the glass to his mouth, he saw an open matchbook balanced on the illuminated surface of the bar. It hadn't been there a second before. Instantly, Victor saw it was the same brand of matches as the ones that had been found in Parc Maisonneuve.

Everything froze as he extended a hand to pick it up. When he opened it, his heart began to race. Under the flap, someone had written:

> 10 23 1964
> there were others

Stunned, he raised his head and looked around. In an instant he was on his feet. The information that had been stored in a corner of his brain now lit up: a shadow had passed behind him a few seconds ago …

The washroom!

Pushing people out of his path, he made his way through the crowd and rushed into the men's room.

Looking around quickly, he saw a couple of guys dousing the urinals' porcelain and a man standing at the mirror, trying drunkenly to cover up his bald spot. None of them, Victor knew, had left the matchbook on the bar.

The stall was closed.

The first kick made the metal door buckle; the second tore out the bolt. The couple inside, who'd been snorting powder and fondling each other, stared in terror at the Glock in Victor's fist. After a hasty apology, he was back in the bar, the pistol jammed into his jacket pocket.

His eyes scanned every inch of the room, studying faces, watching movements. Was anyone behaving unusually or nervously? The man he sought was of medium height and weight. A cap could be removed in an instant, and Victor hadn't seen his features, which were concealed by the brim. But if he tried to melt into the crowd, the detective sergeant would spot him.

The barmaid approached, lips glistening.

"There was a guy in an Expos cap at the bar a minute ago. Where is he?"

She laughed tipsily and pressed her ample breasts against his arm. Her breath smelled of sambuca and mango, which in other circumstances wouldn't have been disagreeable. She ran a hand along his back. "Don't know." She laughed some more. "Feel like a shooter, baby?"

As she attempted to hand him a glass, she spilled liquor on him, then tried to clean up the mess with a rag. Victor took her by the wrist and disengaged himself.

"It's okay," he said, walking away.

His heart was hammering as he stepped outside, looking in all directions. An unlucky Lexus was parked in front of the building; it had to endure the kick with which Victor unleashed his frustration.

The man in the baseball cap had slipped through his fingers.

Holding his phone between his shoulder and ear, Victor groped for his cigarettes. After four rings, as he was taking his first drag, he heard a rasping, semiconscious voice. "You better have a fucking good reas—"

His system was supercharged with adrenalin. He felt goosebumps rise at the thought of what he was about to say. "Shut up and listen, Taillon! I know what the numbers on the fridge mean."

"Ahh, not this shit again …"

The front door of Le Confessionnal burst open. A man wearing a T-shirt came out and projectile-vomited onto the sidewalk a few feet from where Victor stood.

"The numbers represent a date: October 23rd, 1964."

"You could have waited until tomorrow instead of waking me up at one in the morning to talk about some theory."

"It's not a theory, Jacinthe. The killer was here."

64

ARCHIVES

Monday, December 26th

After arriving home from Le Confessionnal, Victor had tried to sleep, but he'd finally given up. His mind was racing, his thoughts skittering between Martin, Nadja, and his dead brother, Raymond. At three in the morning, realizing that the ghosts haunting him would allow him no rest, he'd gotten up and smoked a cigarette at the open window.

After that, he had sat down at his laptop to read the email sent to him by a lawyer named Pageau, who worked at Baker Lawson Watkins. The subject was the Northern file. Pageau confirmed the identities of the three board members who had been tracked down by Lemaire.

The email also provided some technical information about the company, along with a considerable amount of legalese that Victor didn't altogether grasp. But he did eventually figure out that the file had to do with preparing Northern Industrial Textiles for a due-diligence check regarding a transaction that had never taken place.

Pageau added that the file seemed unimportant and would normally have been destroyed a long time ago. This confirmed the conclusion that the Gnome had reached after meeting the former president of the company.

Victor had then spent a fair portion of the night searching the internet and the Quebec Police Information Centre database, hoping to find some link between the various pieces of the puzzle.

In particular, he tried different combinations and permutations of certain keywords: *10 23 1964*, *Kennedy*, *MK-ULTRA*, and the names of the victims and primary witnesses in the investigation, as well as those of the directors of Northern Industrial Textiles. The detective sergeant had also tried to find records of any violent crimes or murders that had been committed on that date on the island of Montreal.

Apart from giving him a headache, the effort had yielded nothing of value, though he had learned that the French writer Théophile Gauthier had died on an October 23rd, that the 1964 Olympic Games had taken place in Japan from October 10th to 24th, and that on the same date — which clearly wasn't a red-letter day in the history of humanity — the number-one hit song was "Doo Wah Diddy Diddy." In a daze, Victor had watched the song on YouTube, performed by a man who wiggled his hips while shaking maracas with both hands.

He slept for an hour or two. When he woke up, his eyelids felt like they were lined with lead. A profound weariness weighed on him. Anxiety was closing in, invading his head. Victor knew from experience that this kind of fatigue was the precursor to a depressive episode. What else could he do but take his medication?

It was an automaton that showered and made breakfast, a robot that rode the metro to Place Versailles. The only good news was that the worst had been avoided: his desire to drink had vanished along with the man in the baseball cap.

He refused to admit to himself that he was hoping for a call from Nadja. None came.

But his phone had started to ring at eight o'clock and hadn't let up since. A reporter assigned to the criminal court beat was trying to reach him. Victor turned off the phone and let the messages pile up in his voice mail.

•　　•　　•

Jacinthe listened without interruption as he recounted what had happened at Le Confessionnal. Feeling helpless, he blamed himself: the killer had been there, under his nose, and he'd let him get away.

"You think it was him, but you didn't see him."

"He was watching me, Jacinthe. The matches were the same brand as the ones we found in the park. Look! You can't tell me that was a coincidence."

Jacinthe was turning the bagged matchbook over between her thick fingers.

"No, but it doesn't make much sense. Have you considered the possibility that the killer paid someone to slip you the matchbook?" She paused. "And besides, why would the murderer be giving us more clues?"

A shrug was the only answer Victor could come up with. After another silence, Jacinthe asked the question that had been nagging at her since she'd learned he spent the evening in a bar.

"I didn't touch a drop," he said firmly.

Despite the fact that it was a legal holiday, the whole team was at work at 11:00 a.m. Jacinthe and Victor were pursuing their discussion. The Gnome was following up with forensics to get an update on the cemetery crime scene. And Loïc, at Victor's request, had set aside his research on the heretic's fork to concentrate on shops that sold archery equipment.

Victor asked Jacinthe to read the email that he'd received from the lawyer at Baker Lawson Watkins concerning the Northern file. Jacinthe couldn't decipher the legalese any more than he'd been able to. Her reaction was summed up in a single question, accompanied by an abdominal rumble. "Are you starting to get hungry?" The detective sergeant asked her to stay focused for a few more minutes. The previous night, while he was dozing, an idea had taken root in his mind, and he wanted to hear her impressions. The Gnome finished up his call and joined them.

Victor took a few seconds to put his thoughts in order before he started to speak.

"Based on what Gilles found out, and on the details we've received from Lawson's office, it seems like the Northern file was insignificant. But we're convinced that the documents Lawson took out of the firm's archives were very valuable to him. So, here's my theory, and I'd like you to tell me if it makes sense. Could a major file have been stored under the name of an unrelated client — in this case, Northern Industrial Textiles — so that it couldn't be found by means of keywords?"

"You're saying Lawson deliberately stored these documents in the archives under the Northern Industrial Textiles name by setting up a fictitious file?"

"You wouldn't need to create a fictitious file. You want to be sure no one stumbles across it by accident, so you go through your old client list and pick out a company that's been dissolved, a minor file, confident that no one will have any reason to poke around in it."

"Northern Industrial Textiles was dissolved in 1974," the Gnome mused. "Does that mean we've been going up a blind alley the whole time we were checking out the company's management?"

Jacinthe was the first to react. "You want to know what I think? If Lawson had really wanted to hide a file, he'd have put it somewhere other than the archives."

"Not necessarily," Lemaire answered. "There are some advantages to putting it there: it's protected from police searches, it's swallowed up in a mass of similar items, and also, sometimes, the best place to hide something is in plain sight."

"And then if you go out of your way to mislabel it," Victor added, "it becomes impossible to trace, except for the person who knows where it's hidden."

"Your idea makes good sense," the Gnome observed.

"I wish I could agree," Jacinthe growled, "but I can't imagine files just lie in the archives forever. At some point, they must get destroyed. So, I'll say it again: I'd be surprised if Lawson took the risk of leaving valuable documents in there."

Lemaire intervened. "Before giving birth to Dwarf Number 5, my wife was a paralegal. At the firm where she worked, they had a policy: each lawyer had to review archived files periodically and decide which ones should be kept. I imagine all the big firms have a similar policy, because the cost per square foot of hanging on to old papers is bound to be very high. Some out-of-date documents are destroyed. Others get transferred to digital platforms so they can be saved without taking up space. Every archived document is regularly reviewed by the lawyer responsible for it. So, yes, Lawson could preserve what he wanted."

The debate continued for a little while, with Jacinthe unwilling to relent. Then they went downstairs to the Place Versailles food court. Because it was Boxing Day and the shopping mall was crawling with bargain-hunters, the cops ordered takeout meals and went back upstairs to eat in the conference room.

To Victor's considerable relief, the delicate subject of Martin's arrest didn't come up.

The Gnome entertained them with an account of his two oldest children's latest adventure: making the basement toilet overflow by putting their turtle in it.

Numbers 1 and 2 had pleaded not guilty, swearing that they'd placed the turtle in the toilet bowl simply to "give him a change of scenery." Then, while playing on the PS3, they had forgotten about the reptile. The trouble had started much later, when Number 4 had tried to flush after a nocturnal pee.

Luckily, Torvald the turtle had emerged from the ordeal unharmed.

After lunch, Lemaire got ready to pay a visit to a pawn shop owner in the Hochelaga district. Mark McNeil's widow had received threats from a man who had showed up at her door, demanding money. Far from being intimidated, the young woman had turned to the Gnome for help. Apparently, McNeil had been borrowing money to stay afloat.

While he buttoned his coat, uncertain how to broach the subject, Lemaire asked Victor if he'd seen the online news reports.

Victor shook his head.

The Gnome stood there, not moving. "Maybe you should have a look," he said, visibly ill at ease.

"I don't want to know about it, Gilles."

Victor was getting ready to consult with Loïc, who had just returned from lunch, when he got a call from Lagacé, the pit bull lawyer he had contacted about representing Martin. Lagacé confirmed that he would take the case. They discussed it briefly, with Victor communicating the limited information he possessed. Lagacé was reassuring: he promised to visit Martin and take the necessary steps to examine the evidence that prosecutors were holding. Then the discussion turned to the matter of professional fees.

"Money is no object. This'll cost what it costs. I'm not a rich man, but I'll give the shirt off my back to keep my son out of prison."

Before ending the call, they agreed to meet later in the day.

Victor sighed. The ten-ton weight had finally been lifted from his shoulders.

Just then, Paul Delaney walked in, wearing a grim expression, and asked Victor to come into his office.

After closing the door, the head of the Major Crimes Unit exploded: "Goddamn jackals!"

65

PRESS RELEASE

For a moment, Victor feared that the higher-ups wanted him suspended, but Delaney put his mind at ease. The police chief and top brass were behind him. Delaney was fulminating, rather, about the online media's sensationalist coverage of Martin's arrest and their moralistic eagerness to link that event with Victor's troubled past.

"Is it really that bad, Paul?"

"Imagine the worst it could possibly be … then double it. Some people want you suspended until the matter is closed. Others want you fired outright. It's a lucky thing most reporters are off this week and the newspapers aren't being printed today."

Victor took a deep breath. He could well imagine what the city's columnists and bloggers were saying: *how could the public have faith in a detective who hadn't noticed that his own son was engaged in terrorist activities?* They would also surely remark on the fact that the son in question belonged to an ultraviolent right-wing group that was seeking to rid Montreal of its immigrants.

Not to mention the old skeletons that would be dragged out of the closet.

"I'm not ready to deal with it yet, Paul."

"I'd understand if you wanted to take time off …"

Delaney read the answer in the detective sergeant's expression: the last thing he wanted to do was brood at home.

"The pressure will intensify over the next few days. You realize how the media will treat this."

"I know, Paul. The classic line: we need to avoid any appearance of conflict of interest. We need to make sure the public has full confidence in the impartiality of Montreal police officers as they investigate the son of a colleague."

"Exactly. The chief wants us to put out a press release to help calm things down. We'll start out by saying you have no knowledge of the facts alleged against your son, and, on a personal level, you intend to offer him the full support that parents naturally give their children in situations like this."

The press release would go on to say that Victor had devoted his career to enforcing the law, and he had no thought of seeking an exception for his son. Depending on the outcome of the case, Martin might have to answer for his actions in court, and Victor would accept the verdict. Without saying anything to Delaney, Victor cringed inwardly at those words: he had taken steps in the past to hide certain offences, protecting his son from arrest. Of course, the crimes back then had been less grave than terrorist conspiracy.

"After that," Delaney went on, "we'll put in a few lines promising that you'll make yourself available to investigators to answer their questions."

Victor cleared his throat and added, "We'll finish up with the usual stuff about the Montreal Police Service reiterating its full confidence in the judgment and integrity of one of its finest officers."

"And that settles that," Delaney said, winking. "Where there's a will, there's a way."

The head of the Major Crimes Unit would finalize the text with the public relations officer, who would then get the necessary approvals before the press release went out for distribution.

For an instant, Victor caught himself thinking that he'd actually dodged a bullet. Someone could have caught him on video as he was attacking Fernandez in the restaurant parking lot, then posted the clip on YouTube. He almost told Delaney what he'd learned about Martin's claim that he'd been working as an RCMP informant, but he decided not to say anything until he had more information.

The conversation then turned to Madeleine's medical condition. Things were stabilizing; her strength was gradually coming back. Delaney and his kids were taking shifts so that someone was always at her side.

With ancillary matters out of the way, the two men got down to business.

"Okay. Tell me what happened at Le Confessionnal last night."

"Let's save that for last, Paul."

In a few sentences, Victor summarized recent developments, particularly the discovery of the arrow in the cemetery. Then he set out the theory that he had proposed to Jacinthe and Lemaire about the Northern file. Finally, he brought Tousignant into the discussion. Delaney pounded himself on the chest, like a man with indigestion or possibly a heart problem. He made a face and burped.

"You still think Rivard was blackmailing Tousignant with the Northern file? Or do you suspect that the senator killed him to get his hands on it?"

"I'm not sure, Paul. But I'd like to bring him in for questioning."

The suggestion was more of a shot in the dark than anything else.

"You've already checked their cell records," Delaney said. "You still believe they might have communicated with each other?"

"Rivard had two phones on him: an iPhone and a prepaid burner. If Tousignant was also using a burner, there's no way to track their calls. Same thing if Tousignant was making the calls from his home phone. And how do we even know they were communicating by phone?"

"Considering the senator's status, I'd like to have something more substantial before poking the wasp nest. We're in enough trouble as it is."

As Victor tried without success to conceal his disappointment, a sly smile came to Delaney's lips. "But that doesn't prevent us from putting his home phone under surveillance."

The detective sergeant smacked the desk. "Where there's a will, there's a way!" He winked at his boss. "I'll talk to Jacinthe. We'll get to work on the warrant now."

Delaney raised his hands to slow Victor down. "Hang on. I want to hear what happened last night."

Victor described his evening at Le Confessionnal in detail and talked about the unsuccessful online search he'd done overnight. "I'm sure the guy in the baseball cap was the killer, Paul."

Delaney rubbed his coarse grey beard, then ran a hand through his hair. "Seems like your guy in the cap wants us to find something. An event that apparently happened on October 23rd, 1964. But where? In Montreal? In Quebec? Elsewhere in the world? We could search forever. Before the seventies, police record-keeping was nowhere near as systematic as it is today. Plenty of old files were never entered into the Police Information Centre database when it was created."

The desk phone started to ring. Without looking away from Victor, Delaney picked up the phone and disconnected the line. The ringing stopped, and the chief reacted with obvious relief.

"That's the problem, Paul. If it's a cold case, there'll be a physical file somewhere. But we have to know what we're looking for."

"If it's a murder case, there should be a file. But — and I'd never say this in public — in the past, regional forces were less organized than in Montreal. Remember the Thérèse Luce murder in Longueuil? Nearly all the major evidence was lost. The lead detective was fired. And this was in the eighties. Imagine what it was like in the sixties."

Victor closed his eyes, discouraged.

"For now, I'm limiting my search to Quebec, even though some clues point elsewhere." Silence. "We can't very well start pestering Interpol or the FBI, can we?"

"You're saying this because of MK-ULTRA and the reference to Kennedy on the hangman drawing?"

Victor nodded. Above their heads, a neon tube flickered and went out.

"There's no point in contacting anyone until we have a better idea of what we're looking for."

Delaney opened his drawer and pulled out a little canister of cloves. He threw several in his mouth and started chewing. "And what does 'there were others' mean?"

"Could it be a series of murders or violent crimes that took place in 1964?" Silence. "You're an old man, Paul. Doesn't the date ring a bell?"

Delaney smiled at the joke. He closed his eyes, put his chin in his hands and scoured his memory. "Nothing comes to mind." Silence. "Maybe you should go see Joe Beans."

Victor's face lit up. He jumped to his feet. "That's a stroke of genius, Paul! Thank you." His eager hand was already on the door handle.

"He doesn't have a phone, but he lives at …"

Victor didn't turn. His footsteps were echoing in the corridor. "I know where to find him."

66

JOE BEANS

His name was Joseph Binet, but everyone called him Joe Beans. During his first months as a Montreal police officer, an older cop had given him the nickname, and it had stuck.

From that moment on, over a career that had spanned more than forty-five years, everyone on the force had called him by that name. It irritated him at first, but if anyone had asked how he felt about it now, looking back, Joe Beans would probably have said he found it funny.

Nearly blind, the old archivist had retired three years ago. At his age, with his years of service, he could enjoy full retirement without any actuarial penalty.

Joe Beans had never entirely succeeded in adapting to computers, which might help explain how he had become indispensable. Instead of relying on technology, he had only ever trusted his own mental faculties.

The man was, in a way, the memory of the Montreal Police.

He could recite by heart the names of the children of the last three heads of the Financial Crimes section. He could tell you about obscure unsolved murders, including ones that dated back three decades, for which files were hard to locate.

Joe could also give you the names of numerous players on the roster of each edition of the Montreal Canadiens, from the founding of the club in 1909 until the firing of coach Jacques Demers in 1995.

He had never accepted that dismissal. From that day forward, he'd ceased to be a Habs fan, transferring his allegiance to the

Detroit Red Wings, a "classy" organization, in his opinion, that was perennially competitive and treated its employees "with respect and consideration." Not to mention the fact that they knew how to make the most of late-round draft picks and put winning teams on the ice season after season.

But that was a separate issue.

Joe Beans had finished his career as principal archivist at the Major Crimes Unit. While other departments didn't want him because of his age, his declining eyesight, and his inability to carry out database searches, Paul Delaney had kept him on as long as possible, because he liked the man and because he knew that when Joe left, he would take a piece of the force's history with him.

Before being demoted to a local station because of the blunder that had cost the lives of two of his men, Victor had known Joe Beans well and had felt genuine affection for him.

The old man lived in a rooming house as shabby as the one in which André Lortie had spent the final months of his life. Joe didn't have a phone, which complicated matters for Victor when he knocked on the door and no one answered.

A man approached and, gazing at a spot on the wall behind the detective sergeant's head, suggested that he might find Joe in the basement of the nearby church, where it was bingo night.

Victor, who had no particular fondness for senior citizens, found himself in a crowd of them when he arrived in the church hall. Indeed, he had a distinct impression that all heads had turned to look at him as he walked in, so much so that he felt obliged to raise a hand and offer a general wave of greeting. But by then the players had already turned back to their cards as the caller announced, "B-12!"

Long tables were set out in rows, with players jammed together at each. Country music was playing softly, and all the players were trying, more or less successfully, to keep their conversations in an undertone, with the result that a sort of booming drone filled the room, making things worse than if people had been speaking in regular voices.

At first glance, Victor was unable to spot Joe Beans among the hundred or so players.

"G-48," the caller announced.

A voice rang out and a hand went up. "BINGO!"

Victor was still scanning the room for the old archivist when a woman came up to him and asked with a smile if he wanted to play. When he responded that he was looking for someone, she suggested that she might know the person ...

"His name is Joseph Binet," Victor said.

The woman shook her head and was about to walk away without another word when he corrected himself. "Everyone calls him Joe Beans."

The woman smiled broadly and signalled for him to follow her. Of course she knew him! Who didn't know Joe Beans?

She led Victor through a warren of hallways into the bowels of the church, stopping at a small, windowless space that served as a storage room but had probably once been a meeting room for priests.

Joe Beans was by himself at a table in a corner, with a stack of documents in front of him. A powerful desk lamp lit up the work surface. As he drew closer, Victor realized that the lamp was actually part of a magnifier that dramatically enlarged documents inserted into it, enabling the old man to read them.

"You have a visitor, Joe," the woman said before turning and heading back to the battlefield.

Joe lifted his head and looked toward the detective sergeant.

Remembering Joe's weakness for Boston cream donuts, Victor had stopped off at Tim Hortons and bought a box of them. He placed the box on the table, but there was no reaction. Surprised, Victor waved his hands in front of Joe's face, but the elderly archivist showed no awareness of them.

The situation had deteriorated since the last time: Joe couldn't see anymore.

A white film covered his eyes. Though his cataracts had been removed surgically, they kept coming back.

"Hello, Joe," Victor said softly.

The old man's brow furrowed, as it did whenever he was concentrating. The two men hadn't spoken in several years, but it took only a moment for Joe's features to light up. His hand reached out and touched the detective sergeant's face. His fingers moved over the rough cheeks.

"Victor? Victor Lessard? Is that you?"

"Yes, it's me, Joe."

Victor opened the box. The donuts' aroma filled the room.

There was a tear on the old man's cheek as he took one of Victor's hands in both of his own. He was skeletally thin.

Eyes closed, Joe chewed each bite with a care that bordered on obsession. Then, using one of the paper napkins that Victor had brought along, he wiped the traces of cream from the corners of his mouth. There was such surrender in his gestures, such appreciation for the pleasure of the moment, that Victor couldn't help being moved.

Joe ate three donuts before taking a pause, temporarily satisfied.

Victor closed the box and set it aside, assuring Joe that the remaining donuts were for him, which brought a smile to the archivist's lips.

Looking at the yellowed documents on the table, Victor asked what Joe was up to. Joe answered that he had agreed to give up bingo for a while in order to help the parish put its archives in order.

The job was difficult, the old man added, because, despite the magnifier, he was finding it harder and harder to see.

Then, like old friends reuniting, they talked about the past.

It was a not-so-distant past in which they had seen each other regularly — a period Joe referred to as the time when he still had eyes.

Without going into too much detail about the investigation, Victor finally set out the reasons for his visit and explained what he was trying to find out.

Joe Beans raised an eyebrow and sat there for a long time, gazing absently into space.

"An event that took place on October 23rd, 1964. Hmm …" He shrugged. There was a long silence. "That was a while ago, my friend …"

The archivist talked about several murders that had been committed in 1964, but nothing in October. Nevertheless, Victor made some entries in his notebook.

Then, after another long silence during which he seemed to have dozed off, Joe added, "The only event that matches that date is a hunting accident. I don't know if it's what you're looking for, but as I recall, it happened in a wooded area, not far from Joliette. If you're lucky, the police will have kept a file. Otherwise, you'll surely find an article in the records of the local paper or the *Journal de Montréal*. Unless I'm mistaken, the accident involved a father and son. At the time, news of the case reached here because investigators wondered at first whether it wasn't a mercy killing followed by a suicide. The son was mentally handicapped."

Victor shook his head, incredulous. "I know you have a great memory, Joe. But how can you possibly recall details of a case that's nearly half a century old?"

The old man smiled sadly. "My older brother died in a hunting accident in 1959. That left a mark."

Dad and Léonard have gone hunting for moose. Charlie wanted to go too, but Mom said no because of Charlie's fever. Sweating, Charlie clutches the sheet and bites a clenched fist in rage. The fever is nothing compared with the heartless remark Dad made as he was leaving, wearing his checked jacket, rifle under his arm: "Besides, Charlie, hunting is for men. And how many times do I have to tell you to take that cap off your head when you're in the house?"

Affronted, wearing an angry expression, Charlie wanted to yell, "Then why are you bringing Léonard along? He may be a man, but he's a retard!"

But Charlie kept quiet, not wanting to make Mom sad. Also, Léonard has never done anything hurtful to Charlie; it would have been unfair to be mean to him when the only guilty person in this situation was Dad. How could he have dared to say a thing like that? It was an insult.

Since those two days in September when Dad went missing and then returned, thrown from a moving car onto the gravel, Charlie has had the impression that Dad is a shadow of his old self. His injuries weren't serious: they healed quickly. Yet, since that time, Dad has stopped getting into the car each morning to go add up numbers at the office. He spends his days shut up in the darkness and silence of his workshed behind the house. Often, when he emerges, he doesn't say a word to the family. Worse, sometimes it seems like he doesn't even recognize them.

Charlie also finds it strange that Dad looks out the window every time they hear a car going by in the distance. He takes his hunting rifle with him whenever he goes out. Charlie can't explain things other than by thinking the body is still Dad's, but there's somebody else inside his head.

Still, little by little, life has gone back to normal. They've almost managed to forget about what happened, though Charlie sometimes hears Mom crying at night, when the lights are on in the workshed.

After more than an hour of applying cool compresses to Charlie's forehead, Mom gives Charlie a kiss and heads for the door. The medication has brought down the fever, but Mom wants Charlie to sleep and get some strength back. While Mom watches from the doorway, Charlie makes a show of nodding off, breathing regularly, the way Lennie does when he falls asleep.

After Mom goes downstairs, Charlie dresses silently and struggles to suppress a cough before grabbing a pillow to muffle the noise. Wiping away the spittle afterward, Charlie knows Mom has gone down to work on her thesis. She won't come upstairs again for hours. Before opening the bedroom window, Charlie puts on rubber boots, a green raincoat, and the ever-present baseball cap.

Charlie has slipped out of the house in secret many times before, meeting Cantin in the woods to smoke cigarettes and trade stories about flying saucers coming to abduct children, and also to talk about René Desharnais and the other jackasses at school.

But that was before Cantin's parents decided to move back to the city, because there were no jobs in the country and money doesn't grow on trees. Now, all those fun times with Cantin belong to the "good old days," an expression Charlie learned from the books Dad used to read out loud each night before bed.

Except now Dad is the one who was abducted by aliens. They did weird things to his brain, and that's why he's stopped reading to Charlie before bed.

Charlie concentrates. From the bedroom window, it's a matter of jumping onto the porch roof without being heard, then, at the edge of the roof, grasping the rainwater pipe — it's very solid — and climbing down silently, rubber boots braced against the cedar shingles. Reaching the ground, Charlie crouches and listens: silence. No one in sight.

Stealthy as a Sioux brave, Charlie crawls beneath the kitchen window to avoid Mom's notice, then, reaching the corner of the house, straightens up and runs toward the field. Seconds later, Charlie is moving through the high grass along the path that disappears into the woods. The trees sway tranquilly in the breeze.

If Dad and Lennie are going hunting, then so is Charlie!

The day is grey and overcast, but Charlie is warmly dressed in a fleece-lined raincoat. The forest, dripping from rain showers, sings and glistens. A carpet of leaves muffles Charlie's footfalls on the moist earth.

Charlie knows by heart how to reach the blind that Dad built with Lennie a few years ago.

From the pond, Charlie veers onto a secondary path that makes it possible to reach the blind by a safe route, never getting into the line of fire, the way Dad has taught, "in case there's an emergency."

Dad will be annoyed, but Charlie has already come up with a story: the fever broke, so Mom had a change of heart and said it was okay to go out to the blind. Charlie knows there'll be a price to pay later, when Mom and Dad figure out the deception.

A gun goes off, its sound echoing through the trees and sliding away among the branches. Charlie jumps, then smiles and hurries onward. Dad is bound to be in a better mood if they've already caught something.

Suddenly, a scream rends the silence. A long, terrified scream that freezes Charlie's blood.

Lennie!

Without thinking, Charlie springs forward, running at top speed, pushing branches out of the way, ignoring the stinging blows of their whiplike resistance. Something serious must have happened to Dad for Lennie to scream like that.

A second scream, more terrifying than the first, shatters the air, followed closely by another gunshot.

Charlie stops short, standing very still. Heavy silence has fallen over the forest.

Dead silence …

Charlie sets off again, running desperately, with a parched mouth and constricted throat that make it impossible to call out. Heart hammering, fighting down a flood of terror, Charlie is trying to repel the thought that keeps coming back: they're dead.

Straight ahead through the brush, a camouflage jacket appears — a jacket that doesn't belong to Lennie or Dad. Instinctively, Charlie dives into a thicket of ferns and takes refuge behind a broad tree. Lying flat, fingernails sunk into the bark, Charlie risks a cautious look out from the hiding place. A man in combat fatigues is approaching along the path. He has a pistol tucked into his belt. His face is streaked with camouflage face paint.

That angular face — it's the driver of the '57 Chevy!

The man stops close by.

Trembling, Charlie doesn't dare move. There's a smell of ammonia and a muffled sound of liquid striking a hard surface.

Wide-eyed, Charlie realizes the man is urinating onto the trunk of the tree, which has become the last line of defence between Charlie and death.

The man clears his throat and burps like a pig. A gob of snot and saliva hits Charlie in the shoulder and trickles slowly downward.

"Goddamn shitty life." The man sighs, closing his zipper. "It was about time."

Biting down hard on one fist so as not to cry out, Charlie sees the combat boots stamp, pivot, and walk off toward the road that winds through the woods less than two hundred metres to the east.

Charlie lies still for a long time, trembling, until the sound of the Chevy's engine fades away in the distance and only the bird calls remain. Numb, stiff limbed, Charlie moves warily along the path. The blind appears through the trees a short distance away.

The wind rises. Raindrops start slapping Charlie hard in the face.

There's a human form on the ground. Lennie is lying at the base of the blind, right leg bent under his body at an impossible angle. Charlie edges closer, lower lip quivering. Lennie's face has been obliterated by the gunshot, reduced to a shapeless mass of bloody tissue.

In shock, Charlie can't look away from Lennie's remaining eye, which shimmers in the forest light. Then, as the brain connections start to work, Charlie retreats, falls backward, and struggles to stand up again, feet slithering in the mud. Charlie's hand falls on an object and grasps it. In the instant it takes to realize what the object is, Charlie throws it to the ground: it's a fragment of Lennie's skull.

Catching a breath has become a struggle. Images are tumbling over one another, the forest is spinning, the wind is keening, and a black shroud is descending over everything. Charlie is about to lose consciousness when a noise drifts down from overhead. A kind of gurgle. Charlie looks up at the blind built into the tree boughs fifteen feet off the ground and listens. It's not a gurgle. It's a voice. A groan.

Dad!

Charlie's hands clutch at the rungs of the wooden ladder, climbing as fast as humanly possible.

The first thing Charlie sees, entering the little space, is the blood. It's everywhere, on the floors, on the walls. From the splatters, Charlie's gaze falls on Dad. Blood is flowing from his mouth. His breath comes in murmurs, punctuated by bubbling. Through the hole in his abdomen, his guts have spilled out. He's lying in a pool of red.

"… arlie …"

Charlie puts a small hand under Dad's neck to cradle him, and kisses his forehead. Dad smiles through his agony.

"Breathe, Dad." Starting to cry, Charlie tries to press the guts back into Dad's body. "You have to hang on, Dad. I need you. You can't leave me."

"Re ... member, Char ... lie. Re ... re ... me ..."

"Breathe, Dad. I'll go get help!"

A long sigh rises in the dying man's throat and floats out through his mouth. His eyes flicker and roll back. The lids droop. His head sags gently to one side.

"Breathe, Dad. Breathe! No, Dad ... Breathe!"

The rain pounds on the roof of the little hut and begins to seep in between the planks.

The cries die in Charlie's eight-year-old throat.

67

SURPRISE GIFT

Victor smoked his cigarette all the way down, stubbed it out in the ashtray near the door, and went inside. His meeting with the pit bull had been brief but encouraging. Martin was in good hands. Before getting onto the elevator, still hoping for a call or text from Nadja, he checked his voice mail. Even though, deep down, he knew the fault was his, he was suppressing the urge to make the first move and call her.

In the kitchenette, while he made himself a cup of decaf, the popping of bubble gum mixed with another kind of popping: Loïc was making microwave popcorn. The kid had an appointment later in the afternoon with the owner of a shop that specialized in archery equipment.

Victor took a handful of popcorn from the bowl that the young detective offered, then instructed him to assemble the investigation team in the conference room.

The whispers fell silent when he entered the room. Jacinthe was slouched in a chair with her feet up on a second chair. In front of her, the bowl that had been full of popcorn moments ago now lay empty.

Lemaire and Loïc were on their feet, bent over a laptop. Loïc snapped it shut when he saw the detective sergeant.

Victor knew they had been looking at online reports about his son.

"So, where should we start?" he asked, pretending not to have noticed.

When no one spoke up, he continued. "Let's start by checking to see if there's a file in provincial police archives in Joliette. With a little luck, there may be an investigator or a member of the victims' family who's still alive."

"Hold on, hotshot," Jacinthe said. She hadn't been totally convinced earlier in the day when she'd heard Victor's account of his meeting with Joe Beans. "MK-whattayacallit, the Kennedy assassination, the Northern file that isn't a Northern file, and now a hunting accident in October of 1964 ... am I the only one who doesn't see how this all fits together?"

She looked pointedly at each of her colleagues.

"You forgot the matchbook with 'there were others' written on it," Victor added calmly.

Jacinthe chuckled and rolled her eyes.

"I'm sure there were others, but other what? We have four murders using two different methods, a suicide, and, if you throw in Will Bennett, a dingbat in a coma. And now you want us to start looking into some prehistoric accident because one old codger says it happened on the same date? Wake me up, somebody," she said with mock desperation, "I'm having a bad dream."

"Let's be clear, we're not neglecting any of the other leads," Victor said, refusing to be provoked. "But yes, we're going to start looking into the hunting accident in Joliette. I spoke to Paul about Tousignant. We've agreed to put a wiretap on him. Someone needs to draft the warrant. We'll deal with other things as they come."

Jacinthe rose to her feet, grumbling, pushed her chair aside and said she'd take care of the warrant. Loïc volunteered to look into the hunting accident, then jumped up enthusiastically and headed off to his desk.

Victor turned to face Lemaire. They were the only ones left in the room. There was an awkward silence. "The kid isn't ready to handle this by himself, Gilles. Would you mind tactfully ..."

The Gnome assured Victor that he'd give Loïc a hand. He also said he'd call Jacob Berger to get an update on the Rivard autopsy, and he'd recontact the forensics team that was handling the crime scenes at the cemetery and Parc Maisonneuve.

Stricken to the soul, Victor was left alone to brood, his head in his hands, wondering whether Martin would be all right and asking himself why Nadja wasn't calling.

He would end his days alone, in a home, sucking lozenges.

Carefully done up in white wrapping paper decorated with chubby Santas and festive green Christmas trees, the package was lying on his desk when he returned, having probably been put there by one of the other cops. Victor smiled, unable to resist the thought that it was Nadja's doing. Then he wondered: why would she send him a gift? Next he thought of Blaikie's assistant at the psychiatry department. Maybe she was sending him additional material. But why would she have bothered to gift-wrap it?

The question hung unanswered in his mind.

With one fingernail, the detective sergeant unsealed the little envelope taped to the wrapping paper and extracted a white card. *Merry Christmas, Mr. Lessard.*

Tearing the paper, he found a small cardboard box, about ten by fifteen centimetres. His eyebrows rose. Intrigued, he opened his desk drawer and retrieved a pair of scissors. Using the tip of one blade, he cut the adhesive tape holding the lid in place.

Victor put his hand in the box and pulled out an object encased in bubble wrap.

With increasing eagerness, he removed the wrap to find a high-quality leather wallet. It looked new. It had been a long time since anyone had given him a wallet.

Opening it, he realized his mistake. For a moment he sat there in shock, staring at a driver's licence as he replayed the sequence of events in his head. They wouldn't be needing a wiretap warrant for the senator.

The name on the driver's licence was Daniel Tousignant.

68

VIRGINIE

Driving at top speed, they were still fifteen minutes from Senator Tousignant's house when Victor spoke by phone to Constable Felipe Garcia, one of the patrol officers who had responded to the urgent call that had gone out to all units over the police frequency.

Garcia had been in the process of sliding a ticket under the windshield wiper of an illegally parked Ford Focus on LaSalle Boulevard when his partner, Denis Beaupré, still in the patrol car, signalled to him with a flash of the headlights before activating the emergency lights and siren. If Garcia had been within vocal range, Beaupré would have said, "Get moving, buddy, we've got an emergency."

Over the phone, Garcia explained to Victor that on arriving at the senator's house, he and his partner had found the front door unlocked and the alarm system disarmed.

Securing the empty house room by room, the two patrol officers hadn't noticed anything out of the ordinary. "Everything seems to be in order," Garcia said. "But his daughter has just arrived."

"His daughter? Let me speak to her," Victor said.

A smooth voice caressed his ear.

"Hello?"

"This is Detective Sergeant Victor Lessard of the Montreal Police. Who am I speaking to?"

"Virginie Tousignant. Is something going on with my father?"

The image of an attractive woman crossing and uncrossing her legs at a press conference moved stealthily through his mind. "The journalist?"

"That's right."

"We're looking for the senator. Do you know where he is?"

"No. I'm looking for him, too. We were supposed to have lunch together." Panic rose in her voice. "Now I'm scared —"

Victor cut her off. "Stay where you are. I'm on my way."

He hung up without waiting for a response.

This was far from good news. Having to deal with family members this early in the process was difficult, but a journalist would be pure hell.

While Jacinthe went around corners at high speed, heedless of the icy streets, Victor couldn't help wondering whether Virginie Tousignant was one of the journalists who had cut him to pieces in the wake of Martin's arrest.

Constable Garcia, who had been watching from the window, opened the door.

In the front hall, Victor and Jacinthe removed their footwear, and Garcia led them to the dining room. When Victor asked where Garcia's partner was, the patrol cop pointed to the back of the house and said he was checking the grounds.

In fact, Constable Beaupré was giving free rein to his inner Jack Bauer, going around the property with one hand poised over the handle of his pistol.

Jacinthe went back to the front hall and put on her boots to look for Beaupré, grumbling, "Dimwit."

Victor watched through the window as his partner walked away through the snow, then turned back to the constable. "Don't touch anything before the forensics team gets here, Garcia."

As Victor was finishing the sentence, Virginie Tousignant came out of the kitchen carrying a tray, which she placed on the dining-room table. The aroma of coffee filled the room, teasing the detective sergeant's nostrils.

"Forensics?" she asked, sounding anxious.

They looked at each other for a moment, and Victor felt the troubling effect of her beauty. She was dressed in close-fitting jeans and a white sweater. Her hair had been gathered in a loose bun, with a stray lock falling onto her forehead. She blew upward to move it aside.

"I can't say more at the moment," he said, trying to sound reassuring.

They introduced themselves formally. Victor saw her eyes fill with tears when he shook her hand. At this point, Constable Garcia got the distinct sense that his presence was no longer required. Grabbing the shoulder microphone clipped to his bulletproof vest, he stepped away to check in with his supervisor.

Victor knew what Virginie Tousignant's next question would be before she even asked it, and he'd have preferred that she not ask it at all. He was no good at lying.

"His disappearance is linked to the string of murders, isn't it?"

To cope with his nervousness, Victor was restlessly playing with his phone. The young woman had a right to know, but he hesitated to bring up the wallet, fearing an emotional reaction that he wouldn't be able to deal with.

"It's too early to be talking about a disappearance," he ventured. "Your father may simply be late ..."

"No," Virginie said. "He's never late. Why are you here?"

Victor's cellphone moved more rapidly between his hands.

"Your date with your father ... was it made far in advance?"

"Dad called me yesterday evening. He wanted to talk."

"Did you find that odd?"

"Why would I? My father is full of surprises. He seemed to be in a good mood. Should I have pressed him?"

Virginie put her face in her hands and began to cry. Since she was only a few steps away, Victor drew near and put a sympathetic hand on her shoulder. To his surprise, the young woman pressed herself against his chest. Not knowing what else to do, he put an arm around her and softly spoke comforting words to her. At the same time, his phone vibrated. Over Virginie's shoulder, he saw that Nadja had just sent him a cryptic text message:

it'll be okay for Martin

Victor tried without success to decipher the message. What was Nadja trying to say? Had she convinced her brother to intercede on Martin's behalf? Or was it just that she believed Martin would prevail with the help of a good lawyer? Should Victor feel relieved?

And as Virginie continued to sob, leaning against him, an important detail suddenly occurred to him: Nadja hadn't written a word about the two of them. She had made no mention of the previous day's events, even though a simple "We should talk" would have sufficed and would have given him cause for hope.

Don't read anything into it, he warned himself, but he couldn't help seeing this as a sign. As far as Nadja was concerned, the relationship they had once shared was over.

Out of the corner of his eye, he saw Taillon remove her boots and cross the front hall in silence, approaching them. When she spotted her partner with his arm around the young woman, she winked knowingly and gave him a sly smile.

With his free hand, Victor gave her the finger.

As he took a sip of water, Daniel Tousignant looked around him once more.

The bedroom was from another era, simple and comfortable: a double bed with a brown-and-orange wool bedspread and a patterned quilt at its foot, dark, prefinished panel walls, a textured poster of a German shepherd crookedly tacked to the wall, a golden-yellow carpet from which humid smells wafted, a nightstand, a straight-backed chair and an old wooden desk. On the desk lay a single-bulb lamp, an untouched pad of paper, several ballpoint pens, a half-filled jug of water, the glass from which he had just drunk, a green-crystal alarm clock, a cassette recorder and, still wrapped, ten TDK cassettes in a careful stack.

Through the window, past the spruce boughs, he could see the river, from which mist was rising, and the corner of a yellow ice-fishing shack.

He would never be found here.

Tousignant smiled — a smile that contained very little bitterness — at the thought that the river would be part of his karma until the moment of his death.

A little earlier, he had enjoyed a hearty meal of spaghetti and meatballs. Now, with the tray taken away, it was time to work.

He glanced at the plate that lay close to hand. He had been thoughtfully provided with a melon cut into wedges, his favourite treat. He nearly gave in to temptation and ate a wedge right away, but then he changed his mind; he preferred to wait until later.

Taking a cassette between his fingers, he pierced the plastic film with the tip of a ballpoint, pulled off the wrapping, and tucked it under the base of the lamp. As he had learned to do years ago, he inserted the pen into the right-hand reel of the cassette and turned it until the brown recording tape appeared. Pressing the STOP/EJECT button, he opened the compartment and inserted the cassette he had just carefully prepared.

From the box, he removed the sheet of labels.

On the A side, he simply wrote:

#1

Leaning closer to the cassette recorder, which was a standard model, rectangular in shape and made of black plastic, he pressed the REC and PLAY buttons.

A red light went on. The numbers on the counter, which he had reset to zero, began to turn slowly. The old man checked to make sure the tape was rolling. Then he took a deep breath.

"My name is Daniel Tousignant. I am of sound mind and body. This is my confession."

70

WHAT IS THAT BEEPING NOISE?

Under Virginie's insistent questioning, Victor had been left with no choice but to reveal the facts, while Jacinthe gazed at the ceiling. For a few seconds, as he described receiving the package that contained her father's wallet, Virginie's nostrils had quivered and he had supposed fresh tears would flow, but the young woman had managed to keep her composure.

Naturally, she had bombarded him with questions.

But what could he tell her? They knew nothing.

In theory, the two detectives should have obtained a warrant before searching the house. But when they explained that the process would be terribly time consuming, and that she could save them trouble by giving her consent, Virginie didn't hesitate for a second. She did, however, insist on being present during their search. Neither cop opposed the idea.

Even if all indications pointed to abduction, it was still necessary to initiate the protocol for a simple missing-person case. Nothing could be left to chance.

It was agreed that constables Garcia and Beaupré would return to their station to coordinate the search effort. Before they left, Virginie gave them a recent photograph of her father, as well as a detailed physical description and details of his health and psychological profile: apart from a cardiac pacemaker, he had no known illnesses or disabilities. He was taking no medication, and he had exhibited no suicidal thoughts or mental problems.

Victor also asked Virginie to draw up a list of public places that the senator was known to frequent. After leaving with the document, Garcia and Beaupré would immediately dispatch patrols to the places where Tousignant was likeliest to go. They would also get in touch with hospitals and emergency services.

Meanwhile, Jacinthe had checked the garage. The senator's two cars were parked there, along with his boat, loaded onto a trailer.

Before the detectives had left Versailles, their efforts to triangulate Tousignant's cellphone had failed. Victor had also put out an alert on the senator's bank cards.

After some consultation, Jacinthe and Victor had decided to wait before bringing in the forensics team and its heavy artillery.

Virginie absented herself for a few minutes to freshen up in the bathroom.

When she returned, her eyes met Victor's, and she smiled. Though Victor wasn't sure his instinct was right, or what the reasons for it might be, he sensed that her attitude had changed.

He wondered for a moment whether it had something to do with the fact that she had put on high heels. Then he shrugged and got to work.

Initially, the search of the house consisted of going from room to room, looking for things that were out of place, details that might provide information about a possible kidnapping.

For example: Had the kidnappers left behind any indication that they'd forced Tousignant to go with them, or that they'd assaulted him? Had the senator managed, without his abductors' knowledge, to hide a note, a message, or any other hint that might assist those who were looking for him?

To speed up the effort, the two detectives agreed to split up, with Jacinthe going upstairs and Victor staying on the ground floor. Virginie decided to accompany Victor. They found nothing that might help them locate Tousignant.

Next, they established a base of operations in the senator's study, where Victor asked Virginie to create a list of people her father might have been in touch with during the last few hours: family, close friends, colleagues.

With surgical precision, Virginie drew up the list and made the calls in a hurry, not wasting time on unnecessary explanations, getting straight to the point, obtaining the information she sought and then hanging up. Apart from Tousignant's assistant, to whom he'd spoken earlier in the day to take his messages, no one had heard from him.

Realizing that he knew very little about the senator's personal life, the detective sergeant had no choice but to ask Virginie for details. He learned that she was an only child, and that her father had been widowed a little over a year ago, after nearly fifty years of marriage to her mother.

Victor got Nadja's voice mail once again and hung up without leaving a message. His frustration was mounting. He had tried a dozen times to reach her since receiving her text, but she wasn't taking his calls. He pocketed his phone angrily and took a moment to calm himself before stepping back into the office, where Virginie was looking through her father's computer.

"Find anything, Virginie?"

Without discussing it, they had shifted to a first-name basis. Virginie looked up at him. "A lot of stuff about the foundation … I'm pretty sure he'd rather I didn't know these things, but I don't think it's the kind of information we're looking for."

After half an hour of combing through documents taken from a metal filing cabinet, Victor's eyes began to hurt. He stood up, yawning, took a few steps around the room and stretched his limbs. Virginie's fingers continued to tap at the computer keyboard.

The detective sergeant looked at the framed documents on the wall. Among the degrees in law and philosophy that Tousignant had earned, Victor saw three honorary doctorates, conferred in recognition of his contributions to the cause of environmental protection, mostly through his foundation.

With some amusement and considerable interest, Victor's gaze fell on the framed dust jacket of a book:

> Virginie C. Tousignant
> *A Comparative Analysis: Buster Keaton vs. Charlie Chaplin*
> Who Was the Greatest Comedian of the Silent Film Era?

"Wow. You wrote a book."

"I did a master's degree in film studies. I was able to get my thesis published."

Victor nodded with unconcealed admiration. Virginie got up and approached him. "My father's very proud of that," she said, looking at the framed book jacket.

"He should be. Getting a book published is a real accomplishment. So who *was* the greatest comedian, Chaplin or Keaton?"

Hands on her hips, head cocked to one side, Virginie feigned annoyance. "You're going to wish you'd never asked." Her pursed lips were irresistible. "Keaton's character is less emblematic than Chaplin's. When you look at Keaton, you see an ordinary man making his way coldly through a series of challenging situations, while Chaplin's character is a situation in itself, a bizarre animal, a magical creature. Compared with Chaplin, Keaton is the man who never laughs. But his sensibility is much more modern than Chaplin's Victorian sentimentality. On the other hand, Keaton's films carry less of a social or humanist message than Chaplin's. All of which is to say that after writing over six hundred pages on the subject, I still don't have a satisfactory answer to the question. Go figure."

Victor searched his memory. He'd seen several of Chaplin's films, but couldn't remember ever seeing one of Keaton's.

"Which is the movie where Chaplin makes fun of Hitler?"

"*The Great Dictator*," Virginie answered.

"Right. That one was really good."

They were both startled by the sound of a throat being cleared. Victor spun around.

Jacinthe was standing in the doorway. "Knock, knock," she said, smiling awkwardly. "Sorry to disturb you. Lessard, can I talk to you for a minute?"

Taillon led him into an adjoining space, one of the house's several living rooms, this one decorated with rustic-themed wallpaper.

"Good to see you're keeping busy, Vic," she said, winking. "I didn't find anything upstairs."

Reddening in spite of himself, Victor mumbled something about having tired eyes from all the documents he'd looked at and not wanting to make too many demands on Virginie, for whom this situation was very painful.

Jacinthe's insinuations shouldn't have bothered him, but the reality was that she'd caught him out like a teenager. She half listened to his mumbled excuses before getting down to business.

"Two things. One, I just spoke to Mona Vézina. She confirms what we suspected. The handwriting on the matchbook, the hangman drawing, and the card that came with Tousignant's wallet all match. The three messages were written by the same person."

Victor took note of the information, which hardly advanced their effort.

"And two?"

"The Gnome just called. Bennett is out of his coma. He's strong enough to talk."

"Is Gilles going to question him?"

"No, he's on the road with Loïc."

The detective sergeant was struck by a coughing fit. "Are they going to Joliette to look into the hunting accident?"

"Not right away. First they have to visit an archery store."

"Right. The arrow we found in the cemetery. I'd forgotten …"

"So, Gilles wants me to go to the hospital to talk to Bennett."

Closing his eyes, Victor nodded several times. "Of course. Go ahead."

"Did you bring your condoms?" Jacinthe asked with a mocking grin.

Taken aback, the detective sergeant frowned, then flushed with anger. "What the fuck is the matter with you?"

"Victor Lessard! We both know you've never been able to resist a good-looking woman. Have you noticed the way she stares at you?" She smiled suggestively. "Anyway, if I were you, I wouldn't beat around the bush. Not after what happened between you and Nadja's brother. If you ask me, that ship has sunk."

The reminder of the previous day's confrontation pushed Victor over the brink.

"Go fuck yourself, Taillon!" he spat.

Jacinthe gave him another wink. "Settle down, big guy. It was a joke. Gotta go."

With the blood pounding furiously in his temples, Victor needed some time to compose himself.

Victor pinched the bridge of his nose between his thumb and forefinger. His eyes felt ready to burst out of their sockets. Another hour of poring over documents had convinced him that there were no clues to Tousignant's whereabouts hidden here. If the senator had wanted to leave them a message, they would have found it by now.

Virginie was still tirelessly going through her father's emails, taking notes as she tried to reconstruct, in the greatest possible detail, her father's schedule over the past few days.

So far, the exercise had yielded nothing. Victor was about to suggest that they take a break and order something to eat when Virginie's ringtone sounded: "Only Happy When It Rains," by Garbage. She stood up and stepped into the hallway to take the call.

After briefly listening to the caller, the young woman mouthed a few platitudes intended to convey sympathy and encouragement. The detective sergeant looked back down at the papers, wearing an expression of concentration, but he couldn't help listening. Virginie was speaking in a low voice, though not low enough to prevent him from hearing.

The caller began talking once again — Victor could tell from the voice that it was a man — but Virginie cut him off, saying yes, she was at her father's house, and no, he shouldn't expect her for dinner. She'd be home late.

Just before hanging up, by way of goodbye, she said, "Don't forget to feed Woodrow Wilson."

Not a word about the senator's disappearance.

Clearly, she had no desire to explain the situation to the caller, nor to get into an interminable conversation on the subject. She came back into the study, rummaged in her purse, and took out a tube of lip balm. Victor kept up his show of being immersed in his reading, but curiosity eventually got the better of him.

"I don't mean to be indiscreet," he said, "but isn't Woodrow Wilson the name of a former politician?"

Virginie applied the balm, then rubbed her lips together to spread it evenly.

"Yes. He was the twenty-eighth president of the United States. Served two terms from 1913 to 1921."

The detective sergeant let out a low whistle.

"Did you take film studies or history?"

"Same thing. And for your information, in the present case, Woodrow Wilson is our dog."

Victor looked at her wedding band, a shining bauble that, on her fine fingers, seemed as large as a Stanley Cup ring.

"You're married?"

Virginie glanced down at her hand. "Oh, this," she said in a disillusioned voice. "Jean-Bernard is a wonderful guy. That's the trouble. If he were an asshole, I'd be braver, and my life would be easier."

In other words: *My husband is a good man, I'm not happy with him anymore, but I can't make up my mind to leave him.* Having no desire to step on the banana peel that she'd just laid out in front of him, Victor decided not to pursue the matter.

"Isn't it a little long, when you call him?"

Virginie looked at him, puzzled.

"Woodrow Wilson, I mean."

The young woman's annoyed expression gave way to a smile. "It's W to his friends."

Victor hesitated momentarily, wondering, before he spoke, whether so much honesty was necessary. Then he came out with it: "My name is Victor Lessard, and I hate dogs."

This time Virginie laughed out loud. "So do I! If you only knew." There was an awkward silence. "Are *you* married?"

Victor answered too quickly for his own taste. "It's complicated."

A noise caught their attention: the beep of an electronic device. Frowning, Victor looked at Virginie. She nodded. She'd heard it, too.

After a few minutes of searching, they realized that the beeping was coming from a steel box equipped with an indicator light, which Victor found attached to the computer tower. With Virginie's permission, he sat down in front of the screen, located the application after a few clicks, and launched it. A control panel appeared on the screen, along with six windows displaying real-time exterior video feeds of the house's front door, driveway, and backyard.

"A surveillance system?" Virginie said, surprised. "Where are the cameras?"

"Hidden outside somewhere," Victor said. He hadn't noticed them, either. "They've gotten so small that you can put them just about anywhere. I've seen cameras in sprinklers, in ceiling lights, even in exit signs." Victor clicked on an icon and pointed at the new window that opened. "You see? Your father configured the system to send SMS alarms to his cellphone. The beeping we heard was just a local signal."

"So as soon as the system detects movement —" Virginie began.

Victor completed the sentence: "The images are sent to his phone."

He clicked on a new tab. "If we're lucky, the images are also recorded and stored." It took Victor only a few seconds to find the folder containing the video footage.

Watching the first sequence, they realized the alarm they'd just heard had been triggered by a car pulling into the driveway in order to turn around on the street. The next three sequences were as Victor and Virginie feared. They watched the images haphazardly the first time, then replayed them in chronological order.

10:15 a.m.: An individual walked into the camera's range. Victor recognized him instantly: it was the man in the red, white, and blue Expos cap, the man whom Victor had tried to catch at Le Confessionnal. The man came up the driveway, holding a package in his hands, and rang the doorbell. Because of the distance from the camera and the cap on his head, it was impossible to make out the man's features. He disappeared into the house.

10:17 a.m.: The senator came out of the house, hands behind his back, as though they were bound. With one hand on Tousignant's shoulder, the man in the cap walked half a step behind him, seeming to press something into the small of his back. Tousignant was offering no resistance. The pair walked out of camera range.

10:18 a.m.: The man in the cap re-entered the frame, dropped two garbage bags onto the snow beside the driveway, then walked out of the camera's view.

Three minutes had elapsed between the arrival of the man in the cap and his departure with the captive senator. Stunned, Virginie asked if there was any footage of what had happened within the house. Victor explained that the cameras covered only the home's exterior.

Although the events on the screen simply confirmed what they had been suspecting from the outset, the young woman was still in a state of shock. "He really has been kidnapped," she said, her voice unsteady.

Victor replayed the last sequence several times. It showed the man in the baseball cap carrying the two garbage bags. The detective sergeant got the impression that before letting them fall, the man had actually raised the two bags in the air, as though wanting to be sure the camera caught them.

Suddenly, Victor gave Virginie an urgent look. "Is today garbage day?"

NOVEMBER 1ST, 2005
THE SPONSORSHIP SCANDAL

Judge Gomery was tasked with rummaging through the trash bins of democracy, and today the commission over which he presides published its report on the sponsorship scandal.

According to the media, the evidence seems to suggest that the program was supervised by the Prime Minister's Office. It also shows that the public service hierarchy was subverted so the program could be more easily controlled, and that the Prime Minister's Office had been made aware of possible problems.

Underlings and hangers-on who pocketed money will go to prison. Who cares?

Judge Gomery would have liked to wring a confession out of former prime minister Jean Chrétien, nicknamed the "Little Guy from Shawinigan," but it was Chrétien who had the last laugh as he showed off his golf balls.

I have to admit that, though I've never agreed with his opinions, I admire the man's methods. As far as he was concerned, Quebec must, at all costs, remain a part of Canada. The end justified the means.

On that specific point, I agree with him: the end justifies the means.

EVERGREEN

71

GARBAGE AND REMOVAL

Victor hurried outside to retrieve the garbage bags; then, with Virginie, laid out their contents on the broad dining room table. The first bag contained two rigid binders, each one as thick as several telephone directories. The second contained five file folders, labelled P-1 to P-5. Each item was sealed with red tape marked NEVER DESTROY.

The detective sergeant could have sworn that the seals looked like they'd been removed and carefully put back in place. "The Northern file," Victor murmured.

He and Virginie stared at their discovery for a moment, not moving, not speaking. Victor's gaze betrayed some uncertainty about what came next. Thinking she knew the cause of his apprehension, Virginie declared peremptorily that there was no way she would let herself be excluded from the examination of the documents.

"You don't have a warrant, and we're in my father's house. You said yourself that you need my consent. Besides, I'm an investigative journalist. I can be helpful."

Victor nodded, inhaled deeply and let the air out of his lungs in little bursts.

At this point, Victor didn't give a damn about her consulting the documents. Contrary to what she supposed, his hesitancy had nothing to do with the fact that she might learn information related to the investigation. The detective sergeant's concern arose, rather, from his desire to shield her from the contents of the binders. How would she react if the files proved that her father was implicated in the murders? Was she ready to face something like that?

Knowing she'd dismiss his arguments out of hand, Victor decided, after a few seconds' consideration, to keep them to himself. "We'll need gloves," he said at last.

Virginie got up without a word and went upstairs, coming back down a few minutes later with a plastic box, which she placed on the table. Inside, there were numerous medical masks and latex gloves of all sizes. Seeing the astonished look on Victor's face, Virginie felt obliged to explain.

"During the bird flu panic, my father didn't take any chances. He followed all the safety precautions that the authorities suggested."

After putting on a pair of gloves, Virginie opened the first of the two big binders. Victor, meanwhile, removed the seal from the file folder marked P-1 and withdrew a sheaf of documents.

As he began to read, a look of surprise appeared on his face. Nathan Lawson had scrupulously preserved part of the correspondence he'd had with Senator Tousignant during 1963 and 1964. For the most part, Victor was able to grasp the primary meaning of the paragraphs he was reading, but he also knew there was a secondary level to these communications, a hidden meaning that eluded him.

Tousignant was clearly skilled in the art of indirectness and the use of coded expressions, which meant multiple interpretations of his words were possible:

```
Montreal
October 12th, 1963

PRIVILEGED AND STRICTLY CONFIDENTIAL

Dear Nathan,

Would you be so kind as to make the initial
payment, effective today, regarding the trans-
action in which we have an interest?

Cordially yours,
Daniel
```

Montreal

November 25th, 1963

PRIVILEGED AND STRICTLY CONFIDENTIAL

Dear Nathan,

Would you be so kind as to make the final payments, effective today, as agreed regarding
the transaction in which we have an interest?

Cordially yours,
Daniel

Montreal

September 15th, 1964

PRIVILEGED AND STRICTLY CONFIDENTIAL

Dear Nathan,

I have been advised that the audit of
Evergreen's financial statements for the fiscal year ending August 31 has resulted in
the identification of "anomalies" in the company's banking transactions — specifically
those dated October 12th and November 25th,
1963 — by the accounting firm that you engaged
to perform the audit.

I must confess that this strikes me as
a source of some concern. Didn't you assure
me that the production of audited financial
statements would be a mere formality? Weren't
you supposed to secure the accounting firm's
co-operation in advance?

In any event, you are surely conscious
of the fact that these "anomalies" would, if

```
they became public knowledge, put everything
at risk.
    In order to nip the problem in the bud and
prevent undesirable consequences, I suggest
that you prepare and distribute envelopes
that will ease the scruples of the individu-
als involved.
    I count on you to take care of this "for-
mality" with all possible speed.

Cordially yours,
Daniel
```

Victor straightened up and uncrossed his legs. As he was shaking the pins and needles out of his foot, the hangman drawing, the one in which Mona Vézina had spotted the hidden *JFK*, came into his mind. Though the sheet was back at the office, Victor was able, by closing his eyes and concentrating, to recall the letters and unfilled blank spaces beside the drawing, along with a couple of accompanying sentences:

```
Let's play hangman: _ V _ _ G _ _ _ N
Hint: Company filled with corpses.
```

The answer to the puzzle was there, within reach, among the paragraphs he'd just read. His pulse quickened as his index finger ran eagerly up to the first sentence of the memo dated September 15th, 1964:

```
I have been advised that the audit …
```

When Victor's eyes fell on it, the secret word exploded off the page:

```
EVERGREEN
```

His mind began to race, his thoughts spinning as his imagination assembled various hypotheses. He reread the memos, and his eye was caught by the sentence referring to payments made by Evergreen on October 12th and November 25th.

President Kennedy had been assassinated on November 22nd, 1963.

But since his conjecture was inconceivable, the detective sergeant chased it out of his head and went on reading:

Montreal
September 19th, 1964

PRIVILEGED AND STRICTLY CONFIDENTIAL

Dear Nathan,

The concern that I mentioned in my most recent communication has now, regrettably, turned into serious anxiety. I am told that at least one of the individuals to whom you had an envelope delivered has returned it.

I understand from your reply that there was no way to foresee the stubborn zeal of this employee (you say he was recently hired?). Even so, I trust I don't have to remind you of the enormous dangers that would arise from the slightest leak of information.

As we are now compelled to take more stringent measures, I am hereby advising you that this employee will shortly become the first "subject" submitted to the professional care of our mutual friend.

Given the importance of taking action as soon as possible, I would ask you to contact her and see to it that she and her facilities remain at our disposal over the next several days.

I have informed Langley about the present
situation, and I have just received confirmation
that a BO asset will arrive at the consulate
shortly to facilitate the transition.

As always, CW will act as liaison.

I have no doubt that you are eager to help
repair the consequences of your earlier mis-
step, and that you will make yourself fully
available to our mutual friend, as well as
to the asset, for all their logistical and
operational needs.

Finally, I count on your entire co-operation
in facilitating their work on the ground.

Cordially yours,
Daniel

Virginie put down the file that she'd begun to read. Victor lifted
his gaze to her. He'd been so absorbed in his work that he had forgotten she was there. Without a word, she rose from the table and
disappeared into the kitchen. Hastily, the detective sergeant scribbled a few notes before returning to his reading:

- Professional care / mutual friend = Judith Harper = MK-ULTRA?
- BO / consulate / Langley???
- Who is CW?

Virginie reappeared a few minutes later, carrying a tray of
freshly made sandwiches, a large bag of salt-and-vinegar chips, and
some beverages. Victor grabbed a bottle of V8, unscrewed the top,
and took a gulp.

Then he bit into a ham sandwich and noticed that she had put
in a slice of processed cheese, just as Ted used to do in the old days.

"Is it okay?" Virginie asked, gesturing at the food.

"It's great," he said, putting a handful of chips on his plate. "Thanks."

She opened her mouth, then hesitated, seeming unsure of how to frame the question she wanted to ask. At that moment, before the words came out of Virginie's mouth, Victor regretted having consented to let her examine the papers with him.

But damn it, he'd had no choice.

Virginie was going to ask about the documents he'd just been looking over, and he was going to have to reveal what he had learned about her father. At best, he supposed, there would be tears. At worst, there would be a meltdown.

"Are you good at tracking down missing persons?"

The question caught him by surprise. He reflected for a moment. If he'd been completely honest, he'd have answered that you always find missing persons in the end, but too often they're not in the condition you had hoped for. But this wasn't an answer he could give without deepening Virginie's worries about her father. Evasively, he said, "Not bad, I guess …"

Virginie interpreted this answer as false humility. "Someday, you'll have to help me find Cormac McCarthy."

Cormac McCarthy? The name was buried too deep in his memory for him to know right away who she was talking about.

Virginie could see him drawing a blank. "The novelist."

Victor slapped his forehead. Of course. *No Country for Old Men.* He had intended, a few years back, to read the book after seeing the Coen brothers' film. "For an article?"

Virginie's eyes wandered along the wood grain of the dining room table, landing at last on Victor's fingers. "No." A long silence. "I'd just like to know what he's up to."

"Except in cases where they're taken against their will," Victor said after a moment, "people don't generally disappear without a trace. A person always preserves a link to his past, even if he doesn't realize it. A motivated searcher could find him."

The silence was starting to thicken when Virginie got up to go to the bathroom. Victor took the opportunity to return to his reading:

```
Montreal
September 21st, 1964

PRIVILEGED AND STRICTLY CONFIDENTIAL

Dear Nathan,

Our mutual friend confirms that the treatments
administered to Subject #1 were successful. I
would therefore ask you to make the necessary
arrangements with AL and CW at the consulate,
so that the two individuals in whom Subject
#1 confided can receive the same treatments
from our friend and her assistant.
    I hope this goes without saying:
    TIME IS OF THE ESSENCE.
    Thanking you in advance for your
ever-reliable co-operation, I am, as ever,

Cordially yours,
Daniel



Montreal
October 20th, 1964

PRIVILEGED AND STRICTLY CONFIDENTIAL

Dear Nathan,

I am informed that Subject #1 has, unfor-
tunately, started making noises once again
about Evergreen's financial statements, and
that he has been trying to persuade Subjects
```

#2 and #3 to help him gather additional infor-
mation for the apparent purpose of bringing
the matter before the authorities.

According to my source, it is only a matter of time before they put the puzzle pieces
together. You will readily understand that we
cannot run the risk of letting them get any
closer to the heart of the undertaking. It is
imperative that the participants' identities
not be compromised.

Langley has just confirmed to me that AL
has received instructions to carry out a
cleanup operation. My source informs me that
CW is opposed to the plan. Given your ongoing
contact with CW, I'm counting on you to let
me know if you learn of any attempt on his
part to impede AL's work.

Cordially yours,
Daniel

Without Victor's being fully aware of it, the pieces were falling
into place. A picture was taking shape. Questions were emerging
with sudden clarity: was the "Subject #1" to whom Tousignant
referred André Lortie? Or was Lortie, rather, the individual
referred to as "AL"? What was Tousignant alluding to when he
mentioned that Langley had dispatched an asset to carry out a
cleanup operation?

The detective sergeant was as fearful of the answer as he was
convinced that he knew it.

When he picked up his pen to make further notes, he felt his
hand shaking. A horrifying vision rose up in his memory. He felt
the same vertiginous sensation he'd had when one of the Red Blood

Spillers had pressed his Beretta into Victor's throat, forcing him to watch as two of his men were coldly murdered.

The memory gave way to the drawing of the hanged man.

At that moment, Victor had a powerful impression that the rope had been placed around his own neck, and at any moment the trap door might open under his feet.

72

EXHIBITS

Eyes closed, hands flat on the table, Victor concentrated on the rhythm of his breathing. Images rioted behind his eyelids, and he let them run free, making no effort to dispel them. Often, when he was beset by anxiety, ghosts from his most distant past came back to haunt him, especially those related to the death of his family.

Walking into the room, Victor sees his father stretched out on the bed. Having killed Victor's mother and two brothers, he has tried to take his own life, too: the bullet has entered below the chin and exited through the top of the skull.

When he realizes that his father is still breathing, Victor is propelled by a force he can't resist. He puts his hands around his father's throat.

He squeezes, squeezes, until the wound stops bubbling.

Then, in a silence that stretches to infinity, Victor looks at the blood on his hands.

As time passed, the images faded. Victor's panic subsided little by little. He felt ready to resume his examination of the file.

In the folder labelled P-2, he found documents relating to the operations of MK-ULTRA, as well as internal memos and correspondence. As far as he could tell, certain documents dating back to 1962 and 1963 concerned the establishment of a private lab under Judith Harper's authority. Victor went through the documents eagerly, noting sentence fragments here and there, searching above all for references to the "subjects" mentioned in the correspondence between Lawson and Tousignant.

But he was unable to find anything about treatments inflicted on specific patients. Victor did note, however, that all communications between Tousignant and Judith Harper's organization had gone through Nathan Lawson.

Judging from the sample he found in the file, such communications had been infrequent.

As he withdrew another sheaf of documents from the folder, a yellowed envelope held together by an elastic band fell to the floor. Intrigued, he bent over to retrieve it and pulled off the elastic. Inside, he found a series of black-and-white photographs in which Judith Harper and Mark McNeil were easily recognizable. In the pictures, the two associates were committing a wide variety of abusive acts. Abetted by her assistant, Harper could be seen mistreating her semiconscious victims.

And in every snapshot, the tormentors wore smiles imbued with a mix of pride and scorn — smiles that Victor knew well, having seen them on the faces of too many psychopaths. These dark images shook him so deeply that he had to leave the table for a few minutes and go outside for a cigarette.

As he stood there, smoking, a single question gnawed at him: how could someone inflict such suffering on other human beings and enjoy it?

When he came back, Victor picked up the coffee pot from the tray that Virginie had placed at the corner of the table a few hours earlier. He filled his cup with cold coffee and took a few gulps.

It was as he went through the contents of folder P-3 that the detective sergeant had the sudden sensation of a veil falling away.

Three newspaper clippings, which he held delicately between his fingers for fear of tearing them, shed new light on the identities of the subjects mentioned in Tousignant's correspondence with Lawson.

On October 23rd, 1964, thirty-nine-year-old Gilbert Couture and his son, Léonard, aged nineteen, had died in the forest near their family home.

Investigators had briefly wondered whether the father had shot his son in a mercy killing before turning his gun on himself. But the Joliette Municipal Police had eventually concluded that the deaths were the result of a hunting accident. Couture had been hired only a few weeks previously as an auditor at the local accounting firm of Bélanger, Monette and Associates.

Lost in thought, Victor raised his head briefly, bit into the sandwich he'd picked up from the tray, and chewed mechanically.

Joe Beans hadn't been mistaken. This was surely the hunting accident that the old archivist had told him about. The detective sergeant turned his attention to the second clipping.

Assuming these newspaper stories were actually about the subjects discussed by Tousignant, they solved the mystery surrounding the written message on the matchbook: *there were others*.

As he read the articles, Victor had a clear sense, now, of who those others were.

On October 30th, 1964, twenty-nine-year-old Mathias Lévesque had been killed in a car accident near the town of Saint-Ambroise-de-Kildare. His car had inexplicably overturned and plunged into a ravine. Lévesque was employed as an auditor at Bélanger, Monette and Associates, an accounting firm in Joliette.

The third clipping was in very poor condition. Victor had to hold it up close to make it out.

On November 7th, 1964, in Saint-Liguori, forty-two-year-old Chantal Coulombe had been killed in a hit-and-run on the town's main street. The driver had never been found. The victim worked as an accountant for Bélanger, Monette and Associates.

The last article had appeared in *L'Étoile du Nord*, which was Joliette's local paper at the time. It also mentioned that this was the third accidental death to strike the firm in the space of a few weeks.

The firm's management expressed its sadness over the spate of unfortunate accidents and promised to "provide grieving families and colleagues with any support they might need."

After rereading the three articles, Victor saw only one possible conclusion: the subjects referred to by Tousignant were indeed the three murdered employees of the accounting firm.

And he couldn't help thinking they had died for nothing.

Gilbert Couture had been killed because he had uncovered something while working on the Evergreen financial statements: a secret whose dimensions he didn't realize, and whose implications he never suspected.

The two others had died because their colleague had taken them into his confidence, thus turning them into troublesome witnesses. Because they had strayed into forbidden territory, a decision had been made: nothing could be left to chance. The three had been eliminated.

Couture's son, Léonard, was simply collateral damage.

◦

Victor rubbed his eyes and ran a hand over his chin. He was tired, but he was also determined to go through the entire file. Folder P-4 contained copies of Evergreen's articles of incorporation and corporate bylaws. The company had been created in 1961 by Daniel Tousignant, who acted as its first president, secretary, and chairman of the board.

Under the heading *Fields of Activity*, there was an entry stating that the corporation was engaged in organizing international trade fairs.

Knowing from experience that corporate bylaws rarely held any useful information, Victor skimmed them, but he paid particular attention to the list of company directors. These included Daniel Tousignant, Nathan R. Lawson, Dr. Judith Harper, and nearly a dozen others whose names Victor didn't recognize, but about whom he would have an analyst prepare a research report.

A single unopened file folder remained in front of him on the table. It was the least voluminous of the group. Wondering what he would find, Victor slipped a finger under the flap of folder P-5 and opened it.

The file consisted of a single sheet of paper, in the middle of which one paragraph had been typed many years ago on an old typewriter, as evidenced by consistent imperfections in the appearance of certain letters. The paragraph indicated the year, 1975, as well as the name and address of an individual in Dallas, Texas.

This contact information seemed to have been subsequently revised. The year had been scratched out and replaced with *2003* in ballpoint pen, along with a handwritten modification of the address. Only the name of the individual, Cleveland Willis, had not been amended.

In his notebook, Victor wrote:

- *CW = Cleveland Willis?*

In light of everything he'd just read, the detective sergeant had arrived at three definite conclusions about the mass of documents lying in front of him. One: this was the file that Nathan Lawson had pulled from his firm's archives hours before disappearing. Two: it had nothing to do with Northern Industrial Textiles, which was simply a cover for Lawson to hide the material he had assembled on Evergreen. And three: the file was incomplete.

The killer was toying with investigators. He had given them part of the puzzle, but he had removed the key piece.

Typically, in a criminal trial, the prosecution would set out the facts alleged against the accused, as well as the offences committed under the Criminal Code, in an indictment. The evidence presented in support of the allegations would be annexed to the indictment in the form of exhibits.

While it was clear to Victor that Lawson had put together a case for the prosecution, it was equally clear that the file contained nothing more than the exhibits. It held only the evidence assembled by Lawson to prove the guilt of one or more individuals.

Yet without a central document to provide the arguments and background logic — without an indictment — it was difficult to grasp the precise nature of the allegations.

Victor looked up from his reading. Absorbed in his work, he had lost all sense of time. He realized that Virginie wasn't in the room, and he remembered that she had gone to the bathroom. The file she had begun to examine, the only one Victor hadn't yet read, lay open on a corner of the table. The detective sergeant reached out to pick up his phone. Looking at its clock, he realized he hadn't seen her in an hour.

"Virginie?"

After calling her name a few times, he searched the ground floor. Was his mind playing tricks on him? The house seemed oddly silent; it was missing the creaks and funny noises that normally populate homes.

Victor stopped for a moment at the living room window and watched the snowflakes whirling like insects in the light of the streetlamp. He was about to return to the dining room when he saw the high heels that Virginie had put on earlier. They were lying on the third step of the staircase that led to the second floor.

He climbed a few steps in silence, then stopped and listened.

At first, he heard nothing. Then, as he concentrated, his suspicion became a conviction: he could hear a voice. It was indistinct, but it was definitely a voice. A man's voice.

His mind began to race, his imagination churning with possibilities. Had Virginie heard a noise upstairs and removed her shoes to catch the intruder unawares?

Breathing hard, with his Glock in his hand, Victor crept upstairs soundlessly and found himself in a dark hallway. A strip of light was visible under a door at the end of the hall. Raising his gun, Victor waited a moment, letting his eyes adjust to the shadows, then

moved forward. Advancing with infinite caution, trying to minimize the sound of his breathing, knowing that a single creaking
floorboard would reverberate like an alarm, he took a full minute
to reach his objective.

The door was closed, but now, on the other side, he could clearly
hear a man's nasal voice: "*I didn't shoot anybody, no sir!*"

Thin trickles of cold sweat ran down his temples. Holding his
breath, bracing his muscles, aiming at a spot near the handle, he
drove his foot with all his strength through the door.

73

PILLOW TALK

The only piece of furniture in the room was a bed. Apart from the black rectangle of the flat screen on the wall, everything was white, pure, immaculate.

Catching his breath, Victor stood motionless in the middle of the room for a moment, then reholstered his pistol. Holding a remote control in her hand, Virginie didn't seem affected by his crashing entrance, nor by the dislocated door.

"Did you get through all the documents?" she asked, her gaze unfocused. "I looked over some accounting statements for a company called Evergreen for the 1963–64 financial year." Silence. "Then I stopped. I was scared of what I might find."

She had hit the pause button. Lee Harvey Oswald's face was frozen, open mouthed, on the screen. The black-and-white image, projected onto the bedspread and onto Virginie herself, created a striking visual effect. "This is about Kennedy, isn't it?" she asked.

Victor's gaze was shifting between the screen and the young woman. She was stretched out on the bed, her upper body propped up on a mound of pillows. The strap of her bra had slipped off her bare shoulder, which emerged from the low neckline of her sweater.

Victor ran a hand through his hair, looking uncomfortable. "Why do you say that?"

"I didn't understand much of what was in those statements, but it wouldn't take a financial wizard to notice that there were big outflows of money in the weeks before November 22, 1963, and in the days that followed. Anyway, I already knew. It was always about Kennedy. That was my father's obsession." She closed her eyes for a moment, revisiting old memories. "I remember back in the early eighties, I used to find him watching this video. He must have thought I was too young to understand. There was one time in particular ... he'd been drinking, and as he looked at Oswald, he kept saying something had gone wrong."

She pressed a button on the remote, and the image came back to life. Looking boyish, visibly afraid of the police officers surrounding him, his lips compressed, Oswald resumed his diatribe: "*I'm just a patsy.*"

Virginie hit the pause button again and lifted her chin in the direction of the screen. "He was twenty-four years old. Look at him. Do you honestly think he could have planned the Kennedy assassination?"

Victor shrugged. He almost asked her a question, but then realized he didn't want to know the answer. Virginie groped under the pillows and retrieved a small metallic box. She opened it and inserted her little finger. When she pulled it out, there was white powder in the crook of the fingernail, which she brought to her nostril. After snorting the cocaine, she looked straight at Victor with shining eyes.

Though his own eyes were drawn to her bare shoulder, he forced himself to meet the young woman's gaze.

She moistened her lips languorously. "Want some?"

Her seemingly complete lack of inhibition had a daunting effect on him. Victor's body felt like an oppressive cage. He felt ridiculous as he stood there in front of her, unsure of what to do with his hands. The longer she looked at him, the greater his discomfort became. "No," he answered at last.

"Are you going to put me in handcuffs?"

Virginie seemed genuinely disappointed when the detective sergeant replied without hesitation that he wasn't a narcotics cop. She pinched her lower lip between her thumb and forefinger. A lock of hair fell in front of her face.

Ill at ease, Victor stared at the floor in front of him.

"Why did he do it?" she asked.

Victor pulled a few threads from the sleeve of his sweater. "The killer? It's what he's been doing since the start. Playing games with us. He put the documents in the garbage bags so we'd find them."

"But why is he trying to ruin my father's reputation? What has he got against him, exactly? Why did he leave these papers for us? What's he thinking?"

Unless he absolutely had to, Victor wasn't going to get into the details of what he'd found in the files. He wanted to spare the young woman.

"Maybe he's not thinking all that much. Unlike the movies, where there's always a ruthless logic behind every action, reality can be disappointing."

"And disturbing," she said. "Always disturbing. Do you think he's crazy?" Virginie's sweater had conspicuously slipped some more, revealing the upswell of her breasts.

Victor's throat went dry; he was finding it hard to swallow. "I'd love to think so, but I doubt that's the case. Whoever kidnapped your father wants to make him talk, or wants to shut him up."

"How are you going to catch him?"

"By trying to figure out what he knows. There's a name in the file. A man who lives in Dallas. Cleveland Willis … Does that name mean anything to you?"

"No. Will you go down there?"

The detective sergeant shrugged. "I don't know."

Virginie took his hand and pulled him toward the bed. "Come here," she murmured.

Victor put a hand on her wrist and freed himself from her grasp.

Though Virginie attracted him, he didn't want this. He had enough troubles already. There was no way he'd do the slightest thing that might compromise what remained of his relationship with Nadja.

Retreating a few steps, he patted his pockets for his cellphone. After a moment, he realized that he'd left it on the dining room table.

He heard a faint thumping, which wasn't coming from his chest, though his heart was hammering.

Downstairs, someone was pounding on the front door.

Victor unlocked the door and Jacinthe burst in, brushing snow off herself. The white stuff flew in all directions. "Too busy to pick up, big guy?" she asked irritably.

Out of the corner of one eye, the detective sergeant saw his phone lying in the midst of the documents on the dining room table, where he'd left it when he went upstairs. "Sorry. I was in the bathroom."

Jacinthe checked her watch, then nodded toward the jacket he'd draped over the banister post on the staircase. "Get dressed. We're leaving."

"What's up?"

"I just spoke to the Gnome. We have a suspect."

Instead of swinging into action, Victor froze. How could Lemaire and Loïc already have a suspect? Between the snowy weather and the bad road conditions, they would barely have had time to reach Joliette. Then he remembered that Jacinthe had said they were going to meet the owner of an archery shop. "Thanks to the arrow in the cemetery?"

Jacinthe nodded as she moved toward the dining room. She glanced distractedly at the papers, then, examining the plate that Virginie had left on the table, she bit into an orphaned piece of sandwich.

Pulling on his jacket, Victor came into the room for his phone.

"The shop owner makes custom arrows," Jacinthe said, her mouth full. "Because of the pink and grey feathers, he thinks this particular arrow came from a lot that he made for one of his customers." She pointed to the documents on the table. "What's all this stuff? Are we leaving it there?"

"Long story. I'll explain later. I'm going to ask Garcia to come and keep an eye on Virginie and the papers until we get back. I don't think she should be alone."

Jacinthe took the bag of chips off the table and they headed for the door. Suddenly, a noise from above made them both turn toward the staircase.

"Victor?"

Virginie had come partway down, but she'd stopped when she saw Jacinthe.

Jacinthe gave her partner a little smile. "Oh, yeah ... You were having a grand old time in the bathroom, weren't you, my friend?"

"It's not what you think," Victor said through clenched teeth.

Virginie had gone back up to the landing, but her soft voice came down: "Victor? Can I talk to you for a second?"

As she was heading out the door, Jacinthe told him in a growling voice to hurry up; she'd be waiting in the car.

The detective sergeant ran up the stairs and found himself face to face with the young woman. Her eyes were puffy. She'd clearly been crying.

"I'm sorry about what happened just now. I don't know what got into me ... I'm not that kind of person."

With the bag of chips jammed between her legs, Jacinthe was driving as fast as she was chewing, but the blowing snow made road conditions difficult.

"Where are we going?" Victor asked.

"A house on Hill Park Circle."

Victor visualized the twisting road that rose from the foot of Mount Royal. He knew the area.

"I asked to have a patrol car sent over there to keep the house under discreet surveillance," Jacinthe said, "but I told them not to go in before we arrive. Hold the bag for me, will ya?"

The detective sergeant held the bag of chips at an angle so she could reach in more easily.

"Are Gilles and Loïc already there, or are they going to Joliette?"

"They're on their way to the suspect's house, but we'll get there long before they do. The archery shop is way up in Pierrefonds."

Victor told Jacinthe about the video footage of Tousignant's kidnapping, then summarized the contents of the files that the man in the baseball cap had left in the garbage bags beside the driveway. When he mentioned the payments that had occurred before and after the Kennedy assassination, and when he described Virginie's conviction that her father's disappearance was connected to that event, Jacinthe bristled.

"Oh, gimme a break! Kennedy ... you've got to be kidding!"

Victor also described the newspaper clippings dealing with the "accidental" deaths of the accounting firm's three employees.

"By the way," Jacinthe said, "Gilles talked to an officer at the provincial police detachment in Joliette. For the moment, there isn't much point in going out there. They can't find anything in their database. They're still checking to see if there's a file in the archives. But I'm not holding my breath. Back then, it was the Joliette municipal force that handled the case, and this hunting accident happened before the Police Information Centre was set up. Since the matter wasn't considered a crime, the file may never have been registered."

"We'll have to follow up with Gilles's contact to give him the names of the other two victims in 1964. Everything's closed on Boxing Day, but I'll call the National Library tomorrow. We need to look at newspaper archives for the dates in question. With a little luck, we'll come up with something. We also need to see what we can find out about Evergreen."

"Your mysterious secret word," Jacinthe scoffed. "Maybe we'll catch a break and none of that will be necessary. We have a suspect, remember?"

The detective sergeant was so busy organizing his thoughts and trying to work out connections among the facts he'd learned that he didn't seem to hear Jacinthe's remark.

"What did you learn from Bennett?"

Jacinthe's head bobbled. "You want the long version or the short?"

"How about something between the two?"

"Bennett was paying for hookers, supplied by a pimp named Daman. He got his kicks from putting a dog collar and leash around the girls' necks, then tying them up before he fucked them. From what I gather, things got out of hand a couple of times, and the girls were injured. The latest one was found last Wednesday, unconscious in a motel-room bathtub. She had a fractured skull. The crazy thing is, Bennett says he got up to all that stuff with Judith Harper's blessing. She even joined in sometimes."

"After the pictures I just saw, that doesn't surprise me," Victor said.

Jacinthe raised her eyebrows. "Pictures?"

The detective sergeant told her about the envelope he'd found in the file folder and the photographs it contained.

"Fucking scumbags, the whole bunch of them," she muttered in disgust. After a moment's silence, she added, "Anyway, the doctor says Bennett has chlamydia, too. So the guy's a nutcase, but I don't think he had anything to do with the murders. Also, Burgers told me the dog collar they found in Bennett's possessions wasn't the same as the one that left marks on Harper and Lawson."

Jacinthe licked the salt-and-vinegar residue from her thumb. The Crown Victoria fishtailed briefly as she swerved into an unplowed lane to pass a car, but she was able to regain control with a few skillful manoeuvres that left Victor's heart in his mouth.

"What do we have on the suspect? What's his name?"

"Finally! I thought you'd never ask. His name is Lucian Duca. Midthirties. No record."

"Do we know what he does for a living?"

"That's the most interesting part."

Taillon's eyes left the snowy road to look at Victor for a second.

"Duca works in the mailroom at Baker Lawson Watkins. He's the dude we talked to on the phone the other day."

75

PURSUIT

At the foot of Mount Royal, Hill Park Circle snaked up from Côte-des-Neiges to Beaver Lake. The patrol officers had parked their car on a hairpin curve a few metres above the house, which was a brick cube with elongated windows resembling arrow slits.

Jacinthe drove past the house, rounded the curve, and pulled up behind the patrol car. Through the windshield, despite the darkness, Victor could see one of the patrol cops speaking into his shoulder microphone. The cop and the two detectives got out of their cars at the same time and stood between the vehicles. Jacinthe squinted to read the cop's name tag: Legris.

In the woods facing the house, snow was swirling among the trees. The wind was blowing hard, forcing them to raise their voices.

"Are you alone, Legris?" Taillon asked, hitching up her pants.

"My partner's in the neighbour's yard, watching the back door."

Victor zipped up his jacket, fished his cap from a pocket, and put it on. "Anybody inside?" he asked.

"Hard to say," the cop answered.

Victor had spoken to Lemaire moments ago. Because of the snow and traffic, he and Loïc wouldn't arrive for at least another twenty minutes. The Gnome had agreed that waiting for them was out of the question.

With her coat open and the tops of her unzipped boots dragging through the slush, Jacinthe rose to her full height, monolithic and seemingly impervious to the bitter weather.

"Okay, Legris," she said in a patronizing tone, putting her hand on the cop's shoulder, "you're going to take position between the car and the house, and let your partner know we're coming. If there's trouble, or if you notice anything unusual, you call us. Got it?"

Taking out his walkie-talkie, Victor told Legris which frequency they'd be using and urged him to be careful. The man they were after was a skilled archer who could put an arrow through a man's forehead at a fair distance.

Unable to hold still any longer, Jacinthe unleashed her war cry. "You're mine, asshole!"

Victor caught up to her as she reached the house and pressed up against the wall, drawing her pistol. His own weapon was in his hand. He took a breath. The blood was pounding in his temples. His whole body was surfing on a wave of adrenalin.

The detective sergeant banged on the door repeatedly. Not getting a response, he tried the handle. It was locked.

Without even consulting him, Jacinthe threw her shoulder against the door, which gave way under her weight.

Victor pointed his gun into the house and yelled: "Police! Anybody there? Duca?!"

As Constable Legris watched the two detectives rush into the house, he cursed his bad luck. He'd been a Montreal cop for nearly two years, and it was always the same old story. Whenever some decent action broke out, he was the one who had to wait outside, freezing his ass off.

Tugging at the elastic leg band on his briefs, which kept riding up between his buttocks, he told himself he should have joined the army like his younger brother, André, who'd done two tours in Afghanistan and seen combat against the Taliban.

An entire wall in their mother's house was covered with photographs of André in the war zone. As for Legris himself, images of his only moment of glory had been captured two springtimes ago, during the mini-riot that had erupted in downtown Montreal after the Canadiens eliminated the Washington Capitals during the NHL playoffs.

And now the fat cow was treating him like he was in kindergarten.

Legris pressed his hands together, brought them to his mouth, and blew between his palms in an effort to warm them up. He patted his pockets, searching for his gloves, and realized he'd left them in the car. Without taking his eyes off the front door, he retreated toward the car.

To his left, in the woods, something moved among the trees. He glanced quickly in that direction, then turned back to watch the door.

Had he seen something? Hard to be sure with all the snow.

Legris stopped moving back. His thoughts were bouncing back and forth between three points: the front door of the house, his gloves in the car, and the shadowy woods.

His eye caught another movement through the trees. The gloves ceased to be a concern. Now only the woods and the front door vied for his attention.

His vigilance rose a notch. All his senses were on high alert. He turned his gaze decisively away from the door. His heart began to pound and his hand slipped down to his hip, unholstering his pistol.

Something was moving in the woods! And it wasn't an animal.

Legris fired at the same instant that his right leg exploded in pain, collapsing under him.

As he fell, the cop saw a silhouette burst out of the woods, a hood pulled over his head. Carrying a bow, the figure ran toward the patrol car. Diving into the vehicle, the archer started the engine and sped away.

A spurt of adrenalin roused Legris. He had to act fast, or his attacker would get away. Lying on his back, he took aim at the car as it raced away down the slope.

Just then, his partner and the fat cow, who had heard his shot, came running. On the sidewalk, the second detective, wearing a furious expression, emptied his magazine into the speeding car, shattering its rear window. Then he broke into a limping run.

Legris had an arrow in his thigh. A red bloom was spreading out on the snow. The pain was starting to come, but that wasn't what fuelled his rage.

"The son of a bitch stole my car!"

Jacinthe turned left onto Côte-des-Neiges and saw Victor a hundred metres ahead, limping as fast as his legs would carry him in the middle of the street. How much time had elapsed between the moment they broke down the front door and the first gunshot? A minute? Two, max? They'd barely had time to determine that Duca wasn't in the dwelling, and that his taste in furnishings left something to be desired. Apart from a bed, a dilapidated couch, an old TV set, and a few kitchen accessories, the place was bare.

Jacinthe pulled up a few metres ahead of Victor and opened the passenger door. As he jumped in, she hit the accelerator.

Out of breath, his lungs on fire, the detective sergeant buckled his seat belt and gripped his bad leg with both hands. "Straight ahead." He coughed. "I lost sight of him as he went past the Trafalgar Building." Still panting, Victor activated the emergency lights and siren, then grabbed the radio mic. "All units." He coughed again. "I have an officer down on Hill Park Circle. Suspect has taken patrol car 26-11. We are in pursuit, southbound on Côte-des-Neiges. Suspect is armed and dangerous."

The Crown Vic's engine roared. Victor looked over and saw that Taillon's jaw was clenched.

"Duca must have been in the woods across from the house," he said as he caught his breath. "I think I hit him."

"Those dumbass patrol cops let themselves get spotted."

Duca had a substantial head start. Even with Jacinthe at the wheel, Victor knew they'd need to take risks to catch the fleeing suspect. At the same time, Duca didn't have Taillon's experience with high-speed driving; nor was he familiar with the car he'd stolen. He might make mistakes at the wheel.

And that was precisely what happened.

Passing the Trafalgar Building, they saw a car farther down the hill, angled crosswise in their path. Duca had spun out after colliding with a Hyundai Elantra, which now straddled the median at the intersection. The fugitive floored the gas pedal on the patrol car, which skidded around until it was facing down the hill once more, then accelerated, zigzagging through the snow. The detectives were now just two hundred metres behind.

Victor grabbed the radio mic. "I have visual contact at Côte-des-Neiges and Cedar. Suspect is approaching Doctor Penfield Avenue."

Victor also relayed the location of the accident.

On the radio, multiple police units were responding, indicating their positions. A fellow cop had been hit — this wouldn't go unpunished. There were now numerous other patrol cars involved in the chase.

Car 26-11 abruptly jumped the median, rolling southbound in the northbound lane of Côte-des-Neiges.

Taillon executed the same manoeuvre. As she slalomed among the oncoming vehicles, Victor saw that she was white-knuckling the steering wheel.

They raced past the Montreal General Hospital, leaving a cacophony of honks and spun-out cars behind them. Fortunately, because of the snowfall and the fact that it was a holiday, traffic was sparse. Even so, one false move would have been enough to cause catastrophe and death. They came perilously close more than once. But miraculously, they arrived unscathed at the merge with Pine Avenue.

Victor let out his breath and began to relax: surely Duca would bear right onto Doctor Penfield and get back into the flow of cars. But instead, the fugitive executed an improbable swerve and headed up Pine, once again into the oncoming traffic. On Côte-des-Neiges, at least, the width of the thoroughfare had made it possible to see cars approaching and steer clear. But now, as Duca sped along the narrow strip of Pine Avenue, dodging vehicles, he was flirting with suicide.

The prohibition against parking on the south side of the street meant it was possible to roll on the sidewalk, which is what Duca did, followed promptly by Jacinthe. It still took lightning reflexes to avoid the lampposts, mailboxes, and fire hydrants that rushed at them.

The hydrant that stood a few metres west of the Polish consulate didn't survive their passage. The Crown Vic was shaken by the impact, but Jacinthe held the car on course. In a trancelike state, totally focused on her objective, she was wrenching the steering wheel left and right, alternating between the brake and accelerator, yelling at the top of her lungs and spewing a steady stream of invective at the man she was pursuing, calling him a wide variety of names, among which *motherfucker* took pride of place.

And with each manoeuvre, she was getting a little closer to car 26-11. Slowly, but surely.

Feeling queasy and, above all, conscious of the insane risk to public safety, as well as their own, Victor placed a hand on his partner's forearm. "Ease up a little, Jacinthe. You're going to get us killed. Worse, you're going to kill someone else."

"Forget it. We're gonna nail him. I'm betting he'll turn onto McGregor. We'll hit him as he goes around."

Sure enough, Duca turned right onto McGregor Avenue.

Victor felt relief to be rolling in the direction of traffic once again. The Crown Vic was now just a few metres behind the patrol vehicle. Jacinthe floored the gas pedal: the car hurtled forward and hit the patrol car's bumper. Duca skidded before managing to get the vehicle straightened out, but not fast enough to avoid the metal guardrail to his left, which he scraped at high speed in a shower of sparks.

Far from slowing him down, though, the impact had the opposite effect, helping Duca get around the corner, which would otherwise have been difficult, since he was rolling too fast to make the turn cleanly.

Jacinthe nodded. She appreciated Duca's daring. "Ohhh, you son of a bitch! You're good!"

Her kick to the gas pedal had brought the Crown Vic into the turn too fast. She followed the fugitive's lead and let the car hit the guardrail, then shot down the slope of the avenue. Desperately, Victor lowered his window ten centimetres.

The wash of cold air braced him. It was either that or vomit.

At the bottom of McGregor, Duca turned left onto Doctor Penfield, heading east at breakneck speed, closely followed by the Crown Vic, its siren screaming. Clinging to his armrest, Victor relayed their position for the twentieth time. The two cars were flying along the avenue, skillfully getting past obstacles and avoiding uncontrolled skids.

Another officer's voice suddenly came through the radio. "This is 37-9. We're setting up a roadblock at the corner of McTavish."

Seizing the microphone, Victor rattled off the street names as they flashed by: Du Musée, De la Montagne, Drummond …

Jacinthe had come up behind the fleeing vehicle and was about to knock it off course, but Duca swerved hard, narrowly escaping the impact.

As they emerged from the long curve of Doctor Penfield, car 37-9 lay dead ahead of them like a nightmarish apparition. Placed transversely in the middle of the avenue, the car wasn't long enough to block it altogether. If Duca decided to try his luck and hit the stopped vehicle, patrol cops seeking refuge behind it would be crushed.

So the two officers of 37-9 had taken up position on the escarpment of Rutherford Park, guns drawn, ready to open fire if the fugitive tried to go around on their side. That was the riskiest option for Duca, who would find himself in a hail of bullets if he went for it.

Which left him the choice of trying to slam right through with a direct hit on the stopped patrol car, or seeking to get past the blockade on the right side by climbing up onto the sidewalk. That was the most tempting alternative, and it was the one the fugitive opted for. As he did so, Victor told himself he would have done the same thing.

Unfortunately for Duca, that was where the jaws of the trap snapped shut.

A semicircular stone barrier, topped with an iron handrail, closed McTavish Street to vehicle access. From the barrier, a flight of stairs allowed pedestrians to descend the five metres from Doctor Penfield to McTavish.

Coming in at high speed, the fleeing patrol car tipped to its right as it hit the edge of the sidewalk. It was a matter of centimetres, but Duca, who must have thought he had leeway, couldn't stabilize the vehicle before it struck the barrier. Because of its speed, the car caromed off the stone surface and was launched into the air, grazing the handrail. It hung in space for an instant, wheels spinning, before plummeting to the street below amid a din of smashed metal and broken glass. The vehicle did several barrel rolls and finally came to rest on its roof.

Jacinthe stopped the Crown Victoria. She and Victor jumped out, leaving the car in the middle of Doctor Penfield, and ran down the stairs. Curious onlookers were already gathering around the stone barrier. One of the patrol officers hurried with the detectives toward the crumpled vehicle, while the other called for backup and began to direct traffic.

Pistol in hand, Victor crouched beside the carcass of the patrol car and was momentarily surprised to see that it was empty. Then he spotted a human figure lying on the pavement ten metres away, near the McGill Students' Society building.

The impact had thrown Duca from the car.

He lay on his back. The detective sergeant knew before reaching him that his body was shattered; all that remained was the broken shell of an unstrung marionette.

Victor knelt beside the dying young man and slipped a cradling hand under his head. Blood was flowing from his nostrils, his mouth, and his ears.

Duca's blue eyes wavered, struggling to focus, then locked onto Victor's as his hands gripped the detective sergeant's sleeve. Duca wanted to speak, but he was struggling to breathe as the blood filled his throat. Victor put an ear next to his mouth, trying to hear his whisper.

Duca's eyes widened. His mouth fought to contract one last time. Then his head fell to one side. The detective sergeant laid it softly on the ground.

"Game over," Taillon said, panting, as she stood over him. "What did he say?"

Victor stood up, frowning, and looked at the bloodstained palm of his hand. He was trying to understand. "I'm not sure I heard right, but it was something along the lines of …" He hesitated. "'I remember.'"

76

"Bedtime, Lessard."

Victor woke up with a start. His elbows were resting on the dining room table. He had dozed off, his chin in his hands. He scratched his face and yawned. Tobacco and caffeine had ceased to have any effect: he could hardly keep his eyes open. Taillon was right. In any case, it would be hours before the forensics team finished collecting evidence and running tests.

After carrying out standard procedures at the scene of the crash, the two detectives had spent the evening and part of the night searching Lucian Duca's house. A pair of skis had been found in the basement. According to the technician Victor had spoken to, the skis' width matched the tracks in Summit Woods and Parc Maisonneuve.

The bow and arrows recovered from the wrecked patrol car were being analyzed at the Forensic Science Lab. The fact that the arrows had pink and grey fletching like the one found in the cemetery left little room for doubt. Duca was their man.

Still — and this was the only reason they hadn't stopped working, despite their exhaustion — they had yet to find any clues that might help them locate Tousignant.

Loïc and the Gnome had been sent to the senator's house to retrieve the documents and put them into safekeeping. Victor had insisted that they handle the job. He had no desire to cope with the destabilizing effect of going back to the house. Because Virginie Tousignant definitely destabilized him.

·   ·   ·

The two detectives had decided to give themselves another thirty minutes before calling it a night. Feeling groggy, the detective sergeant had gone outside for a cigarette in the blowing snow. The ground began to vibrate. He heard the rumble of a snowplow coming up Hill Park Circle several seconds before the plow itself appeared. Between drags on his cigarette, Victor sent a new text to Nadja, a little mechanically. To his great surprise, a reply arrived a few eyeblinks after:

we can talk later ... my brother won't let Martin down ...

Furious, he flicked his cigarette butt into the air. The little red-tipped cylinder was snatched by the wind and carried out of sight. Yes, he should have been happy. He should have been relieved that things were going to work out for Martin. And in fact he was relieved.

But Nadja's choice of words deepened his sense of rejection. She'd made no mention of their relationship. How hard would it have been for her to pick up her phone and tell him to go fuck himself?

"We don't have much to go on, partner." Facing Victor at the table, Jacinthe held a notebook in one hand. In the other, she gripped a ballpoint pen, the end of which she was chewing. "Lucian Duca, born in Quebec, age thirty-three, six foot four, two hundred and twenty pounds. Celtic knot tattoo on his left biceps. No criminal record. Employed in the mailroom at Baker Lawson Watkins for the last two years. His mother, Silvia Duca, born in Romania, died in the late nineties —"

"Say again?" Victor interrupted. He rubbed his temples. His thoughts were foggy. His mind was on information overload. Data storage had become chaotic.

"His mother died in the late nineties."

"No, before that. What did you say before that?"

Jacinthe repeated what she'd said. An idea had bobbed to the surface of Victor's mind, but he had no chance to consider it before it sank out of sight. He asked Jacinthe to continue.

"Silvia Duca owned a ballet school on Sherbrooke Street. It was pretty successful for a while. She also made some smart investments. When she died, her son inherited this house and a fair chunk of money. On his birth certificate, Duca's father is listed as unknown. He had no other family. No sign of a girlfriend … We'll have a complete financial profile shortly. Am I forgetting anything?"

Jacinthe stopped and scanned her notes to be sure she'd covered all the available facts. Then she looked up at Victor. Seeing his face, she knew instantly that something was wrong. "You okay, Lessard? You've gone green."

Since Duca's death, the detective sergeant's stomach had been churning. Now, perhaps from lack of sleep, he was starting to experience a dizzy, bittersweet sensation of floating in space beside his own body. Drops of sweat emerged on his forehead. The room began to spin.

"Oh, by the way, congratulations. You haven't lost your touch. Burgers confirmed that you hit him in the shoulder."

"What? Who?"

"Duca. You put a bullet in his shoulder."

Victor lurched to his feet and hurried into the hallway, desperately opening several doors before finding the washroom. Plunging into the tiny space, he fell to his knees in front of the toilet bowl and vomited.

He flushed several times, and the contents of his stomach were carried away.

How long did Victor stay there, bent over the bowl, catching his breath and recovering his composure as he stared at the wall tiles?

As he was about to get up, he had a sudden feeling of déjà vu. There was a colour variation in the grout between two ceramic tiles near the bowl. He remembered the bathroom in the rooming house where Lortie had lived. An idea took shape in his head — he dismissed it at first.

But then, as he washed his hands, he decided there was nothing to lose.

In his imagination, he could hear Jacinthe's sarcastic voice: *Lessard and his hunches!*

With a pair of scissors taken from the medicine cabinet, he had no difficulty prying out the tile. In the space behind it, he found a little plastic bag. Inside the bag, there was a sheet of paper folded in quarters.

In disbelief, Victor pulled on his latex gloves and carefully opened the bag.

The sheet had been folded and unfolded so many times that the paper had separated in some places. The note was handwritten, the letters pressed tightly against each other:

My darling Lucian, mica mea draga,

I'm so very sorry you had to find out this way. But he wasn't lying. It's true, André Lortie is your father. I don't know what he said that upset you so terribly, but you mustn't listen to him. After the things they did to his brain, he doesn't know what he's saying anymore. I should have told you the truth a long time ago. Can you forgive me before I'm gone?

Your mother who loves you more than anything,

Silvia

MARCH 1981

THE MAN WITH THE DIRTY CLOTHES

"You've gotta let me in! I have nowhere else to go. I'm begging you, Sylvie!"

The banging on the door had gone on for several long minutes. Silvia was standing in the vestibule, unsure of what to do. Should she open up or not?

The man's voice, broken and desperate, touched her heart and brought back memories of a time she had sworn to herself she would never think about again. She looked through the peephole and was hardly surprised at his pitiful condition.

André Lortie had become a homeless man.

The early days of their relationship had been a happy time. Then, one evening in January of 1969, he had vanished without a word of explanation. Six years later, as suddenly as he'd evaporated, he had reappeared, freshly shaven and wearing a new suit. Silvia had just had a painful breakup with her boyfriend at the time, and André's return had been a balm to her wounded heart.

André had always been vague about the reasons for his disappearance. When she'd pressed him, he said he'd spent some time in the United States, looking after a sick relative and working in the insurance business. He'd always had a mysterious side, which she had finally gotten used to.

Silvia gradually became aware that some things about him had changed. The confident, self-assured man she'd known had given way to a taciturn, closed-off individual. Afflicted by night terrors, André had developed phobias: he never stood with his back to a doorway, and he scrupulously avoided walking in front of windows. And at times, especially when he stopped taking his medications, he fell into a terrible state of depression.

Months went by. Silvia and André had some happy times and some dark stretches. In late 1977, after they'd been living together for a couple of years, André had once again left without any warning. She had come home from the dance school one evening to find him gone, having carried off his personal effects in a small leather satchel. His departure had almost come as a relief to the young woman, who was finding it hard to cope with his increasingly frequent changes of mood.

Silvia hadn't known it at the time, but she was pregnant.

Lucian was born in 1978. She raised him alone. Silvia was the kind of woman who put her heart and soul into motherhood and the upbringing of her child, leaving little room for anything else. Lucian made her happy. She had what she wanted, and she was consequently uninterested in burdening herself with a man.

Worn down by the begging and banging, Silvia finally pulled the bolt and opened up. This was the second time since his departure in 1977 that André Lortie had arrived on her doorstep. On the first occasion he had stayed only a few hours, leaving again after she'd fed him and given him some money.

His filthy, ragged clothes reeked of liquor and the street. His tangled hair fell to his shoulders. A beard hid his face and throat, and when he held out his hand, the grime under his fingernails repelled her.

Silvia made him undress right there in the vestibule. Then she put his clothes directly into a garbage bag. After his shower, she brought him clean clothes, and she cut his nails and hair herself, in silence.

Under the child's gaze, Lortie watched with a smile, fingers interlaced across his chest, as his matted locks fell to the kitchen linoleum. Finally, Silvia trimmed his beard down to a length that was convenient for shaving.

Lortie was affectionate with the little boy, but he didn't ask Silvia if the child was his. She didn't bring up the subject.

Sitting on the bathtub rim next to the sink, little Lucian watched the razor move back and forth over the man's cheeks. He liked the smell of the shaving soap, and he liked it when the man tickled his nose with the bristles of the shaving brush. Lortie soaked a washcloth in hot water, wrung it out, and wiped the last traces of foam from his face.

"Feel, Lucian," he said, guiding the boy's hands. "Soft, eh?"

Lucian's small fingers touched the smooth cheeks for an instant. Then Lortie drew a smiley face on the fogged mirror, and the little boy laughed. Lortie crouched down and detached a ceramic tile from the wall at floor level. Into the space, he shoved some documents that he had concealed from Silvia by stuffing them in his underwear before she made him undress. Afterward, Lortie replaced the tile, fitting the pieces of grout back into place.

"That's our hiding place, Lucian." He put a finger to his lips. "It's a secret, just between us. Shhh …"

"Shhh," the child repeated, and laughed.

André Lortie placed a gentle kiss on the little boy's forehead.

Silvia's voice came through the door. "Dinner's ready."

"We'll be right there, Sylvie, honey. We'll be right there."

She'd told him a thousand times that her name ended in an *A*, but he'd never been able to get used to it. André Lortie picked up Lucian and set him down on the floor. They stepped out into the hallway, hand in hand.

77

BRIEFLY REUNITED

Wednesday, December 28th

Victor was walking along the sidewalk with the collar of his leather jacket turned up, his hands crammed into his pockets, a black garment draped over his left arm.

Orange NO PARKING signs had been stuck at intervals into the snowbanks. Once again, Montreal had been outsmarted by the weather. The snow-removal process was dragging on endlessly.

Arriving across the street from the building, the detective sergeant looked left and right a couple of times. No one in sight. It was 6:07 a.m., and the street was as deserted as he had hoped it would be.

Victor crossed the street at an unhurried pace and went through the glass door of the police station. Inside, the corridor was empty, except for one man who was waiting for him.

A cop with ginger hair.

Lucian Duca, the killer they'd been trying to catch for days, was dead.

But a crucial question remained unanswered: had he killed Senator Tousignant before dying, or was Tousignant alive, in captivity somewhere, unable even to move, with a heretic's fork piercing his flesh?

The senator wasn't a young man. Time was passing, and the hope of finding him alive grew fainter by the hour.

The detectives had gone back to square one and spent the morning of the 27th in conference. Rather than treat the matter as a classic disappearance, Victor had insisted from the outset that in order to locate Tousignant, they needed to understand the motive behind Duca's acts. And that motive was clearly rooted in the past.

Victor's view wasn't shared by the other members of the investigation team, who saw Duca's reasons as secondary. Indeed, most of them feared the same thing: that while they were trying to figure out motives, Tousignant would die.

Not surprisingly, Jacinthe was particularly vociferous on the subject. She argued that they mustn't waste time looking into the suspicious deaths in 1964, or continuing their research on the Evergreen files, which, as far as she was concerned, were "ancient history." Her own plan of action had four practical components. One: look into all calls received from people who claimed to have seen the senator, follow up the most credible ones, increase forces in the field, and organize ground searches with canine units along the riverbank near Tousignant's house. Two: since Duca had no apparent family, talk to his co-workers, sift through his bank records, create a timeline for his activities over the last few days, and find out where he spent his vacations and downtime. Had he stayed in any isolated spots recently? Three: continue the work begun by Virginie, contacting people in Tousignant's social circle to find out if anyone remembered anything or if anyone had met Duca. And four: stop obsessing about this shit and enjoy the Christmas holiday. Or what was left of it.

Jacinthe's last point got a big laugh from the group. Even Victor smiled.

Delaney had finally settled on a blend of Victor's and Jacinthe's approaches.

The team had consequently spent a few hours brainstorming in an effort to figure out Duca's motive, not because they needed to know, but because, as Victor had argued, the effort could yield information that would lead them to Senator Tousignant.

Among the hypotheses put forward, the one that eventually became the majority consensus was that Duca had been seeking revenge for the abuses inflicted on his father, André Lortie, under Project MK-ULTRA. Duca's quest had led him to discover the wider conspiracy orchestrated by Daniel Tousignant.

The cops didn't yet know what reasons had driven Duca to kidnap the senator. But they assumed the abduction was linked to Tousignant's involvement in Evergreen.

"The way I see it," Gilles Lemaire said, "his last words were a cry from the heart. In effect, he was saying, *I remember what my father went through, his suffering, his wrecked life*."

A solemn silence had followed Lemaire's comment.

What had happened next?

At this point, the team members were tangled in conjectures. As Jacinthe had observed, they might never know the truth. But it seemed logical to suppose that Lortie had discovered his son's murderous intentions when he found the victims' wallets. Knowing about the crimes that Lucian had committed, and unable to live with that burden, Lortie had ended his life by plunging from a rooftop at Place d'Armes.

Victor pointed out to his fellow detectives that this interpretation had flaws. "If the AL mentioned in Tousignant's correspondence with Lawson really is André Lortie, that raises serious doubts about the role he played in all this."

Was Lortie what he seemed to be? The detective sergeant had conceded to the other cops that "AL" could refer to a host of other things.

But Victor had raised a question that needed to be considered: what was the link between Lortie, Evergreen, and the three deaths in 1964? Had Lortie been employed by the accounting firm in Joliette? And if, as Victor believed, the victims in 1964 had been "treated" by Judith Harper under Project MK-ULTRA before being killed, why had Lortie himself escaped death?

"Maybe that was why he became homeless," Gilles Lemaire suggested. "So he could disappear. Maybe the only reason he survived was that he was living on the streets and couldn't be found."

The filial link between Lucian Duca and André Lortie had also been discussed. DNA tests would be done, using tissue samples taken by Jacob Berger from the two men's bodies. But the results wouldn't be available for weeks.

The detectives had spent the rest of the meeting listing the pieces of information they considered likeliest to help them find Tousignant.

Before ending the discussion, Delaney had handed out assignments. Taillon would look into Tousignant's past, getting in touch with his daughter, loved ones, family, colleagues, and friends. Loïc would do the same with the colleagues of Lucian Duca.

Despite Jacinthe's protests, Victor asked the boss to let him go over the Evergreen files and explore where they might lead. Delaney struck a compromise. He gave the job to the Gnome, who would also be responsible for gathering information about the suspicious deaths of the three accountants in Joliette and for looking at the newspaper articles on the subject, which had been ordered from the archives of the National Library.

Victor, meanwhile, would coordinate search operations with other police forces, and he'd set up a press conference to update the media on the senator's disappearance. It was also agreed — since he was already in the public eye as a result of his son's arrest — that the detective sergeant would not be present at the media event.

Delaney had asked Victor to stay in the conference room while the other detectives went back to their desks. Victor was absently turning a photograph of a buxom, dark-haired woman between his fingers. Sylvie or Silvia — regardless of the name Lortie had scribbled on the white border, the investigators now knew that the picture found in the rooming house was of Lucian Duca's mother.

"Do I need to explain why I've given you less to do than the others?" Delaney asked.

The detective sergeant placed the Polaroid on the table among the reports, photographs, interrogation notes, and information files. Coordinating search efforts would require less than an hour's work, and they both knew Delaney could set up the press conference by himself.

"No, Chief. You don't need to explain. Thank you."

Delaney's reason was hardly a mystery. The news had made the rounds. The rest of the team knew that he had received a call from the chief prosecutor regarding Martin.

"Take the time you need to deal with your personal matters, Vic," the boss concluded. "We've got your back."

Consequently, while the rest of the team spent the afternoon and evening of December 27th doing the required investigative work, Victor had done as his superior officer suggested: he had dealt with his personal matters. He had made numerous phone calls and taken care of all the details, making sure everything would go off without a hitch the following morning.

He had left the office with Taillon around 11:00 p.m. Loïc and the Gnome were still at their desks. Jacinthe had dropped Victor off in front of his apartment, wishing him luck. The detective sergeant had collapsed onto his bed with his clothes still on.

Victor had been waiting in the police station corridor for a few minutes when the ginger-haired officer reappeared, accompanied by Martin.

When the young man saw his father, his face lit up. They hugged fiercely. The ginger-haired cop stepped away to give them privacy. For several seconds, Martin sobbed on his father's shoulder as Victor murmured comforting words in his ear.

After Martin had regained his composure, Victor released his hug and handed over the hoodie he'd brought along. Regretfully, he had to cut short their moment together. There was no time to lose.

"Put this on, son. And pull up the hood, just in case."

In the front hall, the ginger-haired cop was looking out the window. "I think we're good," he said, turning to them.

The cop accompanied them to the door. Before Victor walked out, the two men looked each other in the eye. The cop gave him a nod. The detective sergeant thanked him with a slap on the shoulder, then stepped out into the morning light with his son.

Martin's troubles weren't entirely over, but he was free. At least for now.

Marc Lagacé, the legal pit bull whom Victor had engaged to represent Martin, had called with the good news late on the evening of Duca's death.

The lawyer had added that the release wasn't his doing. The prosecutor's office had called to advise him that they weren't going to bring charges against Martin. Victor was pretty sure he knew what had happened. Nadja had interceded with her brother, and Diego had pulled strings to get Martin off, no doubt invoking his status as an RCMP informant.

Martin's release had come with conditions similar to those imposed during a period of probation: he was under orders to stay away from the friends and relatives of his co-accused. He was also forbidden from entering drinking establishments or possessing any kind of firearm, including legally registered weapons. Martin had also promised to ensure he could be reached at all times, and not to leave the country.

Nevertheless, for his own safety, and in order to let the media storm abate, the young man needed to get out of town for a while. The criminal element didn't take kindly to informants, and news of his liberation was bound to reach his former associates sooner or later. Victor had therefore taken the time to organize Martin's departure, following Delaney's suggestion that he deal with his personal matters. Over the course of the previous evening, Victor had spoken with his ex-wife several times, making all the necessary arrangements.

His conversations with Marc Lagacé hadn't given Victor a clear sense of Martin's legal situation, which remained nebulous. Would he emerge from this without a criminal record? Only time would tell. But for the moment, the detective sergeant had far more important things to worry about. Guiding Martin by the arm, he led him across the street. A black car with tinted windows was waiting for them.

Victor opened the rear driver-side door and looked at his son. "There's something I need to say before you go." The young man raised his glistening eyes to his father's. "I love you, and I'm proud of you. I've always been proud of you."

Victor hugged his son; then, with years of experience seating people in police cars, he put a hand on Martin's head and guided him into the back seat. As the door slammed shut, the driver's window slid open.

The driver was a hard-featured man with curly black hair greying at the temples. Wearing mirrored sunglasses, he gave Victor his best smile, which barely compressed his lips and made his moustache rustle. "Everything's set, Vic. I'll call when we get there."

Victor stepped closer to the window and rested his arm on the car's roof. In the back seat, Martin was hugging his mother. Clearly emotional, she blew her nose noisily.

"I'm grateful to you, Johnny."

Jean Ferland would never win a beauty contest. Some people found him a little corny, or at least old school. The big man, who had become a private detective a few years back, had formerly worked alongside Victor. And in those days, he'd been known as one of the best shots in the Montreal Police.

Victor had absolute faith in his old colleague, even entrusting his son to him. The fact that Ferland could kill a man with his bare hands might also have had something to do with it.

Suddenly, a van came around the corner and sped toward them. Victor knew trouble was on the way. "You'd better leave before they get here. I'll deal with them."

The detective sergeant took a step back, and the car roared away. Placing himself in the middle of the street, Victor gave the media vehicle no choice but to stop. The doors flew open. A camera flashed.

"Detective Lessard! Any comment?"

A second voice rose: "Why was your son set free? Did he get special treatment?"

Victor had succeeded. He had saved Martin from appearing on the front pages of the city papers. Ferland would get him safely to the ranch that his Uncle Gilbert, Marie's brother, owned in northern Saskatchewan. Martin would stay there for as long as it took for the dust to settle back home.

"Do you share your son's views on immigration, Detective?"

Victor wasn't worried. Uncle Gilbert and his men respected the traditions of life on a ranch. They knew how to use a rifle. If any members of the neo-Nazi gang that Martin had infiltrated decided to travel west looking for payback, they ran a fair risk of ending up with a skewer up their ass and an apple in their mouth, turning slowly over a campfire.

Without a word, the detective sergeant turned his back on the reporters and set off on foot toward the Crown Victoria, which he had left parked on a side street. Only when he looked up did he see another car stopped at the curb ahead of him. He recognized the vehicle as it rolled toward him. Through the window, a woman's gaze met his as she went by. Nadja's eyes were full of tears.

Victor didn't start walking again until long after the car had disappeared around the corner.

78

BUSINESS TRIP

Sitting in his office, Paul Delaney had replied to Victor's question by saying that Madeleine was doing better. The detective sergeant, for his part, had informed Delaney that Martin was safe and that Nadja still wasn't talking to him.

Now it was time for Victor to stop beating around the bush and tell his boss the real reason why he had come in to the office.

Delaney took a sip of coffee. When he heard Victor's reason, it came back out through his nostrils. Coughing, he wiped his face with a napkin and used the back of his hand to catch droplets that had fallen onto his fleece vest.

"You gonna pull through, Paul?" Victor asked with a smile.

"Dallas?" Delaney coughed for another long while. "You've got to be kidding. Why do you want to go to Dallas?"

"It's a quick trip. One night, two at the most, and then I'll be back."

Reclining on his chair and putting his feet up on the desk, Delaney unbent a paper clip and started using one of the rounded ends to clean his ear.

"And why do you want to go down there, exactly?"

"To talk to the guy whose name appears in Lawson's file — Cleveland Willis. To understand. Some details are still unclear." The detective sergeant reprised his previous performance, repeating the arguments he'd made during their last meeting.

Delaney waved a hand impatiently. "Okay, okay, I get all that," he said, wiping the paper clip with a tissue. "What I mean is, why make the actual trip? Why not talk to the guy by phone, or contact the FBI or the Dallas Police? They could send a local operative to talk to Willis."

"You know why, Paul. Willis may have information that he's been keeping secret for forty-five years. He won't come clean to some stranger over the phone. If he's going to let himself be approached by anyone, it'll be by someone who knows what he's talking about. I think I know enough to gain his trust."

Delaney laughed softly and drained his coffee. "What if he won't talk? Or you can't find him?"

"That's a risk," Victor conceded. "But the address is valid. There's a Cleveland Willis living there. I checked."

Delaney stopped nibbling the rim of his cup and, over his reading glasses, gave the detective sergeant an annoyed look. "I can't let you go, Vic. The media are on our backs, hoping we'll find Tousignant alive. How am I supposed to explain that my best detective has gone to Texas? At taxpayers' expense?"

Victor looked at Delaney with a small smile, clasping his hands behind his neck. "Easy. First of all, your so-called best detective is a notorious hothead. And then there's the fact that my son just got mixed up in a terrorist plot. Sick leave, vacation — you'll find the right turn of phrase. You're good at that. And I'll cover my own expenses."

Delaney's scowl left no doubt as to how he felt about the plan.

"You've got the whole team here looking for Tousignant. Let me go down there, Chief. What have we got to lose?"

Delaney sat up and returned his feet to the carpet. He put the paper clip and earwax-stained tissue in the cup, then dropped the cup into the wastebasket. "I'll give you two days. That's it. And stop calling me 'Chief.' It's not like anyone around here actually does what I say."

Delaney was only pretending to be an indignant boss, and they both knew it. Victor stood up, clicked his heels, and saluted. "Yes, Chief."

"Ah, get outta my face," Delaney snapped. But there was a smile on his lips.

79

AN X ON THE ASPHALT

Dallas, Texas
Thursday, December 29th

Victor took a moment to contemplate the massive glass sky-scrapers overlooking the John F. Kennedy Memorial Plaza, where a cenotaph had been built in honour of the dead president. The commemorative monument consisted of white concrete columns placed side by side to create a roofless cube, nine metres high, divided in two halves by an opening through the middle.

On the plaque, the detective sergeant read that the monument had been unveiled in 1970, seven years after Kennedy's death in Dealey Plaza, a few blocks away.

The architect had designed the structure to be an open memorial, symbolizing John Fitzgerald Kennedy's openness of mind. Jacqueline Kennedy, who had picked up a piece of her husband's skull from the limousine's trunk on the day of the assassination, had personally approved the design.

Standing on only eight supporting legs, the two concrete half squares seemed to float above the ground, separated from each other by a gap of a few metres. Access to the interior was through this gap. Inside the structure, the only feature was a simple granite block.

After reading the president's name in gold letters on the side of the block, Victor raised his head, shielding his eyes from the sun with one hand.

The temperature was fifteen degrees Celsius. In the blue sky, Victor saw the stripes of a four-engine jet's contrail.

As Victor walked along the sidewalk edging the plaza, he kept an anxious eye on the street. He set the hands on his watch back an hour to account for the time-zone change. He was about to light another cigarette when he was suddenly assailed by doubt: would the man he was supposed to meet actually show up? Feeling his anxiety level rise, Victor reflexively put a hand to his left side, where his service weapon was normally holstered. But he'd left it in Montreal.

What could possibly happen to him in a public space in broad daylight? *The same thing that happened to Kennedy,* breathed a little voice in his brain. To stifle the voice, he shook his head and took a cigarette from the pack.

His fears were ridiculous!

Victor's plane had left Trudeau International at 7:45 that morning. After a direct flight of a little over four hours, the Boeing 737 had touched down at Dallas/Fort Worth Airport at 10:55 local time.

Having swallowed a tranquilizer before takeoff, he had slept the whole way.

From the airport, a single phone call had sufficed to set up the meeting. At the other end of the line, a woman's voice had answered. The detective sergeant had asked to speak to Cleveland Willis. The woman had asked him to hang on a moment. A few seconds later, Victor was speaking to Willis. After introducing himself and explaining that he was with the Montreal Police in Canada, Victor had said, "I'd like to ask you some questions about André Lortie."

A long silence had followed those words.

Victor had pressed on, mentioning the names of Daniel Tousignant and Evergreen. At last, the elderly man had offered to meet him at the John F. Kennedy Memorial Plaza.

Victor had been ready for anything — ready for Willis to hang up, or to say he didn't know anyone by that name, or to protest, or to threaten him. Victor had been ready for anything except what had actually happened: he'd gotten his meeting with ease.

Willis arrived in a white minivan driven by a tall, burly woman in her fifties. She helped him out of the passenger seat, literally taking him in her arms and placing him gently on the sidewalk. He was a small man with diaphanous skin and a sprinkling of age spots on his balding head. His bright green eyes danced behind thin, gold-rimmed glasses. An oxygen tube looped up into his nostrils, and he walked with a cane.

Victor stepped forward and introduced himself. Willis's hand disappeared into his own. The woman stood there in front of him, her bulbous eyes looking him up and down, appraising him. Her expression of displeasure made it plain that she didn't trust him. The old man said something in her ear. She hesitated for a moment, then climbed back into the minivan. She gave Victor one more dark look before driving away.

"My daughter," Willis explained. "Since my wife's death, she's become very protective."

"I understand." Silence. "Is it bad?" Victor asked, pointing to the oxygen tube.

Willis made an effort to smile. "The worst." He pointed toward the concrete box. "Did you get a chance to look inside?"

The detective sergeant nodded.

"How did you find me?"

"Long story."

Victor offered him an arm. Willis took it, and they strolled a few metres to the pedestrian street that edged the plaza.

"Perfect. I love long stories."

And there, sitting in the shade of the trees lining South Record Street, Victor told Willis everything he knew. The account took a full half hour.

Hands crossed over the pommel of his cane, his head slightly bowed, Willis listened closely, letting out an "Mm-hm" of assent from time to time.

Victor wrapped up by answering the man's initial question. "Based on the materials I have in hand, I believe Lawson put together a file on Evergreen's activities, a file that proved Senator Tousignant's responsibility for the events that led to the violent deaths of three people in 1964. It was in this file that I found your name and address. Lawson had tracked down your whereabouts in 1975, and again in 2003."

"Tracked down? I was never in hiding. I sold my house in 2003 after my wife died and moved into a condo. Hence the change of address."

"When I mentioned André Lortie and Evergreen over the phone, you agreed to meet me right away, without asking questions. Just now, as I was talking about Lawson, Tousignant, and Harper, I watched your reactions. I got the sense that all those people were known to you. You don't seem surprised that I'm here. Am I wrong?"

Willis cleared his throat a few times before raising his owl-like eyes to Victor's. "I knew that sooner or later someone would come around and ask me about those events. To be honest, though, I didn't think it would take forty-eight years."

"Tell me what you know, Mr. Willis."

"I'll be happy to. But I warn you now, if you were hoping to get to the bottom of the Kennedy assassination, you're in for a disappointment."

At Willis's request, they walked the short distance to Dealey Plaza, where the assassination took place. They stopped in front of a bronze map showing the route followed by the presidential motorcade on that fateful November 22nd.

"Dealey Plaza attracts an exceptional variety of people, from ordinary tourists to highly qualified conspiracy theorists," Willis said, moving his hand in the air to indicate the two extremes. "And then there are the pseudo-experts, hawking their wares."

And indeed, Victor could see street vendors calling out to pass-ersby, offering them newsletters and books promising the whole truth about the assassination. But the thing that immediately struck him was the relatively modest size of the area, which, from his memories of the Zapruder film, he'd expected to be bigger.

The two men approached a red-brick building. According to the old man, the Texas School Book Depository building, from which presumed assassin Lee Harvey Oswald had fired on the president, looked essentially the same as it had in 1963. Victor followed the line of Willis's extended forefinger to the corner window on the sixth floor where the shooter had been hidden. "They've turned it into a museum," Willis grumbled dismissively, "but there's nothing to see."

Ahead and to their right lay the grassy knoll, with a plaque standing on its tiny patch of green, "near the spot where the fatal shot hit the president," the old man explained. On the ground, a few flowers were swaying in the wind. Victor felt it was simultane-ously ghoulish and fascinating to be in this place.

Willis drew his attention to three white Xs painted on the asphalt of Elm Street, which had been part of the motorcade's route. "Those are the locations where the bullets struck."

Farther down, Victor recognized the entrance ramp to the highway that the limousine had taken to reach the hospital. A man holding a video camera and a microphone with a foam cover asked them in a self-important tone to step aside. He was shooting a doc-umentary about the assassination.

Victor helped Willis cross the knoll and climb the steps that rose beside it. They sat down. The old man gradually caught his breath before starting to speak again.

"I was twenty-eight when I joined the CIA. That was in 1961. I was young and idealistic. I'd worked on Kennedy's senate re-election campaign in 1958 and on his presidential campaign in 1960. For two years, the agency sent me to various countries to oppose Communist activities and promote local democracy. I went to a lot of places: Laos, Paris, Berlin, Latin America. In early 1963,

I was posted to the Ottawa embassy as cultural counsellor; then, in May of that year, I was seconded to the consulate in Montreal. I was one of the resources without an official job description. In other words, the consul sometimes knew what I was up to, sometimes not. My job was to watch the Cuban consulate, which was providing cover for the Soviet spy network, the KGB. The FLQ also had links with the Cubans, as well as with French intelligence services. I was responsible for logistics. I was in contact with Daniel Tousignant and Nathan Lawson, who both worked for the same law firm at the time. They had sources at the Cuban consulate, and we'd exchange information. You have to understand that back then, everyone was spying on everyone else. The intelligence trade was a booming business. For the most part, I dealt with Lawson, who was Tousignant's subordinate. What I didn't know then, but learned later, was that during the period when I was dealing with him, Tousignant was also working for the agency."

Victor's face betrayed his surprise. "Tousignant worked for the CIA?"

Willis leaned his cane against the bench, pulled a handkerchief from his pocket, and began to wipe his glasses. "His code name was Watermelon Man."

Images of the mosaic on which Lortie had written those words came into the detective sergeant's mind.

Willis looked at him before continuing. "Because of his later career, not many people remember that Tousignant was a decorated war hero. He signed up at the age of twenty and fought in Korea with the Royal 22nd Regiment. It was only when he got home that he completed his legal studies. And it was much later that he began his philanthropic work."

Victor took his notebook from his pocket, scribbled a few details, and placed the notebook on his lap.

"In 1961," Willis continued, "Tousignant created a corporation, making himself its chairman and chief executive officer. The company's official activity was organizing trade fairs."

"Evergreen."

Willis nodded. "That's right. Evergreen." The old man coughed and wiped his mouth with his handkerchief. "In September of 1964, when the time came to produce the company's audited financial statements for the fiscal year ending August 31st, one of the auditors discovered an irregularity in the company's books regarding transactions that had taken place in October and November of 1963. Tousignant and Lawson panicked."

The old man had a coughing fit so severe that it bent him over double. He needed more than a minute to collect himself. Crimson-faced, he wiped his mouth once again with his handkerchief, leaving traces of blood on the fabric.

Once he was sure Willis wouldn't keel over then and there, Victor went to a newsstand at the corner and bought a bottle of water.

Thanking him, the retired agent raised the bottle to his lips with a trembling hand and took a few sips. His complexion gradually regained its milky hue. He seemed lost. "Where was I?" he asked, looking at Victor uncertainly.

"You were talking about an irregularity in Evergreen's books."

The light returned to Willis's eyes. "Right. Evergreen had transferred funds to a foreign corporation as payment for excavation work done on the grounds of a trade fair that Evergreen was organizing in Berlin. All the paperwork was in order. The excavation firm had provided valid invoices made out to Evergreen, but the auditor's attention was caught by the amounts involved, which seemed far too high for the nature of the work that had been done." Willis stopped for a moment, as though wanting to get his thoughts in order before going on. "The auditor started asking questions. Dissatisfied with the answers he got, and suspecting the invoices were inflated, he made inquiries about the excavation firm. His inquiries led him to discover that during the period when the work was supposed to have been carried out, in October of 1963, and on the dates of the bank transfers in October and November, the firm had obtained none of the required regulatory permits, and it possessed neither the heavy trucks nor the equipment necessary for that kind of work. It was only in late November, after the assassination, that a permit was finally issued to the excavation firm."

Victor frowned. "It was a fictitious firm, is that it? A shell company?"

"Precisely. Another CIA-controlled entity." Willis's gaze drifted up into the overhanging foliage. "They had moved too fast, without erasing their tracks. Afterward, they'd tried to cover up their mistake by securing the permit. The paper trail was tainted. But no one was supposed to be asking questions. You understand? The accounting firm was already getting brown envelopes."

Victor nodded and closed his eyes. "Why did Tousignant and Lawson feel so threatened that they would order the auditor's execution?"

Willis put an age-spotted hand on Victor's shoulder. "Because he'd found a thread, and they were prepared to use any means necessary to prevent him from following that thread to the heart of the operation. They got rid of him before he could discover the truth."

"What would he have found?"

The old man looked into Victor's eyes, his head rocking slowly. "If he had followed the trail of bank transfers to the excavation company, and then if he'd looked more deeply into that company, its true activities, and its customers, the auditor would eventually have been able to establish a link between Evergreen and certain individuals who had conspired to assassinate President Kennedy. That's why Tousignant and Lawson were scared."

Victor shuddered. "What are you saying, Mr. Willis?"

"I've never possessed the hard evidence that would enable me to prove it conclusively in a court of law, but Evergreen was a front through which the CIA financed political assassinations. What I'm saying is that the agency used Evergreen to pay the shooters who were concealed in Dealey Plaza that day."

80

BLACK OPERATIONS

Willis was talking steadily. Despite the numerous questions that crowded into Victor's head, he decided not to interrupt the old man, for fear Willis might fall silent and the source of information might dry up forever. Victor began scribbling feverishly in his notebook, while trying not to miss a word the retired agent said.

"You have to understand that Evergreen brought together a diverse collection of interests. They were united by a single cause: the struggle against Communism. Among the more notable members, there was a former Hungarian prime minister known for his anti-Communist and anti-Castro views, a lawyer representing an influential U.S. senator with suspected Mob links, an uncle of the Egyptian king, a New York Mafia godfather, a powerful Austrian government minister who might once have been a former Nazi collaborator, and Clay Shaw, who was eventually prosecuted by New Orleans District Attorney Jim Garrison. Shaw had close links with both pro- and anti-Castro elements. All of these people had their own reasons for wanting Kennedy dead. But I'm not going to go into that. It would be pure speculation. I'll stick to what I actually saw. As I was saying, for reasons you now know, Tousignant and Lawson panicked when the accountant discovered a financial irregularity. What was supposed to be a routine audit suddenly threatened the entire structure. You spoke to me earlier about Project MK-ULTRA, which came up a few times in your investigation ..."

Victor nodded to encourage the old man to continue.

"What most people don't know is that when McGill University abandoned the program in 1964, Judith Harper had already taken over from Dr. Cameron as head of the project. The agency had supplied her with funds to set up a clandestine parallel lab, where she performed her own secret experiments. She had a guy working for her ..." Willis tapped his forehead with his fingers. "The name's not coming back to me. A young man ..."

"McNeil? Mark McNeil?"

"Could be. I don't remember anymore. Anyway, do I need to tell you what kind of experiments those two were doing? Mind control and brainwashing, using methods that enabled them to manipulate mental states and alter brain function: administering drugs and other chemical substances, hypnosis, sensory deprivation, isolation, verbal and sexual violence, not to mention various forms of torture. Harper and her assistant were twisted human beings, Detective." For a moment, he gazed intensely into Victor's eyes. "Harper's father had been an Adrien Arcand sympathizer. Arcand admired Adolf Hitler and was a leader of Quebec's fascist movement. Forgive the language, but Judith was the worst kind of nasty-ass bitch. She could commit atrocities in private, while preserving her public image as a respected academic. Now, when that accountant started talking about irregularities, Tousignant and his team first tried to buy his silence. That was standard procedure for them. The senior managers of the accounting firm handling the audit had been on the take for a long time. The audit was meant to be a formality. No one was supposed to raise any difficulties at all. But the accountant assigned to the file was newly hired, and this was one of his very first cases. With a beginner's zeal, he dug deeper than anyone had expected him to. When he refused to take the money and shut his mouth, Tousignant initially turned to Judith Harper to deal with the problem."

"So Harper and Tousignant knew each other?"

"They never let on in public, but behind closed doors, Tousignant, Harper, and Lawson worked as a team. It was through

Lawson that Harper and her assistant were given the job of 'deprogramming' the accountant. At the same time, Tousignant had
gotten in touch with CIA headquarters in Langley to have them
send out a black ops asset."

"Black ops?"

"The agency had a secret roster of killers."

Victor's mind was racing. The image of a face appeared to him.
The pieces fell into place. The fog lifted, and suddenly everything
was clear. Now he understood the references to "BO" and "AL" that
he'd found in Tousignant's correspondence with Lawson.

"André Lortie?"

"The very one. It was Nathan Lawson who called to advise me
that Langley was sending a black ops specialist to the consulate. He
was beside himself. He'd been vehemently opposed to Tousignant's
initiative. Within a few hours, I received confirmation through
official channels that Lortie had arrived. I can still remember the
wording of the message: the mission objective was to 'tie up a loose
end.' Since I was responsible for logistics, it was my job to provide
Lortie with whatever he needed to accomplish his mission. He
was a dual citizen. His father was American, while his mother was
from Quebec. The father had walked out on the family, so Lortie
had taken his mother's surname. He was a former marine, and this
was his second or third black ops assignment. The moment I met
him, I knew he was a sadist. He enjoyed violence. Killing gave him
pleasure."

"He was the one who murdered the accountant and his son,
right?" Victor asked.

Willis nodded. "The afternoon he arrived, I went with him to
the accountant's home. The man lived in the country with his wife
and two kids. If I remember correctly, one of the kids was mentally
retarded. While they were at school, Lortie threatened the accountant and gave him a beating. Lortie said if the man didn't take the
money and shut his mouth, he'd be back, and next time, he'd hurt
the man's family."

Willis's eyes filled briefly with tears of helpless outrage. His lower lip trembled. Victor's throat tightened; he didn't know what to say.

"I sat there and did nothing. I tried to convince myself that I was following orders, but the truth is, I was afraid. Excuse me ..." The old man paused and took a few sips of water. "Unfortunately, the accountant was a brave man. Far from letting himself be intimidated, he told two colleagues about his discovery. That was the beginning of the end. Following Tousignant's instructions, Lortie abducted the accounting firm's three employees, one at a time, and brought them to Harper. She and her assistant administered their treatments. Knowing the agency's penchant for compartmentalizing information, I would bet that they knew nothing about the conspiracy or the stakes involved. They just did what was expected of them: they erased the memories of the three subjects. I'll spare you the details, Detective. Those three people were tortured. They were broken human beings when Lortie dumped them back on their doorsteps."

"But someone must have called the police," Victor said indignantly.

As the detective sergeant raised his eyes, he was constricted by an unpleasant sensation that left a metallic taste in his mouth. Was his imagination playing tricks on him? Twice now, he had seen the same black car with tinted windows roll by, slowing down as it passed them. Victor touched the empty space on his left side. He bitterly regretted not having bothered to fill in the forms that would have allowed him to bring his service weapon across the border.

"You've got to bear the context in mind," Willis said, not seeming to have noticed anything. "The accounting firm was well established in the Joliette area. Tousignant and Lawson were paying hefty bribes to the police chief and subordinate officers to ensure that they'd look the other way. The three employees turned up again within a few days, their pockets stuffed with cash. The whole matter would have sunk without a trace if it hadn't been for that one accountant's stubborn honesty. He stayed quiet for a few weeks, then, despite the fact that he'd been fired from his job, he tried to get back in touch with his two colleagues. Harper's treatment had failed: the accountant's memory was intact. That's when he signed his own death warrant, and those of the two others."

Victor's tension eased: the car with the tinted windows had just disappeared along the highway entrance ramp at the end of Elm Street.

"From the start, there had been animosity between Lortie and me. But at this point, I blew up. I was bitterly opposed to the execution of three innocent people." Willis's lower lip began to tremble again. "One night, I woke up with a knife at my throat. Lortie had slipped into my bedroom. He whispered in my ear that next time, he'd kill me."

A tear ran down his cheek, and then another. The two droplets wound their way to the old man's chin.

Victor gave him time to compose himself before speaking. "Lortie made the killings look like accidents."

"He was a monster, but I can't deny that he was skilled at his work. And, of course, Tousignant and Lawson came along in his wake and made sure the right people got brown envelopes."

Two carefree young women were walking on the grass, their feet bare in the sunshine, holding their sandals in their hands, utterly heedless of the tragedy that had played out on this spot forty-eight years earlier.

"What happened next?" Victor asked.

Willis shrugged. "Nothing. Back then, Montreal was the city of a thousand pleasures. Lortie convinced his superiors to let him make it his base of operations. I stayed as far away from him as possible. But I know that at one point, he infiltrated the FLQ. The U.S. was in the grip of anti-Communist paranoia, and the agency was worried that Fidel Castro might gain control over Quebec's independence movement. Lortie participated in a number of FLQ operations, principally bank robberies. In 1965, the FLQ set off a bomb in front of the American consulate, where I was employed. There were no injuries, but seventy-eight windows were shattered.

I happened to bump into Lortie after. When I asked if he'd taken part in that operation, he answered, laughing, that the consulate's facade had been in need of renovation."

"He also participated in the kidnappings of Pierre Laporte and James Richard Cross, didn't he?"

"No. But I can guess why you think he did. You see, by early 1968, Lortie was becoming uncontrollable. He'd descended into alcoholism. When he was drunk, he'd let down his guard and talk too much. Tousignant and Lawson started worrying. They considered bringing up a second black ops asset to get rid of him, but Lortie had already proclaimed to anyone who would listen that he'd taken protective measures. If he died, the media would learn the truth. Tousignant and Lawson couldn't run the risk that he'd stashed a compromising file somewhere — a file that might surface after his death."

Fresh images appeared in Victor's mind: the space behind the ceramic tile in the bathroom of Lortie's rooming house, and the one Victor had recently discovered at Duca's place. These were some of the locations where Lortie might have concealed the documents Willis had in mind.

"They couldn't risk eliminating Lortie. But they couldn't afford to let him keep talking. So, Tousignant decided to send him to Judith Harper, first in 1969, then again in late 1970, for a tune-up." Willis chuckled. "Lortie was tough. The first time, it took three marines to overpower him." Silence. "Judith had refined her techniques over the years. She erased his memory, and, to create confusion in case he was ever questioned, she planted false memories in Lortie's brain. That's why he was so sure he'd participated in the Laporte and Cross kidnappings."

"Lortie was first admitted for psychiatric care in Montreal in 1969. He had no identification, no family, no past. How did he end up like that? How was it possible?"

"Don't be so naive, Detective. What you're describing is a CIA specialty. It's as easy for the agency to obliterate a person's past as it is for a dentist to pull a tooth. Let's walk, shall we?"

The two men stood and advanced toward the building from which Oswald had fired on the president.

"Things went downhill for Lortie after that. No one had suspected it, but he was afflicted by bipolar disorder. His first breakdown was probably caused by the drugs he'd been given during his treatment by Judith Harper. In fact, it was Harper, acting on Tousignant's instructions, who had him admitted to the psychiatric hospital. By then, Lortie was a broken man, a shadow of his old self. In those days, severe psychotic cases were institutionalized. Harper saw to it that Lortie was kept in isolation for months."

"Was she the one who got Dr. McNeil his job at the hospital where Lortie was being treated?"

"The man you mentioned earlier? I wouldn't know. But if you're wondering whether they could have gone on subjecting Lortie to their secret treatments through the intermediary of an agency-linked doctor, I'd say that was entirely possible."

"What do you mean? I looked at his file. Lortie was eventually discharged, same as any other mentally ill patient in Quebec. He was readmitted a number of times, but he spent most of his life on the outside. Wasn't he a threat, as far as they were concerned?"

Eyes closed, head back, Willis let the sunshine caress his face. When he turned to look at Victor, he was wearing a little smile. "Let's get one thing straight. From the time he was set free, Lortie posed no threat to anyone. His bipolar diagnosis was a blessing for them. It explained all his delusions and undermined the credibility of any claims he might make. I ran into him on the street one day, quite by chance. This would have been in 1973 or thereabouts … I can't recall, exactly. No matter. Lortie was in the midst of a full psychotic breakdown, raving about Pierre Laporte and the FLQ. He didn't even recognize me. He was living on the streets, homeless."

"He had a relationship with a woman at one point. Silvia Duca, a former ballet dancer. Does that name mean anything to you?"

This time, the little smile was supplemented by a wink in Victor's direction.

"Not that one in particular. But Lortie had lots of girlfriends. He used them when he needed to lie low. Somewhat like Carlos the Jackal."

"Do you remember whether Lortie had a child? A son?"

"Considering what I've just told you, I'd be surprised if he had only one!"

Willis laughed before being seized by another coughing fit. He covered his mouth with his handkerchief. When Victor questioned him about the blackout from which Lortie had awakened in possession of his victims' wallets, Willis shrugged. He knew nothing about that.

Victor was in the company of a very sick man who clearly no longer cared about consequences. So why was Willis talking to a Montreal cop and not the media?

Willis was silent for a long time before he answered. "I left the agency in 1975 and moved down here to Dallas, the place where the president was assassinated. I worked in real estate until my retirement. My decision to make this city my home was motivated by a single thought. *Never forget.* John Kennedy was my hero. He was the idol of my youth. I owe my political awakening to him. He's the figure who ignited my patriotic feelings. The news of his death shook me to the core. A few months later, before I'd fully recovered from that shock, I learned facts that changed my life forever. A few lines on a financial statement. A loose end that I was told to help tie up. Since then, I've spent every single day of my life regretting what I did. I was crushed by the machine. I was forced to do things that might have allowed men who plotted a president's death to get away with it. I spent my life in Dallas so that I would never forget. So I'd be reminded each day of my failure to do the right thing."

Overcome with emotion, Willis fell silent, struggling not to cry. Victor didn't speak. He put a sympathetic hand on the old man's arm and waited for him to continue.

"You wonder why I never broke my silence, why I never said anything … What can I tell you?" He paused. "I should have spoken out against evil, but I was afraid. Afraid of retribution — against me, against my wife and children. Afraid that I would die along with my ideals." His eyes were glistening. "I kept quiet because I gave up on my dreams. Because I forgot that it's better to resist than to regret. Because I was, and always will be, suffocated by shame." Willis took a deep breath and regained his composure. "I decided not to say anything. To wait until someone came along and started asking questions. As fate would have it, that someone was you."

Victor didn't speak, but simply lowered his eyes.

The old man was walking with difficulty, leaning on his cane, his back bent. They had left the grassy knoll behind and come to the corner of Elm and North Houston Streets, near the book depository, when Victor saw it again: the black car with tinted windows had just pulled up across the street.

"Wait here."

Driven by an unthinking impulse, the detective sergeant stepped into the street, fists clenched at his sides, arms slightly spread, determined to confront the threat. At the same moment, the driver-side door opened and a uniformed chauffeur emerged.

As Victor approached with a menacing expression, the chauffeur, taking no notice of him, opened the rear door and helped an elegantly dressed woman in her forties get out of the car. Two young children, a boy and a girl, got out after her. The woman spoke into the chauffeur's ear and he nodded. The chauffeur smiled as the woman walked away, holding the children's hands. The little girl waved to him, and he waved back.

Victor had reached the man when he realized his mistake.

The chauffeur asked in a friendly voice if he could help Victor with anything. The detective sergeant stammered a vague excuse and walked away, apologizing. The chauffeur watched him cross the street and shrugged, clearly thinking, *just another weirdo.*

Victor rejoined Cleveland Willis, who hadn't moved from his spot on the sidewalk and seemed to be wondering whether there was a problem. The detective sergeant mumbled something about wanting directions for the trip back to his hotel, then restarted the conversation by mentioning Tousignant's disappearance.

Willis described an ambitious, ruthlessly calculating man whose public image was the opposite of his true nature.

"Was he the one in the shadows, pulling the strings?"

"I don't think Daniel Tousignant and his helpers ever knew who was behind the plot to kill President Kennedy. They were simply instructed by the agency to pay the operatives — which is to say, the shooters. That's as far as it went."

"So, you really believe there was a conspiracy?"

"I've always thought the killing of the accountant and his two colleagues lent credence to the multiple shooters theory, but I've never had hard evidence to prove it. Much of the information I've shared with you was given to me by Nathan Lawson. I don't know why, but he always trusted me." Willis closed his eyes and was silently contemplative for a moment. "The truth is, I've often suspected that he saw me as a kind of insurance policy. You've somewhat confirmed that suspicion by telling me my name and address were in the file he assembled. And it doesn't surprise me at all to hear you suggest that the purpose of the file was to prove Lawson's innocence and Tousignant's guilt. That was Lawson. A lawyer to his core. Whatever the reason, one of the last things he told me about Lortie was that Judith Harper had had a lot of trouble deprogramming one particular sentence. It was something Lortie would repeat over and over, with a mocking laugh, whenever he was drunk: 'I didn't shoot anybody, no sir!'"

In his mind's eye, Victor saw himself in the bedroom with Virginie, watching the frail young man in the video clip.

"This may surprise you. I don't know if Lee Harvey Oswald was one of the shooters on November 22nd, 1963. But I'll wonder to my dying day whether, as the presidential limousine rolled through Dealey Plaza, André Lortie was in a window of a nearby building, holding a rifle."

81

A BIT OF SIGHTSEEING

The white minivan had come to pick up Willis on the tree-lined plaza near the commemorative monument. As she placed her father in the passenger seat, Willis's daughter was hardly friendlier to Victor than she had been upon arrival; she offered him a pale imitation of a smile.

As he thanked the old man, the detective sergeant would have liked to find a graceful way to wish him well at the close of his life, but the words didn't come. In the end, Victor simply urged Willis to take care. They shook hands, and amid the noise of the minivan's exhaust, the retired CIA agent rolled out of Victor's life, just as he had rolled into it a few hours earlier.

The sun was starting to go down. Victor hesitated. Part of him wanted to return to the hotel near the airport and get some rest, but another part wanted to do a bit of sightseeing downtown. His flight home was scheduled to leave early the next morning. There was a pool at the hotel. With a little luck, he'd find trunks for sale at one of the shops in the lobby and be able to swim a few lengths.

On the other hand, he'd never been to Dallas before. He might never come again. His laziness made him feel guilty.

Not wanting to have any regrets later, the detective sergeant decided, despite his fatigue, to walk for a bit. He might find a nice little restaurant and have a bite before turning in.

He wasn't sure what conclusions to draw from his meeting with Willis. A stroll would help clarify his thoughts. The old man had spoken of so many matters that Victor had the vertiginous impression, recalling them, of plunging into a black hole. He needed to sort things out in his head, to categorize the new information.

And he needed a hit of nicotine.

Taking a cigarette from his pack, he went back to the newsstand. The clerk was in the process of putting away magazines. His workday was done, but, for a dollar, he sold the detective sergeant a map of downtown Dallas.

Smoking calmly, Victor went back up Elm Street, along which relatively modest brick buildings alternated with tall, glass structures. The city core was emptying out, little by little. People were going home after work.

Victor nodded a greeting to a man smoking a cigarillo in front of a 7-Eleven. To his left, at one end of a long parking lot, a telecommunications tower rose into the blue sky.

The detective sergeant walked on and soon found himself in a grove of skyscrapers. Eyes lifted, neck bent back, he gazed up at the steel and glass giants.

Hoping for a little variety, he looked more closely at a silver dome pictured on his map: the Dallas Convention Center.

Victor turned right onto a street that didn't appear on his map, but which seemed to be heading in the direction of the Convention Center. Arriving at an intersection that he couldn't locate on the grid, he decided nevertheless to keep going.

If he was reading the map correctly, he would eventually come to Akard Street. From there, he could reach the Convention Center. As he advanced, pedestrians became more and more scarce. He had clearly entered an area that was not only less busy, but also, judging from the shuttered storefronts, less prosperous.

After walking for another few minutes, Victor had to face facts: he was lost. Lighting another cigarette, he decided to go as far as the next intersection. It would be easy to figure out where he was once he saw the street signs. But when he reached the intersection, he was once again unable to find it on his map. That was the trouble with these tourist guides: they only showed the main thoroughfares.

At the corner, a wiry little guy with a toothpick between his lips called out to him. Wearing a Pac-Man T-shirt and leaning against a chain-link fence, the guy had noticed that Victor was trying to find his way.

"Where do you want to go, man?"

"The Convention Center."

The diminutive guy bounced over in his sandals. "Easy. Let me show you, man." The guy bent over Victor's map and, with a grimy finger, indicated the route. Victor realized that he was only a few blocks from his destination.

"Can you spare a smoke, man?"

The detective sergeant was groping for his pack of cigarettes when, with a hard, economical motion, the guy threw a punch that caught Victor just under the left eye. At the same moment, something struck him violently on the back of the neck.

Victor felt himself pitch forward. Everything went black. In the distance, he heard a loud noise blasting through the silence.

82

BABY FACE

Victor opened his eyes and tried to get up. Framed in the yellow glare of a streetlight, a man was bending over him, dreadlocks swaying around his face.

"Easy, brother. You just got flattened."

Victor panicked for a moment, putting a hand to his left eye — he couldn't see out of it. His fingers touched distended flesh. The swelling had shut his eye. It took him a moment to remember where he was, what had happened, and why this stranger was looking down at him.

The stranger's hands slipped under Victor's armpits. "Let's get you back on your feet." The man hoisted Victor into a standing position and led him toward a taxi.

The pavement and the surrounding buildings were wobbling in the cop's field of vision, melting into a blur. He spat, trying to get rid of the mercury taste that filled his mouth. His eye began to throb. Then the pain arrived in the back of his neck. He'd been hit from behind as well.

Staggering forward, Victor patted his pockets. No more wallet, no more phone, and, worst of all, no more cigarettes.

"You were lucky, brother. The man upstairs set Samuel Baby Face Johnson down on your path. Indeed he did."

It was true. Victor had been fortunate.

From the driver's seat of his taxi, Baby Face had seen Victor being attacked. He had put the assailants to flight with several long blasts of his horn. Then, armed with a baseball bat, he had stepped out of the car to lend assistance.

"Where to from here, brother?" Baby Face asked as he eased Victor into the back seat of the taxi. "I can take you home, or to the hospital, or I can call the police for you. But if I call the police, I won't be sticking around to say hello. The truth is, I have a history with the police. And I'm sorry to say it's not a happy one."

Baby Face laughed, revealing flawless white teeth. When Victor explained that he was from Montreal, staying in Dallas for one night, and that he had a room at the airport Hyatt Regency, Baby Face insisted on driving him there.

"I don't want you getting wrong ideas about how we treat strangers around here, brother. I'm not going to let you down. The man upstairs would be displeased if I did."

"I have no money to pay you."

"You'll pay it forward, brother. The man upstairs is watching. He'll know if you've honoured your debt down the line. Amen to that." Baby Face crossed himself.

And while Baby Face continued to talk about the man upstairs, Victor sank into the passenger seat. He watched the highway flow past his window. A Texas Rangers pennant fluttered from the rear-view mirror.

From the hotel desk clerk's expression when he asked for a new key card to his room, Victor could imagine how bad he looked. In the elevator, a couple studiously avoided his gaze.

As soon as he entered his room, the detective sergeant went to the desk, picked up a pen, and scribbled a number on the hotel notepad. Before Baby Face drove away, Victor had asked for a business card so he could send him reimbursement for the unpaid cab fare. But Baby Face wouldn't hear of it. So Victor had memorized the permit number posted inside the car.

Turning his face away from the room's mirrors, Victor swallowed several acetaminophen tablets. Then he went for ice at the end of the corridor while the bathtub was filling.

Immersed to his neck in piping-hot water, he held a bag of ice wrapped in a wet washcloth against his eye. The cold began to numb the pain.

As he considered the trouble he'd have to go through to replace his various cards, one thought provided some consolation: the attack on him had been a simple mugging, unrelated to his investigation. And he could count himself lucky that he'd stored his passport and return airline ticket in the room safe.

Sitting naked on a towel at the head of the bed, Victor hung up with a sigh. His bank cards had been cancelled. The rest could wait until tomorrow.

After several attempts, his call finally got through.

"... lo? Is any ... ere? Less ...? Hel ...?"

"Jacinthe, it's me. I want you to ... Can you hear me?"

"... ard? ... lo? Hello?"

Static. Background noise. A poor connection. Jacinthe was someplace with bad cell reception. The detective sergeant could hear distant, muted sounds: crackling, and a woman's voice speaking a language that was neither English nor French.

"My flight gets in at 11:30 tomorrow morning. Come pick me up."

"Wha ...?"

"Come pick me up tomorrow! At the airport!"

"... port? ... ime?"

Fed up, Victor slammed the handset onto its cradle. Then he pressed the redial button. The line was busy. After several failed attempts, he gave up. At that moment, he realized that he was now sitting beside the towel, with his bare buttocks on the bedspread. He jumped up, disgusted.

He'd always lived by an absolute, inflexible rule, applying it equally to fleabag motels and five-star resorts: never, under any circumstances, touch a hotel bedspread.

The acetaminophen was starting to kick in. Standing up with difficulty, Victor decided to risk a glance in the mirror. Bad idea. Instantly, he turned off the light. A lump of purple flesh enveloped his eye. Luckily, the cut that Nadja's brother had inflicted on the eyebrow hadn't reopened.

Victor looked like Rocky in the aftermath of his bout with Apollo Creed. Feeling desperately alone, he momentarily considered calling Nadja. Then he decided against it. He might as well go all the way with the Rocky impersonation and start yelling *Adrian!* at the top of his lungs, for all the good it would do.

Putting on clean underwear, he reflected on the absurdity of the situation. This had all started with the two wallets Lortie had left on the ledge before stepping into eternity.

And now Victor's own wallet had been taken.

For a fraction of a second, he entertained the notion that the mugging hadn't been a coincidence. Then, in the dark hotel room, he began to laugh quietly.

His wallet was gone. So was his money. His cellphone. His son. His girlfriend. His cigarettes. His face was a battered pulp. And his bare ass had touched the bedspread. Could things get any worse?

The laughter died in his throat. He opened the minibar and closed it. Walked around the room. Opened the minibar again. Closed it again. Those little bottles … No. He wouldn't go there.

He took a pill to calm the anxiety that held him by the throat.

Then he took another.

83

SOMETHING DOESN'T QUITE FIT

Trudeau International Airport, Montreal
Friday, December 30th

With his travel bag slung over one shoulder, Victor navigated around the herd of travellers and exited through the glass doors.

Taillon froze for an instant at the sight of his black eye, which his sunglasses didn't entirely succeed in hiding. "What the hell, Lessard?" she said, laughing. "Did you say the wrong thing to a Cowboys cheerleader?"

"Go fuck yourself, Taillon," he said, trying to smile.

Jacinthe touched his shoulder with one finger and pulled it away sharply, making a hissing noise. "I missed you too, honeybunch."

In the Crown Victoria on the way to Versailles, Victor asked Jacinthe what had happened in his absence. She told him there had been essentially no progress. Then she couldn't resist adding, "A banged head in Summit Woods, a split eyebrow courtesy of your ex-girlfriend's brother, and now a souvenir shiner from Dallas … I'm guessing you'll be glad when this case is over, my friend."

Victor chose not to respond.

His account of the conversation with Cleveland Willis had an effect on his colleagues, especially when he described the retired agent's revelations about Evergreen and the possible involvement of Tousignant, Lawson, and Lortie in a conspiracy to assassinate

President Kennedy. Delaney undertook to contact authorities in the U.S. to pass along the information.

Meanwhile, as Jacinthe reminded the team, they were still investigating a series of murders in Montreal, and they needed to focus their energies on one thing: finding Senator Tousignant. Her own take on the subject was, as usual, categorical. "If you ask me, we're gonna end up in the same place. Okay, so we were wrong about Duca. He clearly didn't commit the murders to avenge his martyred father. But you said Lortie had lots of girlfriends, right?"

"That's what Willis claims," Victor said.

"I'll bet if we do some digging, we'll learn that Lortie's relationship with Duca's mother wasn't all sweetness and light. We may even find out he was beating her. We know Lortie had this nutty habit of hiding papers in bathroom walls. So one day, in the house he inherited from his mother, Duca stumbles across one of Lortie's stashes. He finds documents proving that Lortie and the other people connected with Evergreen were complicit in the torture and murder of the accountant and his co-workers. Imagine Duca's reaction. It's like finding out your father was a war criminal. He's so sickened that he comes up with a plan. He decides to kill those responsible and make it look like Lortie is the killer. Trouble is, when he slips the wallets into Lortie's possession to set him up, things take an unexpected turn. Lortie kills himself. Duca decides to go ahead with the other killings anyway."

A long silence followed Jacinthe's explanation. Victor had to concede that it held water.

"What about Rivard?" the Gnome objected. "He's too young to have had anything to do with the accountants' deaths."

"I'll admit, that part doesn't make sense," Jacinthe conceded. There was a brief silence. "But we've already speculated that Rivard might have been pulled into the affair simply because he tried to recover the Northern file. Or Evergreen — call it what you like ..." Jacinthe was strutting, preening, proud as a peacock of her analysis. "What do you think, kid? Are we on a roll here, or what?" Jacinthe lifted her hand for a high-five, which Loïc, caught by surprise, had no choice but to return.

A deep voice cut through the back and forth. "I agree with just about everything you've said, Jacinthe. I believe we're close to the truth. But still, something doesn't quite fit."

The smile died on Jacinthe's lips. She was about to express her displeasure with Victor when he raised two fingers. "Hang on. Give me two minutes before you start yelling. I have something to show you." Victor got up and went to the metal shelf where the audio-visual materials were stored.

Dozing on the plane during the flight home, he'd had a succession of dreams. In one of them, he'd been at Le Confessionnal, about to take a drink, when Nadja burst into the bar. Unholstering her pistol, she had fired a shot that shattered Victor's glass before he could drink from it.

Waking up with a start, he'd been unable to think of anything except the man in the baseball cap. He saw the man in his memory, staring at him as he leaned against the bar.

Victor played the surveillance footage taken at Senator Tousignant's house, repeatedly showing his colleagues the sequence in which the man with the baseball cap lifted up the garbage bags to be sure the camera caught them.

The detective sergeant couldn't remember the exact measurements that Jacinthe had listed when, on the evening of Duca's death, she'd mentioned his height, but Victor's mind had lingered over that detail.

"Does anyone notice anything?"

The cops on the team looked at each other. Jacinthe was wearing a little smile. Victor knew she was about to invoke the blow to the head he'd received the day before, intending to cast doubt on his credibility. Before she could open her mouth, he addressed her. "Jacinthe, when we were at Duca's house, you gave me his height and weight. They should be in your notes somewhere."

"I can't remember," Jacinthe answered, yawning. She glanced at her watch. "Okay, partner, we've all had fun watching TV and shooting the breeze. But I don't see how we're any closer to finding Tousignant."

"Where are you going with this, Victor?" Delaney asked.

"Lucian Duca was huge, Paul. The man in the ball cap was just average height." Silence. "Doesn't anyone else find it strange that we found no sign of Duca being in possession of a heretic's fork? Everyone's been assuming he was the killer, but we're not looking at a single modus operandi here. We're looking at two."

"You know people who commit several murders often change their methods. And I'm not just talking about serial killers, here."

"Yes, I know that, Paul. But maybe there's another possibility we should be considering."

"That Duca wasn't the only killer? Is that it?"

A heavy silence fell over the investigation team. By raising doubts about the solution of the case, Victor had called everything into question. What if they needed to do more than find Tousignant? What if there was a second killer out there?

"I'm just asking, Chief. But my own view is that Duca had an accomplice. He was much bigger than the man we just saw in the video — the same man I came up against at Le Confessionnal. And last I heard, we still hadn't found Tousignant."

"Height is relative, Victor. It's not easy to judge on video, and you said yourself it was dark in the bar. Also, you weren't in a normal state of mind …"

The detective sergeant was on his feet in an instant. "I won't deny that I could be wrong, Paul, but if you're suggesting that I was drinking …"

Waving both hands in front of him, Delaney tried to calm things down. "Not at all, Victor. That's not what I meant and you know it. I was talking about your fight with Nadja's brother. In any case, the artist's drawing based on the video has already been distributed all over the city."

Jacinthe opened her mouth. Victor knew she was about to make an unpleasant comment. "Taillon, if you say one word about concussions, I swear, I'll wring your neck."

APRIL 5TH, 2010

NAUSEA

Each day holds its share of pain. Fresh scandals arrive, one after another.

A corrupt construction sector. Collapsing infrastructure. Our collective desire for change mired in weariness. Brutal cuts to arts funding. Natural resources sold at fire-sale prices. Political parties financed by dirty money. Systematic apathy. A lack of accountability among our political elites.

The stinking society in which I live disgusts me. It fills me with nausea.

As a simple province, as a sovereign state within Canada or as an actual country, Quebec is free. It is the master of its fate. The only limits upon it are those it imposes on itself.

And while Quebec today continues to seek its identity, I have found mine.

THE MAN IN THE EXPOS CAP

84

I DIDN'T SHOOT ANYBODY, NO SIR!

Victor left the conference room and went directly to his desk. The procurement officer had dropped off Victor's new cellphone, already configured for immediate use. But he still faced the drudgery of entering all his contacts. With a sigh, he opened a drawer, pulled out his noise-cancelling headphones, plugged them into his computer, opened iTunes, and chose a song at random.

"Breathe." Pink Floyd.

Victor had to smile. That was exactly what he needed to do.

Breathe.

His fellow cops wanted to solve the case as much as he did, but they were going about it the wrong way. He had a profound sense of being unjustly treated. His trip to Dallas and his interview with Willis had provided helpful information to the team. He'd received a nasty black eye for his troubles. And now, by way of thanks, his colleagues had reacted skeptically to his legitimate concerns about the path of the investigation.

Two minutes and nine seconds into "The Great Gig in the Sky," as he was drifting, eyes closed, on the ecstatic flow of the soloist's voice, Taillon planted herself in front of him, holding a cardboard box under one arm.

Sensing her presence, Victor pulled off the headphones just enough for her to hear the music.

"*Dark Side of the Moon*?"

"Don't start with me, Jacinthe, because I'm in no mood for —"

"Whoa, settle down there, big guy." She took a deep breath. "I hate to say this, seeing as I thought we'd be able to close the case and enjoy at least part of the holidays, but you were right. I checked my notes and just got off the line with Burgers. Duca was a tall man, built like a brick shithouse. There's no way he was the dude in the surveillance video."

Victor stared at his partner, then indicated the box with his chin. "What's that?"

"Duca's personal effects from Baker Lawson Watkins. Loïc went and got them. I thought we should have a look."

Victor was leafing through archery magazines while Jacinthe pored over a pile of business cards held together with a binder clip. The box contained a variety of odds and ends: an I♥NY mug, movie theatre coupons, buttons, an AAA battery, a tape measure, a bottle of ibuprofen tablets, three unopened packs of sugar-free bubble gum, and two photographs of Duca holding his bow in shooting stance. Victor recognized the background in the photos: they had been taken at Duca's house, probably with his webcam.

"I don't know if you heard, but while you were on vacation in the Texas sunshine, we got Duca's financial profile. Gilles and Loïc talked to his neighbours, and we went through his laptop with a fine-tooth comb."

Victor gave Jacinthe an ironic smile and pointed to his bruised eye. "Oh, yeah, terrific *vacation*. Did wonders for my complexion, don't you think?" He leaned back in his chair and put his feet on the desk. "So, what did you find out?"

"Basically nothing. Duca was careful with his money and had no social life."

With a sigh, the detective sergeant took out the bubble-gum packs to give to Loïc. "In other words, he had no life at all. Cellphone?"

"Prepaid. Forensics tried to access the call log, but the phone was crushed under the car during the accident. It's in tiny pieces."

The two cops continued to rummage in silence. Victor found a cardboard rectangle between the pages of a magazine and turned it over. It was a business card for a courier company. A name and phone number had been scrawled on it. Telling himself it made sense for such a card to be in the possession of a mail boy at a major law firm, Victor put the card on the desk and was about to resume his search when a thought crossed his mind. He picked up the card and turned it over in his hand, looking pensive.

Taillon watched in silence as he tapped on the keys of his computer, did a Google search, clicked on a web link, then sat back, hands clasped behind his head.

"Got something?" she asked, glancing at the card on the desk.

"I don't know … It's a bicycle courier service. I just looked at their website."

"Nothing weird about that. Duca worked in a mailroom. Sending out letters and parcels was his job."

The detective sergeant ran a hand through his hair. "We never figured out how the package containing Tousignant's wallet got here, did we?"

"No. It didn't come in the mail, and no one at reception signed for it."

"If you wanted to send something like that, how would you go about it?"

Jacinthe shrugged. "I have a feeling you're about to tell me."

"You'd give the package to a messenger who already had stuff to deliver here. You'd tell him to leave it discreetly on the counter, in the midst of all the other items, while the clerk was busy signing the delivery slip."

"To pull that off, you'd have to deal directly with the messenger. Slip him a couple of twenties to make it worth his while. Trouble is, those guys all work for companies, with dispatchers keeping track of deliveries. Would your messenger really risk getting into trouble for forty bucks?"

"That's where things get interesting. This service is for independent bike couriers. The site explains that customers are given a cell number for the courier who carries their items. And there's a name and phone number scribbled on the card."

Jacinthe didn't want to get into an argument, but she was clearly unconvinced. "Go ahead and call, but you're wasting your time. Your theory's full of holes. Bike couriers stay in the downtown core. They don't come way out here."

"Can't hurt to try," Victor said, as the ringback tone sounded in his ear. "Hello? Is this Annika? ... My name's Vict— ... Are you on your bike? ... On break? Great. My name's Victor Lessard ... No, it's not for a pickup. I'm a detective with the Montreal Police ... Yes, the police ... What? ... No, I'm not calling about that ... Who cut you off? ... Listen, Annika, I don't care what you did to the guy's rear-view mirror. That's not why I'm calling ... No, relax, you didn't do anything wrong ... I'd rather talk about it in person. Where are you right now? ... Great. I'll be there in fifteen minutes."

Victor turned to Jacinthe. "She's on her lunch break. Corner of Cathcart and University."

"Yeah, well, I'm on lunch break, too. I'm not wasting my time on this."

"We can make it there in fifteen minutes if you drive. And afterward, lunch at Boccacinos is on me. Bring the pictures."

Jacinthe's eyes lit up. "You're a bastard, Lessard," she said, grabbing her coat.

They found Annika on Cathcart Street, sitting on a bench across from Tim Hortons. She was smoking a cigarette, laughing with other couriers. For the first time in days, the sun was out and the temperature was mild.

Victor introduced himself and stepped away from the group with the young woman. Taillon, who had stayed in the car so as not to spook her, now approached. The girl had black lips and fingernails. She didn't seem bothered when Victor introduced his partner.

He stopped counting the piercings in her nose and ears at eight.

"Chilly work," Jacinthe observed, putting a hand on the bicycle seat, getting the conversation started.

"The only way to make money at this job is to work in the winter. You can clear eighty, a hundred bucks a day. When the weather gets nicer, there are more couriers on the road."

Victor showed Annika a photo of Duca. "Recognize this man?"

"Never seen him before," the young woman said, taking a cigarette from the pack Victor held out. "Who is he?"

Victor cupped a palm around the flame of his lighter. Leaning toward him, the courier rested tattooed fingers on his hand as she lit her smoke.

"You sure? We think he knew you. We found your number among his things."

Annika shrugged, at a loss. Taillon rolled her eyes: what a waste of time.

"Have you ever delivered a parcel to Place Versailles?"

"Nah. Too far. We stay downtown. Since we're on bikes, we don't get slowed down by traffic and parking. But for parcels and boxes, customers usually want a car."

Victor pulled out pictures of Duca's victims. He took the top two off the stack — Lawson and Harper — and handed them to Annika.

"Do you recognize either of these people?"

Jacinthe got up with an ostentatious sigh. "I'll wait in the car. I'm hungry. Make it snappy, Lessard."

"I recognize the woman," Annika said without hesitation. "I was hired to go up to her on the street and say something."

Jacinthe stopped and turned. "Say what?"

"A single sentence — 'I didn't shoot anybody, no sir!' Weird, huh?"

The two detectives looked at each other with undisguised interest.

"Tell us what happened," Victor said encouragingly.

"It was all done by phone. I was told it was a joke for a friend's birthday. The person gave me directions to a hiding place in a park. I went there and found an envelope wrapped in a plastic bag. Inside the envelope, there was money and a picture of the woman. There was also a note saying I'd get a call in advance, giving me a time and location to approach the woman."

"That didn't strike you as strange?" Jacinthe interrupted, wearing a suggestive expression.

Victor looked at his partner with a glare that said, *Shut up and let her talk.*

"Kind of. But for five hundred bucks, I had no problem with strange," the young woman said calmly. "Anyway, it's not like I was being asked to do anything illegal, right?"

"Right." Victor nodded. "What happened next?"

"The person called one morning to say the woman would be on McGill College Avenue around seven a.m. I had a little trouble spotting her because of the snow. Then I said the sentence and left."

"Do you remember what day it was?"

"Can't say exactly. It was a little before Christmas."

"The fifteenth?" Victor suggested.

Annika frowned, reminding him of his daughter, Charlotte. If you took away the piercings, there was a definite resemblance between the two. Barely out of adolescence, they were playing at womanhood. "Could be."

"How did she react?" Victor asked.

"I don't know. I think she was surprised. I didn't stick around to find out. I got on my bike and left."

"Do you still have the note? And the envelope?"

"No. I threw them away."

"Describe the man's voice over the phone. Did you hear an accent? Any particular details?"

"It wasn't a man. It was a woman."

She's worked for the Parti Québecois since 1979. For a little over three months now, she's been on the advance team, which handles scouting and preparations for events at which the premier will be present. Her specific responsibility is drawing up detailed event plans, as well as documentation and photocopies.

Stretched out on the white sheets, completely naked, she watches as he tucks his shirt into his pants and awkwardly knots his tie. He approaches the bed and sits down beside her. Accepting the cigarette that she offers him, he takes a deep drag before handing it back. He kisses her tenderly on the forehead, then stands up.

This isn't the first time he's come to her hotel room.

"If I've understood correctly, René, what you're saying is, 'Until next time …'"

Facing the bed, he bows his head slightly and shrugs, closing his eyes for half a second while a little smile plays on his lips. The expression that makes him so lovable …

He picks up an object from the chest of drawers, turning it over in his hands as he looks at her. "I'm very fond of you, Charlie. I may stray from time to time, but my marriage to Corinne is for life. You understand that, don't you?"

They exchange smiles. They both realize he's putting an end to something.

"Good luck next week. We deserve to win. I'll be thinking of you."

"Now we'll see whether Trudeau was more convincing on the campaign trail than I was."

With a laugh, René Lévesque tosses the object he was holding onto the bed. "It's definitely a little boyish," he says as he heads to the door, "but the funny thing is, you look good when you put it on."

The young woman smiles again, but this time her expression is tinged with melancholy. She stubs out her cigarette.

Long after he's gone, she gathers her blond hair in a rough braid and, coiling it, tucks it under the Expos cap.

85

I'VE NEVER DONE ANYTHING LIKE THIS BEFORE

The streets were spooling across his retinas. The blood was roaring in his ears. Victor bit his lip. Everything was compressing, accelerating through his synapses. He'd gotten it right. Duca hadn't acted alone. He'd had an accomplice. Or maybe it was worse than that: maybe there were two independent killers, two monsters, one of whom was still at large, free to continue taking lives at will.

Even if the detective sergeant hadn't entirely dismissed the possibility that the murderers were a couple, the likelihood seemed small to him. For one thing, the murders weren't sexual in nature. For another, serial-killing couples were uncommon. Even so, he couldn't help thinking of Paul Bernardo and Karla Homolka, perhaps because they were the most recent serial-killing couple to make the headlines.

There had also been the Gallego case in the United States in the 1980s.

The Crown Victoria came to rest in a muddy parking area, and Victor looked up at the sign: METALCORP.

He had a feeling of emptiness, of annihilation, of all things vanishing. Then, from a great distance, a voice drew him out of his thoughts, dragging him back to the surface like the bloated corpse of a drowned man.

"We're here, Lessard. Move your ass."

.   .   .

Once the initial shock had passed, they'd questioned Annika. But apart from informing them that the woman on the phone spoke without an accent and sounded like she knew Montreal, the young bike courier had been unable to give them any other informa-tion. She hadn't seen the woman's face; she didn't know her name. They'd left Annika with her piercings and her bike in the middle of the sidewalk on Cathcart Street, and they'd climbed back into the Crown Vic.

Victor was near catatonic, while Jacinthe kept repeating the same words over and over, mantra-like, as she gunned the engine. "Horowitz. We've got to talk to Horowitz!"

A fleeting image of a face had come into his memory: it had taken Victor a moment to recall Horowitz, the warehouse owner who'd had a heart scare when he found Judith Harper's body.

"I knew it all along! Never trust a man. He lied to us about that key. He must have given it to the bitch he was fucking."

Slightly dazed, with a kettle-like whistling noise ringing in his ears, Victor felt like he was walking beside himself, in someone else's body. A surreal feeling. It wasn't painful, just strange, as though he were trapped in a dream from which he couldn't wake up.

In the dream, hand puppets were arguing with each other.

A zebra that wasn't a zebra, but a wolf. Then he was inside Le Confessionnal, rushing to the washroom to catch the man in the baseball cap.

A man who wasn't a man, but a woman …

It was no surprise that he hadn't found anyone. There had never been a man in a baseball cap. He should have been looking for a woman in a cap. He'd been searching in the wrong place.

The knowledge that Duca's accomplice had been hiding in the women's washroom, a few steps away from him, possibly even watching him, filled him with rage. It made his head spin and raised goosebumps on his flesh.

*　*　*

Charging into the warehouse, Jacinthe addressed the man who came forward to greet her. Voices were raised. Gradually returning to reality, Victor began to make sense of the stray phrases that penetrated his mind, eventually understanding that the man was Horowitz's brother, co-manager of the firm, and that Horowitz himself had gone to a sunshine destination with his wife to get some rest.

The whistling in Victor's ears ceased. He became aware that a heated argument had broken out: Jacinthe was insisting that the man place a call to Horowitz. The man was refusing to disturb his poor brother, who'd recently been through a heart scare. The man's objections evaporated instantaneously, however, when Jacinthe declared that in that case, she'd have to call in the forensics team to do another thorough examination of the premises.

It was, of course, a shameless lie. But the fear of seeing his warehouse invaded once again by the police scientific unit prompted him to pick up his office phone and key in the number as they watched. When a voice answered at the other end of the line, Jacinthe put the call on hold, ordered the man out of his own office, and closed the door.

"Wake up, Lessard!" she barked before putting the call on speakerphone.

To prove that his head was back in the game, Victor met his partner's eye, winked, and gave her a thumbs-up.

Thinking the call was from his brother, Horowitz hadn't been on his guard.

But now he was nervously claiming that he couldn't talk to the detectives because he was at the beach with his wife. He didn't realize it, but that was the worst thing he could have said. Jacinthe, who knew no other way to communicate than by blunt force, lit into him.

"Your wife? Great. She should be in on the conversation. Tell me, Horowitz, how does your wife feel about that bitch you gave your key to? You know, the one you were fucking in the warehouse."

A long silence, followed by some throat-clearing and vague mumbling, made it plain that Jacinthe had scored a direct hit.

"Uh … hang on a second."

They heard whispering at the other end of the line. Horowitz was putting some distance between himself and his wife so he could speak more freely. There was a period of silence during which the cops thought the connection might have been cut. But then they heard the sound of footsteps, followed by a door being slammed.

"I've been married for forty years, Detective. I've never done anything like this before, I swear to you!"

Victor whispered to Jacinthe that the last thing they needed was for the guy's heart to act up again.

"Relax, Mr. Horowitz," he said in a sympathetic voice. "We're going to get the whole thing sorted out."

"This is the first time it's ever happened. You have to believe me!"

"We do believe you, Mr. Horowitz."

"We don't believe you for a second, you fucking slimeball!" Jacinthe declared, bringing her fist down on the table.

"It just happened the one time. I couldn't believe there was any connection." Horowitz's voice rose in a desperate cry.

"Give us her name and address and we'll leave you alone," Jacinthe said coldly.

"I don't know it."

"Or maybe you'd rather we had a chat with your wife," Jacinthe hissed. The veins in her neck were bulging.

"I don't know her name! I swear to you!"

Horowitz explained that the woman had introduced herself as a visual artist. She had come to the warehouse one morning in October to buy some scrap metal, saying she intended to incorporate it into a piece she was working on. He had met her that one time. She'd never mentioned her name. One thing had led to another, and they'd ended up on the couch, where they … where they …

"Fucked, Horowitz!" Jacinthe bellowed. "That's the word you're looking for. *Fucked.* Is that when you gave her the key?"

Humiliated, the man began to cry.

Jacinthe rolled her eyes.

"I …"

"You thought you'd see her again, is that it?" Victor prompted.

"I … I showed her where the key was. In case she …" A few words were swallowed up in sobs.

"You showed her where the key was, in case she wanted to see you again," Victor said.

"Yes." He wept quietly. "I was an idiot … But it was the first time in twenty years anyone had shown an interest me."

"This woman," Jacinthe growled, "what did she look like?"

Horowitz described full lips and the most beautiful body he'd ever seen, a woman of medium height, in her forties, with dark hair and green eyes.

"Do you have access to a computer?" Victor asked. "We'll need you to make yourself available. A police artist will be contacting you in the next few minutes to create a sketch of the woman. And you may end up having to cut short your vacation and come back to Montreal."

"Will I go to prison for this?"

Overwhelmed by events, Horowitz sounded like a man who'd just taken a kick to his private parts.

"One thing at a time," Victor said. "For now, our priority is to find this woman, and you're going to help us. After that, we'll see."

"What am I supposed to tell my wife?"

"That's your problem, Horowitz," Jacinthe snapped. "As far as I'm concerned, you deserve to be tarred and feathered. You need to start making decisions with your head instead of your —"

"Mr. Horowitz," Victor cut in, glaring at his partner, "close your eyes and think back. Any detail you can remember may help us save lives."

"She put her bag and keys on the desk. I saw her key ring. There was a little plastic keepsake with a name on it."

"What was the name?"

"Charlie."

Jacinthe hit the mute button and turned to her partner. "Your new lady friend, Tousignant's daughter ... she has full lips, dark hair, and green eyes, doesn't she?"

This time, Victor didn't bristle. The idea had already crossed his mind. Horowitz's description of the woman had shaken him. And he couldn't help but recall Virginie's erratic behaviour on the day of her father's disappearance.

"First of all, she's not my new lady friend. And her name is Virginie, not Charlie."

"But she has a middle initial ... C, right?"

In his mind's eye, Victor saw the framed dust jacket on the wall at the senator's house. Obviously, Jacinthe had noticed it, too.

"You're right. Her name is Virginie C. Tousignant." Victor looked her in the eye. "And she wrote a book about Charlie Chaplin."

86

SHOULD HAVE BEEN A BOY

Through the window of the Café Van Houtte, Victor watched the pedestrians moving along the snowy sidewalk on Notre-Dame near the courthouse. He lifted his cup and sipped the scalding organic decaf he'd just ordered. His phone lay on the table in front of him. There were a handful of customers in the place.

For the fiftieth time, he wiped his damp hands on his jeans. His blood pressure was rising. His eyes felt too big for their sockets. His heart was slamming around inside his rib cage. Anticipation, the period that preceded imminent activity, had always been more difficult for him to bear than the onset of action itself. Every centimetre of his skin itched.

In the car, he and Jacinthe had winnowed down their ideas until they'd arrived at a hypothesis of astonishing simplicity: the children of André Lortie and Daniel Tousignant, two of the prime movers behind the killings in 1964, had teamed up to eliminate all traces of their fathers' barbaric acts.

It wasn't perfect, but it was all they had to go on.

Lacking the time for a file examination at the Register of Civil Status, they had called the office and asked what the C in Virginie's name stood for. The search had turned up nothing.

Victor had no trouble convincing Jacinthe to let him talk to Virginie alone.

Having failed to keep his promise to treat her to lunch, he'd given Jacinthe a twenty-dollar bill, and she'd gone to the McDonald's at the corner.

Victor had said nothing to Virginie over the phone about his reasons for wanting to meet. He had simply said that she needed to come straight over to the Café Van Houtte a few blocks from the editorial offices of the newspaper where she worked. It was the only way to be sure she'd come in a hurry, and to be able to gauge her reaction.

Any attempt to flee would be revealing.

Jacinthe would take up a support position near the building's entrance and follow Virginie discreetly, able to intercept her if the need arose. Obviously, if the young woman had nothing to hide, she'd be overcome with anxiety as she walked into the café, wondering whether her father's body had been found.

Both detectives preferred this approach to a confrontation in the newspaper offices, which they were eager to avoid.

In the end, there were no confrontations or escape attempts. Victor watched Virginie come up Saint-Laurent less than ten minutes later. Her beauty was undiminished, but her features, drawn with fatigue, plainly showed intense worry.

Walking in, she drew near to kiss Victor on the cheek.

Needing to preserve some distance between them for the questions he was about to ask, Victor simulated a bad cough. Virginie retreated.

"Is everything okay? Your call seemed urgent … My God, what happened to your face?"

The detective sergeant put his fingertips to his injured eye. The swelling was almost gone, but the bruise was still sensitive to the touch. Through the window, he saw Jacinthe get into the Crown Victoria, which she'd parked across the street. She was holding a McDonald's bag.

Victor avoided Virginie's gaze and smiled politely. "I'm fine," he said. "Just stumbled into a chest of drawers. Sorry for the sudden phone call, I know it must have worried you. So let me set your mind at ease — I have no bad news about your father. In fact, I have no news, period. We're still searching. How are you holding up?"

"I've been trying not to think about it," Virginie answered. Victor's reassurances seemed to have eased her anxiety. "Working helps. If I had nothing to do but stay home and dwell on this, I'd lose my mind." She frowned. "Are you sure everything's okay? You look strange … Is it because of what happened last time?"

Victor shook his head. "No, that has nothing to do with it. Can I get you something?"

Virginie declined the offer. For the first time since she'd walked in, Victor looked her in the eye. "I have some questions to ask. All by the book, but it won't be agreeable."

The young woman's expression darkened. She took a deep breath and brushed a lock of hair out of her eyes. "This is the stage of the investigation where everyone's a suspect, including the missing man's daughter, is that it?"

"Something like that." Silence. "What does your middle initial stand for?"

Virginie's reaction wavered between surprise and amusement. "It's from my days as a master's student. There was a girl in some of my classes who had the same name as me. I added the C so professors wouldn't get us mixed up."

"So the middle name on your birth certificate starts with C?"

Her lip wrinkled disdainfully. "No. The middle name on my birth certificate is Marguerite. I found it lame. I chose the C for sentimental reasons."

"Meaning?"

"You won't find this very original. It was in honour of Charlie Chaplin."

"The Charlie part or the Chaplin?" Victor asked in a hard voice.

Virginie snatched up her purse from the floor and opened it. On edge, the detective sergeant slipped his hand under his jacket and wrapped his fingers around his Glock. Not seeming to notice, Virginie took out an elastic and tied her hair back.

"What do you mean?" she asked. "What's the difference?"

Her hand advanced along the table toward Victor's elbow, her fingers scuttling like the legs of a spider.

"Answer the question!" Victor said sharply, grabbing her wrist. "Is the C for Charlie or Chaplin?"

"Ow! You're hurting me, Victor. What's gotten into you?" Her eyes were full of reproach.

He loosened his grip. "Can I see your driver's licence and your key ring?"

Angrily, Virginie dumped the contents of her purse onto the table. A man sitting nearby stared.

"Help yourself. I have tampons, too."

Ignoring the remark, Victor checked her cards. The initial appeared nowhere.

"Where were you on December 15th? It was a Thursday."

That was the evening Judith Harper had been killed. Even if Virginie had an alibi, it wouldn't rule out the possibility that she was Duca's accomplice — they'd have to look into his movements that day — but it would be a start.

Virginie tapped briefly on her iPhone, then answered, "I was in Vermont, at a ski chalet."

"Alone?"

"No, with my brother-in-law, my sister-in-law, another couple, and … and my husband." The young woman lowered her eyes, hesitating, as though it was hard for her to speak of her husband. "Do you want their phone numbers?"

"Yes, please."

"Oh, I forgot," Virginie added with cold irony, "the couple's daughter was there. She's thirteen, totally butch. Should have been a boy. But who knows, maybe she's the killer you're looking for. You want her cell number, too?"

Victor's gaze had begun to drift. He wasn't listening anymore; something had clicked in his mind. Virginie noticed. In an instant, curiosity extinguished her resentment.

"What?" she asked. "What's wrong? What did I say?"

Chair legs squealed on the floor as Victor rose abruptly to his feet.

"I've got to go!"

CHARLIE

"I'm looking for Dr. McNeil's secretary."

"Speaking."

"This is Detective Lessard of the Montreal Police."

"I recognized your voice, Detective. What can I do for you?"

"During our first visit to Louis-H., you introduced us to a woman, an orderly who'd spent a lot of time caring for André Lortie …"

"I remember."

"What's her name?"

"Charlie Couture. Why?"

THE END OF THE SHOW

Daniel Tousignant pressed the STOP button on the cassette recorder. The red light went off and the counter stopped turning. When the senator rested his hand on the tabletop, the chains jingled against the wood. Looped through shackles on his wrists and ankles, they were firmly attached to a metal ring bolted to the floor. Tousignant had tested the strength of the contraption; there was no way to free himself.

The woman came in, holding a water jug and a plate of melon wedges. She placed the items on the table. "Good evening, Senator. I came to find out how things are going."

Tousignant was silent for a moment, showing no sign of sadness or panic. Though perhaps not resigned to his fate, he seemed at peace with it. "Good evening, Charlie. We're coming to the end of the show, aren't we?"

The woman nodded. Her expression was unsmiling, empty of emotion.

The old man looked up at her. Despite the severe bun in which she had bound her hair, despite the lack of makeup, despite the hardness that life had etched on her features, Charlie was still a beautiful woman. Her full, round lips were striking; her green eyes shone; and her masculine clothes couldn't entirely mask the sensuous outline of her body.

The senator smiled. Charlie noticed. "Why are you smiling?"

"I was just thinking, as I looked at you, that on the day you kidnapped me, I never would have opened the door if you hadn't been a woman."

Charlie nodded and returned his smile. She knew how to simulate empathy, but she felt none. Tousignant hadn't noticed, but she was holding an odd sort of collar in her hands.

89

THE ASSAULT

Knee deep in snow, Victor moved quickly through the trees, emerging from the stand of conifers on the shoreline. With his senses on high alert, he stopped and listened. The cars on Route 138, winding through the countryside far behind him, were barely audible.

Holding his Glock in firing position, his breath sending puffs of vapour into the cold air, he took a few cautious steps along the hard, crusted snow.

The blackness of the night enveloped him, making his approach easier. A few flakes drifted in front of him.

He kept moving, glancing left at the immense curve of the river, white and frozen beyond the firs. Higher up and to his right, the isolated house was partially concealed by the rising ground and the trees.

Squinting, he thought he could make out a weak, flickering light through the branches, out on the water. His pulse was pounding in his temples.

The Crown Victoria had been racing along Sherbrooke Street toward Louis-H. when Jacinthe executed a hard U-turn. Over the phone, McNeil's secretary had just given Victor Charlie Couture's home address, downriver from Montreal between the towns of Lavaltrie and Lanoraie. Couture had been on sick leave since the 26th, the day of Lucian Duca's death.

Route 138 was more than a kilometre from the shoreline at the junction where they had turned onto the secondary road. Moving through farmland, they'd driven without headlights so as not to be seen, leaving the Crown Vic two hundred metres from the house.

Loïc and the Gnome were also speeding toward the location, but they were still forty-five minutes away: Loïc had been forced to make a detour to pick up Lemaire, who was back at home by then.

"We should wait for them," Victor had suggested as the car stopped.

Jacinthe had winked and smiled. "She saw us pull up and tried to escape. We had no choice but to go in."

And, unspoken, but audible in the tone of her voice: *Are you scared, Lessard?*

As he got out of the vehicle and unholstered his pistol, Victor remarked that she clearly hadn't learned her lesson from the King of Flies case.

"Come on, Lessard! It's just one woman."

Before splitting up, the two detectives had agreed on a plan: Victor would go left, around the house, and approach from the river side. Jacinthe would wait in the car for five minutes, then she'd move in along the path that led straight through the open field to the back door of the house.

It took Victor a moment to realize that the light on the water was coming from the window of an ice-fishing shack about a hundred metres from shore. The glow was yellowish, flickering like a lantern flame, creating an illuminated rectangle that reflected diagonally off the ice. The shack's entrance seemed to face the far shore. All that was visible from this side, as far as Victor could tell, was part of the structure's rear and right walls.

Looking at his watch, he saw that five minutes had elapsed. Jacinthe would be on the move. The time had come for him to turn and climb the rising ground before closing in on the house.

Instead, he took a few steps onto the ice and stopped. Something had moved out there, briefly entering the yellow light.

Peering into the darkness, he finally understood what he was seeing: there was a human figure on the ice, standing up straight, hands bound behind his back.

Victor began to walk toward the light.

"Lessard!"

Jacinthe's voice. Desperate. Heart-stopping.

The detective sergeant didn't hesitate for an instant. Turning away from the shack, he retraced his steps, running hard. His partner was in trouble.

The house was dark. The wind was shrieking as Victor moved forward. Drawing nearer to the house, he saw its decrepit condition. The peeling, filthy aluminum siding; the warped clapboards.

The detective sergeant ascended a rotting wooden staircase to the porch. On his right, he saw a glint of glass: a sliding door was visible in the shadows.

Crouching against the wall, pistol raised, he opened the door as softly as he could. It slid along its track without a sound. Holding his breath, he slipped into the house and closed the door behind him. He stopped for a moment so his eyes could adjust to the darkness. The pounding of his heart was a steady roar.

Thinking the space was clear, he stepped forward.

Shards of glass crackled under the soles of his high-tops. Suddenly a light ignited, its beam aimed at him, blinding him. For an instant he considered firing, but not knowing where Jacinthe was, he couldn't risk hitting her.

A woman's voice, calm and deep, rose from the darkest corner of the room. "I've been waiting for you, Detective Lessard. Put your weapon on the table. You have nothing to fear. My gun is pointed at my own head, not yours."

The beam swung through the air and, for a fraction of a second, illuminated a steel barrel pressed against a red, white, and blue Expos cap. Then it swung back, blinding him again.

A table stood near the sliding door. On it, he saw a tape recorder and several TDK cassettes, still in their plastic wrapping, as well as a small cardboard box and a pair of binoculars.

With his finger curled tensely around the trigger, still pointing his weapon, he released the safety catch. Without seeing the woman, he knew where she was. One well-aimed shot would end this.

"What do you want?"

"I'm ready to give you a confession, Detective. Everything you need to record it is on the table in front of you." Silence. "But if you make one wrong move, I'll blow my brains out. And you'll never learn anything more than you know already."

A little voice in Victor's head, the voice of reason, was urging him to refuse this crazy offer and pull the trigger.

"What about my partner?"

"Don't worry. She's in the other room. After Tasering her, I gave her a small injection. She'll wake up in a couple of hours, feeling fine. At worst, she'll have a mild headache. It's your call, Victor. Shoot me now, or put down the gun … You don't mind if I call you Victor, do you?"

"And Senator Tousignant?" he demanded, ignoring her question. He cocked his head in the direction of the river. "Is it him I saw on the ice?"

"It is. But if you make any effort to rescue him before our conversation is over, you'll lose on both counts. He'll be dead before you reach him, and when you get back, I'll have ended my own life."

A doubtful frown twisted the detective sergeant's brow. "How can you kill him from here?"

"You may not know this, but he has a pacemaker. I've placed a series of electrodes on either side of his heart. See this little gadget?" A hand slid into the beam of light, holding a black electronic device barely larger than a cellphone. "It's a wireless electrostimulator.

People use these things to build muscles without having to exercise. They're strongly contraindicated for anyone who wears a pacemaker. With this instrument, I can send out an electric signal strong enough to stop his heart."

"You sure about that?"

"Fair question. No, I'm not sure. But if you're ready to risk it," she said in a bantering tone, "so am I. Shall I push the button?"

The woman didn't sound like she was bluffing. Without seeing her face, it was impossible to be certain.

"How do I know you won't hit the button after we talk?"

"That's a chance you'll have to take. But I give you my word that when we're done, Tousignant will be yours. I have no interest in seeing him dead. Open that box on the table."

Victor lifted the lid and saw several cassettes labelled with dates and numbers.

"I've recorded his confession because I want him to face justice for his crimes."

The detective sergeant's mind was racing, weighing the available options. Time stood still. The voice of reason in his head pleaded with him to pull the trigger. A well-aimed shot would prevent the woman from pressing the button, and then he could save Tousignant. Even if the man was a ruthless monster, Victor had a duty to protect him. But in that case, Victor would never get a confession. To be sure the woman didn't activate the electrostimulator, he'd have to shoot to kill.

And then if his aim was off, apart from the fact that the woman would be able to hit the electric signal, there was the possibility that she'd return fire. Still, that danger hardly worried him. Even if he couldn't see her in the shadows, Victor knew exactly where she was. At this distance, a couple of bullets would be enough to end the threat. The problem was, he tended to follow his instincts rather than listen to the voice of reason.

Victor knew the danger was great. He might be wrong. Even so, he was convinced that the woman posed no threat to him. He decided to take the chance.

The silence was broken by the click of the safety as it slid back into place on his pistol. He laid the gun on the table, taking care to leave it where he could seize it and fire in an instant if the need arose.

"You put the heretic's fork on Tousignant?" he asked.

"You've done your homework, Victor. Pick up the binoculars and see for yourself."

The detective sergeant did as he was told and located the figure on the ice; he was visible from behind. The senator was in a standing position, his hands bound behind his back with restraints attached to a heavy chain. The other end of the chain was bolted to the floor of the shack, making escape impossible.

Tousignant was encased in a broad-brimmed metal yoke. A gap in its centre exposed the back of his neck. Two metal rods connected the edges of the yoke to a little black box between the shoulder blades. A single rod linked the box to the manacles around the wrists. The result was a Y-shaped assembly behind the senator's back. Above this assembly, a kind of metal spider stood poised over his head, its legs attached to the rods connecting the collar to the black box. A black dart about fifteen centimetres long projected lethally from the spider, pointing straight at the gap in the yoke, through which it could strike the neck.

With the senator's back to him, Victor didn't see the metal points piercing his chin and chest, but the positioning of the man's head, tilted back at an extreme angle, left no doubt as to their presence.

Iron bars duct-taped to Tousignant's ankles and thighs prevented him from bending his legs or sitting down. Looking through the binoculars, Victor now had the answers to two questions that had dogged him. First of all, he knew the origin of the adhesive residue that had been found on Harper and Lawson. Second, he understood why there was no physical evidence of their having been suspended above the ground: the bars had made that unnecessary.

A wooden log lay on the ice in front of the senator.

"The key is on the log?"

From the other side of the room, the woman answered in a cool voice. "Very clever, Victor. If I'd said yes, you would have known I had no intention of letting the man live. The key is on the table, under the cassette recorder."

The detective sergeant checked and found a key.

"I didn't arm the mechanism. The pain and discomfort are intense, but his life is in no immediate danger."

As long as his heart doesn't fail, Victor thought.

"How long has he been out there?" he asked.

"About an hour."

"You were expecting us, Ms. Couture?"

"It would be more accurate to say I was hoping you'd come," the woman answered, seemingly unaffected by the fact that the detective sergeant knew her name.

"Don't play games with me," Victor said in a calm but uncompromising voice. "How did you know we were coming? Did McNeil's secretary warn you?"

"Audrey is a colleague. We often took our lunch breaks together at the hospital. You mustn't be angry at her. She was shaken by your call and wanted to do the right thing by warning me that the police were interested in me." Silence. "There's tea on the stove behind you. Would you mind pouring two cups?"

Victor hesitated, then retreated a few steps. He found cups on the counter, took the teapot off the stove, and poured out the steaming liquid. Holding the two cups, he came forward again, toward the table. The beam of light swung down to the floor in front of him.

He took the opportunity to look around and memorize as many physical details of the space as possible.

"Put my cup on the floor, in the light, then sit down at the table," the woman ordered.

Victor obeyed.

A veined hand came out of the darkness and took the cup. "Thank you. I'll let you handle the situation if your fellow officers

are waiting for a signal to move in. As I warned you, if I so much
as hear a strange noise, I'll put a bullet in my head, and you'll learn
nothing more."

The detective sergeant looked at his watch. It would be another
twenty minutes before Loïc and the Gnome arrived. "Should I start
recording?" he asked.

"Yes. There's already a cassette in the machine."

The beam of light moved again. The woman reoriented it so
that it no longer blinded Victor, but she herself was still enveloped
in shadow. By squinting, he could make out her silhouette, but he
couldn't see her face.

"You know my name. But do you know who I am?"

The police officer shrugged. "During the drive out here, I racked
my brain trying to recall where I'd seen your surname before. Then
it came to me. The name was in the Evergreen file that you left in
the garbage bags at Senator Tousignant's house. Unless I'm mistaken, you're Gilbert Couture's daughter. One of my colleagues is
looking into it as we speak. Your father was an auditor employed by
the accounting firm of Bélanger, Monette and Associates in Joliette.
He and two other employees were killed by André Lortie in 1964,
on the orders of Daniel Tousignant."

"Your colleague needn't have bothered, Victor. You've got it
right. They also murdered my brother, Lennie, but we'll come
back to that. Before continuing, may I ask what it was that gave
me away?"

"One detail ... a trivial detail ... Earlier today, someone was
talking to me about a couple she knew whose teenage daughter should have been a boy. At that moment, I realized that the
woman who slipped me the matchbook at Le Confessionnal wasn't
disguised to look like a man. She had a masculine appearance in
everyday life. Then you came into my mind, and I remembered
what you'd said to me at the hospital when I commented that it
took incredible strength to do your job."

"I said my father always wished I'd been a boy."

"Exactly. I remembered that conversation by chance. But it was only a matter of time. Our research into your father's life would have turned up your name." Victor sipped his tea.

Charlie went on. "As you surely realize, parents who are dissatisfied with the gender of their child can exert a powerful influence, even if it's unintentional, on the child's development. My brother was intellectually handicapped. My father never accepted his limitations. And he always treated me like a boy. So much so that I ended up dressing and behaving like one."

The little voice in Victor's head spoke up again: *why was he sitting here, drinking tea and making quiet conversation with this woman as though she were an old friend, when he should be grabbing his gun and putting an end to the charade?*

But the voice evaporated when he realized he was lying to himself. He knew perfectly well why he was sitting here. The woman was giving him a chance to fill in the remaining holes in the story, to satisfy his curiosity, while still retaining the ability to save Tousignant.

Suddenly, an obvious fact occurred to him: her desire to make her confession here, rather than in a police interrogation room, was revealing.

Charlie Couture had no intention of facing trial or going to prison.

90

THE RED LINE

Victor would remember these moments until his dying day, until his last breath.

Four walls. The scent of tea. The floorboards creaking under his chair. The sliding door, through which the river was visible; and, out there on its frozen surface, a human silhouette framed in a yellow glow. Two people, a man and a woman. A police officer and a murderess. A conversation forever altering the arc of time. And, all the while, life flowing away like water in the kitchen sink, drop by drop, second by second.

"Lucian Duca gained proximity to one of the victims by getting a job at Baker Lawson Watkins. You did the same thing by working at Louis-H., where you were able to watch McNeil and Lortie. Am I right?"

"Yes. I was hired as an orderly at Louis-H. in 2008, then I got myself assigned to the ward where André Lortie was an occasional in-patient."

"You wanted to pin the Harper and Lawson murders on him."

"Above all, I wanted to tip him into complete madness."

"Or even steer him toward suicide."

"It was hard to know whether he'd go that far, but after I'd spent some time observing him, I knew which buttons to push, which switches to throw to unbalance his mind."

"As I recall, during our conversation at the hospital, you told us about his having woken up from a blackout in possession of wallets, with bloodstains on his clothes."

"Lortie never had my father's wallet or those of the other victims. Those were suggestions that I planted in his head during his delusional phases, and that finally took root among his other fixations. I used to talk about the subject each day, during his periods of hospitalization. And each day, I'd murmur the words that drove him deeper into psychosis."

"You were getting him ready for what would come next …"

"I was preparing the ground so that, when he found the wallets of Harper and Lawson among his possessions, he'd be convinced that he was falling back into the same nightmare a second time, and that would amplify his instability. He was utterly taken in. Lucian paid a young homeless man to hide the wallets among Lortie's things. When Lortie found them, he was convinced that he'd killed Lawson and Harper."

Victor frowned. He remembered Constable Gonthier's report. Before jumping, Lortie had said, "It's starting again. I'm sick of it." Then Nash's face appeared in Victor's memory. Was he the young homeless man Charlie had just referred to? She answered that she didn't know.

"But then, why did you tell us about the wallets, if you were the one who'd planted the suggestions in his mind? Were you trying to send us down the wrong track?"

"The information was in his file. I gave you the clinical facts. That's what any of my colleagues would have done. Otherwise, you might have suspected me."

"As for McNeil, your job allowed you to be in contact with him, too …"

"To be honest, my real intention was to get close to Lortie. I didn't realize at the time how deeply involved McNeil had been in the abuses that Judith Harper inflicted on my father. I also didn't know that McNeil had continued to practise a form of surveillance on Lortie. I hadn't planned to kill him at first."

An idea came to Victor. It meant interrupting her, but he decided to speak.

"When the opportunity presented itself, you took the number magnets from McNeil's refrigerator. And you called him from Judith Harper's home phone on the day you killed her."

Charlie blew on her hot tea and took a sip. Then she nodded.

"I hung up as soon as he answered. I had taken the magnets some time ago, during a party that McNeil had hosted for the employees of the ward. I just wanted to make him a suspect, to cause trouble for him. Not to kill him. Not until he realized that I had falsified Lortie's medical file."

Victor remembered the handwritten note on the tab of the homeless man's psychiatric file. "The reference to Dr. Cameron ..."

"Yes. I wanted to point you subtly in the direction of Project MK-ULTRA. Since I was the last person who'd handled the file, McNeil confronted me. But then, to my great surprise, he proposed a financial arrangement in return for his silence. He said he'd taken precautions in case something happened to him. He was bluffing. I set up a meeting with him in Parc Maisonneuve. I think he wasn't worried because I was a woman and he knew me. What he didn't know was that Lucian was concealed nearby, with his bow." Silence. "I'm not sure whether he understood that I was Gilbert Couture's daughter. He was so obsessed with money ... I guess you know the rest."

Victor remembered seeing, in McNeil's office, something in the psychiatrist's expression when he'd mentioned the handwritten note. Without meaning to, the detective sergeant might have been the one who had tipped him off.

"What about the number magnets on the fridge? I know they had symbolic importance for you — the date of your father's death. But how were they significant to Judith Harper?"

"The night Dad was killed, Tousignant and Harper had dinner to celebrate his elimination. Lortie was there. He took pictures." Silence. "Lucian showed them to me."

Victor committed the information to memory, then asked for permission to check the messages on his phone, which had just rung.

Charlie Couture granted it.

The Gnome had sent a text: he and Loïc had been delayed and wouldn't arrive for another twenty-five minutes. Though Victor didn't like to admit it to himself, this was good news for him. He was totally absorbed by the conversation.

Wondering whether he should reply, he decided at first to do nothing. Then he changed his mind, typed a quick *OK*, and put the phone down.

Every minute he spent with the murderess was increasing his store of knowledge. He also wanted to avoid wasting precious time bringing the Gnome and Loïc up to speed on the situation. Charlie Couture wasn't asking for status reports. She had given him fair warning. He must act accordingly.

"You were talking about Lucian ... how did you meet him?"

"Each time he was discharged from Louis-H., Lortie lived on the streets or in a seedy apartment. Earlier in his life, he'd had several mistresses. When he needed money, he'd make the rounds, showing up on their doorsteps late in the evening. A lot of the time, he'd be chased away by a new boyfriend. Once in a while, he'd receive a little sympathy and a few dollars. Silvia Duca, Lucian's mother, was one of those mistresses. She had taken pity on him now and then, putting him up for a few nights. Lucian was a young boy at the time. Silvia had never told Lortie or Lucian that they were father and son, but Lortie figured it out. At one point, during a delusional episode, he told Lucian that he was his father and opened up about his past. Lortie described the mistreatment he'd suffered at the hands of Judith Harper and McNeil. He talked about his participation in FLQ operations, and about his involvement in the plot to kill President Kennedy. Lucian remembered that during previous visits, Lortie had concealed documents and photographs behind the bathroom tiles. Documents that Lortie himself seemed to have forgotten about, but corroborated his accounts."

Victor recalled his conversation with the retired CIA agent. Cleveland Willis had spoken about those documents, which Lortie had held up at the time as a threat. On impulse, Victor said, "Those documents also described the torture of your father and his fellow employees by Judith Harper, and their subsequent execution by Lortie."

"You're right," Charlie said. "That was part of it. Lortie hadn't only concealed papers relating to the missions he'd carried out for Tousignant and Lawson. He was also in possession of documents proving he'd spent time with Oswald."

Victor's gaze strayed as his brain assimilated the information that Charlie Couture had just given him. She went on.

"When Lucian became aware of all this, he was devastated. He never talked much about his feelings, and I don't know a lot about that period of his life, but I can imagine his reaction. In the space of a few weeks, he had learned not only his father's identity, but also that the man was a killer, capable of the most atrocious crimes."

"So Lucian confronted his father?"

"Lortie denied all of it. He claimed he couldn't remember a thing. When Lucian pressed him, holding up the documents as proof, Lortie said it wasn't his fault. He claimed that he'd been brainwashed, that he wasn't responsible for his actions. The file contained papers relating to his treatment under MK-ULTRA. Those papers cited certain sentences that he kept repeating until they were erased from his mind by Judith Harper. One of those sentences had been spoken by Lee Oswald at the time of his arrest."

"I didn't shoot anybody, no sir," Victor quoted.

"Exactly. But Lucian was no fool. The papers established clearly that Lortie had undergone the treatments in 1969 and 1970, long after the murders in 1964. Lucian broke off relations, and Lortie fell off the radar."

The conversation was giving Victor an ever-clearer picture of the case.

"Then, using the information in Lortie's file, Lucian tracked you down ..."

"It was in 2007. One evening, Lucian showed up at my door and started giving me this information. He was insistent, saying I was the first person he'd talked to about these things, telling me I had a right to know, and that he had documents to back up everything he was saying. At first, I couldn't understand. I thought he was crazy. I threw him out, not wanting to hear another word. But in the days that followed, Lucian refused to give up. He kept calling and knocking on my door. Finally, I gave in. I thought about the things he was saying. In the end, I was completely overwhelmed. And revolted."

"You'd believed until then that your father and brother were killed in a hunting accident?"

"No. I knew Dad and Lennie had been murdered. I'd seen the killer myself on the forest path, though I had no idea who Lortie was at the time. But when I told Mom what I'd seen, she made me swear not to go to the police, because if I did, we'd both be killed, too. I never found out how much she knew about what had happened. Until her dying day, she refused to talk about it." Silence. "I know she did it to protect me. As time went by, I put my life back together. I tried to forget, to put it all behind me. Do you understand?"

Victor still couldn't see the woman's face, but he could hear the emotion in her voice. She paused for a long time before continuing.

"I asked Lucian why he had come to me instead of going to the police. He didn't know, exactly, and couldn't answer. I decided to go to the police myself, but each time I got in the car to do it, I ended up turning back. Who would believe me? I sat in the car in front of the house for hours at a time, crying. During the first few weeks, I saw Lucian every day. I needed to talk to him, to understand. Little by little, a relationship developed between us, and we became lovers. It seemed unreal that he was interested in me. I hadn't had a man in my life in a long time. And the age difference was substantial. But the relationship did me good. I tried to convince myself that the best thing I could do was live in the present and forget the past."

"Yet you were unable to do that …"

"If I've learned anything over the years, it's that the past always catches up with us. When Lucian came into my life and I learned the truth, my wound, which had scarred over, burst open again. Something broke, and this time it was irreparable."

Victor found himself nodding in agreement. Charlie's observations about the past had a particular resonance with his own experience.

"So you and Lucian set about planning your revenge ..."

"It didn't happen the way you might suppose. You don't get up one morning and say, 'Let's get payback.' It isn't even something you discuss. But a day comes when you open your eyes and it's there in front of you, and you accept it without question. Time had gone by. I'd started to monitor the movements of Tousignant, Harper, and Lawson. I was sickened by their professional and financial success, but above all, I was disgusted by the fact that they'd been able to keep moving forward, to live their lives with impunity, never facing any consequences for their crimes. A plan had begun to take shape in my mind. But I didn't mention it to Lucian. Then, sometime in 2008, I think, I walked past a homeless man begging in the street. When I refused to give him money, he grumbled, 'Goddamn shitty life,' and spat on the ground. It was Lortie, I was sure of it. In my entire existence, I'd only ever heard one person say those words. I told Lucian about the encounter when I got home." Silence. "I didn't know it, but he spent the next several days searching for his father in the city's homeless shelters. A week later, he gave me a list of the places that his father frequented. That was when I shared my plan with him for the very first time. Lortie was often admitted to Louis-H. I already had nurse's training, which meant it was easy for me to get a job as an orderly. One by one, things fell into place. When Lortie was readmitted to Louis-H. in 2010, I was ready. The final phase of my operation began."

Victor could well imagine that Charlie had acted out of a complicated mix of overlapping motives, but he still decided to ask the question directly: "You were driven by more than a simple desire for retribution … weren't you?"

"I know people will only talk about revenge when they analyze my crimes. Because atrocities are so hard to understand, there's a tendency to latch onto simplistic notions of good and evil, to place those two things in separate, watertight moral compartments." Silence. "But you're right, Victor. The deepest motive for my actions wasn't a desire for vengeance. In Dad's eyes, honour was to be prized above all else. It was the value he instilled in me with the greatest passion and conviction. I did what I did to honour his memory. I wanted to show him that I remembered." A long silence. "Revenge came second. A distant second. It came when I saw the terrible fear and pain on the faces of my victims. When the sight of their suffering gave me pleasure."

Victor nodded. Hearing Charlie talk about the blackness of her soul plunged him into a profound despondency, but, knowing what she had lived through, he couldn't help feeling a kind of empathy for her.

"Was it to honour your father's memory that you needed to get Tousignant's confession? The documents that Lucian had brought you weren't enough?" He paused. "Wouldn't it have been possible to avoid all these deaths?"

"The documents implicated Tousignant as the man in charge, but only in a roundabout way that might not have guaranteed his conviction. I had to make sure there was no possible ambiguity. Tousignant is a man of means. I wanted to be certain that he wouldn't be able to hide behind a battery of lawyers. In order to get past all his lines of defence, to make him confess, I needed the others to be dead. Tousignant had to know that I'd stop at nothing, that I was prepared to kill him if he didn't comply. I needed him to be convinced that he had no choice."

"You could have stopped when you got your hands on the files that Lawson put together on Evergreen. They clearly incriminate the senator."

"There was no way of knowing that Lawson had the files in his possession. It's true, those documents answered a lot of questions. But by then it was too late to turn back."

"Why did Tousignant open up to you? He couldn't be sure you'd let him live after he confessed. The proof is, he's out on the ice right now. And I promise you, he thinks he's going to die."

"That's true. But we're all the same when the end is staring us in the face. We're willing to do a lot to postpone it, even by a few seconds. The senator chose to talk in the hope that he might live, rather than shut his mouth in the certain knowledge that he would die."

The detective sergeant nodded. He was aware that the woman in the shadows was watching him, sizing him up. "Confessions obtained under duress are worthless in court," he said.

"I'll trust the judges to do their duty." Silence. "You should have seen the fear that came over Harper and Lawson every time they got close to the red line."

In response to Victor's question, Charlie Couture explained what she was talking about: the length of red duct tape that ran along the floor in front of the surface that the key was lying on.

"They perceived the red line as a threat, a sign of imminent danger. You can't imagine the joy on their faces when, having thought they'd die as soon as they crossed the line, they took the key in their hands and imagined they were saved." Charlie laughed: a demented, chilling laugh. "But instead of liberating them as they'd hoped, the key triggered the mechanism that condemned them."

The detective sergeant realized at that moment that she had watched her victims die. The red line, the key releasing the lethal dart — she had seen it all. Had she gone so far as to capture the horror on video? She was insane. Brilliant. Psychopathic.

"Why did you choose that weapon?"

"It was a kind of homage. Mom was a historian, a medievalist. Her doctoral thesis was on the use of the heretic's fork, but she never finished it. Dad's death shattered her life. She died of cancer afterward."

"How did you get it?"

"The fork? Lucian made it. Before being hired at Baker Lawson Watkins, he'd worked in a foundry. He was very good with his hands."

"And he created the mechanism that shot the dart through the victims' necks?"

"When the system is armed, the dart is released by the victim turning the key to unlock the manacles. I used to joke with Lucian that he should patent his invention." Silence. A quiet cough. "As it turned out, I felt no satisfaction after Judith Harper's death. It was too fast. She was resigned to dying and picked up the key after a very short time. It was all over in a few hours."

"Was Lucian with you?"

"Not for the kidnapping. After paralyzing her with a Taser and injecting her with anaesthetic, I put her in a wheelchair to get her out of the building. Then I put her in my car. It was easy. She was small and thin."

Victor remembered watching at Louis-H. as Charlie had helped an obese patient to roll over on his bed. She was accustomed to such manoeuvres.

"You brought her to the warehouse. You had seduced Horowitz, so you knew the company's business hours."

"The warehouse is closed on Fridays. Horowitz explained to me that they'd been doing things that way for twenty years." She laughed. "Seducing the old pig wasn't very hard."

"You wore a dark wig, didn't you?"

"Yes," Charlie murmured.

"In the case of Nathan Lawson, you held him captive for a few days before killing him …"

"I was ready to take some chances with Lawson, even if that meant he might escape. It turned into a game. I wanted to give him time to be frightened, but I also wanted him to hope he might get away. I followed him at a distance by car after he left the office. I knew he wouldn't call the police. As a last resort, I'd have intervened with the

Taser if I thought he was going to escape. At one point, I drove past him in my car, and I saw the relief on his face as he watched me go by. Just a harmless woman …" Silence. "When he stopped off at a business centre and then drove to the cemetery, I started to worry, but Lucian had let me know that he'd helped Lawson put a file in the trunk of his car. While I was following Lawson, Lucian made sure the file really was hidden in the cemetery. I knew Peter Frost's house. I'd already followed Lawson when he took the young man there to have sex a few weeks before. When I realized that the house was Lawson's hiding place, I knew I had all the time in the world."

The woman took a deep breath. She was speaking freely now. She needed no prompting from Victor. Was she unburdening her conscience as she talked, setting her mind at ease? The detective sergeant had no way of knowing.

"After Lawson hid the documents, Lucian and I looked through them. Then I had him put them back. I knew they were Lawson's insurance policy, his tradeable asset, and that someone would come for them with the intention of contacting Tousignant and threatening to make them public. As far as Lawson was concerned, the calculation was simple: he was convinced that the senator wanted him dead. I kept Lawson on a sedative drip while I waited to see how things developed. Logically, it could only be Rivard who would come for the file. Lawson trusted no one else. When I saw Rivard speak to the media after the press conference, I understood."

"Rivard was sending a message to Tousignant, saying he had what the senator was looking for."

"At that moment, I knew Rivard had betrayed Lawson and decided to sell the file to the highest bidder. Which, of course, was Tousignant. Lucian started following Rivard. The day after the press conference, Rivard went to the cemetery to recover the file. In Tousignant's confession, he describes the methods he and Rivard used to communicate."

"Then Lucian killed Rivard to prevent the file from falling into Tousignant's hands?"

"Lucian and Rivard worked in the same office. Rivard was arrogant and heartless with support staff. Lucian already hated him. When Rivard came for the file …" Silence. "Lucian was a competitive cross-country skier and an experienced bowhunter. Rivard never had a chance."

Flashes of insight were lighting up and fading out in Victor's brain. He would need to play back the recordings to be sure he had explored every corner of the labyrinth.

91

STRUCK DOWN

The words carried by Charlie Couture's voice were dissolving, the phrases melting, the thoughts cracking open, giving way, in Victor's head, to images of pain and death, but also to glimpses of love and nostalgia.

A sudden click startled him, rousing him from his absorption in the narrative. The tape had run out on the A side of the cassette. The detective sergeant ejected it, turned it over, and resumed recording. Charlie Couture had been talking for half an hour.

"How long until your fellow officers get here?" she asked.

Victor looked at his watch. "Ten minutes."

He and Charlie looked at each other, not needing to say a word.

"There's something else I'd like to know," he began. "Since the outset, you've left clues in your wake. The fridge numbers, the CD in Lawson's car, the handwritten reference to Cameron on Lortie's psychiatric file, the matchbook at Le Confessionnal, the Evergreen files in the garbage bags, and Tousignant's wallet, which you sent me. You've repeatedly taken chances so as to point us in the right direction. Consciously or not, you wanted us to catch you. Am I wrong?"

"The CD was a mistake, an oversight. Lucian was on his way to recover it when you spotted him in Summit Woods. As for the other items, I'll say this: my long-term goal was to have the conversation that we're having right now. But I had hoped that Lucian …"

Charlie didn't finish the sentence. A fraught silence hung in the room. Victor took a long pause before continuing.

"Though I won't say I agree with your motives, I think I understand them. But what were Lucian's?"

"Would you be able to accept being the son of a monster?"

The question hit Victor like a slap in the face. The woman could have no idea of the effect her words had on him.

"Life is full of contradictions … Lucian carried terrible violence within him. He became convinced that this violence was his genetic inheritance from Lortie, and that he was doomed to follow in his father's footsteps. Faced with what he thought was an inevitable end, he chose to dedicate his life to what he believed was a just cause." Silence. "And you know," she said, her voice trembling, "we loved each other."

Victor heard her sobs and felt his own throat tighten. After a moment, the woman spoke again.

"I'm sorry." Silence. "I was glad it was you who led the investigation. I'd seen you on television in the past. I knew I could trust your judgment and integrity."

"You used me. You knew that as I investigated the murders you and Lucian had committed, I'd eventually become interested in the killings that occurred in 1964. That was what you wanted, wasn't it? For me to reassemble the picture, in a way."

"If I had come to you with my story, you never would have believed me. You'd have advised me to get a lawyer, who would have battled their attorneys for years in order to prove my allegations. I would have been sued for libel, and in the end, everyone would have decided I was crazy. As you searched for the person who killed Harper and Lawson, you pursued an independent investigation, which now enables you to confirm the truth of my claims. You'll find my diary in the bedroom. Maybe it will provide the answers to other questions you may have."

Victor drank the last of his tea, put the cup on the table, and let several seconds pass before speaking again. He was unsure of how to phrase what he wanted to say next, because it arose more from the realm of feelings than of logic.

"You spoke earlier of being driven by the desire to honour your father's memory. But there's something else at work here, isn't there, Charlie?" He hesitated. "Something deeper than honour."

The answer came quickly, suggesting that his intuition had been right.

"I wasn't lying to you about Dad." She paused. "But I've allowed the barbaric actions of Tousignant, Lawson, and Harper to hamper me for too long. I've spent my life in search of myself. Now that I've defined myself by my own actions, I can take my leave in a state of liberty and independence. Do you understand?"

Victor bowed his head, gazing at the floor in front of him. He couldn't see Charlie Couture, but he knew she was watching him with piercing intensity. "You haven't given yourself an escape route, have you, Charlie?"

"This isn't something a person walks away from unscathed. You're an excellent police officer, Victor. Above all, you're a good man. I won't be here, but you can tell them …" Silence. "You can tell them that Charlie Couture remembers."

His hand shot out, reaching for his Glock, but the detective sergeant wasn't fast enough. A Taser discharge overwhelmed him, knocking him to the floor, leaving him paralyzed, unable to stand.

92

THE RIVER

Victor struggled to his feet. The door was open. The wind whipped his face. Down below, on the river, he could see a light moving along the ice beyond Senator Tousignant. Still reeling, the detective sergeant grabbed his gun off the table, rushed down the porch stairs, and descended the snow-covered slope. Charlie's head start was between forty-five seconds and a minute.

Holstering the Glock, he was at the river's edge in a few steps. His feet skidded momentarily on the ice, and he reached the shack.

Senator Tousignant was in pitiful condition.

His face contorted with pain, his eyes bulging, he was drooling and shaking. Blood trickled beneath his chin, which was penetrated by two iron points, and ran down his neck, accumulating in a viscous puddle on the coat fabric over his chest, into which the other end of the fork had been driven.

"… lp me … help me," he gurgled, gasping.

"I'll be back, Senator."

"… ard! Don't … eave me … here! Less … ard!"

Charlie's light rose and fell gently ahead of him. He was moving through the darkness as fast as his bad leg would allow. Unable to see his feet, he stumbled frequently over the little mounds of snow that dotted the frozen expanse.

The distance between him and the light was shrinking. Encouraged, Victor stepped up his pace, his breath snapping in the frigid air.

After a hundred more metres, he felt the surface change under his high-tops. It was becoming more porous. He realized suddenly that his feet were wet.

This early in the winter, the ice sheet hadn't entirely blanketed the river. It had begun to form over the shallower stretches near the banks. How far out had he and the woman come? Were they already in the danger zone?

When he heard the first cracks, he knew death lay ahead.

"Charlie! Stop!"

Victor had narrowed the gap to fifty metres. But the light was moving forward relentlessly. The ice was starting to sag under his feet, forcing him to slow down. Because he was heavier than she was, the surface might not hold up under his weight as it had, moments earlier, when Charlie passed over it.

Suddenly, with horror, he heard a deafening crack as the ice gave way in front of him.

"Charlie!"

He watched as the light sliced through the air, fell, and was gone.

Victor stepped on something that made a metallic noise. Aiming his phone light downward, he saw the chain that had held the senator: it was lying on the ice near the shack. A flashlight beam struck him in the face, dazzling him. He shielded his eyes with one hand.

"You okay, Vic?"

The Gnome had come to meet him at the shoreline. Lowering his gaze, Victor realized that his jeans were as soaked as his shoes.

"Is she …?"

The detective sergeant shook his head, drawing a finger across his throat. The Gnome froze, his mouth open, bewildered.

"Where's Tousignant?" Victor asked.

"Inside, with Loïc. We managed to get the fork off him. He's weak, and he's lost a fair amount of blood. The ambulance and forensics team are on their way. Jacinthe is just coming to. What the hell happened?"

The detective sergeant let out a deep sigh. "Long story, Gilles ..."

The loud bang of a gunshot tore through the quiet air.

After a stunned instant, the Gnome was rushing toward the house, pistol in hand. Victor didn't move. He didn't need to. He knew what had just happened. Charlie Couture had left her gun inside the house.

Tousignant had used it to kill himself.

The prospect of his confession becoming public, and the awareness of all the repercussions that would ensue, had snuffed out his desire to live. Not only would his taped admissions reveal that he'd been behind the murders in 1964; they might also prove that he had participated in a conspiracy to assassinate President Kennedy.

Victor's hands were shaking as he lit a cigarette. He took a hard drag, making the tobacco crackle.

And suddenly, nothing remained but the darkness and the silence and the snowflakes dancing around the orange firefly between his fingers.

93

DIARY

As Charlie had told Victor, her diary was in the bedroom, placed conspicuously on the bed. While Lemaire consoled Loïc, while Jacinthe recovered her wits under the ambulance attendants' care, while the forensics techs started working over the crime scene, Victor found a quiet corner in the basement and began to read.

He lingered for a long time over the last entry, which had been made a few days earlier:

December 27th
I Swear to You, Dad

You can scream to the world that you're free
But your chains must be broken from within
I am the right of my cells to choose their fate
I am free and sovereign, and I choose how I am governed
I am independent of outside influence
I will not live to see the new year: time is spilling over
I am leaving this place, which I have loved so dearly
I am departing to walk barefoot upon the world
And I swear to you, Dad, that for all eternity

I remember

94

SAD SONGS

Saturday, December 31st

The door opened a few centimetres. Between locks of unkempt hair, a glistening, puffy eye looked back at him.

"I can come back later, if this isn't a good time."

"No, come in. But I warn you, I've been crying and listening to a playlist of sad songs."

As he entered the house, he didn't notice the picture windows with their view of downtown Montreal, or the raw concrete walls and ceiling, or the designer furnishings, or the thick white carpet, or the artworks, or the mess.

Rather, while he removed his high-tops, he was unable to take his eyes off Virginie's breathtaking body as she walked to the far end of the room, bare-legged, in panties and knee socks, one camisole strap falling off her shoulder.

She put on a form-fitting robe and walked back toward him, wearing dark glasses.

"Are you by yourself?" Victor asked.

"I sent Jean-Bernard to his brother's place for a few days, with the dog."

"And here I'd driven over especially to meet Woodrow Wilson," the detective sergeant said, making a face.

The joke elicited a smile from Virginie. The cop's glance strayed to a coffee table nearby, where a line of white powder was visible.

"Got any cigarettes?" the young woman asked.

Victor put two between his lips, lit them, and gave one to her.

"I won't stay long. I just came to give you something." He handed her the small box that had been in his hand since his arrival.

"What is it?" Opening the box, Virginie found audio cassettes inside.

"It's your father's confession. The woman who … Charlie Couture … wanted him to stand trial. But now that they're … I mean … I thought you had a right to know …" Silence. "These are copies. You can do what you want with them."

Emily Haines's vaporous, heart-rending voice filled the room, singing about her baby's lonesome lows.

What would Virginie do with them? Destroy them, or publish the truth in a newspaper story? Victor had no idea. He would have been hard pressed to predict who would prevail between the journalist and the woman grieving for her father.

Virginie's lower lip started to tremble. The box slipped from her fingers and the cassettes tumbled out onto the carpet. Taking off her glasses, she looked up at him, her eyes burning with distress. She stepped forward and pressed herself to his chest, weeping. Gradually, her sobs subsided and she was quiet in his arms. The world was reduced to their two faces and the silence and the tears running down the young woman's cheeks.

Rising to the tips of her toes, Virginie tilted her head back slowly to look at him. Victor felt his spine tingle as his reflection grew in her dilated pupils. Her lips were poised, suspended in the air, centimetres from his own.

"You and I will never kiss each other," she murmured. She put a finger over his mouth to prevent him from answering. "But we'll always wish we had."

95

NEWS FROM TROIS-PISTOLES

Sunday, January 1st

Victor turned off the Blu-ray player, left the flat-screen TV tuned to an all-news channel, and got up. The outcome of the boxing match in Kinshasa in 1974 hadn't changed. Yet, despite the fact that he'd watched it dozens of times, every viewing still left Victor incredulous. Muhammad Ali had withstood George Foreman's savage early round assaults, then flattened him in the eighth.

Victor picked up the tub of Polyfilla and the spatula from the kitchen table. With deliberate movements, he started applying a third layer of the compound to the hole that his fists had opened in the drywall on the evening he'd beaten up Nadja's brother.

When the work was done, he rinsed the utensil in the sink and briefly ransacked the kitchen, opening the refrigerator, freezer, and cupboards in turn. The search was fruitless. He'd have to go out for something to eat.

The clock on the stove indicated 5:12 p.m. The walk to the living room window felt like a trek across a desert.

At the window, with the streetlight's orange glow filling the room, he lit a cigarette. Outside, a man was shovelling his car out of a snowbank.

Victor reacted with a start — a scrawny, yellow-haired dog was slowly crossing the street, its head swinging limply between bony shoulders.

A car coming up the street honked impatiently, but the yellow dog didn't change its indolent pace, taking an eternity to reach the other side. At last the animal clambered over the bank created by the snowplow and sat down on the sidewalk in front of Victor's apartment door.

Dog and detective exchanged a long look.

"It's been a while," Victor whispered at last, watching the beast struggle to its feet and amble out of sight at the end of the street.

Despite the tablets, his stomach was knotted with anxiety.

The weather girl came on, wearing a pink outfit. With a click of the remote, Victor shut her up before she could open her mouth.

He was still standing there, communing with the dark screen, when his cellphone rang.

Martin had called an hour earlier, from Saskatchewan, to wish him a happy New Year. Father and son hadn't spoken in some time. Victor had had trouble hearing Martin over the noisy festivities that were in full swing at Uncle Gilbert's house.

Judging from the background racket that threatened to drown out their conversation, it was clear, at least, that the young man wasn't bored. Before hanging up, the detective sergeant had learned that Martin was doing fine and that his mother, Marie, was still out west, keeping him company. Victor had ended the call with a promise to get in touch again in a couple of days, and to come out for a visit soon.

Now, puzzled, he looked at the caller ID: it was a confidential number. Hoping, without really believing it, that the caller might be Nadja, he answered.

"Victor?"

"Mmm?"

"Hi!" A cheerful voice. "I wasn't sure it was you. It's Simone … Simone Fortin. Happy New Year!"

Hearing his old friend's voice brought a half smile to his lips. "Simone! What a surprise. Happy New Year to you, too … and to Mathilde and Laurent … What's new?"

"Oh, not much, apart from one thing …" A joyful yell came over the line. "I'm pregnant!"

Victor lifted his head.

How long had he been sitting here, head down on the kitchen table?

Had he really seen the yellow dog and talked to Simone Fortin, or had those events unfolded in his imagination?

In any case, the bottle of Glenfiddich now stood before him. Still inviolate, it was singing its dark siren song of oblivion. In the bucket, which he had filled a few minutes earlier, the ice was beginning to melt.

Nadja's absence haunted him. It wrung his heart.

Seizing his cellphone, Victor sent her a text. He'd had no word from her since seeing her through the car window on the day Martin was released:

forgive me

After sending the message, Victor picked up the Scotch bottle unceremoniously, uncorked it, fished a few ice cubes out of the bucket and, after tossing them into the glass, filled it to the brim with amber liquid.

"All this distance travelled," he muttered to himself, holding up the glass, "just to end up where I started."

The ring of an incoming text message stopped the drink short of his lips. His face brightened. Nadja had finally replied. Putting the glass down, he grabbed the phone and hurriedly read the message:

hey dad, just wondering what you're up to … feel like coming over? my roomies are out for the night … we could have new year's dinner together

luv, charlotte xx

Victor bit his fist until it bled. Then he put his head in his hands. Shame washed over him; tears filled his eyes. How had he let himself get so wrapped up in his petty miseries that he'd forgotten to call and wish his daughter a happy New Year?

Especially since, with Marie and Martin on the other side of the country, Charlotte had no other relatives in town but him. He had let her down horribly. What a useless father he was.

Victor had actually reflected on the phenomenon in the past. It tended to come up in the lives of parents who were coping with a problem child. The siblings often grew up in the shadows, deprived of the attention they deserved.

Martin had taken up all of Victor's attention, had sapped all his energy. And in the meantime, in silence, Charlotte had grown into a magnificent young woman.

Victor rose quickly to his feet, picked up the glass and the fifth of Scotch, emptied them into the sink, and dropped the bottle into the recycling bin.

Throwing on his jacket, he dialed Charlotte's number.

"Hello, beautiful … Yeah, I just got your text … You bet I'm up for it! … I'm leaving now. What can I bring?"

As he closed the front door behind him, Victor wiped his eyes. He was wearing a broad smile.

UNTIL NEXT TIME

Victor tilted the pitcher and watered the plant that he'd rescued from André Lortie's hellish room. Then, with a damp cloth, he delicately wiped the dust from its leaves.

The morning had gone by quickly. There had been a few early meetings, after which, with Mogwai's *Mr. Beast* in his headphones, he had worked on the report that would close what had come to be known as The Couture Affair.

The river ice hadn't yet given up Charlie's body.

One day — tomorrow, perhaps, or when the spring came, or two years from now — the detective sergeant knew his phone would ring. He would go to the morgue, and the white sheet would be pulled back, and he would look at the swollen, decomposed body, the slack, discoloured remains of Charlie Couture.

Sometimes, even though he knew it was impossible, he found himself imagining that she'd survived, that she had succeeded in swimming to the far shore before hypothermia overtook her.

Or that she'd climbed into a Zodiac that she'd left moored a short distance away, and had let herself drift in the darkness before starting the motor a few kilometres downstream.

Despite the terrible things she had done, her boundless love for her father had affected Victor.

Their blood had dried, their sins had been purged, their souls had been delivered from suffering for all time, yet Charlie, Lortie,

Tousignant, and the others lived on. With time, their memories would begin to fade.

Some would disappear forever from his thoughts, while others would return now and then to populate his gallery of ghosts.

There were moments when Victor wondered whether he ought to fear what he had become, or whether he had become what he ought to fear.

His gaze rested on the leaf in the palm of his hand. He turned his mind away from his thoughts and focused on the reality before him: nature, palpable, in all its simplicity and splendour. Nature, which, unlike human beings, never disappointed him.

Placing the pitcher and cloth on a metal trolley, he gave himself a shake and sat down at his desk. His mood was darkening, but he was refusing to surrender to it.

He glanced at his watch. He'd have to leave soon. Pulling a blank sheet from his printer, he placed it on the desk and penned a brief note:

> Dear Baby Face,
> If you ever come to Montreal, call me.
> I owe you, brother.
> Thanks,
> Victor

Using the permit number posted in Baby Face's taxi, the detective sergeant had found the address of the driver who'd saved him in Dallas. Folding the note, he slipped it into the envelope along with a pair of tickets that he'd bought online for a Texas Rangers game in May.

He was putting a stamp on the letter when Jacinthe came up.

"Hey there, Sleeping Beauty."

Jacinthe's period of unconsciousness in Charlie Couture's house had made her the reluctant owner of a new nickname.

"Go fuck yourself, Lessard," she said, smiling and raising a middle finger. "We're going for lunch. Want to come?"

"No, thanks, I already have something."

•   •   •

Victor patted the pockets of his jeans and searched his jacket. Where had he put the damn key to the service vehicle he'd reserved? Probably on the desk somewhere, under the piles of documents.

He lifted the interrogation report that Loïc had submitted to him. The young detective had gone back to see Nash, the homeless former maths Ph.D. student. At first, Nash had sworn that he'd never given anything to André Lortie. Under persistent questioning, however, he had finally admitted to accepting money from a man in return for hiding an envelope among Lortie's possessions. Swearing that he didn't know what was in the envelope, Nash had identified the man from a photo array laid out by Loïc. The man was Lucian Duca.

Victor's search continued in a toxicology report. The report indicated that no trace of anaesthetic had been found in the blood-streams of Judith Harper and Nathan Lawson. This came as no surprise. Going through Charlie Couture's house, the investigation team had found vials containing a substance that was undetectable in the blood after a few hours. Using her access to the drug cabinet at Louis-H., Charlie had stolen everything she needed.

Shit. If Victor didn't find the key soon, he'd be late. The detective sergeant pushed aside the thick pile of sheets containing a transcript of Tousignant's confession. Victor had listened to every second of the recordings, but hadn't learned much beyond what he already knew. The same was true of the indictment drawn up by Lawson, which investigators had found among Charlie's possessions.

Next, Victor's eyes fell on the autopsy report concerning Daniel Tousignant. The report confirmed that Tousignant had killed him-self with the pistol that Charlie Couture had left in her house. The document didn't mention that the senator had turned the weapon on himself seconds after Loïc had intervened to stop him from destroying the recordings of his confession.

All the materials gathered by investigators — specifically the Evergreen file, Tousignant's confession, and Charlie's diary — had been turned over to the FBI by the Montreal Police. Victor didn't yet know what the consequences would be. Would U.S. authorities want to question him?

He patted his jeans again. What had he done with that fucking key?

Then an idea struck him. He put a hand in his back pocket, the one in which he ordinarily kept his wallet. The key was there. Sometimes things were where they should be. You just had to pay attention.

The wind was scouring the streets of Chinatown; the sun was concealed by clouds.

With his collar upturned, hands in his pockets, the bruise under his eye having turned an ugly shade of yellow, Victor was moving fast, his stride purposeful. Turning onto La Gauchetière Street, he stopped at a mailbox and inserted the letter addressed to Baby Face. After double-checking the slot to be sure the letter was gone, Victor walked another hundred metres and entered a nondescript building.

He went up the stairs, reached a hallway, and turned right. Coming to the third door, he knocked and, without waiting for an answer, stepped into the room.

At the end of the hallway, Jacinthe Taillon smiled in triumph. She advanced to the door that her partner had just closed behind him. No sign. No buzzer. Now, at last, she would learn what he was up to in Chinatown.

Expecting to walk into an opium den or an unregistered massage salon that specialized in happy endings, Jacinthe turned the door handle and marched inside. Lessard was stretched out on a massage table, shirtless.

Disturbed by Taillon's sudden arrival, the elderly Chinese man stopped inserting needles into the detective sergeant's skin, glared at the intruder, and began speaking to her in an angry tone.

Jacinthe didn't understand the language the man was speaking, but she had a pretty clear sense that he wasn't paying her any compliments. Victor, meanwhile, was returning her gaze with undisguised annoyance.

Lessard was getting acupuncture treatments!

"It's to help me quit smoking," he said, in response to his partner's unasked question. "Close the door on your way out."

Emerging from the treatment, Victor set out on foot for a dingy little place nearby whose dumplings and Tonkin soup he particularly enjoyed. As he was walking along, his phone vibrated. Putting a hand in the pocket of his leather jacket, he withdrew his cigarette pack before retrieving his phone.

The sun came out from between two clouds for a breath of fresh air, but the brighter shine was on Victor's face. The text message that had just arrived was from Nadja:

i miss you …

Pocketing the phone, Victor wondered: where was she? What was she doing? Had she finally made it to the cottage that they'd rented for the holidays? The thought broke through his armour and made his heart swell with hope.

Perhaps, after all, she would give him a second chance. Perhaps life would go back to the way it had been before.

Perhaps, this time, he would figure it out.

Standing there on the sidewalk, he was about to toss his cigarette pack into a trash can when he saw a young homeless man at the corner, begging.

Victor stopped in front of the young man and handed him the cigarettes. Then he set off toward the end of the street.

"Thank you, sir! Thank you! Keep smiling!"

AUTHOR'S NOTE

Every crime novel is rooted in the reality of the society it describes, bearing witness, in some measure, to a given era or series of events, past or present. This novel, however, doesn't convey historical or political reality. The novelist's task is to imagine what could have happened. And since this world is not a real but a fictional one, the characters' thoughts, in context, are intended to serve the story and to be true to their own logic.

In a novel, details must be rendered with precision on subjects as varied as medical prescriptions and archival policy. A significant number of people helped me clarify these details. I've named them in my acknowledgements.

Now and then, reality needs a helping hand. I've added two floors to the Stock Exchange Tower. In 2008, penthouses were built atop the New York Life Building, from the roof of which one of my characters commits suicide. I've reconfigured certain locations in the city of Montreal, and I've taken some liberties with historical facts and persons.

Behind each of these departures from factual accuracy, there are precise reasons too complicated to go into here. One common principle unites them all: they serve the story.

Everything, always, must serve the story.

Martin Michaud

MATERIALS

I've always enjoyed reading the acknowledgements in rock bands' liner notes, where each musician lists the instruments used in the making of an album. Obviously, a writer's toolkit is more modest. If you ever come across me writing in a café, you'll see me wearing my reliable Audio-Technica ATH-M50 headphones. I know, I know, I look like a Martian with those things on my head. (Incidentally, I highly recommend them to parents who need a break from their children's yelling.) Permanently installed beside my desk, there's an old Gibson acoustic lent to me by my good friend Marc Bernard. (And which will never be returned — there, I've said it.) That guitar is essential to maintaining some semblance of sanity when I'm working on a project. What else? Too many litres of espresso. An iMac, a MacBook, a printer that works when it's in the mood, a yellow highlighter, and a knapsack. Wow. Totally glamorous, eh?

ACKNOWLEDGEMENTS

Writing this novel has been a long, solitary journey to the end of myself, and it's been an enterprise in which a great many individuals have contributed significantly to the creation of the story. I am indebted to every one of them. I extend my warmest thanks:

To the friendly, collaborative, and enthusiastic team at Dundurn. It is an honor for me to be part of the family.

To Arthur Holden for understanding and respecting my characters and style in a very subtle way. When I read my book in English, I hear my voice. And that is because of your talent and sensitivity, my friend! You are the artist.

To my dear agent, Abigail Koons, for putting in the hard work and her faith in me at the start of this new journey, and for her ongoing guidance, passionate support, and ability to make me laugh. You are a gift.

To Catherine McKenzie for being a thoughtful friend and a facilitator in opening new horizons.

To the whole team at les Éditions Goélette for their support.

To Ingrid Remazeilles, who was the first editor to believe in me and in my ability to tell stories.

To Benoît Bouthillette, winner of the 2005 Saint-Pacôme Prize (best Quebec crime novel of the year), for helping me refine the style and effectiveness of this book. It was an honour to have you in my corner, Mickey.

To Patricia Juste and Fleur Neesham, for applying their fine proofreading talents to my text.

To Constable Geneviève Gonthier of the Montreal Police, who, in telling me about a personal experience, was the origin of an element of the novel's plot, and who, thereafter, generously offered her insights on questions relating to police matters.

To Jacques Fillipi, who devoted countless hours to reading and commenting on my manuscript with sympathy and attention to detail. Best wishes to your boys, Jacques. (Here's hoping that next time, the weather will be warm enough to take advantage of the pool!)

To Marie "Mémé Attaque Haïti" Larocque for reading my manuscript and offering comments, live from Jacmel, with enthusiasm, humour, and talent.

To Dr. Robert Brunet, psychiatrist, who generously invited me into his house, patiently taught me about bipolar disorder and its pharmacology, and helped me create a psychiatric profile for André Lortie.

To Jean-François Lisée, for receiving me in his home days after the birth of his youngest child, for answering my questions about the role played by U.S. intelligence services in Quebec during the 1960s, and for helping me give a past to Cleveland Willis.

To Michel Boislard, for explaining the practical aspects of archival policies in major law firms.

To Isabelle Reinhardt for her insight on questions relating to the Enterprise Register.

To Ariane Hurtubise, for sharing her experiences as a worker in the field of mental health.

To Carole Lambert and her sister for information regarding finance.

To Billy Robinson, Morgane Marvier, Johanne Vadeboncœur, and other booksellers across Quebec, whose passion and love of books make all the difference, helping novels like mine to find a readership.

To my friend Marc Bernard, with whom I've developed the habit of discussing the broad strokes of my novels.

To my parents, for the lessons they taught me; to my father, for the sentence I heard ceaselessly when I was small: "When you do something, do it well, or else don't do it at all."

To my children, Antoine and Gabrielle, for your support and your love, and for all the hours you let me steal from you so that I could bring this project to fruition.

To Geneviève, my love, my muse, my proofreader, my rereader, my keyboard artist, who's there in the good times and the less-good times, who picks up what I let fall, who offers me mad quantities of time and who too often neglects herself for my benefit. Your name deserves to be on the cover of this book as much as my own.

To all of you, I offer my thanks. And I promise you: I remember.

Responsibility for any errors that may subsist in this novel is, of course, entirely my own.

Read on for the first chapter of Martin Michaud's
next Victor Lessard Thriller

Coming October 2020

MARCH 31ST, 2005
QUEBEC CITY

Darkness.

Behind his eyelids, he tried to recreate a mental image of the face, but the vision kept slipping away.

For a fraction of a second, he thought he saw the outline of the eyebrows, then everything went blurry. However hard he tried, he couldn't visualize the eyes.

When the eyes absorb death, they reflect only emptiness. I can't find a way to picture that void.

He shook his head. All that remained of his life was a dream, buried in another dream.

Waiting.

Tapping steadily on the tiles.

The rain ended a little before 8:00 p.m.

Crouched in the darkness behind the kitchen counter, he re-inspected the arsenal arrayed in front of him: a hockey bag on wheels, a metal suitcase, a pile of towels, and a bottle of all-purpose cleaner. He was invisible from the entrance. All he would have to do was charge forward to get the man.

Two hours ago, he had parked the car on the street and neutralized the alarm system. Before leaving the vehicle, he had slipped his laptop into a knapsack and stowed it under the back seat.

He had proceeded methodically. Everything was in its place.

He stroked the handle of the knife strapped to his ankle.

Soon, he would extract death from death.

He knew the well-regulated life of the man he was about to kill, down to the slightest detail. This being Thursday, the man would leave work at 8:30 p.m. He'd stop off at the supermarket for a frozen dinner. When he got home, he'd microwave his meal and eat it in front of the TV, sprawled in an easy chair.

He had slipped into the house several times while the man was out.

He had looked over the row of DVDs on the man's bookshelf and noted with disdain that they consisted entirely of American TV shows.

People dull their minds with crude, derivative entertainment.

He had also remarked that the immense, luxurious house was at odds with the frugal habits of its owner. He had noticed a marble chess set in the living room,. He had observed the detailed ornamentation on the finely carved pieces.

A house like this should have been home to a family with children, not one person living alone. People were losing touch with real values. The cult of the individual, of every man for himself, disgusted him.

People don't take responsibility for their actions anymore. They think they can let themselves off the hook by pointing fingers at others whose actions are worse than their own.

This man would pay for his mistakes. He would see to it.

He heard the car's engine outside, then a key sliding into the lock. The door opened softly and a hand groped in the darkness, searching for the switch.

A final doubt assailed him. He brushed it aside.

His plan had no obvious flaws, apart from the possibility that a third person might be present. The man lived alone and didn't seem to have any relationships outside his work. The fact that the house was isolated provided a degree of extra protection in case a problem should arise. It would be unfortunate to have to eliminate an innocent victim, but sometimes collateral damage was unavoidable.

He held his breath, tensing his muscles, ready to burst out of the shadows.

He'd been waiting a long time for this moment.

As soon as he'd spotted the photograph of the young woman, as soon as she had resurfaced, he'd done his utmost to avoid attracting attention.

He had forced himself not to buy more than a few items in each store, seeking out the anonymity of large retail outlets. He'd been compelled to visit a dozen different establishments, all located outside a two-hundred-kilometre radius from his home. He had never asked a store clerk for assistance.

Once his purchases were made, he had removed the labels and eliminated all markings that made it possible to trace the items.

These precautions had struck him as elementary.

On March 20th, his birthday, he had loaded up his old truck and set out for the hunting lodge at Mont-Laurier, north of Montreal.

Since the lodge was inaccessible by road, he had transported his materials using the snowmobile and utility sled that he kept in the town's storage warehouse. The warehouse had a separate access door. No one had noticed him coming or going. In any case, it wouldn't have been unusual to encounter him in the area at this time of year.

He had decided to transport his victims by night, to minimize the risk of being seen. Not wanting to leave anything to chance, he had made this advance trip to the lodge in darkness. There would be no room for error when he had actual bodies to deal with.

That night, he had put away the food before going to bed. With the cupboards full, he could count on several days' autonomy before needing to resupply.

He'd spent most of March 21st sleeping and recovering his strength. In the evening, he had gone snowshoeing in the forest and heard a solitary wolf howling at the moon in the frigid darkness. It had occurred to him that he was like that wolf: the last prophet on the hill. He too would stand alone and howl out his gospel to the world.

The next day, he had carried out the necessary modifications. The lodge was divided into three sections: a main space, a private room, and a dormitory.

He had emptied the dormitory of its four bunk beds, which he had disassembled and stored in the shed. Next, he had boarded up the windows with slats of plywood. Using chains, he had affixed metal manacles to the wall at the end of the room. Then he had tested the apparatus. Once locked, it was escape-proof. Finally, he had installed the projection system.

Two freezers purred in the main space. Each one was big enough to hold a body.

The hunting would be good.

On March 23rd, he had returned to Quebec City, eager to begin.

The alarm system didn't emit its usual beep. The man was surely wondering why it wasn't working.

The light blinded him for a moment, but he blinked without concern. In a few seconds, his eyes would adjust and he would kill his prey.

The old man would have been proud of him.

The old man's been drinking in the truck all morning. Suddenly, a door slams. The boy feels a hand on his back. He's expecting to get hit, but the blows don't come. The old man hands him a rifle with a telescopic sight. The boy knows how to find his way in the woods. He knows how to track a moose. But at this particular moment, all he wants to do is cry. He has no desire to venture into the forest alone. "Quit whining like a baby. Do your father proud." He heads off with an ammunition clip, his hunting knife, a canteen and a knapsack containing a few sandwiches.

He leaped from his hiding place before the man, who had picked up the telephone, could call the alarm company to report the outage.

For a second, everything seemed suspended, frozen, as though time were folding in on itself.

He drove the knife into the rib cage with a quick, brutal motion. The man staggered backward. The killer pulled out the blade and struck twice more, two blows as rapid as they were lethal.

He was surprised at that moment to discover how easily the weapon pierced flesh, severed muscles, sliced organs.

A sound of splintering bone confirmed that he had perforated the sternum.

With distorted features, the man gurgled like a bathroom drain.

"We all have to pay for our mistakes," the killer said in a soft, almost compassionate voice.

It's crazy how the brain works.

The man didn't even wonder why this fate had befallen him.

Instead, he reflected on the fact that he would never meet the baby his sister was expecting in May. He also thought about the lakefront property that he'd wanted to buy, though he had never taken concrete steps to make his wish a reality. With a hint of panic, he realized that he would miss an important meeting and that he wouldn't be able to take out the garbage.

And finally, his life ended on a question mark: who had spread that plastic sheet on the floor?

At that moment, the killer drove the knife blade upward, causing irreversible damage to the internal organs.

The man collapsed onto his attacker. Their foreheads came together, giving them the brief appearance of grotesque Siamese twins. They stared at each other wordlessly.

The hunter saw only surprise and distress in the horrified gaze of his prey. On the threshold of death, the man's lips parted as though he were about to say something, but a final spasm emptied him of breath.

The killer slit his victim's throat, and the lifeless body slid gently to the floor.

A jellyfish of blood wriggled on the plastic sheet.

It had all happened so fast that he barely had time to grasp what he had done.

He opened the metal suitcase and took out a Nikon digital camera. He photographed the body from every conceivable angle, taking several close-up shots of the face and wounds. When he was satisfied with the images, he put the camera back in the suitcase.

He pocketed the dead man's ID cards and rolled up the body in the plastic sheet. As he'd expected, getting the corpse into the hockey bag was the hard part.

Now it was time to clean up. He used the towels to wipe the blood spatter off the tile floor, then scrubbed everything thoroughly with disinfectant.

He removed his gloves and coveralls. He put them in a plastic bag with the dead man's ID cards and the bloodstained items. He put on a pair of clean gloves and rolled the hockey bag to the garage.

After parking his car beside the victim's, he leaned the bag vertically against the bumper. Then he grabbed it from underneath and lifted it until it tipped over into the trunk. Finally, he unzipped it and shoved in plastic ice bags on either side of the body.

Done. No one around.

He downloaded the photographs to his laptop, then erased the Nikon's memory card. He looked at the photographs as one might look at a painting. They were his work of art.

The images would be perfect for his blog. And for everything else.

He burned the photographs onto a blank disc, then attached a preprinted label to the disc. He slid the disc into a case, went back into the house, and left the case on the counter. On his way out, he reactivated the alarm and locked the door using the dead man's keys.

He started the old black BMW 740i that he'd stolen the day before from the long-term parking lot at Quebec City's Jean Lesage Airport. Insurance companies spent a fortune each year on theft prevention, but some drivers were simply stupid. If you knew where to look, you could easily find a hidden duplicate key. The BMW's owner had shown exceptional consideration in leaving the parking stub on the dashboard.

Despite his excitement, he forced himself to drive slowly. After a few kilometres, he started to relax. Everything was going according to plan. His victim lived alone and wasn't expected at work until the following Wednesday. Barring unforeseen circumstances, no one would miss him before then, which meant there was ample time to carry out the rest of the plan.

He would stop somewhere for a fast-food meal. Not the healthiest choice, but this evening he was prepared to make an exception. He didn't want to fall behind schedule.

Should he take the body directly to the lodge or get some rest on the way?

He considered the matter.

If he drove at a reasonable speed, he could expect to reach Mont-Laurier around 3:00 a.m. Taking out the snowmobile, loading the sled, and making the trip in darkness would require at least another hour. Everything would depend on how tired he was.

He'd been driving for twenty minutes when a dull thud shook the car. He looked in the rear-view mirror and saw nothing out of the ordinary. He had probably rolled over a pothole.

In the middle of Highway 20! This country is going to hell in a handbasket.

By the time he was five kilometres out of Saint-Hyacinthe, he was struggling to stay awake.

He stopped in the town for a bite to eat and took the opportunity to have another look at the photographs on his laptop. Then, in a vacant lot, he burned his victim's personal effects and the soiled items.

He dispersed the ashes with the tip of his shoe.

His adrenaline level was falling again by the time he saw the glow of Montreal in the distance.

On the Champlain Bridge, with the skyline in view, he decided that it would be wiser to get some rest in the city. He didn't want to risk falling asleep at the wheel.

He remembered a motel on Saint-Jacques Street where he'd stayed in the past. It was the sort of establishment that took cash and didn't ask for ID. If he remembered correctly, there was also a pharmacy nearby. Perfect. He'd kill two birds with one stone.

He parked in the motel lot. Knowing he'd be back in Montreal in a few days, he paid for a full week. He stowed his belongings in the dingy room and walked unhurriedly to the pharmacy.

After pulling a ski mask over his face, he drew a hammer from the folds of his coat and smashed the front window. The alarm went off instantaneously. He'd have to work fast. A police car would be there within minutes.

He used the hammer to disable the two security cameras, then walked quickly to the prescription counter. He broke the lock on the cabinet containing restricted medications, took thirty seconds to find what he was looking for, then grabbed several vials and a syringe.

He sprinted out into the deserted street. After a minute, he slowed down to catch his breath.

In the distance, he heard a siren.

He strolled back to the motel. Walking helped him put his thoughts in order.

He was ready.

Tomorrow will be a great day.

The label on the disc was dated March 31st, 2005. A web address was printed on it.

So were two words and eight digits.

Error message: 10161416.

31901065623037